going bovine

LIBBA BRAY

going
bovine

Delacorte Press

Copyright © 2009 by Martha E. Bray

Library of Congress Cataloging-in-Publication Data
Bray, Libba.
Going bovine / Libba Bray.—1st ed.
p. cm.
Summary: Cameron Smith, a disaffected sixteen-year-old who, after being diagnosed with Creutzfeldt-Jakob's (aka mad cow) disease, sets off on a road trip with a death-obsessed video gaming dwarf he meets in the hospital in an attempt to find a cure.

ISBN: 978-0-385-73397-7 (trade) ISBN: 978-0-385-90411-7 (lib. bdg.)
ISBN: 978-0-375-89376-6 (e-book)

[1. Creutzfeldt-Jakob disease—Fiction.   2. Mad cow disease—Fiction.
3. Dwarfs—Fiction.   4. People with disabilities—Fiction.   5. Automobile travel—Fiction.]   I. Title.
PZ7.B7386Go 2009
[Fic]—dc22   2008043774

The text of this book is set in 11-point Galliard.
Book design by Trish Parcell Watts
Printed in the United States of America
10 9 8 7 6 5 4 3 2

First Edition

For my parents with love.
This one's also for Wendy.
And, as always, for Barry and Josh.

acknowledgments

I would like to thank everyone I've ever kissed or punched* and anyone who has ever kissed or punched me.

I'd like to thank the guy who once validated my parking ticket when I had no money, and the homeless lady who said my hair looked like a dandelion with pieces blown away. I'd like to thank the people who save the whales and the whales themselves, especially the whales stuck in middle management, because that is tough. I would like to thank the people in this world who are weirder than I am—all three of you, plus Crispin Glover. I'd like to thank people who read and think and people who have made me think and read and those who think while reading and read while thinking, but you shouldn't read while driving because that's a safety issue. If I possibly met you in some parallel universe, I would like to say welcome and thank you, too, and, you know, sorry about not calling—that time-travel thing's tricky with my rollover minutes—and also, is there a way to get that sticky stuff from the Higgs field off the bottom of your shoe? I'm asking.

I issue these copious thanks because I'm always afraid I'll forget somebody. By the time the pages are in copyediting, and my brain feels like it's gone a few rounds with Ali in his prime, I have a hard time remembering to pick up milk, let alone remembering the

*For the record, the only person I have ever punched was my older brother, Stuart. And he had it coming. No one should get to wear the Batman cape all the time. The word is "share." I'm just saying.

many wonderful people who helped midwife the book. This is a commentary not on their much-appreciated contributions but on my beleaguered mind, which—if I may offer this in my defense—did live through the 1980s, which was a hell of a decade.

So, you know, thanks. To everybody. Everywhere. Well, maybe not the guy who vomited on my new shoes after the True Believers concert that time in Austin. I don't want to thank him. But most people—thanks.

Still. In acknowledgments pages, they like you to get specific with your shout-outs. Otherwise, people stop inviting you to dinner. And I like dinner. So, with that in mind, I would like to thank the following very specific people:

My publishers, Beverly "I Am Woman, Hear Me Roar" Horowitz and Chip "Animal House Was Based on Me" Gibson. Much respect.

My beloved editor, Wendy Loggia, whose faith never wavers and who pulls me off the crazy train even when my bags are already on board and the conductor (who looks an awful lot like Jack Nicholson in *The Shining*) is offering his hand. Thanks, Wendy.

My agent, Barry Goldblatt, who believed from the beginning, and who has the misfortune of being married to me, so it's hard to escape the neurosis.

Pam Bobowicz and Krista Vitola for their support and input. Also, the chocolate.

The über-talented Trish Parcell for another boffo cover.

The ever-lovely Lisa McCourt and her dad for the Disney World insider info. Thank heavens it really is a small world after all.

Clive Owen for continuing to have an imaginary affair with me.

Rachel "Chelbaby" Cohn, Susanna "Superfoxy" Schrobsdorff, and Jo "Just Because I Haven't Come Up with Your Annoying Nickname Yet Doesn't Mean I Won't" Knowles for reading an early draft of this novel and offering great critiques and encouragement and just generally making me feel minty fresh. Great do you all rocketh.

Justine Larbalestier (who doesn't get a nickname because I fear her) for pushing me to push myself, and for telling me to give the gnome more screen time.

Maureen Leary. Maureen Effing Leary! (Really. That's her middle name. It's on all her monograms.) Maureen Leary, Writer Extraordinaire, who gave me incredible advice and helped me slaughter my "little darlings." Those Midwestern vegans. Surprisingly savage with a pen.

Adam McInroy for talking me through all the physics. Also, for teaching me how to do a layup when you were nine and helping me pass College Math for Idiots when you were only eleven. But I kicked your ass at Axis & Allies a couple of times, bucko, and don't think I don't hold on to that to salve my petty ego.

Laurie Allee for being there and for the physics links. In any parallel world, I still want you as my wing (wo)man.

Brian Greene, Nima Arkani-Hamed, Hugh Everett III, Lisa Randall, Steven Weinberg, Ed Witten, Michio Kaku, Neil Turok, and Julian Barbour for their amazing work on unlocking the mysteries of our universe and providing me with inspiration. (Albeit only through bookstores and the Internet because I don't actually know any of you, but you seem lovely.) Any liberties taken, science gotten wrong, or weird stuff completely made up and perhaps trademarked are solely the fault of the author, who can barely program her DVR.

My insane friend Brenda Cowan for the genius that is Shithenge. I'm not worthy.

John Nevius for the paper-clip analogy and the discussion about Creutzfeldt-Jakob disease.

Vivien Schultz and Debo Hendrix, old friends and natives of New Orleans, for helping me remember that you get saltines and hot sauce on the table, not spicy peanut mix. I don't know what I was thinking.

The Tea Lounge on 7th Avenue, 2001–2008. R.I.P.

The baristas at 'Wichcraft, Southside, and Red Horse Café, also.

Pete Townshend. I don't actually know Pete Townshend either, but I've just always wanted to be able to thank him in my acknowledgments pages.

The makers of Rock Band, because it's cheaper and more fun than antianxiety meds.

The Camp Barry crew for their encouragement.

For listening to me piss and moan beyond all reasonable limits, purple hearts to Maureen Johnson, Robin Wasserman, E. Lockhart,

Holly Black, Cecil Castellucci, Cassandra Clare, Justine (again), Scott Westerfeld, and that guy who sits at the table next to us wearing a weary expression worthy of Camus.

My son, the awesome Joshua, who was patient enough to survive yet another deadline with Mom. For the record, honey, I think your idea about Zombie Bunnies™ rocks out loud.

Last, but most definitely not least, this novel wouldn't exist without the velvet whips and "make it work" attitude of Cynthia and Greg Leitich-Smith. *Going Bovine* was written for their wonderful WriteFest workshop in Austin, Texas, in 2005. Thanks, Cyn and Greg. In the pasture of life, you are both prettier than speckled cows—the bombshells of bovines, I am told. (It's good to know that in case you're ever playing "What's My Category?" Death Round quiz and that question comes up.) A big thanks to all the WriteFesters who participated but especially Brian Yansky and Anne Bustard, who were saddled with the entire manuscript and didn't complain once but offered insightful, invaluable critique. You rule.

Take my advice and live for a long long time,
because the maddest thing a man can do in this life
is to let himself die.
—CERVANTES, *Don Quixote*

Hope is the thing with feathers.
—EMILY DICKINSON

It's a small world after all.
—WALT DISNEY

CHAPTER ONE

In Which I Introduce Myself

The best day of my life happened when I was five and almost died at Disney World.

I'm sixteen now, so you can imagine that's left me with quite a few days of major suckage.

Like Career Day? Really? Do we need to devote an entire six hours out of the high school year to having "life counselors" tell you all the jobs you could potentially blow at? Is there a reason for dodgeball? Pep rallies? Rad soda commercials featuring Parker Day's smug, fake-tanned face? I ask you.

But back to the best day of my life, Disney, and my near-death experience.

I know what you're thinking: WTF? Who dies at Disney World? It's full of spinning teacups and magical princesses and big-assed chipmunks walking around waving like it's

1

absolutely normal for jumbo-sized stuffed animals to come to life and pose for photo ops. Like, seriously.

I don't remember a whole lot about it. Like I said, I was five. I do remember that it was hot. Surreal hot. The kind of hot that makes people shell out their life savings for a bottle of water without even bitching about it. Even the stuffed animals started looking less like smiling, playful woodland creatures and more like furry POWs on a forced march through Toonland. That's how we ended up on the subterranean It's a Small World ride and how I nearly bit it at the place where America goes for fun.

I don't know if you've ever experienced the Small World ride. If so, you can skip this next part. Honestly, you won't hurt my feelings, and I won't tell the other people reading this what an asshole you are the minute you go into the other room.

Where was I?

Oh, right—so much we share, time aware, small world. After all.

So. Small World ride, brief sum-up: Long-ass wait in incredibly slow-moving line. Then you're put into this floating barge and set adrift on a river that winds through a smiling underworld of animatronic kids from every country on the planet singing along in their various native tongues to the extremely catchy, upbeat song.

Did I mention it's about a ten-minute ride?

Of the same song?

In English, Spanish, Swahili, and Japanese?

I'm not going to lie to you; I loved it. *Dude,* I said to myself, this *is the shit.* Or something like that in five-year-old speak. I want to live in this new Utopia of singing children of all nations. With luck, the Mexican kids will let me wear their *que festivo* sombreros. And the smiling Swedes will welcome me into their happy Nordic hoedown. *Välkommen,* y'all. I will ride the pink fuzzy camel in some vaguely defined Middle Eastern country (but the one with pink fuzzy camels) and shake a leg with the can-can dancers in Gay Paree.

Bonjour.

Bienvenido.

Guten Tag.

Jambo.

I was with the three people who were my world—Mom, Dad, my twin sister, Jenna—and for one crazy moment, we were all laughing and smiling and sharing the same experience, and it was good. Maybe it was too good. Because I started to get scared.

I don't know exactly how I made the connection, but right around Iceland, apparently, I got the idea that this was the afterlife. Sure, I had heatstroke and had eaten enough sugar to induce coma, but really, it makes sense in a weird way. It's dark. It's creepy. And suddenly, everybody's getting along a little too well, singing the same song. Or maybe it had to do with my mom. She used to teach English classics, heavy on the mythology, at the university B.C. (Before Children) and liked to pepper her bedtime stories with occasional bits about Valhalla or Ovid or the River Styx leading to the underworld and other cheery sweet-dreams matter. We're a fun crew. You should see us on holidays.

Whatever it was, I was convinced that this ride was where you went to die. I would be separated from my family forever and end up in some part of the underworld where smiling kid robots in boater hats sang nonstop in Portuguese. I had to keep that from happening. And then—O Happy Day! Salvation! Right behind the Eskimo igloo (this was before they

3

were the more politically correct but slightly naughty-sounding Inuits), I saw this little door.

"Mommy, where does that door go to?" I asked.

"I don't know, honey."

We were headed for certain death on the River Styx. But somehow I knew that if I could just get to that little door, everything would be okay. I could stop the ride and save us all. That was pretty much it for me. My five-year-old freak-out meter totally tripped. I slipped free of the seat and splashed into the fishy-smelling water, away from the doe-eyed, pinafored girl puppet singing, *"En värld full av skratt, en värld av tårar"* (Swedish, I'm told, for "It's a world of laughter, a world of tears").

The thing is, I didn't know how to swim yet. But apparently, I was pretty good at sinking. You know that warning about how kids can drown in very little water? Quite true if the kid panics and forgets to close his mouth. You can imagine my surprise when the water hit my lungs and I did not immediately start singing, "There's so much that we share."

The last thing I remember before I started to lose consciousness was my mom screaming to stop the ride while crushing Jenna to her chest in case she got the urge to jump too. Above me, lights and sound blended into a wavy distortion, everything muted like a carnival heard from a mile away. And then I had the weirdest thought: *They're stopping the ride. I got them to stop the ride.*

I don't remember a whole lot after that, just fuzzy memories filled in by other people's memories. The story goes that my dad dove in and pulled me out, dropping me right beside the igloo, and administered CPR. Official Disney cast members scampered out along the narrow edge of EskimoSoon-toBeInuit-land, yammering into their walkie-talkies that the situation was under control. Slack-jawed tourists snapped pictures. An official Disney ambulance came and whisked me away to an ER, where I was pronounced pukey but okay. We went back to the park for free—I guess they were afraid we'd sue—and I got to go on the rides as much as I wanted without waiting in line at all because everybody was just so glad I was alive. It was the best vacation we ever took. Of course, I think it was also the last vacation we ever took.

It was Mom who tried to get the answers out of me later, once Jenna had fallen asleep and Dad was nursing his nerves with a vodka tonic, courtesy of the hotel's minibar. I was sitting in the bathtub with the nonskid flower appliqués on the bottom. It had taken two shampoos to get the flotsam and jetsam of a small world out of my hair.

"Cameron," she asked, pulling me onto her lap for a vigorous towel-drying. "Why did you jump into the water, honey? Did the ride scare you?"

I didn't know how to answer her, so I just nodded. All the adrenaline I'd felt earlier seemed to pool in my limbs, weighing me down.

"Oh, honey, you know it's not real, don't you? It's just a ride."

"Just a ride," I repeated, and felt it sink in deep.

The thing is, before they pulled me out, everything had seemed made of magic. Like I really believed in this crazy dream. But the minute I came to on the hard, glittery, spray-painted, fake snow and saw that marionette boy pulling the same plastic fish out of the hole again and again, I realized it was all a big fake. The realest thing I'd ever experienced was that moment under the water when I almost died.

And in a way, I've been dying ever since.

CHAPTER TWO

Wherein the Cruelties of High School Are Recounted, and the Stoner Dudes of the Fourth-Floor Bathroom Offer Me Subpar Weed and a Physics Lesson

"Who the heck is Don Quicks-oat?" That's what Chet King wants to know.

It's early February, six weeks into the new semester, and we're in English class, which for most of us is an excruciating exercise in staying awake through the great classics of literature. These works—groundbreaking, incendiary, timeless—have been pureed by the curriculum monsters into a digestible pabulum of themes and factoids we can spew back on a test. Scoring well on tests is the sort of happy thing that gets the school district the greenbacks they crave. Understanding and appreciating the material are secondary. For the record, our friend Chet King has read exactly three books in his life, but I'm not sure that sitting through *The Happy Bunny Easy Reader* twice should count. The other book was, no doubt, about football.

"That's *Don Quixote*," Mr. Glass says, pronouncing the "x" as an "h," the proper way.

"Don Key-ho-tay," Chet repeats, exaggerating Glass's somewhat effeminate enunciation. The other jocks snort in laughter, like backup singers on steroids. They've got their jerseys on. Chet does too, though he won't be playing today or any other day. Ever since a bad slam on the practice field cracked two vertebrae near his neck, our former all-state quarterback has been permanently sidelined. Another guy might've gone out drinking over the loss of a big-time sports career. Not our guy Chet. He went to the other extreme, claiming that the accident must have been God's will, a way to steer him toward a new direction in life. He gives this little motivational speech, "God took away my football scholarship but I'm still happy, happy, happy," at Kiwanis club dinners, pep rallies, churches, youth groups, any place that will clap and cheer for him. I guess when your drug of choice has been applause and adoration from the stands it's kind of hard to give that up.

Anyway, it gets him laid, I hear. Doing the horizontal mambo with sympathetic cheerleaders is, apparently, a-okay in God's book, and it doesn't upset your spine like football. Of course, now he's dating my sister, Jenna, so I'll just be flipping on the denial meter for that one.

Mr. Glass is undisturbed. "Okay, settle down. I haven't dismissed you yet."

You dismissed us on day one, I think. It's the kind of sardonic comment that would be good to share with a mate, a pal, a sidekick and coconspirator. If I had one.

"¡Hola! ¿Quién puede decirme algo sobre Miguel Cervantes?" It's Mrs. Rector, Calhoun High School's Spanish teacher, to the rescue. This year, the administration has

7

decided to have coteachers on certain segments. The idea being that we need to cross-pollinate our educational experience with tidbits from history *and* literature, social studies *and* foreign language skills, chemistry *and* home ec, which might prove valuable if we get the urge to make a highly volatile banana cream pie.

Mrs. Rector translates some of the text from Spanish, adding the proper "r" rolls and flourishes. She's got a reputation as the town lush. *¿Quanto costa una grande margarita, por favor?* The fluorescent lighting is zapping out its periodic Morse code of odd sounds: We are hungry. Send us more of your bug kind. All in all, I'm ready to ride out the class under the radar. Just another ten minutes till I can blow through Calhoun's front doors, past the school buses lining the drive for the away game, past the phalanx of cars and trucks ready to follow them anywhere Texas sporting loyalty demands, and hotfoot it downtown to Eubie's Hot Wax—half-price CDs and old vinyl.

"Is Don Quixote mad or is it the world that embraces these ideals of the knight-errant that is actually mad? That's the rhetorical question that Cervantes seems to be posing to us. But for our purposes, there is a right answer, and you need to know that answer when you take the SPEW test," Mr. Glass says, pointing to the board, where STATE PRESCRIBED EDUCATIONAL WORTHINESS test is underlined twice. Mr. Glass's monotone is lulling me into slumber. *Zap, buzz,* goes the overhead lighting. I've put my head on my desk, where I can hear the minute hand ticking hard in my ear. My eyelids are heavy. Almost . . . Asleep . . .

The room is on fire. A row of flames shoots up into my field of vision. I leap out of my chair, knocking it over. It hits the ground with a loud thwack.

"Mr. Smith? Are you okay?" Mrs. Rector asks.

When I look up to the front of the room, everything's fine. No fire. Nothing but every pair of eyes trained on me, which is a strange sensation. Usually, I'm famous for being looked through or over or some other preposition besides at.

Mr. Glass crosses his arms. "Yes, Mr. Smith?"

"Uh, no. Sorry. It was a . . . um . . ."

Mrs. Rector's pursed lips seem to be holding back the words *"Usted está un pendejo."*

The silence is filled by the ego-pulverizing laughter from the gaggle of gum-popping girls on the right. Somebody singsongs, "Fuh-reak . . ."

"It was a cockroach on my desk," I blurt out. "A big one. Like, SUV big."

A few of the girls scream and pull their legs up. Our resident class clown makes slurping sounds, which grosses out the Korean exchange student next to him.

"Nice going, Smith," one of Chet's doughy football buddies says, laughing. Steve or Knute or Rock. One of those *muy macho*–sounding names. A name that says "I can waste you on the Astroturf." Not like Cameron, which sounds like the person who gets wasted on the Astroturf.

Mrs. Rector claps for attention. *"Mi amigos, silencio, por favor.* Settle down, please. Señor Smith, I will give you *un pase de pasillo* so that you can find *el conserje* to come spray."

"The rest of you," Mr. Glass pleads, "please turn in your SPEW test prep books to Chapter Five: Why Thinking Can Cost You on Test Day."

I take the Get Out of Jail Free pass and head right to the men's bathroom on the fourth floor. The Conspiracy Theory & Gaming Society—Stoner Kevin, Stoner Kyle, and Part-time Stoner Rachel—is in residence. Technically, girls aren't allowed in men's bathrooms, but since only the losers, present company included, ever use this one, it's a nonissue. Besides, Rachel's five ten with six tattoos and seven piercings. Nobody gives her shit.

I guess we're sort of friends. If getting high in high school bathrooms and occasionally sharing a table in the caf counts as friendship. We exchange "heys" with limited eye contact— my preferred greeting—and they offer me some of the weed they're using their bathroom huddle stance to try to disguise, as if the smell isn't a dead giveaway.

"Thanks, man," I say, getting in two large hits to take the edge off. I'd toss off the bizarre flame vision I've just experienced as an acid flashback except that I've never done acid, finding it hard to go willingly to a place that could be frightening, hellish, and totally beyond my control. A place much like high school.

Stoner Kevin starts in like a TV program suddenly coming off pause. "I'm just saying, the cat is either dead or alive. It can't be both."

Rachel snorts out the hit in her mouth. "You're wrong, dude. The cat's both alive and dead until you open up the box and take a peek at it. Until then, all possibilities exist. You create the result."

"Look, my friend." Kevin sticks his head under the faucet, takes a drink from the tap, and wipes his mouth on the sleeve of his Frank Zappa tee. "I don't make up the rules of quantum mechanics; I just play by them."

Rachel passes me the joint, looks at me. "You know about Schrödinger's cat, right?"

I shrug.

"Awww, dude!" the three of them say in unison.

Kyle's eyes are bloodshot slits in his grinning face. "This

10

will blow your mind! Okay, so this scientist guy, Schrödinger, did this trippy thought experiment in quantum mechanics where he was all, 'Hey, what if you've got a cat in a sealed box along with, like, a radioactive substance . . .' "

"Not that you should put your cat in a box with poison; that's why it's a thought experiment . . . ," Rachel points out.

". . . and the atom either decays and kills the cat—or it doesn't. Until you open up that box and observe, everything's a probability."

"Wrong," Kevin says. "You're hung up on the observer effect. You don't control the outcome. You don't create the reality. Face it—the cat's either alive or it's dead."

Rachel blows her nose on a paper towel. "If a tree falls in the forest and there's no one there to hear it, does it make a sound?"

"I thought it was 'If a bear shits in the woods,' " Kyle says.

"You can't hear a bear shitting in the woods," Kevin insists.

"How do you know? Have you ever heard a bear shit? Maybe they're loud."

"Dude, you're missing the point." Rachel tosses the wadded paper towel. It misses the trash can and rolls under the sink. "The point is probability and reality. And that's where parallel universes come in. Reality splits into two possible outcomes—one where the cat lives; another where the cat dies. From every choice you make, another world is created where a *different* reality happens."

"So you're saying if the kitty dies in our reality—boom!— there's another reality born where Whiskers is alive and well and chasing mice in the garage?" Kyle tucks his long, stringy blond hair behind his ears.

"Totally."

11

There's a flush from one of the stalls. Weird, because I didn't hear anybody come in, and I didn't see another pair of feet under the doors. The door bangs open, and a really small dude with a huge 'fro comes barreling out, pushing up his sleeves. It takes me a minute to realize he's a dwarf. He pumps the soap dispenser hard several times.

"There's no soap? Are you kidding me? That's a health code violation—totally unsanitary."

Stoner Kyle waves his hand in front of his nose. "What's unsanitary is what you just did in the stall, Gonzo."

The Gonzo guy toddles over to the ancient window and cracks it. "You guys mind not smoking that shit around me? I've told you I'm asthmatic."

Rachel shrugs. "Dude, designated smokers' lounge. Find another bathroom."

Little Dude catches me staring at him and I can feel my face reddening. I hope I haven't pissed him off; it's just that I've never seen a dwarf before.

Kevin makes introductions. "Gonzo, Cameron. Cameron, the Gonz-man."

Gonzo walks straight up to me, folds his arms over his chest and sizes me up like knives are going to be drawn, positions taken, and the orchestra is tuning up for the big fight-at-the-gym musical dance number. "You a gamer?"

"Sometimes."

"Huh," he says, still checking me out.

In the mirror, Kevin puts drops in his eyes. "Gonzo's gonna try to beat the Captain Carnage high score at the arcade today."

"Oh," I manage. "Cool."

"Yo, what's that?" Gonzo nods toward the floor at a slab of balsa wood covered in what look like weird sand-art formations. It's ugly as hell, whatever it is.

12

"This? This is the social sciences project that's gonna keep me from doing summer school." Kyle holds it up for examination.

Gonzo cocks his head to one side. "What the fuck *is* that?"

Kyle snorts. "Hello? It's *Stonehenge?*"

"Looks more like Shithenge to me," Gonzo says, turning away.

Rachel and Kevin bust out laughing.

"Oh my God! That's it! Dude, that is totally Shithenge!" Rachel says.

"Shut up, you guys," Kyle mumbles.

"Hey," Gonzo says, slapping his hand against the door just as I'm trying to slip out. "You should game with us today. 'S gonna be insane."

"Gonzo rules at Captain Carnage!" Kevin shouts between snorts of giggling.

"It's 'cause I always grab the ticket that protects health. You grab that ticket and you're golden for a few levels."

"Sorry, man. Can't go," I lie. "I've got this . . . thing I gotta do. After school. You know."

He knows I'm full of shit but he nods. I nod. And there we are.

"Shithenge," Kevin snickers. "Dude, you are so screwed!"

"I said shut up, man!"

Gonzo takes his hand away. "Sure. No problem. Catch you next time."

He goes to give me a fist bump, a token of bathroom stoner etiquette. I give a sort of wave that looks more like I'm holding up a stop sign. Our hands slide off one another in an awkward fist bump/wave collision. And then I'm out the door.

CHAPTER THREE

Which Treats of the Particulars of High School Hallway Etiquette and the Fact that Staci Johnson Is Evil; Also, Unfairly Hot

The pot's kinda lame, but I've got enough of a buzz going to coast through the amount of time required to drop my books in my locker and wait for the end-of-school bell. It's my misfortune to have a locker on the first-floor main hallway on Park Avenue, so called because it's where all the popular types congregate to formulate their plans for world domination: planning secret parties, leaking the info that there is a party that most of the student body isn't cool enough to attend, deciding who's in or out or in need of torturing that week. It's a busy schedule, and it requires a lot of hallway. I do my best to accommodate them by being unnoticeable, which, basically, involves my just having mass and occupying space.

My smart and universally adored sister, Jenna, is among the attractive evil cabal. She's standing beside the water fountain with her dance squad, her dark blond hair pulled up into the requisite ponytail and cascading ribbons. They've got their colors on today, the snappy blue-gold combo of our fearless team, the Calhoun Conquistadors of Hidalgo, Texas.

Hola, Calhoun Conquistadors! I admire the use of alliteration, but somehow I doubt the school board really got what the Conquistadors were all about when they chose them for a mascot. Maybe the whole raping, pillaging, looting, suppressing cultures thing just blipped off their social consciousness radar. Whatever. It makes for a nifty T-shirt logo. Who doesn't love men in metal hats?

Jenna's seen me but she's pretending she hasn't. When you're pre-majoring in perfection, having a brother who's a social paramecium is a real drawback. While our tense family situation has forced me further into my shell, it's made Jenna into a shining example of teen perfection. Perfect hair, perfect grades, perfect social standing. Through her endless pursuit of the perfect, she's trying to erase us all—the dad who lives through his work, the mom who lives through her children, the scattered way our family communicates through notes left on the fridge and cell phones and no real face time. In a way, I admire her ability to swim against the tide. Me, I'm a drifter—right downstream and over the falls along with the rest of the driftwood.

I should just let it go, this social snub. I should just hang on to what's left of my high and motor on to Eubie's, but I can't help myself. I may suck at football, basketball, tennis, and just about every other sport out there, but I can absolutely letter in cruelty.

"Hey, Jenna. Were those your birth control pills I found in the bathroom this morning?" I say, full of pep.

15

The other dance teamers gasp. One lets out a giggly "Oh my God."

Jenna's a cool customer, though. She's used to my brotherly hijinks. "No, I think those were the ones Mom meant to take before you were born. Don't you have a meeting of the Social Outcast Society to attend? If you hurry, you can get a good seat."

Point Team Jenna.

Everybody laughs, and it would be boffo if I could just fade into the lockers right now. But against the uniform pert tan-blondness that is the dance team, my shaggy dark hair, British-musician-on-the-dole pale skin, and six feet of seriously awkward body stand out like a strip of film negatives plopped down on top of their happy group photo.

One of the Hotness Crew smirks. Staci Johnson. I'm not too proud to tell you that it makes me go a little expansive in my Fruit of the Loins. Staci Johnson is a shallow social climber who would never allow me within a ten-foot radius of her rather magnificent body. I know this. But what can I say? My penis is a traitor.

"You've got mustard on your shirt," Staci points out.

"It was cheeseburger day."

"Oh my God, you don't actually eat in the cafeteria every day?"

"I have a thing going with one of the lunch ladies. Bernice. She's the one with the hairnet *and* the mustache. But mum's the word. Wouldn't want to spoil the big prom surprise."

Someone whispers, "God, your brother is so weird."

"Just ignore him," Jenna says with a sigh. "*We* do."

Chet strides up, all six feet of him, and drapes his arms over my sister like a big daddy gorilla. It's a clear message to the hallway—She's mine. Chet nods at me in that ages-old macho greeting: I have acknowledged your existence, peon. Do not ask for more.

"What are y'all doing for spring break?" Staci asks, arching her back so that her butt sticks out in a noticeable way.

"I've got a mission ski trip with my church," Chet says. "Trying to get Jenna here to come, too."

Jenna beams. It would be so tempting right now to say something like, Wait, Jen, don't you have an abortion scheduled for that week? But Chet would probably kick my ass. Hell, Jenna would probably kick my ass.

Staci twirls her hair around one finger. "Well, me and Lisa and Carmen are going to Daytona for the YA! TV Party House."

"Omigod, you are not!" one of the wannabes squeals. "If you get to meet Parker Day I will be so jealous!"

YA! TV—Youth America! Television—is the barometer of cool for teens everywhere, and Parker Day, with his highlights, vintage rocker clothes, souped-up sneakers, and sly smile, is its most telegenic host. Half the kids in school walk around spouting his trademarked phrase, "You *smoked* it!"

"Actually, we need a fourth to make it happen," Staci says. "Jenna, you should come with us."

"To Florida?"

"It would be fun."

"Yeah," Jenna says. "But expensive."

Staci sticks her butt out just a little farther, which I didn't think possible, and my penis, the mutinous bastard, fires up again.

"Well, think about it," Staci says. "It's gonna be completely mammoth."

"Yo, Cam," Chet says. "Nice stunt with the cockroach."

17

"What cockroach?" Jenna asks.

"The Cammer here pulled a fast one. He said he saw a cockroach to get out of English class."

Jenna gives me a look. The look says, You are disappointing Mom and Dad.

"You didn't miss anything, just more *Don Quixote*. My pastor thinks we shouldn't be reading that stuff. Said it can give kids the wrong ideas, make 'em question everything and get all weird. It happened to this one kid he knew, and the parents had to get him straightened out."

"Oh my God," Staci says, like this bullshit Chet's telling her is as sad as some little kid dying of cancer.

"From books? I don't believe that," Jenna says, and I feel a glimmer of hope that she will not fall to the forces of evil.

"It's true!" Chet insists. "Anyway, it's all good. His folks sent him to this church that's got everything from a school to a restaurant, so you never have to go outside all that much, and he's pretty much there all the time, away from negative influences. It's like what happened to me with my injury."

Here we go. The girls practically swoon.

"I could've questioned stuff. I could have let it change me. But I didn't." He grins. "You've gotta stay positive. Right, Cam?"

Oh, absolutely. I'm big, big, big on the thumbs-up to the positive. I can't go a day without wanting to draw a happy face on every surface I see.

"Right," I say.

"You coming to the game, bro?"

"Can't. It's against my religion."

Chet smirks. I'm pretty sure the Bible says Thou Shalt Not

18

Smirk, but that could be a rumor. "Yeah? What religion's that?"

"Apathy."

Jenna looks like she could cheerfully strangle me. Staci Johnson turns to her posse and giggles. "What*ever*!"

"See? That's what I'm talking about," Chet says to the others like I'm not even there.

And in a way, I guess I'm not.

CHAPTER FOUR

In Which a Brief Sanctuary Is Found, I Fail to Comprehend Jazz, and I Am Forced to Have a Conversation with My Asshole Father

Eubie's Hot Wax sits one block away from the university, nestled between a head shop disguised as an incense and candle store and an art studio famed for its stained-glass cat selection. It's a little oasis of sounds sans the attitude of the mega music store in the mall. It's my favorite place in this dusty Texas town.

At Eubie's there are no six-foot risers announcing the latest release from a pouty-lipped nymphet with only one name. No college music majors earning extra beer money while snorting out pretentious statements like "Well, sure, I guess the Copenhagen Interpretation's an okay band, but they wouldn't have been anything if *Pet Sounds* hadn't come out first." Just bins upon bins of obscure LPs and CDs from newer bands mixed in with jazz and novelty stuff like my personal fave, the Great Tremolo, whose songs about the pain of life were written solely for recorder and ukulele. You have not felt angst till it's been filtered through Portuguese and nose-thrumming vibration. Plus, he has the highest voice I've ever heard in a dude. When he reaches for that one ball-breaking note in every song, I can't help losing it every time.

I was first introduced to the Great Tremolo via one of those satellite radio shows that exists just to play obscure, freaky shit you could swear the producers made up during the break. As I was lying on my bed with my headphones on—the ones I decorated with space stickers from Tomorrowland—the DJ dropped the needle on the Great Tremolo and a song called *"Para Mí He Visto Ángeles,"* which, according to the liner notes, translates to something like "For I Have Seen Angels." I sat straight up, laughing. It's like the Great Tremolo's voice is from space, and he's on the verge of crying while he sings, but like crying with happiness if that makes any sense at all. I mean seriously? How can you not lose your shit over that?

The Great Tremolo made close to twenty albums, and with Eubie's help, I've managed to collect seven of them. I take comfort in the fact that there is someone out there who's more of a loser than I am, and believe me, the Great Tremolo is a total emo loser, tilting at sonic windmills.

Eubie hears the bells tinkle over the door when I come in and looks up from his perch behind the counter, where he's playing store DJ. He's got a big smile for me. "Heeeey, Cam-*run,* where you been, my man?"

"Nowhere," I say, stepping up to the counter. Eubie's growing a little soul patch. It looks good with the dreads and the multicolored T-shirt emblazoned with the face of some famous reggae star.

"Nowhere's a bad place to be. I been there. How come you got no girlfriend?"

I pick up a copy of the free weekly newspaper I have no

intention of reading. "Ahh, you know. The Cam-man is meant to be shared by many, held by none."

Eubie laughs. He's got a laugh like a machine gun firing through velvet. "That's some serious bu'shit, man. Do yourself a favor, friend. Leave my shop and go live a little."

"I am living. A little. Got any new Tremolo for me?"

"Come on back." Eubie leads me through the purple curtains at the back of the store that hide the storage area where the employees take their breaks. It's not much of a room. Couple of chairs. A long counter covered in plastic take-out containers and backpacks. There's a large cork bulletin board on one wall. It's loaded with pictures of the employees dressed up for Halloween and Christmas parties. Ticket stubs from concerts and hard-to-read flyers for band members needed poke out at odd angles, overlapping. A torn piece of notebook paper advertises a carload of guys going to the YA! Party House for spring break who are willing to give somebody a ride for cash. Mardi Gras beads hang from a thumbtack beside a picture of Eubie in a feathered mask, whooping it up on Bourbon Street. Down in the right-hand corner is a picture of an old man in a suit, a hat, and black sunglasses. He holds a trumpet in his weathered hands.

"Who's this guy?"

"Junior Webster. Best horn player in New Orleans." Eubie sucks in air and shakes his hand like he's burned it. "That cat is *outside,* I'm telling you. You ever get to NOLA—and you should—go check out the club he used to play at, the Horn and Ivory."

"He doesn't play there anymore?"

"Hard to play when you're dead. Here, check this out."

From a black plastic milk crate, Eubie pulls out an LP so old and worn that I can see the outline of the vinyl in a white ring on the cardboard cover, which shows Junior Webster standing in front of a painting of the galaxy. In the center of those stars is a black hole.

"Huh," I say.

"Huh," Eubie mocks. "You won't say 'huh' in a minute, son. I'm-a school you." Eubie eases the record lovingly from its sleeve and places it on his turntable. " 'Cypress Grove Blues.' If you had on a hat I'd ask you to take it off, 'cause you 'bout to hear some church."

He drops the needle. A mournful horn blows, high and sharp, like a woman's wail at a funeral; then the whole thing crashes into a wild jazz ride that has Eubie, eyes closed, head forward, hitting some imaginary cymbals like the drummer I know he is on weekends. I don't get jazz. It always sounds to me like a bunch of toddlers let loose in a music room. I try to be polite, though. When the song ends, Eubie pulls the needle off and waits for my reaction.

"Pretty cool."

Eubie arches an eyebrow. "Damn right it's cool. That all you got to say?"

"Really cool," I say, hoping it passes for enthusiasm.

"Cam-run," Eubie says, shaking his head so his dreads wiggle like dancers. "You need help, my man. You hearin' me?"

"Yeah."

"I'm tellin' you, if I had another life to live, I would live it in New Orleans, making music with Junior Webster, makin' holes in space with a wall of sound. Music has the power to save the world." Eubie rubs at his soul patch for a second before breaking into a grin. "I tell you what, I'm-a let you borrow this album for the weekend. You listen to the whole thing and see what you have to say then."

My palms start to sweat. I don't want to be trusted with

Eubie's favorite album, especially since I know I'll never listen to it, and I'll have to come up with some excuse for why I didn't. I put up my hands, back up a little. "I don't want to take your best album, Eubie . . ."

Eubie tries to hand it off, like a baton in a race he's the only one running. "Go on, it's okay."

"I don't know, Eubie. That's a big responsibility."

"No, my man. Child support is a big responsibility. This is a record."

I shake my head. "What if it gets broken?"

"I'll kill you." He winks. "But it won't get broken. You'll treat it like a baby girl."

I know Eubie. He is anal about his LPs. The fact that he is offering it to me is a Big Deal. But I'm not comfortable with the Big Deal. I just want to keep things as they are—no expectations equals no failed expectations equals no hurt feelings equals everything's cool.

I put my hands in my pockets and rock on my heels. "You know, things are kinda busy at school this week, and I'm working an extra shift at Buddha Burger and stuff, so . . . you know. But thanks anyway." I give a half-assed smile. "So . . . did you get that new Tremolo I ordered?"

Eubie's disappointed. I can see it in the way he puts the LP back and sighs, and I feel kind of crappy about it. I'm used to disappointing everyone else, but not Eubie.

He shimmies an album out from under a stack on his desk. The cover is a picture of cheesy perfection: two wineglasses, soft candlelight, and a feather. *Viver É Amar, Amar É Viver.* There's a little asterisk after the title along with the English translation, *To Live Is to Love, to Love Is to Live.*

"What is it about this guy?" Eubie asks.

"I have a secret thing for the recorder." When Eubie

doesn't laugh, I explain, "Have you ever listened to this guy? He's a joke."

"So you buy it to mock him." Eubie plops his long frame down in one of the folding chairs and bites into a health-food bar he's had in his shirt pocket.

"No. Not really. Sort of. Well, yes."

"To him that shit's sacred, you feel me? He's writing about pain, about the loss of love, the injustice of life. About hope. I'm not gonna sell you this if you're just gonna make fun of it. That's not what music's about, my man." He gives me a disapproving look.

"Well," I say, swallowing hard. "He does play a mean recorder."

Eubie shakes his head. He polishes off the last of the health-food bar and pushes me out through the curtains and toward the cash register with my new Tremolo record. "Here. Take the damn album. And get yourself a girlfriend."

It's warm and sunny when I step out on Mambrino Street. Across the four lanes of traffic sits the university where my dad works. My dad is a physicist. He works with people who deal in all kinds of weird cosmic shit. String theory. Parallel universes. The viability of time travel. It's not going to build you a better toaster, but it is trippy stuff that makes you spend all day trying to figure it out.

Actually, what I should say is that my dad works *against* the cosmic. He's a semifamous debunker of anything that isn't old-school physics. He calls all the new theories "The Emperor's New Clothes of Science." I'm not kidding. He actually submitted that as a paper for *Scientific Masturbation Quarterly*. Okay, so it's not really called that, but trust me

25

when I tell you that it is filled with articles of solo pleasure. The rest of us are bored shitless. "They can't prove any of that, Cameron," he always says. "And until there's proof, it's not science to me." That's my dad for you.

Since I'm so close, I could stop in. A quick cost analysis lists the pros and cons of this move. Pro: I might be able to finagle use of the car for a few hours. Con: I would have to have contact with Dad. It's a real toss-up, but my jones for the car wins out. It's one of those amazing early spring days you get in Texas sometimes, the kind with a hint of summer to it, a preview of coming attractions, and driving around with the windows down would be mighty fine.

The Bohr Physics Complex is a dingy prewar building on the outskirts of campus featuring neat, ordered rows of classrooms and offices. A huge bulletin board in the center hall is littered with invites for intramural soccer, projects on alternative fuel sources, and buttloads of discussion groups: "Which Way to Higgs Field: Does the God Particle Exist?" "Feel our vibration! Meet in room 101 to discuss the latest in string theory, multiverse theory, and the theory of everything!" "Hail, Putopia!" "Exploring the unexplored—the mysteries of dark energy. Dulcinea Hall. 7 p.m. There will be a keg, so come early and get your strangelet on."

Dad's office is behind the last door of a long corridor that hasn't seen a paint job since Einstein was alive. The door is open a crack. I hear voices, so I peek through. One of Dad's TAs is in with him. She's been to the house before. Her name is Rachel or Raylie, some "R" name. She's sitting in a chair across from my dad, leaning forward, laughing at something he's just said. My dad doesn't seem like my dad. He doesn't sound angry or annoyed like the dad at home who does the yard work, pays the bills, rotates the tires, and looks like he hates every minute of it. He's actually smiling, which is just weird. I knock on the half-opened door, and Dad stands up quick.

"Hey there, Cam. What a surprise. You remember Raina, my teaching assistant?"

Raina. She gives a little wave. "Hi."

"So what brings you over here at four-thirty on a Friday afternoon?"

"I was at Eubie's. Thought I'd drop by."

"Great," Dad says, smiling like he wants to sell me a used car. "Uh, Raina, if you could have those papers ready by Wednesday morning."

"Sure, Frank."

Frank? She calls him Frank? What's wrong with Dr. Smith? Raina and I brush each other on my way in. She has big brown eyes and her hair smells like oranges. For a split second I imagine her naked. But then I think that maybe my dad has done the same thing or even seen her naked and I'm wishing I had a big doobie to take that thought right out of my head.

Dad offers me a seat. "Well, this sure is a surprise."

"So you said." I plop down into the no-frills chair on the other side of the desk, the place where his students sit. This is how they see him: Tall, fit guy in a starched white button-down and khaki pants. Big desk. Big chair. Big diplomas on the wall behind his graying-around-the-temples head, making him look like one of those religious icon paintings. A black box with an angel snow globe Jenna and I gave him for Christmas one year. The base broke off a while back, and now the angel leans against the glass with both hands like she's trying to get out. One of those metal pin sculptures that molds to your hand and holds the shape. Two neat stacks of papers—graded and yet-to-be-graded. Lamp on one side, phone on the other. Order. Symmetry. Authority.

"Raina is a really smart woman. Great physicist. Those freshmen don't know what they're up against. She could have gone to MIT if she wanted to."

"Cool. Hey, can I borrow the car?"

Dad's smile sags and now he looks familiar—like a birthday balloon four days after the party.

"Is that the only reason you stopped by?"

I press my face against the metal pin sculpture. When I pull it away, my expression is caught in a scream. "Well, it's not like you're using it right now."

"When your grades improve, we can talk about the car." Dad shakes the sculpture out, erasing me. "Hey, you'll probably like these."

From a desk drawer, he removes a stack of photos and shoves them into my hands. They're vacation pics—a couple of guys in Gold Coast University T-shirts backpacking in the mountains. A trio of girls at some mega bowling alley. A crew of rowdy college kids on the beach during spring break. I don't know any of these people. "Some of my students have this project. They stole a yard gnome from somebody's lawn and have taken him on vacation all over the world. They pass him off to whoever's going on a trip next."

Now I can see the little guy peeking out in each picture, all fat red cheeks, white beard, and twinkling eyes. Well, if he could twinkle. He looks like he wants to. He also looks like he could cheerfully beat the crap out of his smug kidnappers. Or maybe he likes to travel. Maybe he sends postcards to the other yard gnomes: *Having a great time. No sprinklers here.*

"Funny," I say, throwing them back on his desk, where they fan out in a photographic arch.

"You didn't even look at them."

"Yeah, I did."

Dad sighs. "You know, Cameron, you might at least pretend to be interested in my life."

"Dad, I looked at them."

He tidies them up and puts a rubber band around them so they're contained, like him. That's my dad. Never yell when you can simmer. Never scream when you can cut somebody with a look. Never go ahead and have that fight when you can feel righteous about walking away and giving them your back. I've seen a lot of my dad's back.

"About the car. I was thinking I could just use it to run a few errands and then I could come back for you, you know, whenever you're done." I throw him a father-son-bonding bone at the last minute. "Maybe we could get some pizza."

"What errands?"

"You know," I say, shrugging.

"No, I don't know. That's why I asked."

"Just some errands. For school."

"What do you need for school?"

"Nothing."

"Cameron. That doesn't make sense."

"I just need to borrow the car. To get some stuff. No big deal."

"Stuff," Dad says, playing with his pen. "Books? Clothes? Sports equipment?"

Dad would cream himself if I said sports equipment. "I was kind of thinking of going out for lacrosse this year. Might look good on the college apps."

"A solid GPA would look better," Dad shoots back. He and Mom can't figure out how two professors ended up with such a C+ average of a kid.

"So can I borrow the car?"

"No. I'm working late tonight."

Working late. With Raina, no doubt. His T and A.

"Fine," I growl. "Can I at least borrow your ID card so I can get a discount at the campus bookstore? I need to pick up a copy of *Don Quixote* for English class," I lie.

"No problemo." Dad smiles and hands me his ID card. To the untrained eye, it looks like he's happy to help me out. But I know he's only happy that he's won. I take the card and pocket it.

"You're welcome," Dad says.

"Great. So I'll see you later."

"Would it kill you to say thanks?"

"Possibly. And since I could end up dead, it seems like an extreme test. Don't you think?" Who's winning now, Dad?

"Only the one book." He turns around to face his computer screen. Hello, Dad's back. I've missed you. What took you so long?

The arrival of the Back means it's officially time to go, but my foot has fallen asleep. It's all pins and needles and I can't quite feel it under me when I stand on it. I try to stop myself from falling by bringing my hand down hard on the desk. The snow globe topples over and shatters, soaking the yard gnome pictures.

"Cameron!" Dad shouts, pushing his chair back and away from his wet desk. A little hits his pants in a bad spot.

"I tripped, okay? My foot was asleep! Wasn't my fault."

"Nothing ever is." Dad opens his desk drawer and pulls out his collection of convenience-store napkins. He's dabbing furiously at the pictures, assessing the damage. "It's okay," he says.

I don't know if he means the pictures or me.

*   *   *

I pick up a copy of the *Don Quixote Fake It! Notes* and a bottle opener with a padded handle that reads SCREW ME just to piss Dad off. It's a long bus ride out to our subdivision, so I thumb through the free weekly rag I picked up at Eubie's.

Strange Fires Sighted in Several States. "The world is ending for sure," says Reverend Iggy Norant.

Roadrunner Bus Company: Just Follow the Feather to Your Next Adventure.

Missing Scientist May be Time Traveler to Other Worlds.

Troubled Teens? For everlasting satisfaction, send them to our church.

Did you suffer adverse effects from Human Growth Hormone? If so, you could join our class action suit today.

Secret Super Collider Could be Breakthrough—or Swallow Our Planet in Black Hole!

X Marks the Spot, Says Top Disease Dr.: "I've cheated death, and so can you!"

Ragnarok On! Learn ancient Norse in the comfort of your own home: call now and get bonus rune pendant absolutely free!

Need a Job? Exciting opportunities exist with United Snow Globe Wholesalers: Freezing life behind glass. Call 1-800-555-1212.

I finish the paper. There are still a few miles to go, though, so I read the first few chapters of *Don Quixote*. The *Fake It!*

Notes tell me that Cervantes is satirizing the culture of idealism. The only thing I know about Don Quixote is that he and his sidekick go off and have imaginary adventures, battling windmills disguised as giants and that sort of thing. No windmills outside the bus window. Just rows and rows of houses that all look pretty much the same. Sure, some are two stories; some are ranches. A few even have that big round turret for a garage like some kind of ridiculous suburban castle. But they're the same house spaced out every five houses or so by other houses that have matches throughout the neighborhood. When I was a kid I was always afraid I'd wander into the wrong house and the wrong life by mistake. Now that sounds pretty good.

The sky's amazing, though. Bright blue, like paint right out of the tube before you water it down. The clouds are bouncy little mattresses up there. Something flutters past my window, making me jump. It's a flock of birds taking off for the cloud beds. They must have come a little too close to the bus for comfort. I watch them till they're nothing but specks. And for a second, I see something else in the sky, a flutter of wings too big to be anything I can name.

CHAPTER FIVE

Wherein I Have a Very Strange Encounter While Stoned and Employ a Frying Pan in My Defense

There's a note on the fridge: *Cam, home by 10:00. Lasagna in freezer. If you use the toaster oven, unplug it afterward. It overheats. Mom.* There's a hastily added *Love you* squeezed in before her name in a different-color ink. It's the personal touch that means so much.

Mom teaches English comp, single-celled organism level, at the community college. She could be teaching a challenging English lit class somewhere good, but she never finished her dissertation or whatever it is you need to become a bona fide PhD. Mom has trouble finishing stuff. The house is crowded with half-scribbled-in crossword puzzles, books with the bookmarks in the middle, bags of knitting, scarves she got halfway through and then abandoned.

The lasagna is totally freezer-burned, cold and inedible, so I dial up a pizza. True to their ad campaign, Happy Time

Pizzeria delivers within thirty minutes—complete with bonus mega-ounce sodas and cinnamon-frosted-bread dessert product—and I'm camped in the recliner, scarfing down my slices in the middle of our large, empty family room.

I have a special relationship with the remote control. I like to think of it as my own personal divining rod, taking me safely past nighttime soap operas, used car commercials, tel-evangelists, and medical trauma shows. It stops briefly on a repeat showing of *Star Fighter*, the cult metaphysical action movie all kids between the age of nine and thirteen have to see at least ten times before they can pass into puberty. No kidding—there are kids who can quote the whole damn thing.

I let the screen idle on the news while I roll a J. Quick pictures stretch out across our TV's full forty-two inches: young guys in camouflage holding guns while guarding a desert. Bloody kids crying in the blown-up streets of some foreign city. A follow-up story on a store bombing last Christmas. A commercial with Parker Day's suntanned face hawking Rad XL soda. Back to the grim report and a local story, a fire in a neighborhood across town. The flames make me think about my weird dream in Spanglish class today, and I get a funny feeling inside, like when you're driving around a sharp curve on a one-lane road and you can't see what's coming. The reporter says something about similarities to another fire and the authorities' fears that an arsonist is on the loose. And then they switch to a story about celebrity baby names and some starlet who named her bundle of joy Iphigenia.

I smoke just enough to make me slow down inside, like I'm part water bed. Then I hide the roach and spray a toxic amount of air freshener just in case anyone gets the crazy idea to come home early for some "quality time." Finally, I flip on the ConstaToons channel so I can watch a marathon of my favorite animated classic, the one where a poor, bedraggled coyote chases a roadrunner around a tumbleweedy landscape. Every single time, this poor guy gets his ass handed to him by TNT gone wrong or falling anvils or other backfiring ruses. But he never stops chasing that damn roadrunner.

I've seen this one a million times. The coyote rigs a skewed-perspective backdrop of a long hallway with many doors painted on it. It's just a painting, but somehow, the roadrunner zooms right into the picture as if it's real, opens one of the doors, and escapes. The coyote's got a big "Wha . . . ?" on his face. He runs into the painting, and they chase each other in and out of doors, just missing each other. Finally, the coyote opens a door and a train runs him right over, poor bastard. Even though I've seen it a zillion times before, I laugh my ass off, because I'm stoned, and it's my right to laugh at things that, in the cold hard light of day, would not be all that funny.

A blur of white zips past the open doorway into the kitchen. It takes my weed-fogged brain two seconds to register what this means: Somebody's in the house.

"Mom?" I call. "Dad?"

Nothing.

"Jenna, is that you? You better cut it out. I'm warning you."

Shit. I hope I sprayed enough Citrus Rain to take away the pot odor. From the kitchen comes a faint rustling sound.

"You should know we've got an alarm system!" Our alarm system is basically me screaming my head off if I see this guy, but he doesn't have to know that. Quietly, I slip into the kitchen. Nobody's there. I do a quick scan for a weapon. Plastic napkin holders. Place mats. Steak knives so dull they

35

can't cut through butter. I grab the frying pan soaking in the sink and slink into the living room just as something darts up the stairs.

Oh shit, man. My blood pounds the sides of my skull, and I feel woozy. Should I call the cops? My parents? What if I'm just stoned and paranoid?

Be cool, Cameron. Just check it out first.

I creep up the stairs with a fry pan as my only defense, and despite the fact that my heart is beating like a humming-bird's, it strikes me as funny. Greetings, ax murderer! I was just wondering how you like your eggs?

I reach the landing. Mom and Dad's room is empty. So's Jenna's übergirl lair. No doubt any serial killer would take one look at the lavender walls covered with sensitive girl songwriter posters and dive out the window anyway. Bath-room's clear. That leaves my room.

The door's half closed, so I kick it open with my foot. My room is exactly the way I left it: Rumpled clothes on floor. Stereo equipment and miscellaneous computer wires lying about. Unmade bed. Stacks of LPs, CDs, comic books. Closet doors are open. Okay, weird. I don't know what kind of pot this is—Imagine There's Some Badass Dude Coming to Kill You pot—but never again, man.

Something catches my eye. The window's open. That's new. And there on the windowsill is a feather. I pick it up. It's huge. Bigger and thicker than any bird's feather I've ever seen. Soft and white with pink at the edges. Huh. I turn it over in my hand and I swear, I must be going mental, be-cause there on the snowy surface of that gigantic feather is one word, a greeting.

Hello.

CHAPTER SIX

Wherein My Part-time Gainful Employment Proves to Be a Hell Beyond All Imagining and I Make a Most Curious—Okay, Really Weird—Sighting

"Cameron?" Someone's banging on my door. Banging equals Mom equals easily ignorable. I roll onto my stomach and bury my head under my pillow. The banging continues, muffled somewhat by the layer of synthetic down filler over my head.

"Cameron?"

No. No banging. No Cameron. Cameron sleep now.

The pillow is ripped savagely from my head.

"Cameron? It's ten o'clock."

I open one eye and see that yes, yes, it is ten o'clock. Ten zero zero. Zero, my favorite number. As in zero expectations, zero disappointments.

"Ten o'clock. Good time for growing boys to get their sleep," I mumble. "Night, Mom." I try to grab behind me for the pillow but Mom's still got a firm hold on it.

"You promised your dad you'd mow the lawn today."

"I did?"

"Yes, you did. Last Saturday, when you forgot to mow it after you'd promised to the week before."

I vaguely remember this, but honestly, all I can think about is the taste in my mouth. I've got the kind of pot hangover where I swear little road crews of pixies have been hard at work all night painting my tongue with dirt-enhanced pitch.

"Right. Do it later," I mumble.

"He'll be back from tennis in an hour."

"So I'll start then." I make a swipe for the pillow and miss.

Mom holds it just out of reach. "Honey, you have to go to work at Buddha Burger."

My joyous part-time fast-food gig, which the 'rents forced me to take. I've only worked there four weeks, and already it feels like a soul-sucking spiral of pain.

"I'll call in sick."

"Cameron, do you think that's such a good idea? They might think you're unreliable."

It seems a bad time to point out that I am unreliable. Or I'm reliable when it comes to being unreliable.

" 'Sokay. Somebody'll cover me."

I take possession of the pillow again. Mom's still standing in my room. I can feel her hovering. Some other mom might get angry, blow up, or drag me from my bed with a purposeful "Young man, it's time you learned some responsibility!" In the TV movie version, that would be "the big turning point." And at the end of the movie, when they showed me with a decent haircut and a graduation cap on my head, accepting the special scholarship/presidential seal/call to cure cancer, I'd thank my mom, and there'd be a glossy close-up of her tearstained face while everybody stood to applaud her.

This is so not my mom. She's like me—driftwood. After a few seconds, I hear her shoes squeaking a retreat.

"All right," she says, before pulling the door shut. "But at least use the Weedwacker around the front walk."

"Sure thing," I promise, and fall right back to sleep.

I wake up at eleven-fifteen, which is fifteen minutes before I'm supposed to be reporting for my six-hour shift at Buddha Burger, a twenty-minute drive across town. Shit. I grab my uniform—black pants, white button-down shirt with a meditating Buddha cow floating atop a hamburger bun, dorky faux Tibetan monk hat—brush my teeth, and look around to see if there's anything I'm forgetting. That's when I see the long feather on the floor and last night's weirdness announces itself in my memory. What the hell was that? *Hello.* The feather said hello.

But there's nothing written there now. For all I know, that feather's been on my floor for a long time, and last night was some random ganja flip-out. I throw it in the trash and run downstairs.

After some minor-league pleading with Mom, she agrees to let me take the Turdmobile, her crap-brown box of a car. It's ugly but it runs, and it's better than the bus when you're late. All down the block, the lawns are alive with men on riding mowers. They gallop across their yards, whipping them into shape, in control of those few square feet of ground. All hail the suburban action heroes! Do not tangle with those men—they have Weedwackers and they know how to use them! I mean, honestly, I'm supposed to get good grades, go to a good college, not screw up, so I can get to do this shit someday? Thanks, I'll pass.

Dad, still in his tennis whites, pushes the power mower around our already pristine lawn. Our eyes meet for a nanosecond, and then Dad stoops to examine a particularly hearty clump of weeds. As I back the Turdmobile down the driveway, he's running the mower over the same spot again and again, forcing the rebellious patch to bend to his will.

I'm through the doors of Buddha Burger seven minutes past my shift start time, which, if you ask me, is within the realm of acceptable. But not so for our manager, Mr. Babcock. He's waiting by the clock, his bushy mustache scrunched into a hairy M above a tight frown. He makes a point of looking at the clock, then at me.

"Hi, Mr. Babcock," I say, punching in.

"You're late, Cameron." Wow. And you, sir, are incredibly observant.

"Yes, sir. Sorry about that. I had to take my mom's car and it kept stalling out. . . ."

"Cameron, I'm gonna give you a piece of advice, son. Never explain, never blame."

He stares meaningfully at me. I think the human interaction manual says that I'm supposed to supply a comeback here, something to show I have "understood the message."

"Yes, sir. That's good advice, sir."

He puts his arm around my shoulder like he's my life coach. "Son, I don't know what your home situation is." In his thick Texas drawl, "situation" has about ten syllables. "Maybe you don't have a daddy at home. Maybe you do. But here at the Buddha Burger, I like to think of us as family. You know what that means?"

There's yet another place where I can feel awkward, resentful, and out of touch?

"It means that while you work here, I'm like your daddy. I make the rules. And when I say you need to be here on time or even ten minutes early for your shift, I mean it. You got me?"

"Yes, sir," I say. Mr. Babcock pats my shoulder. He smiles, and the caterpillar mustache—the envy of state troopers everywhere, I'm sure—straightens out again. I hear that on the weekends, he's a part-time security guard with mirrored sunglasses and a gun. He probably poses in front of his bathroom mirror to see how he looks saying "Freeze!"

Mr. Babcock is pleased that I have "heard his message." I'll bet he feels all cuddly inside that he may have "put another youth on the path to responsibility." I make a mental note to write *Kick Me* on the back of his shirt sometime.

I'm working with Lena today. Just great. Lena's the most literal person I've ever met, with the heart and soul of a district attorney. When Lena is shift manager, she expects you to work your ass off—no skipping off to the walk-in for a secret smoke or pretending to clean the bathrooms for thirty minutes. It's by the book all the way.

She hands me a rag. "Late again, Cameron."

"Just by seven minutes. That's not really late, Lena."

She swivels around, hands on hips. "Yeah? That's seven minutes I had to cover for you. Not cool."

"It's not that big a deal." I busy myself stocking the napkin holders on the counters, but I can feel her eyes on me, like she sees straight through to my inner assholian, irresponsible core. I look up and she's studying me.

"Can I ask you a question, Cameron?"

"I think you just did. Or did you mean an additional question?"

Lena doesn't even bother to dignify this with a new facial expression. "My question is this: What's wrong with you?"

She's staring at me with those big brown eyes, waiting. And what I want to say to her is *I don't know. I honestly don't.*

"Right. I'll just go wipe down."

Lena shakes her head slowly, judge and jury. And then she does that thing I can't seem to do. She shakes it off, puts on a smile, and turns to the next customer. "Hi, welcome to Buddha Burger. How can I help you?"

Only six more fun-filled hours to go.

The tables are a mess. Every inch of the fake bamboo tables is covered in the sticky, mushy remnants of Buddha Burgers, Meditation Fries, and Fresh Fruitiful Frothies. People come here because they think it's healthy and they're saving the environment while they chomp their fast food. There are lots of framed pictures showing smiling indigenous peoples who are *absolutely not being exploited* by the corporate office. In the back is a Zen water fountain supposed to induce feelings of peace. Mostly it makes people have to go to the bathroom. New Agey chant music is piped through the speakers. Rug rats run around playing with their Buddha cow toys, making moo sounds and fucking up all my cleaning efforts.

Lena summons me to the front over the mike. It's her break time, and she is very, very serious about taking her break at the same time every shift. I take over the register just as Staci Johnson and her crew walk in. On the bell curve of high school humiliation, this rates the top grade.

"Lena," I beg in a whisper. "Can you take this one for me, please?"

"Ha! Funny." She holds up her *Star Fighter* graphic novel. "I'm on break."

"Look, I'm sorry I was late—"

"That makes . . ." She counts heads. "Five of us."

"Really, really sorry. It won't happen again. Just please take this one."

She makes a show of drumming her fingers on her chin like she's thinking hard. "Hmmm. Let me see. Um. No."

"Lena. Please. Pretty please. I'll be your best friend."

"I have a best friend. Her name is LaKeesha. You'd know that if you ever paid attention to anyone else."

"Okay. I'm a jerk. A self-involved jerk. But I swear, if you just take this one order, I will get the soy cheese from the walk-in for a week. Promise."

For a minute, I think she's considering. Then she flips her book open to the ribbon-marked page. "Sorry. I'm at a good part. The fate of the universe hangs in the balance." Lena shoves her card into the time clock. I hear the gunshot-hard *click-punch* of it seal my fate.

"Excuse me, could we get some help?" Staci calls out.

Lena jerks her head in their direction. A smirk pulls at her lips. "Sucks to be you."

Shit.

Resigned, I trudge over to the register, wondering if girls can smell your total fear, like wolves or very experienced serial killers.

"Hi, welcome to Buddha Burger. Can I take your order, please?" I say, pulling out a plastic tray and putting a one hundred percent recycled paper liner on it. I avoid eye contact by staring at the useless factoids: *DNA, or deoxyribonucleic acid, is the genetic code that makes you uniquely you! Before they're your cruelty-free burgers, Buddha Burger cows are raised with sunshine and happiness. That's why they taste so* moo-*velously good! Recycling is good for the planet—and you and me. Let's all get recycled!*

43

"Excuse me?" one of the girls says, snapping her fingers to get my attention.

Staci Johnson and I are separated by a cash register and two feet of counter. "Wow. It's Cameron Smith. I didn't know you worked here." Staci stifles a giggle. "Nice hat."

Here's a heaping plate of I Hate You. Would you like fries with that?

Staci & Co. change their order four times just to mess with me. They all want Fresh Fruitified Frothies, which are a pain to make. It's February, girls. Order coffee. I'm at the blender for what seems like hours, developing carpal tunnel syndrome, or aggravating the carpal tunnel syndrome I've already brought on by frequent self-abuse, which I suppose I could cut back on. Then again, everyone needs a hobby. The Frothie-making must have been harder than I thought, because when I bring out the tray of drinks, my hands start to twitch and jerk. Every muscle in my arms is break dancing. I can't hold on to the tray. It goes flying, splattering Staci in blueberry-strawberry-peach soy moo.

Staci lets out a little scream. "You did that on purpose, Cameron Smith."

"I swear I didn't," I say. My left arm is still shaking. I use my right to hold it steady, which makes it look like I'm trying to hug myself.

"He totally did do it on purpose," one of the wannabes says. She rips four or five eco-friendly napkins from the pop-up dispenser and hands them to Staci.

"God, he is such a freak," Staci mutters just loud enough for everyone to hear. Even the ankle-biters in the joint have stopped running around screaming, more interested in the action going on up front.

Mr. Babcock struts around the fry vats, hiking up his pants. "What seems to be the trouble?"

"He threw our Frothies at us." Staci shows off her wet shirt.

"Cameron? Do you have a problem?" Mr. Babcock says, tearing his eyes away from Staci's Frothie-drenched chest.

"No. It was an accident. I don't know what happened. It's like I lost control of my arms or something and—"

Mr. Babcock holds up his silencing finger. "Never explain or blame, Mr. Smith. Ladies, at Buddha Burger, we take safety seriously. Your meal is on the house. Lena, could you retake these girls' order?"

Lena doesn't look up from her graphic novel. "I'm on break. Fifteen minutes. By law."

Mr. Babcock sighs. "Fine. I'll do it myself. Cameron, I'm gonna have to ask you to hand in your Buddha badge."

Every pair of eyes is on me as I hand over my Meditating Buddha Cow pin and hat. Only one person isn't watching. A bronzy girl with pink hair in the far corner eating a Buddha's Bounty Hot Fudge Sundae. She's all lit up from the afternoon sun. And she has wings. No, that's . . . ohmygodyes! There they are—white, fluffy, big-assed wings tucked behind her back. No, dude, that can't be right. People do not have wings.

"Cameron?"

"Huh?" I say, turning back to Mr. Babcock.

"Take your things and leave now. Don't forget to clock out."

Staci and crew form a little huddle. They make it seem like they're trying not to laugh, but really, they're enjoying the show. And when I turn back to look at the table in the far corner, it's empty.

CHAPTER SEVEN

In Which I Am Subjected to the Slings and Arrows of Dinner with My Family

"I thought maybe we could all go to Luigi's for an early dinner tonight," Dad announces. He makes these announcements periodically, the "let's act like a family" edicts. For all I know, he may make them a lot, but it's rare that we're all gathered in the same place at the same time to hear them. We're like electrons both attracting and repelling each other.

"Sorry, Daddy. I can't," Jenna says. She bothers to sound apologetic. "I'm going to the movies with Chet and everybody."

"What time?" Dad asks.

"Eight o'clock."

"It's only five now. You could eat dinner with us and then go."

Jenna's mouth falls open. "By myself? I can't show up by myself. That's lame. What if they're late and I'm sitting there all alone looking like a loser, like . . ."

Cameron, my loser brother.

"Besides, Lisa and Tonya are picking me up at six. We're meeting the guys for pizza first."

"Do you need money?" Mom asks.

"Why?" I snap. "She doesn't actually eat the food. I'm sure she's got enough for a diet soda."

Jenna glares at me.

"All right, settle down. Well, guess it'll just be the three of us, then."

"I'm not hungry," I say.

"Would it kill you to spend a little time with your family, Cameron?"

I don't know. Would it kill you to stop doing the nasty with your TA? Why don't you admit that's the real reason for this sudden family powwow? You've been home late every night for a month. Is Raina on vacation?

I could say this out loud, but I don't.

"I'm really behind on my reading for Spanglish. That Don Quixote is one funny guy. Wouldn't want to miss a minute of it."

"You're reading *Don Quixote*?" Mom asks. "Did you know Cervantes is considered the first modern novelist?"

"No. Wow. Well. I better hop to." I disappear upstairs but I can still hear them in the kitchen arguing.

"So, do you want to go to Luigi's?" Dad asks, sounding irritated.

"Oh, I don't care," Mom answers.

"We could get sushi."

"That would be fine. I could just order a salad."

"Mary, if you don't want to eat sushi, just say so."

"No, no, that's fine. You know me. I hate to make decisions."

I know how their evening will go. It's like a rerun of a

show you've seen a million times. They'll end up going to Luigi's, where they always go, where Dad can hold court and be the big man and Mom can have a hard time deciding what to order until Dad finally orders something for her that she'll hate and pick at and make him mad. He'll mutter something about how if she doesn't like it she doesn't have to eat it and she'll make a big show of taking a bite and saying no, no, it's good, she's just not all that hungry after all. They'll exhaust their topics of conversation—his work, her work, us kids—before the appetizers come and spend the rest of the meal in silence, looking for other people they know who could come over and rescue them from each other.

Yeah. Think I'll be skipping this one, thanks. But apparently, Dad has other ideas. He knocks on my door as he opens it, a habit I find beyond annoying. Really, why bother knocking at all?

"Cameron, get dressed. We're all going to Luigi's for dinner."

"I thought Jenna has that thing?" I sputter. "If Jenna's not going I should be exempt."

"This is family," Dad says. "No one's exempt."

Luigi's is billed as the place "for families and fun!" I have a hard time putting those two things together in the same sentence. Luigi is a nice enough guy—short, balding, originally from New Jersey. His wife, Peri, is a blond Amazon with a thick Texas accent. Unlike my parents, Luigi and Peri are a unit, crazy about each other, and I wonder what that's like, why some people stay in love and others don't.

"Hey, y'all! Welcome to Luigi's," Peri says, greeting us at the door with laminated menus.

"Well, hey there, Peri. When did you start working the door?" Dad teases, pouring on the charm.

Peri laughs. "I know! Can you believe Lou's finally lettin' me play hostess? I've only been askin' fer about a year! Made me take a test and ever'thin'. Can you imagine?"

"Only so I could figure out a way to spend more time with you," Luigi says, and kisses her cheek.

Peri beams. "Always the romantic."

"Enjoy your dinner!" Luigi tells us.

Peri leads us past the trompe l'oeil wall made to look like a garden in Italy, and the red and white checkered tablecloths decked out with carnations and bottomless baskets of bread-sticks. I think an alarm goes off if anyone is without a starch product at any time. Peri takes us to a table right by the faux gas fireplace, which flares with this sort of weird blue-orange flame that doesn't even pretend to look real.

"Here you go. Your server will be right with you. Thank you, and enjoy your meal," she says, like she's a graduate from a hostessing school.

"Isn't this nice?" Dad says, opening his menu, blocking us out. Mom does the same. Jenna looks miserable, but she's too much of a good girl to risk disappointing Dad. That's why she gave in. She doesn't have the close personal relationship with his back that I do. I wish I'd taken the time to get high first so I could at least find this all somewhat amusing.

"Who's got something good to tell us?" Dad says, once the orders have been placed and the overflowing bread basket has been raided. We all need something in our mouths to keep what we want to say from jumping out.

"I've got something," Jenna says, smiling, right on cue. "You know how spring break is coming up? And you know how I've always wanted to learn how to ski? Well, Chet's church group has a ski trip planned, and they have an extra place for me."

"Church group?" Dad says.

"I don't know, honey," Mom jumps in. "Skiing is very expensive."

"It wouldn't be that much. They got a great deal, and I could use some of my savings. . . ."

Oooh, bad move, Jen. Mentioning the use of college funds for anything other than that purpose is an automatic disqualifier, but thank you for playing.

Dad gives one of those oh-you-silly-girl smiles meant to show his good nature. But since he doesn't have a good nature, it mostly comes across as assholian. "Those savings are for college."

"Dad," Jenna says, exhaling loudly, eyes toward the ceiling.

"No. Now, honey, you know the rule about that."

"I never get to do anything."

"You could use my savings," I say, biting into buttered onion bread. "I don't think there's a college that would take me."

Dad stifles a sigh, tries to put a smile on it. "Well, we're gonna work on those SATs starting this summer. That way, you'll be prepared come next year."

"Here's hoping," I say, fingers crossed.

"Top-say eing-bay an erk-jay," Jenna singsongs in the Pig Latin we used to use as our special twin language. Back when we were pals.

My father takes a belt of his Scotch. "Hope has nothing to do with it, Cameron. It's hard work. If wishes grew on trees we'd all be rich."

"That doesn't make sense, Dad."

"Neither does a kid with your IQ nearly failing high

school," he says, and there's nothing smug about it. He really looks pained.

"Did I tell you all that I'm going to be teaching a course on the poetic and prose *Eddas* next semester?" Mom says, trying to change the subject. "Remember how much you kids loved those Viking sagas when you were little? Odin and Freya, Balder and Frigg."

Dad's eyes are still on me, like I'm something he just can't find a theorem for. "I know you want me to give up on you, Cameron. But I'm just not built that way."

I could say thanks. The words are on my tongue. But, apparently, I'm not built *that* way. He'll make me care and then he'll give me his back.

"Could you pass the salt?" I say, and I give my spaghetti a dousing, even though it doesn't need it.

After dinner, we walk along the strip mall. The shops are getting ready to close. People make their last-minute purchases. Mom and Jenna go into the bookstore, while Dad steps into the athletic shoe store three doors down. I stand out on the sidewalk, waiting. Lightning pulses in the distance like cosmic Morse code. *Beat-beat, flare.*

An old homeless dude in a tinfoil hat pushes a squeaky shopping cart through the mostly empty parking lot, tossing cans in when he finds them. He stops in front of me, nods toward the sky.

"Something's brewing. Can't you feel it?"

"Rain," I answer.

"No, sir. Lot more 'n rain." He points to his hat. "Better get you one of these."

"Will do."

51

"The world's going to hell. It's all gonna end." He points to his hat again. "Get yourself one of these."

He fishes a flattened Rad soda can out from under a sewer grate. A truck cuts through the lot, its headlights pushing against the dark. The wind shifts, bringing a faint smell of smoke. The old dude drives his cart down the sidewalk, the wheels shrieking the whole way.

CHAPTER EIGHT

Two Weeks Later

**Of What Happens When I Punch Chet King
in the Stomach and Not Even Intentionally**

"Dude, you okay?"

I'm doubled over the bathroom sink, trying to quiet the weirdness in my head. Stoner Kevin's voice sounds like it's coming from deep inside a tunnel.

"Seriously, you don't look so good."

"I think I ate something bad," I manage.

Something really bad. Something that might be warping me on a genetic level.

He gives me a knowing grin. "Awww, *duuuude*! Are you 'shrooming? Oh, man, you are totally taking the Psilocybin Express to Club Mushroom Med, admit it!"

In the bathroom mirror, my face is paler and more gaunt than usual. My eyes are huge and haunted. Under my skin, my nerve endings seem to twitch and burn, smoldering match heads just blown out and wispy with smoke.

"You look wrecked, my man. Why don't you ditch? Take off, enjoy the ride."

"Can't. I'm nearly failing Spanglish. One more absence and I'm gone."

"Dude. Sucks."

The bell rings. It clangs in my head like a gong played through a megastack of amps.

"Come on," Stoner Kevin says. "I'll sit next to you in class. Help you out."

"You're in my Spanglish class?" I ask.

"Uh . . . yeah." He grabs my backpack for me.

"The whole year?" I try to picture him in there and can't.

"Dude. Yeah." Kevin shakes his head, laughs. "Whole year. Don't you remember?"

No. I don't.

"Yeah. Just messing with you," I say, and let Stoner Kevin lead the way to class, because I'm having trouble remembering that, too.

"You should have all read the assigned chapters in *Don Quixote* over the weekend. Remember this will be on the state SPEW test," Mr. Glass says, erasing the blackboard and writing the word THEME in the center. He underlines it just in case we missed it. "Who would like to start today's discussion?"

"Can't be a discussion if we're just supposed to spit back what the state's looking for on the SPEW," the Goth girl behind me snipes.

Mr. Glass scans the room, seeking out those who are friendly to his "let's get jazzed about forced reading" rap. He knows to overlook me. The weird muscle twitches in my leg haven't stopped. And from the corner of my eye, I think I see flames licking at the walls. When I turn my head, they're sucked back in. It's the lack of sleep, I tell myself. Unless I get good and wasted, I can't manage more than an hour or two. I'm so exhausted I'm seeing shit.

"Anybody?" Mrs. Rector asks when no one answers Glass's prompt. "Miss Rodriguez?"

Our future valedictorian doesn't disappoint. "Sampson Carrasco comes up with a way to trick Don Quixote into accepting his life and his place in society and, eventually, his death."

"Yes, very good, and how does he do that? Remember—you must cite examples from the text. That's what you'll do on the test. Don't overthink it—too much thinking will kill you on the SPEW test."

"Well, instead of telling him that he's crazy or he can't do this, he can't do that, he encourages him to go on all these adventures. But Sampson disguises himself and goes along."

"Yes. And why does he do that . . . Mr. King?"

"Me? Aw, I'm sorry, Mr. Glass. I didn't read it."

"Why not, Mr. King?"

"I object on religious grounds."

Mr. Glass rolls his eyes as Chet's football buddies snicker. My head feels like it could explode. Like I need to scream or hit somebody. And just like that, my left arm gets a rogue message and jerks out.

Mr. Glass squints in my direction. "Yes, Mr. . . ." He has to consult his class roster to remember who I am. "Smith? You must have had something you wanted to add?"

"No. I . . . ." The buzzing in my ears is getting worse. "Stop it!"

The football guys start humming the annoying theme song

from a classic sci-fi show. A fresh wave of laughter travels over the class and Mrs. Rector has to shush them; it's all like a detonation to my ears. Press my palms to my head. Stop, stop, stop.

"Come on, Mr. Smith. Venture out of your shell." Yeah, fuck you, too, Mr. Glass. Man, my head. "Why does Sampson Carrasco travel with Don Quixote in disguise? To trick him?" Stop. Please. "To lure him? To help him? Why . . ."

"Because . . ." The buzzing inside me is so intense I can't take it anymore. "Because . . . *fuck off!*"

Mrs. Rector's mouth hangs open. Mr. Glass, for once, is speechless. Somebody gasps, "Oh my God."

Mr. Glass's mouth snaps back into a tight line. "Mr. Smith, you will leave the classroom."

"I'm sorry, I . . . aaaaahhhh!" My body's on fire with pain. "Goddammit!"

Mrs. Rector points to the door with dramatic flair. "Leave. My. Classroom. Now."

"It's okay, *Señora* Rector," Stoner Kevin says. "Cameron's cool. He just ate some wicked mushrooms, that's all."

Yeah, thanks for that, Kev. I try to grab my backpack, but it's like my muscles are from another planet, jerking and twitching in a bad robot dance that gets more snickering from the class.

Mrs. Rector's voice takes on that I'm-above-it-all tone. "I've had quite enough. Could someone please escort Mr. Smith to Principal Hendricks's office?"

"Sure thing, Mrs. Rector." Chet King gets out of his seat and towers over me. "Come on, bro. You're not being funny anymore."

On an ordinary day I would hate Chet King both for his prison guard stance and for calling me "bro." But this is not an ordinary day, and all I can feel is totally freaked out that my body isn't getting any of my brain's frantic commands to move. His hand lands on my arm, and it's like a burn.

"Ahh, shit!" I scream. My spastic arm flies out and whacks Chet in the gut. He's a big guy, but the punch catches him off guard. His knees hit the floor, followed quickly by the rest of him. The jocks are on me at once. Every touch feels like it's connecting with raw nerve endings. I'm vaguely aware that I'm screaming things that are "inappropriate to a peaceful classroom environment."

I guess that's why Chet finally hauls off and socks me.

The Calhoun High School behavior code sheet we all have to sign at the beginning of the year is pretty firm about the dos and don'ts of personal conduct. Punching beloved football players in the stomach is definitely a don't. I'm suspended for five days for unruly behavior and, thanks to Kevin, suspicion of drug use.

Mom has to come pick me up in the Turdmobile. She's so mortified and, knowing Mom, worried, that we drive in total silence—total silence being the parental barometer of just how screwed you are. But the real fun is yet to come. There's the phone call to Dad, which results in his early arrival home (sorry, Raina), which leads to a closed-door discussion, which takes us to the four of us sitting in the family room: Mom, Dad, me, and the disappointment. It's like I'm a camera cutting from close-ups of Mom—worried, vaguely detached, certain this is all a reflection on her uncertain mothering—and Dad—tight, controlled, pissed off, determined to fix things.

57

Mom: We just want to know if you have a problem, Cameron.

Dad: It's obvious he has a problem, Mary. That's not the issue.

Mom: Well . . .

Dad: What are you on, Cameron? Did you think it would be funny to get expelled like that?

Mom: Is it marijuana, honey? Did you get some bad pot?

Dad: When colleges look at your transcript now, do you think they're going to be putting out the welcome mat? Jesus, we'll be lucky to get you into community college.

Mom: Honey, you're not sniffing glue or anything like that, are you? Please. Because that stuff can rot your brain.

Dad: And punching a kid in the stomach? That's great. Just great.

Mom: Oh God. It's not meth, is it? I saw a special on that. People had to have their noses reconstructed.

The camera cuts to a close-up of teen boy as he debates whether to tell his parents the truth, as he weighs whether they will believe him or not.

Me: Mom. Dad. I'm not on drugs. I just—

Cut to wide shot.

Mom: Is this why you got fired from Buddha Burger? Because you were doing drugs? Honey, you have to be careful when you're working with hot oil.

Dad: Mary. Please.

Mom: I just wanted to know.

Dad: It's beside the point.

Mom plays with her artsy earrings. Her hair needs a dye job. The roots are frizzy and gray.

Me: I don't know what happened. I felt sick, okay?

Dad: So you started cursing and punched a classmate. Cameron, that doesn't make sense.

Medium shot of teen boy as he struggles with what to say. It has been too long since he has tried to communicate with his parents, and it's like they are on the other side of the ocean, speaking a different language. Cut to Mom.

Mom: Maybe he needs to talk to a therapist, Frank?

Dad: This is manipulation, Mary. We've got to be the parents, here. Tell us the truth, Cameron. Who's selling you the drugs?

Mom: Oh, Cameron. *You're* not selling drugs, are you?

Me: Mom. Dad. I'm not on drugs. Well, not this time.

Mom: Not this time? Oh, Cameron.

Me: Can you guys just chill for a sec—

Dad: (laughs) Chill? Chill?

Mom: Honey, we're just . . .

Dad: That is rich. . . .

Mom: . . . worried about you.

Dad: Fine. You are officially grounded. The door's coming off your room. You've lost your privacy rights for now. Do you understand?

Cut to close-up of teen boy as he stares at a spot on the wall.

Me: Yeah.

Mom: Do you have anything you want to say, honey?

Extreme close-up of spot looming like a hole.

Me: No.

The camera angle goes wider and wider till it's so out of focus we're nothing but a blob of color on the screen.

Once I've had my ass handed to me Dad style, and it is determined that I *will* go see a drug counselor *and* a shrink, I sit at the kitchen table, reading, since that's pretty much all that's left to me, being that I am grounded for the foreseeable future. Jenna prances past me on her way to the fridge to look at food she won't eat because she's afraid it will make her fat, and fat is a big old black smudge on the storefront window of perfection.

"I hear if you even look at the ice cream for too long, it'll turn you into a porker," I say.

"I'm not talking to you."

"I'm crushed."

"You punched Chet!" Jenna's so pissed she actually takes out a non–fat free pudding cup.

"Don't take it out if you're not going to eat the whole thing," I say.

She slams the fridge door and pulls off the foil top with dramatic flair. "You know why you don't like Chet?"

It's a rhetorical question, but I can't help answering anyway. "You mean besides the fact that he's a self-involved blowhard?"

"You don't like him because he cares about other people. I mean, his speeches at Kiwanis help save people's lives! Have you ever done that, Cameron? Have you ever done anything for anybody else just because you actually cared about them? No. You probably don't even know what that feels like."

This is the part where I jump in and say, *Why, that's not true. I care about all sorts of people. And the environment. And endangered farm animals. Secretly, I've been working up a plan to give an endangered farm animal to every person I care about just so they will know the depth of my feelings.* But the truth is, she's got me on this point. Chet's not the angel that she thinks he is, but I'm in no position to say shit about anybody.

Jenna takes my silence as a concession. "You will not wreck things with Chet and me. From now on, you are not to talk to me or acknowledge me in any way. Got it?"

60

"You. Me. No interaction. Me got."

"Good."

She takes one bite of the pudding, licks every speck from the spoon, puts the cup back in the fridge, and drops the spoon in the sink with a clank.

CHAPTER NINE

Wherein I Am Subjected to Visits with Two Therapists and an Epic Fail with an Ergo-Chair

THE VISIT WITH THE DRUG COUNSELOR

"Hi, Cameron, I'm Abby."

Her office is a study in bland. Soothing green walls. Plastic chairs set in a circle. A messy desk that seems to say, "Hey, you can trust me—I'm busy and kooky just like you kids!" The obligatory, inspirational, cute-pet posters on the walls: STAY STRONG—STAY OFF DRUGS! BE HAPPY, NOT HIGH! There's a half-finished fruit smoothie in the middle of the desk.

"So," Abby says, with an I-already-know-the-answer-to-this-question smile. "Tell me, why are you here today, Cameron?"

"There was nothing but reruns on TV."

Abby nods sympathetically, but her eyes say, Just You Try Me, Asshole. "Cameron, I'd like to help you with your treatment, but you're going to have to start by being honest with me. Tell me about your drug intake in a typical week."

I shrug. "The occasional joint."

She makes a *tsk* sound in her throat like she doesn't believe me, when, actually, I'm telling the truth. "No hallucinogens? Because I hear you really tripped out."

"No. Nothing like that. I think I got some bad pot, though? 'Cause I've been seeing weird stuff lately."

"Mmmm, flashbacks," Abby says, nodding. "That can happen with hallucinogens."

"But I didn't—"

"Oh, man," Abby interrupts, laughing. "I remember this one time, I was traveling around following the Copenhagen Interpretation with my ex-boyfriend . . ."

Thirty minutes later: ". . . dancing polar bears and tracers coming off my body like the freaking aurora borealis! Crazy! Anyway, what I'm trying to say is, I've been where you've been."

No, Abby. It is now clear that you have been many, many places I have not.

"And that's why I say, you have everything to live for, Cameron. Every reason to be happy. Why would you want to hurt that? You need to stop self-medicating and start talking about your feelings," Abby insists. "Get them out. Express what's inside."

"Okay, well—"

She holds up a finger. "So that's why I'm going to send you to my colleague, Dr. Klein. Would you like to do that, Cameron?"

"I guess—"

"Oh, I'm sorry, Cameron," she says, wrinkling her nose. "We're out of time for today. But I think you did very well."

"Hi, Cameron. I'm Dr. Klein."

His office is a study in bland. Soothing vanilla-colored walls. A few ergonomically correct chairs in muted shades of brown. A wooden desk that seems to be whispering, "Don't mind me; I'm just observing," tucked into a corner. And a long leather couch pushed against one wall. I decide right away that I will not go on that couch.

"You can sit anywhere you like," Dr. Klein says, settling into a big *Star Fighter* villain-worthy chair. I sink into one of the ergo-chairs. It's so low my knees come up to my chest.

"You can raise that," Dr. Klein says, seeing me. "There's a handle on the side there."

I struggle with the hydraulics of it, bouncing up and down like a low-rider till I finally land in the same squatty position where I started.

"Good?" Dr. Klein asks.

"Yeah. Golden."

"So," Dr. Klein says, giving me a smile as vanilla as the walls. "Why are you here, Cameron?"

"Aren't you supposed to tell me?"

Dr. Klein nods. The nod says, I Know All About You, Asshole. "I know what your parents have said. I want to know why *you* think you're here."

"Chronic masturbation."

Dr. Klein raises an eyebrow. "If that were a character disorder, I'd be seeing the entire high school. Anything else you want to tell me?"

Turns out, there is. It feels good to talk, and once I start, I don't stop till I've told Dr. Klein all about the weird flame dreams, the feather message I found, the winged Valkyrie girl with pink hair at Buddha Burger, and the feeling that my body has basically been invaded by pain aliens who stab me in intervals and make it hard for me to remember stuff.

Dr. Klein jots down notes, and then he stops writing and just sits, ramrod straight, looking small and a little scared in his big boy chair. In the end, he hands my parents a script for antipsychotic medication and schedules some serious sessions. So, now I've been to see a drug counselor who told me I needed to lay off the drugs and talk about my feelings, and a shrink who heard what I had to say and immediately put me on drugs.

Thank God I've still got some weed left.

CHAPTER TEN

Of What Happens When I Find Myself
on a Dark Country Road and the Sky Rains Fire

The anticrazy meds make me really tired, but still I can't sleep. The insomnia's gotten worse in the past week, and I'm up every night until four or so watching late-night TV. Last night, I was so bored I actually watched a public television special about some scientists building their own big bang machine—some kind of super-duper, atom-smasher, super-collider thingy they want to use to discover strings and super-strings and parallel worlds our brains aren't wired to see yet; worlds that could be as small as a snow globe or as big as the Milky Way. Eleven dimensions. That's what they say there might be.

Right now, the dimension I'm in is extreme boredom. I've basically been under house arrest since the Chet incident. But tonight, Dad's got a lecture at the university, Mom's at book club, and Jenna's spending the night with her girl posse. I feel kind of shitty—my muscles ache like I took a body slam from the entire football team—but I'm not wasting my freedom. I smoke enough to get loose and bike it over to Eubie's.

"Hey, Cam-run!" Eubie says when I walk in the door. "Where you been?"

"Nowhere."

"Still? That's not right." He takes a good look at me. "You look worn, my friend. Zombified."

"Yeah. Thanks."

"Got no color. You need to get out. Experience things. Play music. Fall in love."

"Yeah, I'm on it. Night and day," I say, flipping through a bin of novelty records.

"Why you giving me that smart-ass shit? I'm serious," Eubie says. "Life is short, my friend."

"So they say. Got anything new for me?"

Eubie puts his hands on the counter and leans forward. "No," he says. "Unless you want to borrow that Junior Webster record."

"Maybe some other time."

"All right. Not gonna push you. But you missing out. Hey, ch-ch-check it out," Eubie says, waving a travel itinerary at me. "Got me two tickets to New Orleans for Mardi Gras."

"Who's the other ticket for?"

Eubie puts a hand to his chest and staggers backward in mock shock. "Cam-run? Did you just ask a personal question? Did you express an interest in your fellow man, in someone other than your own miserable self? Lord, Jesus! It's a miracle—that's what it is!"

"Yeah, yeah, yeah," I say, pretending it doesn't bother me. I'm interested in other people. I'm interested in having sex with Staci Johnson. That's a form of interest.

"I'm taking my new lady," Eubie says, kissing the tickets. "Misty Deanna. Miss D."

I wipe a hand across the back of my neck. I'm sweating and clammy at the same time. "Sounds like a porn name. Or a drag queen."

Eubie holds up a finger. "Don't start. You got plans tonight?"

I shrug.

"What's that mean?"

Nothing. That's the glory of a shrug. Totally noncommittal.

"There's a sweet show going down at Buddy's. Jazz. Some tight cats. I'm sitting in. You want to come? I'll put you on the list as my guest."

"Nah, thanks. I got stuff I gotta do."

"Uh-huh. Like what?"

"You know. Stuff."

"Okay, Mr. I Don't Go Nowhere I Don't Ever Try Nothin'. But you're missing a hot show."

"Next time," I say.

"Yeah. Next time," Eubie says, rolling his eyes.

I leave with some blank CDs so I can make copies of my Tremolo LPs. By the time I finish the other half of my J, the streetlights have all twinkled into action. The weed is most excellent, and I've copped one hell of a serious buzz that makes everything, including me, seem like it's both wave and particle. I pedal past campus housing, hopping my bike between street and sidewalk, ignoring stop signs and dodging traffic lights. At the last corner of Mambrino Street, a truckload of drunken college guys careens around a corner, nearly wiping me out.

"What's your problem?" One of the guys is yelling at me, but mostly I hear my heart beating like a mofo in my ears. They hurl insults and empty beer cans.

"Get out of the road, dude!" somebody shouts before they peel away chanting, "Par-ty! Par-ty! Par-ty!"

I'm too altered for in-town cycling, so instead, I shoot off onto an old country road that winds past cow pastures and lonely farms. The route's longer but there's less traffic, and I can enjoy my buzz in peace. The road's bordered on both sides by flat, open fields dotted by bales of cotton. The long white rectangles remind me of those newspaper pictures of soldiers' coffins unloaded from army planes.

I stop pedaling and enjoy the feel of the damp wind on my face. It's going to rain, but I don't mind. It's like I'm the only person in the universe right now. Soft rain pecks at my face. I stick out my tongue and taste it.

The wind picks up and pushes harder. Over the cotton fields, the clouds are thickening into a mean gray clump. They're moving really fast. It's as if they're being pulled into the center of the sky by a huge invisible magnet. Seeing it makes my heart double its beat. Suddenly, I don't want to be out here by myself. It's about a half-mile to the turnoff that leads back to my house. I'm out of the seat, pumping hard as I can, putting my full weight into each pedal stroke.

That dark cloud mass starts swirling. *Tornado,* I think. Shit. But it's weird, because the clouds aren't pushing out and down; they're pulling *in*. There's a boom of thunder, a zigzag of electricity, and a small, dark hole opens up in the murky center of those clouds, a black eye giving off no light at all. The rest of the sky crackles like a laser light show. A neon spear of lightning strikes a small tree close to the road. With a huge pop, the tree explodes in a shower of flames.

I'm startled and lose my balance. My bike skids out and away, and I roll on the gravel, thudding my head against the road. With a hiss, I sit up. My vision's blurry. The horizon's doubling. My head aches and my knee's bleeding.

The tree's still burning, blooming with fire leaves. As I watch, bits of fire leap free and then, man, I must be higher than ever or my brain got banged up, because what I'm seeing now cannot be happening. Those leaves of fire grow and change, like something's inside waiting to be born. The one closest to me evolves as quickly as one of those time-lapse photography experiments in science: the small, hunched-over form unfolds, spreads out, takes on mass, intention. It stands, stretches taller and taller, maybe seven or eight feet high. A huge, burning man with eyes black as the hole opening above us. Oh God, there's three, four, now five of them; they burn so brightly, flames licking off their bodies like blue-orange sweat. They sweep their arms out this way and that, and where they pass, the land curls up in blackness. This makes them laugh, which is a horrible sound—like the screams of people burning to death.

One of the fire giants notices me. Our eyes lock. My blood pumps a new rhythm—*runrunrunrunrun*. It's like the fire giant can sense it. Screeching, he points a fiery arm in my direction, and the heat blows me back. Holy shit. Head ringing, face sunburn-warm, I scramble for my bike and try to pedal like I'm not hurt and fucked up. The bike wobbles, then straightens. The smell of smoke is strong in my nostrils. Behind me, I can hear that horrible screaming.

Just make it to the turnoff. That's all. Just. Don't. Stop.

Somebody's standing in the road.

I hit the brakes, nearly skidding out again. It's dark, and hard to see, but somebody's definitely there. And he's big.

"Hello!" The panic in my voice freaks me out. "Call the fire department!"

The guy doesn't move.

"Hello? Can you help me?"

A sonic boom of thunder drowns me out. Lightning crackles around us, and I get a glimpse: Big dude. Black armor glistening like oil. Spiked helmet, steel visor. Sword. The light bounces off the sword in arcs that hurt my eyes. Sword. He's got a fucking sword! Darkness falls again, and after the intense lightning, the night seems thicker than before. I can't see, can't move, can't think, can't do anything but breathe quick as a fish washed up on the beach, hoping to catch a wave back to safety. Lightning shreds the dark for another two seconds.

He's gone. The road ahead's clear.

Rain crashes down hard and fast; it spurs me into action. With my heart going punk in my chest, I tear up the road, putting as much distance as I can between me and whatever that scary weirdness was back there. Only when I'm safely around the turnoff do I look back: In the downpour, the burning fields are smoking down to charred ruins. The fire gods and the big dude are gone. And up in the sky, there's nothing to see but clouds and rain.

The empty oblong bubble with its question-mark icon stares back at me, white and unknowing. "Trust me," I want to tell it. "I don't even know how to *start* this search." Humungous, futuristic knight dudes standing in the middle of the road? Menacing, seven-foot-tall fire giants? Black holes over suburbia?

Maybe it was a tornado or some optical illusion or that pot

was laced with some Grade-A Hydroponic Strange. Under the glare of the computer screen, I type in "bad pot experiences." What comes up is page after page of people who've passed out at parties and had *Asswipe* written on their foreheads in permanent marker, kids who ended up getting busted by the 'rents and grounded for life. Nothing about what I've seen. I hit Refresh, and suddenly, a new link pops up: www.followthefeather.com. And there's a picture of one of those weird feathers like I found in my room.

My mouth is so dry it's like my saliva's been burgled. Finally, I tap the bar, and the screen goes dark for a second. An image of the It's a Small World ride comes up. The song bleeds from my speakers. A line of script floats to the middle of my screen and settles into focus: *Follow the feather.* Beside it is a little feather icon. I click on it, and a video clip plays.

A guy in a lab coat sits at a desk cram-packed with stuff—papers; a strange light-up toy that looks like it's part seashell, part pinwheel, with little tubes all over it; a framed photo of a smiling lady with light hair and freckles; an old-fashioned radio. I recognize the song playing—something by the Copenhagen Interpretation. A shelf behind the guy's head hosts an impressive snow globe collection. He leans in to adjust something on the camera, his face going blurry. Then he's back and smiling, hands clasped.

"Hello," he says. He has a nice voice. Soothing. It's hard to say how old he is, older than my dad, though. He's Asian, with long, salt-and-pepper hair, and bushy black eyebrows framing eyes that seem both exhausted and surprised, like one of those people who's seen just about everything and still can't believe it.

"I will find it. Time, death—these are only illusions. Our atoms, the architecture of the soul, live on. I'm sure of it." He holds up the weird toy. "Somewhere in those eleven dimensions we cannot yet see, lie the answers to the greatest questions of all—why are we here? Where do we come from? Where do we go next? Is there a God, and if so, is He unconcerned or just really, really, really busy?"

There's a blip, and the video jumps to some footage of people playing soccer on a field near wind turbines. *Click.* Quick cut to the same guy with his arm around the smiling, freckle-faced woman from the photo on his desk. She presses her lips to his.

"Ah," he laughs. "There's eternity—in a kiss!"

The video cuts out for a second, and when it comes back, it's the same man, but he's older now, his long hair gone mostly to silver, his eyes wearier. The Copenhagen Interpretation song still plays. He holds up a big, pinkish-white feather.

" 'Hope is the thing with feathers that perches in the soul.' Emily Dickinson. Why must we die when everything within us yearns to live? Do our atoms not dream of more?" His hand closes around something that looks like a ticket or key card. "Tonight, I embark for other worlds. Searching for proof. For hope. For a reason to go on. Or a reason to end . . ."

That's it. There's nothing more. I try to play it again, and all I get is the bit that plays at the end of every ConstaToons cartoon: a picture of a twinkling galaxy and suddenly, the roadrunner pokes his head right through space, puncturing a hole in it. He holds up a sign that says MEEP-MEEP. THAT'S IT FOR NOW, KIDS.

The next thing I know, a siren's blasting in my ears.

"Cameron!" someone shouts, competing against the brutal electronic scream that won't stop. "Cameron!"

With a gasp, I wake, drenched in sweat.

"Cameron! We'll be late!" Mom. Yelling. Downstairs.

The alarm clock's still shrieking. Digital numbers assault me with their red blinking: 7:55 a.m. I'm in my bed, still dressed in yesterday's clothes.

"Be right there!" I punish the alarm clock with a hard whap. I feel like shit. My clean clothes are in a heap on the floor. When I reach for them, every muscle aches. Definitely a school nurse day.

Downstairs, the house whirrs with busy household noises, all that to-ing and fro-ing people seem to love so much. Mom's more frazzled than usual. She's wearing one earring and searching for the other. "Cameron, we have to go, honey! Grab a breakfast bar."

"Not hungry," I say, taking half of Jenna's bagel from her plate.

Jenna snatches it back. "Mom, could you please remind your son that he's not to have any interaction with me?"

Mom throws up her hands. "Could we not do this today? I have a very important meeting with the Dean."

"He started it." Jenna pouts.

The kitchen smells like smoke, and for a minute, I panic, remembering my pot-induced episode from last night. "Mom, you left the toaster on. It's burning."

"No I didn't. Where on earth is that earring?"

"Mom-dude. I can smell it overheating. It's making me nauseated."

Jenna holds up her bagel for inspection. "Hello! Not toasted, okay?"

"Ha! Made you talk!" I'd gloat some more but even that exchange hurt my brain.

"You guys, please. Jenna, could you help me find my earring?"

The stench of burning plastic is getting stronger. I know Mom has used the toaster and forgotten to unplug it. If it overheats, Dad will have a cow.

"Fine, I'll unplug it."

A low, pressurized hiss escapes the toaster. Tendrils of smoke seep out around the sides. There's a flicker of orange that makes me jump back. Before I can pull the plug free, the flicker morphs. Long, curved fingernails of fire inch out from behind the smoking toaster and rake deep black scars into the wall there.

"Mom . . ." My voice cracks.

The toaster bursts into flames, shooting a stream of fire all the way up to the ceiling. Mom and Jenna yelp, but I can't stop looking. The flames have eyes—hard black diamonds in a face of blue-orange heat, and they're staring right at me.

"Get the fire extinguisher!" Mom shouts.

They're not real. They're not real. They'renotrealnotrealnotreal. It's another dream, Cam. Just wake up. But I can't. In my ears is the hiss and pop of flame coming closer. My knees buckle. I'm on the floor, shaking. Above me, the fire giants laugh, and I feel it in my body like a virus I can't eject.

Help me. Help me. Help me.

"Cameron? What's the matter? Cameron!" Mom yells. "Jenna—get your father. Frank! Frank!"

Mom falls on top of me with her full weight, but I'm fighting her. I'm not trying to. I just am. Stop. My brain's screaming the order, but my legs aren't getting it.

"Cameron?" Mom's eyes are wide with fear. I want to tell her, warn her, but I can't make the words. And the fire giants are so close. Feels like I'm melting from their heat. One bends down, cocks its head. Its flickering tongue snakes out

75

and licks along my arm to the shoulder, sending hot shards of stabbing pain through me. It laughs that terrible laugh I heard in the cotton fields. I can't wake up and I can't make it stop.

And then the only sound I hear is my own terrified screams.

CHAPTER ELEVEN

In Which I Recount the Untold Joys of MRIs and Open-Backed Hospital Gowns

"Okay, Cameron, just hold still for a second."

I'm lying on the conveyor belt part of an MRI with the feel of cold medical stainless steel against my bare ass. They've made me wear this ridiculous, open-backed hospital gown that I swear is made out of tissue paper, and my buns are freezing. They let me keep my socks on, though, like that's supposed to make me feel better.

This is my third doctor's visit in four days. I've had questions asked, blood taken, reflexes tested, MRIs examined, and one biopsy sent off. I've been poked and prodded in places I'd always prided myself on keeping untouched for that one special doctor who gives me a ring and a promise someday. "We just want to rule some things out," they all say—doctor code for "brain tumor/cancer/meningitis-TV-movie disease of the week."

The conveyor belt moves me through the metal circle till I'm mostly inside. My body's shaking, and I don't know if it's whatever is wrong with me or just the fact that I've been nearly naked for hours on end. The disembodied voice from the MRI control tower reverberates in the cone. "Cameron, we need you to lie perfectly still, okay?"

"Okay," I answer, but my voice doesn't go farther than the metal over my head.

The thing starts up, taking snapshots for some doctor's photo album. Nobody warned me about the sound. *Kerchung-kerchung-kerchung*, like a giant stapler traveling across my skull. Shit. I can't wait to get out of this thing. After what seems like ten minutes past forever, a tech comes in, takes the IV out of my arm.

"You're done," he says. "You can get dressed."

I'm sitting on my bed, reading *Don Quixote* when Dad comes home. He knocks and lets himself in.

"Hey, buddy." The last time Dad called me buddy I was eight and had the measles.

I look up briefly. "Hey."

"How're you feeling?"

"Okay."

"Yeah?" He asks like he really wants to know.

"Yeah. You know. Okay."

"Yeah." He nods and picks up a Great Tremolo LP and pretends to read it. "This guy any good?"

I shrug.

"Your mom told me about the, ah, the doctor's visit. I swear those guys don't know their asses from their elbows. Anyway, Stan in my office—you know Stan Olsen?—he gave me the number of a specialist in Dallas. I made an appointment for Tuesday."

"Okay."

"I'm sure it's nothing, Cam. Viruses can mimic all kinds of things. The doc will probably throw us out for wasting his time." Dad puts the Great Tremolo LP down. He looks at the junk-strewn floor like it's causing him actual pain but he only clears his throat. "Cameron, what did you see? When the toaster caught on fire? Your mom said something about fire giants."

"I guess I was just getting sick."

Dad thinks it over, nods. "Speaking of fire, maybe I'll build us one tonight. We could toast marshmallows, watch a movie?"

It seems like a bad time to point out that it's sixty degrees, not exactly cozy fire weather. "Sure."

"Okay. Well. I'll, ah, just . . . chop some wood. Okay, buddy?"

I hear the sliding doors into the backyard open and close. When I peek out my window, Dad's standing in the yard with his hands on his hips, just looking around like he's never really seen our backyard before. He picks up the ax, takes a halfhearted swing at a puny log. Then he drops to his knees and closes his eyes for a minute. I'd almost swear he was praying. But my dad's a scientist. He doesn't believe in religion. He leaps up and swings the ax down hard on the log, putting his whole body into it again and again till there's nothing left but a mess of splinters.

The specialist's office is in a huge glass-and-stone complex near the hospital. I'm starting to think there's an interior decorator who specializes in medical décor. Somebody responsible for choosing the so-fake-they-almost-look-real plants and the beige striped wallpaper I've seen in every doctor's office I've been in lately. She probably even fans out the magazines on the side table, the copies of stuff no one ever reads like *Let's Fish!* and *Mazes for Kids* and *Automobile Quarterly*.

"How are you feeling, sweetie?" Mom asks me for the fourth time this afternoon. She holds my hand.

"Fine."

Dad drums his fingers on his knees. "Maybe we could go to Sancho's for enchiladas after. Would you like that?"

"Sure," I say.

Mom stares straight ahead. "They have good guacamole."

"Very good guacamole," Dad seconds.

I pick up a copy of *Automobile Quarterly* and pretend to be interested in an article about a guy with a used car lot specializing in refurbishing old Cadillacs. Anything to avoid talking.

A nurse pokes her head in. "Mr. and Mrs. Smith? The doctor would like to see you first."

It's another fifteen minutes before I'm summoned to Dr. Specialist's office. Somebody's X-rays are up on a light box behind his head. I don't know if they're mine or not. At this point, they almost seem like they could be part of the medical décor arranged by that same decorator. Dad's sitting in one of the chairs. His face is gray. Mom's clutching a tissue.

"Hi, Cameron. I've just been talking to your parents here. You've had quite a week, I hear," the specialist says like he's trying to be jocular, like this is a social call. Fuck him. I try to fold my arms over my chest but they won't cooperate, so I let them twitch at my side. *Just a virus. Viruses can do all sorts of things.*

"Your case is very unusual, Cameron." The specialist taps his pen against a folder on his desk. "Have you ever heard of Creutzfeldt-Jakob disease?"

"No. What's that?"

"It's a neurological disease. It affects the brain. You might have heard it referred to as mad cow disease in animals."

I glance at Dad, who looks like he's posing for Mount Rushmore—not a single eye twitch.

"Mad cow disease," I repeat. "Doesn't that affect . . . cows?"

"Yes. Well. This is the human form. But it works in much the same way."

I vaguely remember hearing a news story about mad cow disease. Some cows got it from bad feed and went insane, hence the mad cow. But I'm pretty sure I haven't been munching on any bad feed, unless you count what they serve in the Calhoun cafeteria. So I don't see how I could have this Creutzfeldt-Jakewhatever. Sounds like a brand of kick-ass speakers.

My right hand's trembling. I can't make it stop. I feel like unzipping my body and crawling out.

"You see, there are these infectious proteins called prions that aren't normally a threat, but sometimes they go awry. And when that happens, it's trouble. For instance . . ." He pulls out a paper clip. "This paper clip holds papers just fine. But if I bend it, like so"—he pulls out one leg of it—"it no longer functions in the same way." Dr. Specialist Man shoves a sheaf of papers into the messed-up paper clip and the papers scatter across his desk. "Then those prions—the bent paper clips—reproduce like that, bad copies of a wrong protein, taking over your brain, destroying it over time."

"Oh. Uh-huh," I say, because I can't really take in any of what he's saying.

"This is nuts. Where could he have gotten it? You tell me how a normal sixteen-year-old kid ends up with CJ!" Dad barks.

"Could have been anything," Specialist Man says with an unconvincing shrug. "Could have been tainted beef or even something genetic waiting to happen. The truth is, we'll probably never know."

"Unacceptable. This is pure conjecture," Dad snarls, and for the next few minutes, he and Dr. Specialist confer in some secret language—Dad basically telling the doc he's full of shit, and the doc making a case for why he's not. I don't understand a lot of it because my head hurts and it feels like there's an army of ants doing an aerobics class under my skin and I don't want to be here anymore.

"So, what's the treatment?" I ask.

Dr. Specialist taps his pen against his desk lightly. Dad goes quiet. Mom squeezes her tissue. Something terrible twists inside me.

"There's a cure, right?"

Nobody says anything for a few seconds, and those feel like the longest seconds of my life. Dr. Specialist sits up straighter, morphing from man to doctor-machine. "We're still exploring options at this time," he says in that calm voice they teach you in medical school along with crappy handwriting.

"But, like, the other people who've gotten this Crew, croix . . ."

"Creutzfeldt-Jakob disease . . ."

"That, the, um, mad cow thing, what happens to them?"

The doc clears his throat. "It depends on the progression of the disease. But there are some things you need to know, Cameron."

Dr. Specialist finally finds his voice, and now I just want to tell him to shut up. It's like the information is a big wave rushing over me, and I can only grab at certain words and phrases to hold me up. "Progressive muscle weakness," "uneven gait," "dementia and delusions," "four to six months," "hospital," "experimental treatments."

I don't hear anybody mention it's going to kill me. Probably because no one actually comes right out and says it. In fact, Dr. Specialist does everything he can *not* to say it.

And that's when I know I must be in some deep shit.

CHAPTER TWELVE

**Wherein, Now That I'm Officially Screwed,
a Pep Rally Is Celebrated on My Behalf, and
Staci Johnson Gives Me the Time of Day**

What happens to us when we die: an informal poll.

Theory #1: The Christians are right. There's a big guy with a white robe and a long, flowing beard and a devil with a pitchfork, and depending on whether you've been bad or good (oh, be good, for goodness' sake!), you'll wind up playing a harp with the angels or burning in the everlasting fires of hell, both of which sound sucktastic.

Theory #2: The Jews are right, and when you die there's nothing, so you better have gotten plenty to eat in this life.

Theory #3: The Muslims are right, and I am in for some serious black-eyed virgin time. Then again, I've got black eyes and am a virgin, so I may be in for some serious trouble once I kick.

Theory #4: The Buddhists and Hindus are right. This life is one of many. You just go on working through your karmic baggage till you get it right. So be nice to that cockroach. That could be you someday.

Theory #5: The UFO crazies are right, and we are all one big experiment for a race of superaliens who like to sit around in the alien equivalent of the Barcalounger, sipping a brew and watching those wacky humans get up to the nuttiest sorts of hijinks. And when we buy the farm, they swoop down in the mother ship and take us back to Planet Z and the primordial ooze.

Theory #6: Nobody knows shit.

This is just one of the many nifty lists I've been making up over the weekend since I got my diagnosis and entered it into that devil's playground, the Internet. Turns out I'm in for a fun ride. I've learned a lot of spiffy new information.

For instance, if you want the technical term for what I have, it's Creutzfeldt-Jakob variant BSE. BSE stands for Bovine Spongiform Encephalopathy. Should I tell our studio audience more about it, Jim? Sure, let's tell 'em what I've won. Well, folks, it's a fatal virus that eats holes in your brain, turning it into a sponge. The tying-shoes brain cell? Sorry, this item permanently out of stock. We regret to tell you that your gross motor skills and neurological functioning will no longer be in your control. Here's your econo diaper pack. Watch out for those hallucinations, and have a nice day.

It's all got a sort of pathetic, TV-movie-of-the-week treatment. How our hero started off as a good kid/under-achiever-with-promise/hardened-by-life-but-marshmallow-soft-in-the-center type who managed to get hooked on drugs/make the debate team/tutor a disabled kid and everything turns around the minute he accidentally kills his best friend in a car accident/scores the winning point/nearly loses the kid to "the system" and comes to realize how much he loves the little tyke. Cut to denouement, where everyone *has learned a lesson and comes out a stronger, wiser person for it.* The kind of shit that makes parents and politicians coo over the "positive," "life-affirming" message that gosh-darn-it our young people need more of today. Insert Theme Tab A into Plot Tab B, fold and fluff, and you've got yourself a nice little book that also makes a beautiful display for your holiday table.

Yeah, fuck that.

You know what works? Denial. As a coping tool, denial is severely underrated. Hey, maybe it's a mistake and I've just got a wicked bad flu. Doctors make mistakes all the time. Psych—just kidding!

For a long time, I thought it would be cool to die young. Honestly, things weren't going so well in the life department. Death seemed infinitely more glamorous and, you know, kind of hard to fuck up. I confess that most of the dying fantasy involved watching every girl who'd ever dissed me throwing herself on my coffin, sobbing over my early demise and confessing that she'd always wanted me and wished she'd had the chance to claim my virginity while I was alive.

Problem is, I won't be around to sample the goods. I'll be turning into a sponge head. This is the sort of stuff I think about with the few brain cells I've got left. Of course, Mom and Dad are convinced the diagnosis is wrong. And I want to believe them. Just like I want to believe that Staci Johnson secretly wants me and uses constant hostility to mask her lustful impulses.

Like I said, denial. Now served 24/7.

* * *

By the weekend, news of my possibly imminent demise is all over town, and the house has been Fruit Basket City. It's like now that I'm checking out, I actually matter. And, for some reason, this demands cute baskets loaded with kiwi animals and apples carved into flowers. Calhoun High School has gone into overdrive for me. Rumor has it that the school board fears a lawsuit and they had people in sci-fi-worthy suits tearing apart the cafeteria in case that's where the BSE came from. I hear the new menu features a lot of tofu. But to make up for all the gosh-darn inconvenience of my having a terminal disease, they have organized a pep rally in my honor. I'm hooked up to wires and cameras so that my face will be transmitted over the JumboTron in the gym, and I get to watch the Rally of Pep happening live over my TV.

"Hi. Testing. Is this thing on?" Staci Johnson's bodacious bod is front and center on our forty-two-inch screen. The fates taketh away but they also giveth. Once she figures out she's on, Staci gives the command to her wannabes and they fan out behind her in cheerleader fashion, giggling and smiling. But Staci smiles biggest. "Hi, Cameron!"

"Hi, Cameron!" the girls say, high kicking until one of them accidentally flicks Staci's ponytail with her foot.

"Goddammit, Tanya!" Staci growls, slapping the clumsy girl's leg. She turns back to me, all smiles. "Omigod, Cameron, everyone here misses you, like, so much, and we are totally organizing a fund-raiser for you."

"I'm making a crepe paper cow. For the poster," a smiling wannabe says. She's wearing a CAM'S MY MAN T-shirt.

"A cow?" I choke out.

"Omigod, Debbie!" Staci growls between clenched teeth. "Like, hello? That was supposed to be a surprise?"

Debbie's face falls. "Sorry."

Staci leans forward. Her face is huge. "You are so brave,

Cameron. You just gotta stay strong, okay? See you at the pep rally." Staci walks away, giving me one of those glances over the shoulder that she's famous for, the ones that make guys think they might have a chance.

Jenna's on camera next. She's actually been very nice to me lately, which is almost as weird as having CJ. "Hey, Cameron. I hope you can feel the love. Everybody's pulling for you. I mean, everybody." She glances over at Chet, who's hanging out with the principal in the background. "Chet's got his whole youth group praying for you. They read passages from the Bible together every morning."

"Wow. Do their lips move while they read? Do they have to use their fingers?"

She rolls her eyes. "Be nice," she whispers close to the mike.

Jenna has to introduce me via camera to the principal, who doesn't remember suspending me. That's a drag. I was hoping to play on the guilt there. Finally, it's showtime. The gym doors open, and everyone pushes in, laughing, talking, eating processed snacks—the official food of high school. Funny, I used to hate the kids in my high school for any number of small and big annoyances; now I hate them only because they get to be alive longer than I do. The turnout's surprisingly big. Apparently, seeing the Mad Cow Kid is a better draw than girls' volleyball or guys' lacrosse, which isn't saying much.

Chet King's doughy face pushes into the left side of the TV. He looks worried. "Cameron, hey, it's me, Chet. You know, bro, I'm sorry about that punch in Rector's class. I didn't know you were sick."

No. Of course not. It's only Christian to hit people who are well.

I should let him off the hook, tell him not to sweat it, but

I can't help it. I really hate that Chet King gets to keep living and I don't. I cough long and hard for effect and watch him wince, terrified he's made God grumpy.

Principal Hendricks steps up to the mike. "Take your seats, people, please." He waits for things to settle down to a dull roar before continuing. "As you know, we're here to honor a very brave student today and show him our support. Cameron Smith."

The gym explodes in sound. It's meaningless. I'm going to die.

Principal Hendricks shouts over the din. "Cameron, we know you're gonna beat this thing. And every single one of us is pulling for you. Just embrace the positive."

"Amen," Chet King says, and I wonder if he's pissed that I've surpassed him on the God Will Test You Because He Loves You scale. He didn't get a special pep rally shout-out when he broke his vertebrae.

"Let's give Cameron a special cheer," Principal Hendricks says, applauding.

Eight cheerleaders turn the gym floor into a blur of athletic tumbles and pumped fists. They clap and yell and motion for the crowd to get on their feet. Grudgingly, kids stand. Now that they can see I don't have three heads or large boils covering my body, they probably want this over with so they can get out, go home, go smoke a J, get in the chat rooms, game it, whatever. The rah-rahs lead the crowd in a rousing chant of my name. "Cam-a-run, Cam-a-run, Cam-a-run!" The sound bounces around the rafters and off the bleachers in a thick roar that hurts my ears. Some jackass moos and the principal of vice takes the mike to warn them they will be "subject to disciplinary action," plus what they're doing "isn't nice."

February 20 is officially declared Cameron Smith Day at

Calhoun High School. Teachers say nice, generic things about me at the mike. They can't say nice, specific things because that would entail actually knowing and caring about me. Mom and Dad sit on the bleacher closest to the basketball net. They look gray and flat, clapping along when they're supposed to, but never smiling. Every now and then, Mom ducks her head and I see her hand go up to her face, wiping. The visiting nurse pats my shoulder, and I want to tell him to stop. His comfort is too much. I take some ragged breaths, holding back the tears, because I don't want my last high school moment to be me sobbing on a cheesy JumboTron.

Fuck you, I think instead. *Fuck you for living.*

The wall of gymnasium sound thrums in my head like a g-force. I just want this to be over. And then, up in the stands I see her—a girl with short pink hair, torn fishnets, black lace-up punker boots, and a tarnished breastplate like some Wagnerian heroine. From behind her back, two white buds appear on either side of her arms and begin to bloom like enormous daisies reaching for the sun, stretching out for what seems like forever. Wings. She's staring right at me and smiling. Her smile is the biggest thing on her face, like it almost doesn't fit. And I swear she's glowing. Getting brighter by the second. The light drowns out the other sights and sounds in the gym. The wings reach their maximum span, and now I can read the message written there: *Hello, Cameron!*

And just like that, everything inside my head goes dark.

CHAPTER THIRTEEN

In Which I Check into the Hospital and Have an Encounter with an Angel and Other Strange, Annoying Things

"Cameron?"

The voice sounds like it's coming to me from inside a tunnel. *Ow, shit! Could you get that light out of my eyes?*

"Cameron, can you hear me?"

Yes, I can hear you. Can you hear me, because I was really fucking serious about that instrument of torture disguised as a penlight that for some reason you seem to find it amusing to shine directly into my pupils. I'm pretty sure they prosecute people as war criminals for this kind of shit.

The dulcet tones of Dr. Asshole float back to my ears. "If you hear me, Cameron, just make a sound."

Hello! Are you not listening? I've been talking.

Haven't I?

"If you don't want to speak you can squeeze my hand or nod if you understand."

I nod and my brain throbs in my head.

"Good. Very good, Cameron." The light stops, thank God, and I'm able to drift in and out, catching snippets of conversation between Dr. Asshole and my 'rents.

"We're giving him . . . for discomfort . . ."

I'm floating in space. It's nice here. A comet zooms past. A star. The Buddha Cow twirls by on her lotus-flower hamburger patty. She raises a hoof in Zen salute. I've been blessed by the Cow. Amen.

"We'd like your permission to try something experimental, something that in trials has had some success with destroying the prions that attack the brain and may slow the progression of the disease."

Sounds good to me, Doc. Let's kick some serious prion ass. Any time is good. And a little more morphine wouldn't suck. Oooh, I just flew through the Milky Way. Awesome.

". . . some side effects . . ."

"I don't know. . . ." It's Mom's voice.

Something's pulsing up ahead. *Huh. What is that thing?* It's round and dark.

". . . twice a day . . ."

". . . doesn't even know we're here . . ." Dad's voice.

The Buddha Cow zips on and disappears into the big black hole up ahead. *Me no likee this. Time to reverse thrusts, Captain.*

". . . Just sign here and we can get started. . . ."

Sign what? Hey. I hit reverse. *How come that hole's getting closer? No fair. Mom? Dad? Dr. Asshole? Somebody? Pull me back. I'm getting too close to this thing for comfort, man. Seriously. I'm nodding. Anybody out there see me nodding? Anybody out there? Anybody?*

Day Three

I open my eyes. On the wall opposite me is a framed picture of an angel. St. Jude's. Right. I'm in the hospital.

A lady in pink scrubs is beside me, fiddling with a bag on an IV pole. She's solidly built, like she could kick my ass if she wanted, and her skin's the color of coffee without a trace of milk. She wears a lanyard around her neck. A bevy of angel pins have been tacked to it. The lanyard holds her hospital ID, which reads GLORY BEAUVAIS.

"You wakin' up?" she asks me. She's got a strong accent.

"Yeah," I croak. My voice is scratchy.

"Good, I need to get your vitals." Glory's not big on the chitchat and endearments, it seems. She puts the blood pressure cuff around my arm, pumps it up and watches the meter ticking off numbers. When she's satisfied, she tears the cuff off in a loud rip of Velcro. "One twenty over seventy. Good. Little bit of fever. I'll tell the doctor, see if we can get you somet'in for it. You in pain?"

Oh goody. The candy store is open. "Yes," I gasp. "A lot of pain."

Glory purses her lips, which are unadorned by any lipstick at all. "I'll put in an order for some aspirin."

"I think I need more than that," I say.

She doesn't budge. "I'll tell the doctor. Your breakfast will be here soon."

Day Four

The old geezer across the hall coughs all the time. I started counting them. Twenty-eight in one thirty-minute period. To drown out the sound, I've taken to watching soaps. It doesn't really work, but now I'm captivated by a storyline about this woman and her evil twin who, for some reason I can't figure out, looks nothing like her. Old sick guy is coughing up a lung over there.

God, if you exist, can you take him instead of me?

DAY FIVE

It's official. I hate oatmeal. Hospital oatmeal is gray with the consistency of glue. You can pour two packets of sugar substitute and a whole carton of milk into it and it still won't have any taste. If this is what my last days are going to be about, put the pillow over my face now. Dad was here this morning. Now Mom's on duty. She brought me some new comics, which was cool. I must have drifted off. When I wake up, she's sitting in the ugly hospital chair, slipping pictures into a big book. She gives a half-smile. "I thought I might finally finish that photo album of our Disney trip."

"Mom. I was five when we went to Disney."

"I know. I kept saying I'd get around to it." She puts a picture in my hand. "Do you remember this?"

It's a picture of us standing outside Tomorrowland. I'm grinning maniacally like my face might break with joy.

"You loved that place. Made us go on everything you could ride at least four times."

"Was this before or after I tripped out on A Small World?"

"After," she says with a sad little smile. Mom sifts through the shoe box of pictures. She picks up and abandons one after the other. "I don't know where to put all these things."

Finally, she closes the box. She slips it and the half-finished photo album into her book bag to be forgotten.

The stoner trio has come today. Their conversation is like watching a volleyball match where you can't tell the players apart.

Rachel: Dude, some of those nurses are smokin' hot. The one with the dark hair in a ponytail? Is she into piercings and science nerds?

Kevin: Does she ever come in and, like, take her hair down and be all, "Oh, Cameron, I never dreamed it could be like this!"

Rachel: Pig. Stop talking about my future girlfriend that way.

Kyle: That could totally be like, one of those last wish things, though. Do it. Put in for hot nurse sex before you kick.

Kevin: They hooking you up with good meds? My uncle went in for gallbladder surgery and they gave him, like, Make-Me-See-God-Ocontin or something. It was the only week he wasn't a complete asshole. We wanted to put it in his water supply.

Rachel: Did you hear? The student council is selling gold ribbons to raise money and everything. Whole school's wearing 'em. Mrs. Rector dipped into her margarita money to buy one, and she doesn't even like you.

Kevin: It was supposed to be black-and-white, you know, like a cow pattern? But that was already taken for some other disease.

Kyle: Sorry you've gotta be in the hospital, dude.
Rachel: Sucks.
Kevin: Yeah, definitely the big suckage.
They nod in unison.

Kevin: Speaking of suckage, ask Kyle what he's doing this summer.

Kyle: Shut up, Kevin.

Rachel: Summer School City, man. Shithenge didn't cut it after all.

Kyle: I said, shut *up*.

Kevin: I told you I woulda hooked you up with a paper off the Internet, dude. I know sites the teaching bots never even think of checking. Oh! We brought you the new Director's Cut of *Star Fighter,* episodes one through four—

Kyle: The only ones worth watching—

Rachel: —Sorry the plastic's off, but we tested 'em out last night. Figured you wouldn't mind. Dude, the print is so clear, you can see everything. Like when Star Fighter is battling it out with Dark—

Kevin: —Matter? The glow of his ultimate peace weapon doesn't even look computer-generated. Awesome.

Rachel and Kyle: Yeah. Awesome.

They leave the boxed set on the end of my bed, where it balances on my toes.

Rachel: So. Dude. Seriously. Before you croak, you think you could put in a word for me with that nurse?

DAY ELEVEN
_____

The door opens and a tiny bird of an old lady shuffles in, using her IV pole like a cane.

"Um, I think you're in the wrong—" I start.

She puts her finger to her lips, silencing me. "They won't look for me here."

"Who?"

Her eyes widen. "Them! I'm going to get out of here. I'm running away."

96

Her hair is a long tangle of wiry gray down the front of her hospital gown, and I wonder if she's an Alzheimer's patient or something and if I should call for the nurse. I feel around for the call button but it's just out of reach. She doubles over, coughing, and I recognize that cough from across the hall.

She settles into the chair beside my bed and puts her bony hand on my arm. "This is not how I'm supposed to die."

"So how *are* you supposed to die?"

Her eyes take on a faraway sheen. "In a house by the sea in an upstairs bedroom. It's late spring, and the open window lets in the smell of lily of the valley. And there's a garden outside. It's decorated with paper lanterns, and the children, the children chase after fireflies while their parents laugh and talk as if they have all the time in the world. In a house by the sea, it will end, and I will slip from this life as if it were no more than a sweater grown too large and threadbare with years, something no longer needed. That is how it should be. Not here. Never here." She fixes me with her gaze. "I don't think you should die before you're ready. Until you've wrung out every last bit of living you can."

This lady is, like, ninety, if she's a day. I'd say she's pretty well wrung it. I want to yell at her for having had that long. "Well, I guess there's not much we can do about that," I say bitterly.

"Bullshit! That's what they say so you'll give up without a fight." She leans in so close I can smell the old-person odor on her—musty and old-fashioned, like a room no one goes into much anymore. "I've seen them outside, burning on the lawn. Tall as houses and so bright, so bright."

The hair on the back of my neck stands at attention. "You've seen those freaky fire giants?"

She nods, her eyes wide and fearful.

"What are they?" I whisper.

"They are chaos. Destruction. The end of hope. Oh, these are frightening times. I have to get away!"

An orderly appears in the doorway. "Mrs. Morae, come on, now. You're not supposed to be in here."

"I'll go where I like!" she snaps.

"Now, Mrs. M, don't be like that." The orderly comes closer, looming like a shadow, and for a second, in that shadow, I see the outline of something terrible, and then it changes. It's just a dark blur against the blandness of the wall.

The old lady's lungs rebel. Long, coughing spasms rattle her frail frame.

"See? Gotta get you well. Back to bed, Mrs. M," the orderly says, taking her arm.

"It's okay," I tell the orderly. "She can stay. Really!"

"Tell them they've got it wrong," she hisses between coughs as he leads her gently away. "A house by the sea. Tell them!"

I fall asleep, but my dreams are full of bad things—fires engulfing the world. A black hole opening above us, pulling everything in without a trace, as if we never even existed. Diseased cattle falling in the fields like gassed soldiers in some long-ago war. The angel in the tarnished armor banging her hands against a window while flecks of snow coat her lashes and hair. I wake up with my heart pounding, unsure of where I am or what's happened, whether I dreamed the conversation with the old lady.

A house by the sea. I'd like to be there now. And I wish there were a button I could press that would get me out of here, that could make this all go away.

Glory's been off for two days. Today she's back in her pink scrubs that look good against the dark of her skin. I'm not feeling so great. Sometimes I think I see the punker angel sitting in the corner of the room, reading a comic book with the ill-fated coyote on the cover, an anvil racing for his head. But when I mentioned it to Mom, her eyes got teary, and I haven't said a word about strange angel sightings since.

"Time for your meds," Glory announces in her no-fanfare way.

I wash them down even though they're getting hard to swallow. My body seems like it's failing me by degrees.

"Okay," Glory says, once my vital signs have been recorded for posterity. "You need anything else?"

"No," I say, watching her push the cart toward the door. "Yes."

Glory stops, looks at me. There's no "What is it, sweetheart?" or "Oh, my poor brave bunny." Nope. She just stands, waiting. And I can tell she's even a little annoyed. Kind of makes me like her. We speak the same language.

"Am I going to get better?"

Glory's ramrod body softens for a minute. "You got to ask your doctor that, Cameron." I like the way she says my name, like it has three syllables instead of two.

"It's just . . . nobody tells me anything, you know?"

Glory glances toward the hallway, where she has charts to file and patients to check. "That's cause nobody knows not'ing about how it all works out or why. Why God takes the good or the young or why we suffer. I don't know why he took my little girl with the cancer when she was only five."

She takes a deep breath, like the pain is still fresh. "I don't know and I guess I never will."

All the air has left my lungs. I feel like I should say something, but somehow I don't think Glory's the I-want-your-sympathy type.

"Just push the button if you need something," she says, a little softer this time.

DAY FIFTEEN

Chet King's come for a visit. Even though CJ isn't really contagious, he's decked out in full protective gear—white paper gown, mask, and gloves—like a giant medical paranoia snowman or some eccentric pop star addicted to bizarre fashion choices. He raises one hand, and it reminds me of those good luck pandas you see in Chinese restaurants.

"Hey there, champ," he says at last. "Jenna asked me to stop by. Not that I didn't want to come, you know . . ." His voice is muffled behind the mask. "Hey! Did you hear? The coaches are letting us dedicate this week's all-star game to you. Everybody's praying for you, bro."

I up the volume a bit on the TV. Wouldn't want to miss a scintillating second of my soaps.

Chet clears his throat. "So, uh, how are you doing?"

"Good, except for that pesky dying thing."

"That's sort of what I wanted to talk to you about today." Chet sounds so serious I actually hit the Mute button. "You know, Cameron, no one ever really dies. Not if they've accepted Jesus Christ as their lord and savior."

Chet drops to his knees by my bedside and, with a prayer for protection from my noncontagious disease, takes my hand in his massive gloved one, which is, holy shit, like some kind of freaking paw. How come I don't have manly hands like that? If there is reincarnation on tap somewhere, I'm putting in for big hands.

"Lord, I pray that you will lift the fear from Cameron's mind and forgive him his sins. In the name of your son, our savior, Jesus Christ, Amen. Cam," Chet says in a low church voice. "You have anything you wanna add?"

"No, I think you covered all the bases."

"Don't you want to confess your sins and ask Jesus to forgive you?"

I don't know why this is the thing that pushes me over the edge. I wish I could rip out every tube and wire and punch Chet King for real this time instead of by accident.

"Shouldn't Jesus ask *my* forgiveness? I mean, seeing as he's taking me out of the game at sixteen without even letting me get laid first."

Chet shakes his head. "Cameron, I know that anger's just a front."

"No, it's not. I'm actually very pissed off."

"It's just a front for all the hurt in your soul. I can see it. So can God."

The TV is an enticing carnival barker of color and form. I want to scream, *If God can see my hurt then why the hell doesn't he take it away? If God really exists, why would he allow all the terrible, unfair things to happen? I mean, what kind of sadistic creep is he?*

"You think I don't know what it's like to lie in a bed feeling sorry for yourself, wondering why something terrible is happening to you?" Chet says. "I wasn't even sure I'd be able to walk. Football was my life, and I'll never play the game ever again. But it's okay with me now, Cameron. And you know why it's okay?"

"Because you've realized it's a retarded sport?"

Those gloved hands of Chet's ball into fists at his side for a second before going limp. "Because I've accepted Jesus Christ into my heart and my life. And I know that what happened to me happened for a reason. God has a bigger plan for me, and I have to trust in that."

The question's out of my mouth before I even have a chance to think it. "What if it's not God's will, Chet?"

"But it is. I know that."

"No, Chet, what if it's just a shitty thing that happened? What if it's just bad luck, some random thing like a butterfly flapped his wings in South America and you broke your neck? What if there is no divine plan at all and we are totally on our own?" I don't know what kind of answer I want or if there even is an answer. "You ever think about that, Chet?"

"No. No, I don't," he says with assurance. "And I feel sorry for you if that's how you feel."

Yeah, I think, closing my eyes to the Chet Kings of the world. *I feel sorry for me, too.*

DAY SOMETHING

The coughing across the hall has stopped.

SOMETIME LATER

Hey, Cameron. Pssst. Wake up.

No. No wakey. Sleep. Tired.

Caaaammerrrronnnn! Come on. We've got to talk. We've got lots to do, okay?

She's taking shape in my mind. A small, pixieish face with

102

that wide, full mouth. The hair's short, spiky. Pink. And yep, those wings are spread out. They've been spray-painted with stencils of the Buddha Cow.

Watch this, she says.

She flips a switch on her breastplate, and the Buddha Cows on her wings float up, over and over, like a crazy digital billboard.

Cool, huh?

Who *are* you? I ask.

Why don't you find out?

How?

She puts her hands to her mouth like she's going to shout. Instead she whispers. *Wake up.*

SOMETIME AFTER THAT

Can't sleep. Every time I start to drift off, I think about the old lady, Mrs. M, and what she said. If she said it. Maybe I dreamed it.

My head hurts. Lungs hurt. Arms. Legs. Everything.

Turn on the TV to pass the time. Same old shit on YA! TV. Some show called "The Inside, Outside, and Backside of Music." Parker Day's the host. He's tricked out in his "serious outfit": black pants, black turtleneck, black-rimmed glasses, even though the fucker for sure has perfect eyesight. They've even photographed him on some gloomy, windswept heath to give it that tragic oomph.

"Unless you've been in a time warp, you know the story of the Copenhagen Interpretation," Parker says as they go to voice-over. "From an Inuit fishing village to international music stardom, the Copenhagen Interpretation was living the dream as musicians and messengers of world peace. The release of their debut, *Small World*, launched them into the spotlight. It was quickly followed by their masterpiece, *Words for Snow*. Many claimed the vibrations produced by their music brought on a feeling of well-being, even euphoria, and their concerts promoted harmony. As lead singer Thule said, 'What's so hard about being kind?' Traveling with their ever-present interpreter"—there's a still of some guy in a Hawaiian shirt at a microphone—"the CI toured the world, and the world would never be the same again."

A quick-cut montage of images set to a Copenhagen Interpretation sound track zips across the screen: a blurred shot of the four band members covered head to toe in heavy coats and hoods, like Antarctic explorers; another blurry image of them in the same outfits playing some festival; another indistinct photo of them in the snow.

"And then, one day, at the height of their fame," Parker's voice continues as the screen fades to black, "they were simply . . . gone. In the middle of the Big Benefit Concert for Peace but Against Non-Peace and People Generally Being Not Nice, in the middle of what everyone agreed was a bitchin' set, they simply vanished. Were they the victims of foul play? Had they grown weary of fame? Were they aliens visiting from a musically advanced planet? Or, as some suggest, had they eaten each other in a drug-induced, hate-fueled orgy of excess—the dark side of celebrity? When we come back, we'll explore. . . ."

That's all I can take of that. Flip to the news. A shellacked anchorman giving the daily grim. Teenaged soldiers carrying guns. Bombed marketplaces tattooed with blood. Crying villagers. Melting ice caps, confused polar bears. Kneeling guys in black hoods behind razor wire. A wildfire in another state. Guys watching it burn, the fire reflected in the mirrored lenses of their sunglasses. Jeez, someone needs to push the reset button on this planet.

The anchorman smiles and they cut to a cute story about a Captain Carnage championship going down.

NIGHT

I can't breathe.

Shit. My lungs. Tight. Can't take in. More. Than a gasp. Of air. Pain.

Dad. Getting up. Scared. "Cameron? Cameron!"

Can't say his name. Can't ask for. Help. No air. Dad's eyes. So scared. Running out. Shouting.

Dad. Back. Glory, too, and. Some guy in green. Pulling a cart. Serious machine.

Glory. Snapping on. Gloves. Lightning quick. "Okay, baby, hold real still for me."

She's never. Shit. Never called me. Baby. Guy in green. Plastic tubing. More people running. Body seizing. Shaking. Can't. Can't stop.

"Gotta get him tubed," Glory barks. "Give him that shot, now."

Arms. Holding me. Down. Roll to side. Pain. My hip. Shot going in. Medicine. Hot like fire.

Breathe, Cameron.

Glory's face. Determined. Grim. "Hold him good." Fingers. Opening my mouth. Tube. Coming in. Oh fuck. Snaky plastic. Too much. Makes me choke. Want to. Scream. Gagging. Choking. My heart. Frantic general. Screaming. "The hell's going on out there? Report, soldier, report!"

Stop. Can't. Stop. Shaking. All over. Panic. Like a wave. Taking me. Under.

105

Glory. Near. "Easy, easy, it's okay, baby, don't fight it, just a minute and it'll all be over."

Scared. So scared. Make it stop. Must stay. Awake. Fight. The old lady said.

Focus. Picture. On the wall. Angel.

Meds. Make my head. Heavy. Then light.

The picture. The angel. Focus. See.

Wings. Move. Flutter.

Like snow.

Falling.

CHAPTER FOURTEEN

In Which I Wake Up

White.

All I see is white.

Blink.

White.

Blink, blink.

White, white.

The white has little pockmarks, like the surface of the moon.

Blink again, and the spongy square tiles of the hospital ceiling come into focus. The hospital. *I'm still here? What if I'm not? I'm afraid to look. Okay. Take this slowly. Slide eyes to the left. Window and a wall radiator. Eyes to the right. Visitor chairs. Mom and Dad. Sleeping.*

Mom and Dad. Still here. All still here.

Thank you.

It's night when I wake again. The first thing I notice is that there's no tube in my throat anymore. It's sore and dry, though. Like I've been eating gravel for two days straight.

"You awake?"

A new face appears above my head. I shriek, surprised by the sound of my own scratchy voice.

"Oh, sorry, dude. I thought you were awake."

I close my eyes and silently will the hallucination to go away. When I open them again, his face is still next to mine.

"You okay, amigo?"

I try to talk but my throat is sore and dry. "Could you. Water. Please?"

"Oh. Sure. No problem, dude."

In about three seconds, there's a cup in my hand. I take a few sips and feel my throat balloon with each one. Better. "Thanks. Sorry if I scared you. It's just . . . I thought I might have, um, died. Or something."

"Yeah, no kidding. I was a little freaked out about it myself," he says.

"You were here then?"

"Just wheeled in."

I take a really good look at him. He's got a cherubic face, all round cheeks and pug nose. Big, dark, almost-girl-pretty eyes guarded by eyebrows knit together in an expression of annoyance and suspicion. It's all topped off by a huge mushroom cloud of kinky hair. Calhoun High. Fourth-floor bathroom.

"You're the gamer," I say.

"Four-time Captain Carnage champ. It's Gonzo, if you don't remember. Well, my full name is Paul Ignacio Gonzales, but everybody calls me Gonzo."

"Cameron. Smith."

"Yeah, I know." Gonzo scrambles up onto his bed, which is like watching somebody's kid brother try to do it. "So. You're the guy with mad cow disease. Wow."

"Yeah. Wow."

"Wow, wow, wow." Pause. "That is some crazy shit, dude. How'd you get that?"

"Nobody really knows," I say.

"Hey, no offense, but isn't that fatal?"

Nobody's come out and said it so directly. Gonzo's just gone up a notch in my book. "Yeah. Supposed to be. They've got me on some experimental stuff."

"Man. That sucks." Gonzo adjusts his bed. The back rises up with a mechanical groan till he's at a ninety-degree angle.

"So . . . what are you in here for?" I ask.

"Me? I'm in here a few times a year."

"Oh," I say, not sure if it has something to do with his Little Person status.

Gonzo pours his can of Rad XL soda into a plastic cup and swigs it, following up with an impressive belch. "My mom's always convinced that there's something terrible wrong with me and that I'm going to die. If I get a rash, she thinks it's beri-beri. If I lose a little weight, she thinks I've got colon cancer or a tapeworm. If I get a cold she thinks it's pneumonia. I think I hold the record for most chest X-rays ever performed on a single human being under the age of twenty."

"How old are you?"

"Sixteen."

"Me too." I take another sip of my water. "What are you here for this time?"

"I took this growth hormone?" he says, like he's not sure whether he took it or not. "It was supposed to help me get

109

taller. Didn't work. You probably figured that out already. Anyway, the stuff was made from cows—there was this whole class-action lawsuit—so when my mom read about you in the paper, she kinda freaked, wanted them to, you know, test my blood and stuff, make sure I wasn't gonna . . . you know, go bovine." His smile pushes his cheeks up like Venetian blinds, till his eyes have nowhere to go but into a squint.

"So," I say. "What's the word? Is your brain sponging out even as we speak?"

"No, dude. I'm good. But I've had this bad cough, too, so you know, gotta do the old chest X-ray and rule out pneumonia. Or TB. Or lung cancer."

The phone beside Gonzo's bed rings. He lets it ring twice, like he doesn't want to pick it up, but the third ring he cuts short.

"Hi, Mom. Nah, I'm okay. Lunch? Some kind of gross, pureed chicken thing with mashed potatoes and carrots, a little pudding. Mom, how could the chicken be poisoned—it's in a hospital? I'm not being mean. ¡No soy malo! Okay. Okay, okay, siento. Yes, they took me for the spinal. No. No meningitis, so I'm cool. Mom, I don't have a brain tumor. I don't! What do you mean? What article? Well that doesn't mean . . . but not every dwarf gets it!"

Gonzo shifts down low in the bed. "When are you coming by? Can you bring me some books? My Big Philly Cheese Steaks CDs? Oh, and my *Star Fighter* DVD."

Of course he's a *Star Fighter* guy.

"All right. You too. Mom. I can't. *I can't.*" He sighs, then lowers his voice. "Love you, too."

The minute Gonzo hangs up, he grabs an asthma inhaler from his bedside table, puts it in his mouth, and takes two huge puffs, finally letting everything out in a big exhale and a few dry hacks.

110

"You okay?" I ask.

He nods. "Yeah, dude. My mom was just freaking me out a little, that's all. I'm her only kid. She raised me totally on her own and shit. My dad wasn't up for kids, especially not a dwarf kid."

"Oh," I say.

"Hey, you like the Copenhagen Interpretation?" Gonzo asks. "Got the remix of 'Words for Snow.' Did you see the commercial they cut to that song for Rad XL: 'For when you're too much for any other soda!'? Dude, it is *severe*! Hey, do you like *Star Fighter*?"

"Who doesn't?"

"Dude, I have that whole movie memorized! My favorite part? When Odin—right? He's the old master?—when he says, 'These Star Fighters are not worth the trouble. You will help them escape,' and totally mind-numbs the guards into letting those guys go. Man, I wish I could do that to Mrs. Rector. 'These are not the grades you wish to assign me, teacherling. You will reach for a higher letter or taste the righteous mojo of my Ultimate Peace Weapon.' Awesome. Hey, do you—"

The phone goes off again. Gonzo's jaw tightens. He stares at the phone like he's afraid of it. He makes it to four rings this time. "Hi, Mom," he says with a deep sigh. "You what? Mom. Why? Why did you look up the nutrition content of the hospital food on the Internet? No way. No, they *don't*. They have to clean the table free of peanuts before they make the chicken, okay? I mean, it's a hospital. I'm sure they're super careful. *No hago esto.* I'm not asking for an EpiPen. Mom! You're not listening to me . . ."

I turn over and slip my headphones on, scroll through the dial till I find my cache of Great Tremolo songs. One press, and Gonzo's increasingly desperate arguing with his mom is drowned out by the familiar recorder-and-helium voice of my favorite cheesy musician. The notes swoop and fall, like someone trying to sing while being tickled. It's the only thing that's made me happy in the past two weeks, and I'm not letting go of it.

CHAPTER FIFTEEN

**Of What Happens When I Am Assigned a Mission
of Crazy Importance or Just Plain Craziness.
Because Sometimes It's Hard
to Know the Difference.**

When I wake up, Gonzo's asleep, and my parents must've stepped out. The edges of the room soften with a white glow that grows so bright I have to put up my arm to block its radiance.

"Hello, Cameron."

The glow dies down, and she's standing at the end of my bed—the one who's been following me around leaving feather messages. I take in the torn fishnets, plaid mini-kilt, shiny, riveted breastplate with leather straps at the sides and a worn, Great Tremolo decal near the left shoulder. Her wings are a crazy black-and-white-checkered pattern, like they've been spray-painted at a body shop to look like hipster sneakers.

Blink and the hallucination will go away, Cameron. Shut my eyes tight and open them and she's still there, all bright and shiny and smiling.

"Hullooooo," she trills, waggling her fingers at me.

"Please," I croak out. "I—I'm not ready."

"Not ready for what?" She sits next to me on the bed and hooks the heels of her combat boots on the metal frame. She pulls a bag of candy from behind her breastplate and offers it to me. "ChocoYum?"

An involuntary laugh-squeak escapes me, and then I go right back to being freaked out. "You're not real. I'm hallucinating."

"Do I seem real to you right now?"

I nod.

"Well, there you go." She gobbles down a handful of ChocoYums. "Oh my gosh, these are seriously amazing. So often there's no truth in advertising. But these really are both choco *and* yum." She catches me staring at her wings. "Go on. Touch them, if you want."

"Huh-uh," I say emphatically. If I don't touch her, she doesn't exist.

She scoots closer, singsongs, "You know you want to. . . ."

"Okay, could you not do that? Makes me feel dirty."

She makes a show of zipping her lips.

"No offense, but this is just"—I swallow hard as my fingers move toward that broad expanse of wings—"just, um . . . sometimes my brain kinda throws a switch, see? And . . ." They're the softest thing I've ever felt, velvety as a baby duck. "Shit!" I snap my hand away. "Oh God. Oh crap. Felt real. Oh wow."

" 'Wow' is a palindrome! The same word backward and forward. Isn't that cool?"

I stare at her. "Who . . . who are you?"

The room grows brighter with her smile. "I'm Dulcie. Pleased to meet you."

"My hallucination has a name." I try to grasp at some semblance of sanity. "Right. You—you've been following me," I say like some annoyed headmaster reprimanding a student. "First at my house. At Buddha Burger. In the school gym. You left me a feather."

"And still you didn't call. Men." She points to the unopened pudding cup on my hospital tray. "Are you gonna eat that?"

"No," I croak.

"Do you mind?"

I can only shake my head.

"Thanks. Oh, hey, watch this." She puts the spoon on the end of her nose and slowly takes her hand away. It balances there for a second before dropping into her waiting palm. "Cool, right?"

"Yeah. Cool." I've got a lump in my throat the size of Chet King's manly hands. "So . . . are you just, like, visiting? Or is this . . . am I . . . ?"

"What?"

"Dead?"

Her eyes widen in surprise. "Oh yowza! No! Don't be such a Goofy Gloomer." Her smile fades fast. "But we've got a lot to talk about and we don't have much time."

"What do we have to talk about?"

"Your mission," she says through a mouthful of chocolate pudding.

"My . . . mission."

"Your mission. We need your help, Cameron."

I can feel my heartbeat in my skull. "Define 'we.'"

She writes in the air with her spoon. "We. Plural form of 'I.' 'Nos' in Latin. Wow, I miss Latin. So much fun—all those exciting verbs that don't come until the end of the sentence.

It's like a movie trailer for language." She downs another spoonful of pudding, rolls her eyes in bliss. "Sure you don't want some of this? It's surprisingly edible."

"Mission?" I prompt.

"Right." She stares right at me. "You ever hear of a guy called Dr. X?"

"No," I say.

"No Dr. X?" she asks again.

"There are several Dr. Assholes who come in here every day to scribble on my chart and poke me with sharp objects so they can collect points for their Sadism Scout Badges, but so far, no Dr. X."

"You know, you are very funny!"

"That's because I'm hallucinating."

"Dr. X is a brilliant scientist. Like beyond genius. Branes, parallel worlds, time travel, wormholes, superstring theory, M-theory, Y-theory, Double-Z-theory, the Theory of Everything Plus A Little Bit More. This guy was at the forefront of it all."

Just trying to follow her is making my head hurt. "My dad says that stuff isn't real science, that it can't be proven."

Her left eyebrow shoots up. "Hmmmm. *Anyway* . . . Dr. X finally did it."

"It."

"Yeah." She licks the spoon clean. "Personal pronoun, non-gender-specific, third-person singular."

This is officially my weirdest and most annoying hallucination yet. "What did Dr. X finally do?" I say slowly.

"He figured out how to break through, to travel through time and space. He's been parallel world hopping, raking up quite a few cosmic frequent flier miles. But that's not the problem. He's come home again." Her dark brows are furrowed. "And he brought something back with him."

116

"Something meaning like a T-shirt or coffee mug?"

"Not quite." She puts the spoon down. "Ever hear of dark energy?"

"No. What is it?"

"Beats me. Nobody really knows what dark energy is except that it makes up most of space. It's an eternal mystery. When Dr. X traveled through space and time and stopped to smell the roses in the Higgs Field, he tapped into that stuff. Something was created, and it followed him back to this world. Now it's massing into something new, expanding and accelerating events, destabilizing everything." Her expression is grave. Chocolate's smeared around her mouth like a clown's lipstick. "You've got to find Dr. X, get him to close the wormhole before the whole planet goes up in flames. Before everything is obliterated."

"Whoa. What do you mean *I've* got to find Dr. X? Shouldn't that be your jurisdiction? Use your angel superpowers or whatever. Leave me out of it."

She fixes me with a stare. "Cameron, do you wonder how you got your disease?"

I've spent, like, a billion hours wondering that very thing. "They say it might have been a bad burger."

Dulcie makes a disgusted growl in her throat. "So unimaginative. No. Everything's connected, Cameron. There are no accidents. Your disease isn't a virus or a bacteria—it's something completely different, something that actually alters your DNA. Those prions are like car body shop guys pimping the ride of your mind, my friend."

"Thanks. That's very encouraging."

"Don't you get it? The prions attacking your brain right now? *They're from the same unstable, dark energy.* That's why the doctors can't figure it out. Because what's attacking you is from another world."

117

"But how—"

She holds up a finger. "I'm getting to it. Don't rush a girl in the middle of her exposition. But it's also what's going to allow you to find Dr. X. Those prions can help you see what everybody else would miss. By not working 'right,' your brain is actually capable of seeing more than anybody else's, including mine." She taps the side of my head. "What's going on in here right now will help you make sense of the signs and find Dr. X's secret location."

"Signs?" I repeat, because I've only understood about three words she's said.

"Yes. Yes! Signs!" She leaps up in excitement and nearly sends my plastic water pitcher to the floor. "Tabloids, billboards, 'coincidences'—things no one else pays attention to. These are the clues for your journey. It's up to you to decipher it, to connect the dots and find the meaning."

I squeeze my hands against my head as if I could make this stop. "This is officially the craziest shit I've ever heard."

"Really? Man oh man, I could tell you a few things . . ." She laughs, then stops. "Right. Not important. So. Anyway. There's a lot going on in those tabloids. You'd be surprised. It's like alternate universe code. And that's how Dr. X has been communicating. Through tabloid code. He needs help, Cameron—he's not a well man."

"But that's so totally random!"

Dulcie tucks a piece of hair behind her ear. "In a world like this one, only the random makes sense."

"Wait, I thought you just said everything's connected. How can it be both—"

"Randomly connected, connected very randomly," she says, examining Jenna's stuffed cat, Mr. Bubbles Kitty. "Cute. So soft. Cotton? Hey there, kitty. Do you think

Cameron should go on this mission and save the world from complete destruction? Just nod for yes." She makes the cat nod.

I tear Mr. Bubbles Kitty out of her hands. "I still don't understand how it is that you can't find this guy. You're an angel. Aren't you? Don't you have any angel superpowers—appearing to shepherds in fields where they lay, blowing trumpets? Laser eyes? At the very least, you should have some kind of angel GPS for locating missing people."

"I'm just a messenger. That's all."

A prickly feeling works its way up my arms. "Wait, are you an alien? Where'd you come from?"

"Great question! Anyway, I don't want you to fret. I'm not gonna abandon you to tabloids and billboards. I'll be checking in, here and there."

"Checking in?"

"Here and there."

I fold my arms over my chest. Out in the hallway, an orderly pushes somebody on a stretcher. "Tell me one reason why I should do this?"

She sucks on the plastic spoon again. When she pulls it out, it's coated in what's left of her lipstick. "I was saving the best for last. There's a bonus round. Dr. X is the one person who can cure you."

I sit straight up. "Wait, they said there is no cure—"

"—That *they* know of," Dulcie interrupts. "But there *is* a cure. And Dr. X has it."

A cure. It seems as ridiculous as those spray-painted feathers she's sporting. But a cure . . .

"I don't know if you've noticed, but I'm hooked up to an IV. I can barely move."

"Yeah. I can help you out a little there, cowboy. I've got

119

something Dr. X left behind. One of his early experiments. Hold out your wrist?" I do and she hooks what looks like a big plastic watchband around it. "Your temporary pass. It'll keep the symptoms at bay and stabilize you for about two weeks. After that . . ."

"After that, what?"

She's not smiling anymore. "The prions will take over. They'll tear your mind apart the same way that dark energy will tear the world apart."

Hearing her say that makes my heart beat a little faster. The watchband has something inside—a laminated green card with writing on it. *Walt Disney World. Magic Kingdom. "E."* *Adult Admission. Good for Choice of One.* On the left side is a list: *Adventureland, Frontierland, Liberty Square, Fantasyland, Tomorrowland.* "What is this?"

"An E-ticket," she says excitedly.

"An E-what?"

"E-ticket. They used to have them at Disney World a million years ago. They got you a straight shot to the best rides. So awesome! Of course, those tickets are discontinued now, so you should be careful with that one."

I stare at it. It's just a green ticket in a bracelet around my wrist. "And this would protect me . . . how?"

She licks the rest of the pudding spoon clean and drops it on the tray. "Sorry. That *is* top-secret angel info."

All the hope I'd felt vanishes. In a minute, I'll wake up. I'll wake up and it will be another day in which I'm living a dream of dying slowly, a dream I hope I'll wake up from, on and on till it's over.

"Okay, you know what? I'm clearly having some kind of pain-meds-induced hallucination, and I'm sure you're a very nice hallucination with a supergreat, nonreal personality, but

I'm going to go back to sleep now, and when I wake up, you'll be gone."

She puts her hand on mine, and it's as soft as her wings. "Cameron, we've exhausted every other option."

"You still haven't told me who 'we' is!"

She sucks air through her teeth, nods. "Yeah. I know. Cameron, you're our last best hope. I'm asking you to save the world, cowboy."

"Wait," I say, pushing myself up again. "That's a line from *Star Fighter.*"

She gives me that big goofy grin. "Yeah! I couldn't resist. Great movies, right? Well, the early ones. The later ones . . . ehhh. Oh. Almost forgot. There's just one more thing," she says, biting her lip. "You need to take Gonzo with you."

"What?"

"You need a pal on this trip. Everybody needs a friend."

I drop back against the pillow, fold my arms over my chest. "Not me. I travel solo or not at all."

Her eyes crinkle. "Now who's quoting *Star Fighter?*" She deepens her voice, swaggers. " 'Not me, princess. I travel solo or not at all.' Right. Not the point. The point is, you're gonna need a mate, a pal, a sidekick and coconspirator. And frankly, Gonzo could use a little help, too. I mean, look at him."

She parts the curtain a crack. Gonzo's asleep, mouth open, snoring slightly, a Captain Carnage video game guide crumpled under his chin.

"You'd be providing a valuable public service," Dulcie says.

"No, no, and no." I tick off the reasons this is a bad idea. "One, he's a compulsive talker. Two, he calls his mom, like, five times a day. Three, he snores. Four, he's completely phobic and thinks everything's going to kill him."

Dulcie shrugs. "Nobody's perfect."

"The other day he said there are chemicals used in the processing of toilet paper that can give you rectal cancer. So now he's bringing his secret stash of special recycled toilet tissue in with him in the mornings. He will never say yes."

"You won't know until you ask. Besides, his fate is tied to yours. Everything's connected."

"There's no such thing as fate."

"Except for random fate."

"That's . . . insane."

"Yeah." She grins. "Insanity. Brilliance. Such a tough call. Look, Cameron, I'm just a messenger. I don't know everything. But I do know this: you're being given a chance. Take it and you might live. Stay here and you will surely die." Dulcie cuddles Mr. Bubbles Kitty, fluffing him with her fingers. "Whaddaya say—you, Gonzo, connecting the dots, finding Dr. X, getting a cure, saving the universe? You down, cowboy?"

My head hurts; it's almost time for my pain meds. Where's Glory? I want to check out for a while. Not think or feel. I roll onto my side, away from her. "I'll think about it."

"Okay." Dulcie reaches over me and tucks the cat into the crook of my arm. "But Cameron? Don't think about it too long."

NIGHT

Mom and Dad and Jenna are here, camped around me. They're all watching some stupid episode of an even stupider show on YA! TV called *What's Your Category?* where kids have to answer questions to prove they know more than anybody else does about a particular stupid topic, and if they get too many wrong, they're dunked in a stinking pool of mystery yuck.

"Dude," Gonzo whispers without taking his eyes off the TV. "You ever watch *I Double Dog Dare You?*"

I shake my head. It throbs, and I can't help thinking about what Dulcie said, about those prions attacking my brain being some mysterious agent from another world. It would be so nice to blot this all out with a big fat dose of pain meds, but I can't have any for another hour, according to Glory, who was here . . . when? I don't know.

"It's awesome. Once they made this guy shave his butt on national television—and the guy did it! Totally rocked the house."

How long till the pain medication? I could count the minutes. Go to sleep and not wake up. I could stay here and wait for the inevitable.

Saving the world. That's impossible. Insane.

Still.

A cure. I could be cured. That's what she said. And some little atoms come awake inside me, swirling into a question I can't shake: "Why the hell not?"

I could have a chance.

And a chance is better than nothing.

CHAPTER SIXTEEN

Wherein I Try to Convince the Dwarf to Leave Behind the Comforts of Recycled Toilet Paper in Order to Accompany Me on a Mission to Possibly, Maybe Save the World

Once my family thinks I'm asleep and they step out for dinner, I wake Gonzo.

"Hey, dude. What's up?" He sits up and wipes the drool from the corner of his mouth. The newsprint from his video game manual has smeared over half his face from where he fell asleep on it. This is the guy Dulcie thinks I should take with me on the road? Holy crap.

"Um, look, I know this is going to sound completely crazy, but I had this, I don't know exactly what you'd call it. A vision, maybe."

"What kind of vision?" he asks, yawning.

"This angel spoke to me and—"

Gonzo stops mid–eye rub. "Hold up. How did you know she was an angel, amigo? What did she look like?"

"Uh . . . wings. Breastplate. Pink hair. Fishnets and combat boots."

"Awesome! Punk-rock angel! You think God's a metal-head?" Gonzo gives me a thrashing air-guitar solo while banging his head and flicking his tongue in and out of his mouth. It's like watching a snake die slowly and painfully. "What's angel girl's name?"

"Dulcie. So—"

Gonzo frowns. "Doesn't seem like an angel name to me. My mom's really big on the saints, and I've never heard of a St. Dulcie. You sure you weren't just dreaming, man?"

"Yes, I'm sure," I say, though I've never been less sure of anything. "She gave me this mission, Gonzo. The most important mission of our time."

"Awesome. Lay it on me."

"Well . . ." I tell him everything Dulcie said about Dr. X and his time traveling and the cure and the end of the world approaching if we don't locate him and get him to close the wormhole.

Gonzo stares at me. "Dude, you sound like those geezers who hang around the bus station wearing tinfoil hats and pissing into empty soda cups."

"I know it sounds crazy, but I'm telling you the truth. I swear. She was here. She ate my pudding snack." The spoon. Her lipstick. I run for the trash. "I can prove she was here. Hold on."

The linoleum's bitter cold against my feet. The postal workers in my brain finally come off break and send the message to my legs that it's okay to walk, and I stumble over to the trash can. Nothing's in there but my mom's half-finished crossword puzzle.

"They must've taken it with the tray," I say.

"Sure they did." Gonzo holds up some fingers. "Let's do a quick sanity check. How many fingers?"

I flip him the bird. "How many fingers am *I* holding up?"

"Harsh."

"I'm not crazy, okay?" I say, even though what I'm saying has every hallmark of a stadium-sized crazy concert.

"Okay. So how do we find this miracle guy, this Dr. X?"

"She said we have to look for signs—billboards, tabloids, personals."

Gonzo stares at me. "Seriously, what are they putting in your IV? Wack on tap? Even if we entertain the idea that a winged being in combat boots gave you a secret mission to find a doctor with a magical cure, how are you gonna go anywhere, dude? In case you haven't noticed, you're in a hospital bed at St. Jude's and sometimes you have trouble just getting to the bathroom. Did 1-800-Punk-Angel give you some pointers there?"

"She gave me this." I show him the laminated wristband. Gonzo puts his face near and reads.

"An E-ticket?"

"It's got some cosmic, stabilizing mojo to combat the prions."

"Cool! Punker Angel gave you more health."

"Yeah, exactly. But it's only good for two weeks."

Gonzo whistles. "Man. Bummer. Well, good luck, dude."

"I'm supposed to take you with me," I say very fast.

His hand flies up. "Oh, hell to the no."

"Gonzo—"

"No, no, no, and no with a side of no."

Gonzo plops down on his bed and makes a big show of opening his video game manual, turning pages way too quickly to read them.

"I told her you were too chickenshit to go." It's a low blow, but I'm pissed that Gonzo *is* such a chickenshit and that Dulcie set the bar so high right away.

126

"I'm not a chickenshit," Gonzo says, sounding hurt. "I'm not an unnecessary risk taker."

"Gonzo," I say, playing my final card. "She said this dark energy Dr. X brought back is bringing about the end of the world. You. Me. This. Everything will be gone if we don't find him."

He sits up and dangles his legs over the side of the bed, swinging them so that his heels bang softly against the metal railings like a chime. "Everything everything?"

"Yeah," I say softly. "Dulcie said you're part of this, too. That you'd find your purpose on this trip, and that's why we were put in the same room together. No accidents. Everything's connected. In a random sort of way."

Gonzo's eyebrows crease into furry caterpillars of concentration. "So, like, when's this big mission supposed to go down?"

"Tonight. Right now."

Gonzo stares at me. "Dude, this is insane! You know, we probably need shots wherever we're going. I've only got one roll of my special toilet paper—"

"We can get more. Gonzo, this is my only chance to stay alive, okay?"

"I don't know, man. I gotta talk it over with my mom." He reaches for his cell and I pull it away.

"No. Sorry. If we go, we can't tell anyone. They'll try to stop us. It has to be a secret."

"Dude, my mom will freak." Gonzo's breathing gets shallow and wheezy. He grabs for his ever-present inhaler, his version of a blankie, and puffs away.

"Gonzo, if Dulcie's right, in two weeks, your mom will be dead." I toss his cell at him. "Do what you want. But I'm going to find Dr. X. And I'm leaving tonight."

127

I throw my backpack on the bed. All I've got are a few pairs of clean underwear and the clothes I came in with. My jeans feel strange against my legs; they wake my skin up. I grab the puke-yellow bin with its array of helpful products— toothbrush, toothpaste, scratchy tissues, mouthwash, comb, and lotion—and dump the contents inside, tossing the bin back on the bedside table.

Gonzo's got his chubby hands on his hips like a weary camp counselor. "Dude, you are insane."

"Yeah. Documented."

"All right," he says with a sigh. "Give me a minute to get dressed. I'm going with your bovine ass."

CHAPTER SEVENTEEN

Which Treats of Our Daring Escape from St. Jude's and Our Talk with a Stinky Dude in a Tinfoil Hat

Nurses are a little like cops—they're never around when you need them. But when you want to avoid them, they are everywhere.

"How are we gonna get past the nurses' station?" Gonzo asks, panicked, as we open the door a crack and peek into the long corridor that leads from our room, past the nurses to the bank of elevators around the corner.

He has a point. This would be an ideal time for somebody around here to flatline like they always do on TV shows, all the bells and whistles going off and creating a big, noisy distraction. But this isn't a TV show; it's an actual hospital with sick people doing what sick people do best, which is largely to lie around with a minimum of fanfare.

"This is a bad idea. Let's blow it off," Gonz says.

"Don't chicken out on me."

"I'm not! It's just, I mean, come on, dude. This is so not possible."

My eyes scan the corridor for something useful. Glory's standing at the nurses' station, gossiping with two other women sitting behind computer screens. She's wearing her mauve scrubs today. I know the angel pins ring her neck. Someone says something amusing, and Glory laughs. "Oh Lord, help me, girl," she says in that accent that sounds like music. Off to our right is a red Exit sign that I know has to lead to stairs.

"Come on," I say, pulling Gonzo out behind me. "Don't look up. Just keep moving."

The bright lights of the corridor wash over us in waves. A maid comes by with her disinfecting cart. A doctor strides past, trailing residents like a kite's tail. Visitors wander carrying overly festive flowers and balloons. The gifts are a lie meant to disguise the fear and worry hiding in their eyes.

I don't want to die here. That's the only thing I'm sure of.

My right leg twitches and I will it to keep functioning. For now, it's gotten the message. We round the corner and there are the stairs.

For some reason, I turn back for a final sweep of the hall, and when I do, I see Glory has left the nurses' station. Clipboard in hand, she's heading for her rounds. In fifteen minutes tops, she'll pull into our room for a temperature/blood pressure/pulse rate check and all hell will break loose. I'd hoped for a longer head start. Shit.

"What's the matter?" Gonz asks.

"We need to move," I say, pushing into the stairwell for the long climb down.

*　　*　　*

When the hydraulic front doors of St. Jude's release us into the world, the sky is the blue-going-to-purple of late sunset. Above the praying-mantis-style lights of the parking lot, bashful stars flutter like they're not sure whether it's okay to show their full light just yet. The air is warm and sweet. I breathe in as much of it as my lungs will hold. It hurts in a good way, like my insides are holding a deep stretch.

"Ah shit. Taste that air, man. So good."

"Yeah, yeah, yeah. Now what?" Gonzo asks, looking left and right like a wanted man.

"We need to get out of here. Got your cell?"

He pats his bag. "Yeah."

"Great. Call for a cab."

"What's the number?"

"I don't know. Call Information."

"That's, like, a dollar seventy-five. My mom will kill me."

"Gonzo, she's gonna kill you for breaking out of the hospital and going on an unscheduled road trip with me. Calling Information's kind of incidental, don't you think?"

"I knew this was a bad idea," Gonzo grumbles, but he punches in the three digits anyway, and ten minutes later, a battered cab picks us up on Eldorado Street, two blocks from the hospital.

"Where to?" the guy asks, flipping on the meter.

"Good question." Gonzo glares at me.

This would be a good time for Dulcie to show herself, give us a little divine intervention, put her money where her "there are no accidents, my friend" mouth is.

The meter goes up another fifteen cents and we haven't even moved. I'm waiting for a sign. This is what it's come to: I'm now believing in supernatural visions of punk-rock angels and last-ditch missions to save the universe/my life and random signs to point the way forward. Right. I'm just about to say, "Okay, you got me—game's over. Let's go back to the hospital and laugh it up about this over a nice cafeteria tray of gelatinized mystery meat" when I see something glinting over the rooftops. It's a sign, all right. A large, peeling billboard advertising the Roadrunner bus depot. The smiling roadrunner is in a full run, going so fast that one of his feathers flies loose behind him. JUST FOLLOW THE FEATHER TO BIFROST ROAD, the sign says.

Follow the feather.

It's not trumpets or thunderclaps, but it's the best we've got right now.

"Bus station," I say at last, hoping the prions in my brain are right.

The bus depot has been carved out of dirty tile, ancient plastic benches, half-empty candy machines, and overflowing trash cans. It's run by people who were offered a chance at a job in hell or the bus depot and lost the coin toss. Also, it smells like piss.

Some grizzled man in a janitor's uniform is swishing dirty water around on the floor with an even filthier mop. An empty information board hangs from the low ceiling, taking up most of the middle of the mostly deserted room. No buses. No info. Nothing to go on.

"What now?" Gonzo asks.

The clerk at the ticket counter doesn't even move his little partition when we get up there.

"Hi," I say. "Um, there's nothing on the information board."

"A-yup." He flips the page in his comic book without looking up.

"Great. Thanks for that," Gonzo mutters.

"When's the next bus?" I ask.

"Not till seven-o-five tomorrow mornin'. But y'all cain't stay here. Ten minutes till closin'. Won't open up again till six a.m."

"Okay, thanks." I leave the window and sink onto a bench.

"I told you this was wack." Gonzo sucks down a mouthful of asthma medicine.

Signs, signs. Dulcie said to look for the "seemingly random." How do you look for the random? Doesn't the random generally find you and that's what makes it random?

A hollowed-out, gray-skinned dude who smells like pee sits next to us. It's the same guy I saw in the parking lot the night we went to Luigi's. He's still wearing his tinfoil hat. "What are you boys doing?"

"Saving the world," Gonzo says, scooting away.

"Ah. Good. It's going to end, you know. It's all going to shit. That's why I got me one of these." He points to his wrinkled silvery cap.

"Hank, you need to let these boys be, now." The guy with the mop has reached us.

"Piss off," the old guy snaps. He takes out a bag and inspects the things inside.

" 'Scuse me," the janitor says. "Could you lift yer feet, please? I need to get that spot."

Dutifully, Gonz and I raise our legs, drawbridge style, and he mops underneath.

"Dude, there's no bus tonight," Gonzo says. "Give it up."

The old homeless guy stops rummaging through his bag. "Yes there is. There is one! It's downstairs waiting."

I look to Mop Guy for confirmation. He stops long enough to wipe his sweaty brow with his arm. "Well, there is one tonight, but it ain't on the regular schedule. It's private. The Fleur-de-Lys."

"That sounds like a porn thing," Gonzo whispers nervously. "Does that sound porny to you?"

I ignore him. "Where's it go?"

"Where you think it goes?" the homeless guy says. "New Orleans. That there's the Mardi Gras bus, son. It's Mardi Gras time."

"Thanks."

"You welcome," he says. "Might as well have fun before it all ends."

"Gonz," I say, digging in my pocket for cash. "How do you feel about New Orleans?"

"What? You don't know for sure that's the right bus."

"No. I don't. But it's the only bus. Look, I know this seems a little half-assed . . ."

"No, dude. I'd be thrilled if this plan were half-assed. This is, like, *no*-assed."

"You're right. It's the most no-assed thing I've ever done in my life. So am I getting two tickets or one?"

Gonzo rubs his inhaler pump like a talisman. "All right. I'm in. But if we don't find this Dr. X in New Orleans and see what he's got for me, I'm on the first bus back."

"Fair enough."

I open up my wallet. My credit card, the one my dad gave me to teach me fiscal responsibility, is still there. I've got a whopping credit limit of five hundred and fifty dollars.

I run to the window and rap on the bulletproof glass. The clerk barely looks up. "Yup?"

"How much for two tickets on the Fleur-de-Lys?"

134

With a sigh, the clerk puts his book down. "That'll be two hundred seventy-eight dollars and fifty-two cents with tax," he says.

He processes the charge and hands us two tickets, and Gonzo and I race for the last bus of the night.

CHAPTER EIGHTEEN

**In Which We Make a Stop in New Orleans
and Gonzo Refuses to Eat Fish,
Annoying the Crap out of Me and Our Waitress**

I mostly sleep on the trip from Texas to New Orleans. Occasionally I open drowsy eyes and catch dreamlike glimpses of the world. Gas stations hawking plastic cups with every fill-up. Cram-packed strip malls featuring the same stores and restaurants. Skeletal dogs picking through trash. Litter-strewn marshes. Crumbling roads snaking under half-finished highways. Factories belching toxic smoke clouds. I take it all in, and for a second, I wonder whether this planet is worth saving. Close to morning, I wake up long enough to see that we're crossing over some ginormous bridge that seems to stretch out forever. We're surrounded by water. It's sort of cool, like I'm floating.

"Lake Pontchartrain Causeway," the lady across the aisle says. She's wearing a WORLD'S BEST GRANDMA T-shirt, and under her flowered skirt she has on panty-hose support socks that only come up to her knobby knees. She offers me some of her peanuts. I decline, and she puts them away, pulling out a long thin cigarette that she tucks over the top of her ear. "You got family in Nu'walins?"

"No."

"Ever been there?"

I shake my head.

"Well, it's a mighty special place. Or was. What they let get done to it . . ." She shakes her head. "But we survive, we survive." She starts singing a little bit of a song to herself. It sounds old and sad and promises a better day. "Law, I hope we get there soon. I can't wait to have me a smoke. They say smoking kills you, but I been smoking my whole life and I'm healthy as a horse."

Coughing hard, she turns a matchbook over and over between her fingers, working it like a worry stone. The image on it is familiar, and I cock my head to get a better look. It's the cover of the Junior Webster album Eubie showed me.

"You heard of the Horn and Ivory Club?" the old lady asks, holding up the book of matches.

"No," I lie. I don't really want to get drawn into a conversation.

"Good place. Here. You take these, honey." She puts the matches in my hand.

"That's okay." I try to give them back.

"No. Go on and take it. Souvenir of your first trip to the Big Easy. You never know when they might come in handy."

"Thanks." These matches look ancient. They probably can't light anything for shit. On the flip side the cover reads *The Horn & Ivory Club, 141 N. Rampart Street,* with a telephone number that starts with letters. I put them in my pocket, lay my head against the seat back, and stare out the window at that bridge that just keeps going on. After a minute, the lady starts to sing her song again, lulling me to sleep.

We roll into the city about dinnertime. The skyline glitters under a hazy, late-afternoon sun. New Orleans looks as if it's just appeared out of the water like a myth, a modern Atlantis that shouldn't exist. The bus hisses into the depot, which is as desolate and dirty as the one we've just left. Gonzo and I pour out onto the streets with the other pilgrims. Even though it's late February, the air's warm and sticky and a little aggressive—just another character in what promises to be a town full of them.

Gonzo and I are starving, so we find a diner close to the depot. It's a total tourist place with lots of fake alligators on the walls and Mardi Gras beads hanging from every hook. It's noisy and crowded, too, this being Fat Tuesday. After a hellishly long wait, the hostess takes us to a tiny table near the back. The menu is huge and has about forty-eight different kinds of seafood specials on it. I make a quick decision and munch down on the saltines and butter they've got on the table. Gonzo's still hidden behind the accordion door of his menu. His fingers tap nervously against it. A waitress with poufy blond hair puts two waters down in front of us. She has a charm bracelet with about a million charms that jangle when she moves. Around her neck is a cross necklace the size of Rhode Island.

"What can I get you fellas?" she asks, taking out a pad and pencil.

"Boudreax's Seafood Special with fries," I say.

"Ketchup with your fries?"

"Yes, please."

Gonzo finally lowers his menu. The waitress takes note of

his Little Person status. It's like it stalls her out for a minute and she needs to reboot, but the forced smile comes back.

"And what about you, dawlin'?"

Gonzo's eyes are like saucers. He's sweating and coughing a little bit, pulling at his collar. I sense a full panic tsunami coming on, though I don't know why just yet.

"Excuse me," Gonzo says. He puts his menu up in front of his face. It doesn't block the waitress's view. It just makes him look like an idiot. "I can't eat anything on here, man."

"Why not?"

"It's all fish."

"Yeah, no kidding. It's a seafood restaurant. Jambalaya Café. Says so right out front."

"I can't eat shellfish. My mom says I could be allergic."

"Could be or are?"

"It's a helluva way to find out, dude. I could go into anaphylactic shock and die right here within seconds, no do-over."

The waitress's smile falters. No doubt she's picturing herself losing tips while she runs for the CPR kit under the counter. Under the fluorescent lights, she looks tired and lined, like one of my mom's old book bags, and I feel sorry for her and totally pissed at Gonzo.

"So order the fried catfish," I say.

The waitress agrees. "The catfish's real good. It's my fav'rite." Her pen hovers, ready.

Gonzo shakes his head. "Mercury, man."

I make a show of examining the menu. "Sorry . . . don't see the Mercury Special anywhere . . ."

"No, the mercury. In fish, amigo. Some fish have a high concentration of it. It can cause brain and liver damage and all sorts of wicked reactions."

"You know, Gonz, it's not like they're back in the kitchen opening thermometers all over the food. Get a grip."

"Dude, this is serious. Do you know how many people die of mercury poisoning each year? It's some serious sh—" Gonzo steals a glance at our waitress. "It's a growing concern."

People are being seated in our section. People who might want to order lots of fish from the seafood menu and ostensibly leave big tips to go with that. Our waitress taps her pen on her pad. "I can give y'all another minute if you need. . . ."

"Gonzo," I hiss under my breath. "I'm freaking starving. Just order something, okay?"

The hostess whispers to the waitress that Table A3 is ready to order. She nods.

"We've got a good salad bar. It's all-you-can-eat." The waitress gestures to a food island in the middle of the room where vats of brightly colored food sit on little ice hills under protective glass lit by a jillion lightbulbs. It's like a small salad city.

Gonzo narrows his eyes. "How often do you clean that thing?"

"Every night," the waitress answers. Her smile is strained.

"That's it? Do you know how long it takes for *Listeria* to grow under those hot lamps, even with ice?"

Here we go.

"It can happen in just five hours. Five hours and you've got the salad bar of death!"

The waitress looks confused. "From Listerine?"

"*Lis-ter-i-a*. It's bacteria that can cause anything from food-poisoning symptoms to coma."

The waitress's smile has completely vanished. "Well, my goodness. Are you boys from the health department? 'Cause

140

we passed with flying colors just two months ago. My manager's got the certificate on file."

"No, ma'am," I say, flashing Gonzo an I-will-kill-you-if-you-speak look. "Just bring him a grilled cheese sandwich."

"And coffee," Gonzo adds.

"And coffee," I say.

"I'll put that order right in for you!" The waitress takes our menus and practically runs from the table. A bus boy drops off a cup of steaming java.

"How did you get the name Gonzo anyway? Were you born in St. Irony Hospital?" I ask once our waitress has gone to the coffee station where she's telling the other waitress on duty about Gonzo. She pokes her head around to gawk at us.

"Dude, you have to be careful. They say they clean stuff, but they really don't." Gonzo empties three packets of sugar into his coffee and stirs it with the end of his fork.

"You know, Gonzo, that's kind of the least of our worries," I say.

"That's what you say now. When you're puking up your stomach lining in an hour, you'll think differently."

I push the saltines away. "Thanks for that visual."

"For real, dude, my mom read a magazine article—investigative journalism—about what goes on in restaurant kitchens. You don't want to know."

"You're right. I don't. Maybe your mom should stop reading stupid crap that exists only to keep people in a state of constant fear."

Gonzo's expression darkens. "You talking shit about my mom? Maybe if your 'rents had been more on their game you wouldn't have gotten a bad burger or whatever and ended up with holes in your brain."

"Nice."

"I'm just saying."

We stare at each other over the mostly empty cracker bowl. "You know what? Let's just not talk," I say.

Gonzo shrugs. "Fine by me, *pendejo*."

The waitress brings our food and I eat like a man possessed. We haven't really had anything other than JellyJuice Bears, convenience-store hot dogs, and Corny Doodles since we left the hospital. I'm not usually one of those people who gets all rhapsodic about food, but this fish is amazing—like the first time I've ever tasted anything. Gonzo sniffs his grilled cheese sandwich repeatedly and takes tentative bites.

By the time we finish dessert and make our way on foot to the French Quarter, it's nighttime. Now that my stomach is full and there's so much excitement on tap, I forget to be annoyed with Gonzo, and I guess he's over my shit, too. We just keep giving each other these goofy "Whoa! Check that out!" grins. It's like another world down here—all these old houses with galleries where people sit and watch parades of tourists going by. The streets of New Orleans are like a collage—all kinds of people, things, and colors bumping up against each other, overlapping till they make something new. College kids stagger out of bars still holding hurricane glasses. A ponytailed girl leans against a garbage can, puking. Street musicians compete for attention: a guitarist in a top hat tries to outsing the lady violinist, and both of them are drowned out by the washtub band a few feet down.

"Dude, I can't see a fucking thing," Gonzo complains.

There's an opening in the crowd. I squeeze through, pulling Gonzo along, and we position ourselves in the front. When the couple we've pushed aside starts to complain, I point to Gonzo. "His mom's on one of the floats. I promised to bring him down," I lie, and the woman, who's drunk, gets

142

all sentimental and starts singing nursery songs to Gonzo, which makes no sense, but if there's anything I'm starting to learn about people it's (a) that they are fundamentally suspicious and afraid of anyone who is "different," and (b) that fear makes them do and say asinine things.

Gonzo scowls. "Is she kidding me with that?"

"Ride it out, little dude," I say. "We're here and you can see everything."

Gonzo can't argue with that, so we stand on the parade route, taking it all in. Revelers in tall, wack-a-doodle hats and neon-bright wigs dance and sing as the floats pass by. They shout for beads and the krewes on the floats answer their calls. I nearly get beaned by a handful of bright purple necklaces. I slip some over my neck and offer the rest to Gonzo, who shakes his head like I'm giving him Bubonic Plague in jewelry form.

"You don't know where that's been, man."

Eubie was right—Mardi Gras is amazing. A guy in a skeleton costume, his face painted like a skull, dances down the street while acrobats in glittery harlequin outfits tumble and jump around waving long paper streamers. On a float painted like a flood, a drag queen in a sash that reads MISS LEVEE waves to the crowd and they go wild. A funeral band marches right past us. The musicians come first, playing trumpets and banging drums. Behind them, the people raise their hands and dance, whooping it up like it's just another celebration. Farther down the line, the partiers roar their approval, signaling that the next float is a winner. It's the most elaborate float we've seen, a good ten feet high with these huge gates in the middle, one white, the other gray with the faint outline of a horn on it. A tall dude in a feathered bird mask stands on the edge and spreads his arms wide.

"I am Morpheus, king of dreams," he says, and the speakers

carry his deep voice for blocks. "We *all* walk in a land of dreams. For what are we but atoms and hope, a handful of stardust and sinew. We are weary travelers trying to find our way home on a road that never ends. Am I a part of your dream? Or are you but a part of mine? Welcome my brother, Phantasos, for this is surely a phantasmagoria, a fantasy world, and we are all players."

"Dude!" Gonzo yells over the din. "That is so seriously fawesome. I want to drive one of those to school! Whoo-hoo!" He's grinning and dancing in place. "When I kick, this is exactly how I want to go out. Just pure party. You know?"

"Yeah, sure," I say, but there's a catch in my chest while I watch those funeral dancers marching down the street. For the first time since we got off the bus, it strikes me how crazy this all is. How scary and uncertain. I'm at Mardi Gras, sandwiched between beer-soaked drunkards, with nothing more to go on than some vague, probably delusional belief that I'm where I should be. My legs get a weird tingly sensation, and I try not to panic.

Signs. Coincidences. The random.

Frantically, I search for clues. Is there a "Dr. X is Here" banner on one of these floats? A billboard with an arrow pointing the way? I rub a hand over the E-ticket wristband and hope that it will protect me from those rogue prions long enough to find Dr. X, wherever he might be.

The streets erupt with a fresh wave of cheering, pulling me back to the parade.

Morpheus laughs and blows some sort of glittery powder at us, coating our shirts in sparkles that make me sneeze like crazy. I reach into my pocket for a tissue and my fingers find the matchbook given to me by the lady on the bus. *The Horn & Ivory Club. Junior Webster. 141 N. Rampart.*

Signs. Coincidences. The random.

"Come on," I say, whapping Gonzo's arm. "Time to go."

"Go? But we just got here! Go where?"

"Here," I say, flipping the matches to Gonzo, who fumbles and recovers them.

"What's this?"

"Where we're headed next."

CHAPTER NINETEEN

Wherein We Have an Encounter with a Drag Queen and the Most Famous Jazzman Alive or Dead

"So let me get this straight—we're guiding our path based on a matchbook cover?" Gonzo asks.

"Just keep walking." I pick up my pace on the narrow, cobblestone street.

There are only a few people milling around, and they're headed the opposite way. The houses we pass are dark and shuttered and plastered with old, torn flyers that show grainy pictures of smiling people and hand-scrawled pleas for help—*Missing! Have you seen? Our grandma/brother/sister/father. Please call!* They're so worn they seem to fade into the brick like paper ghosts.

Gonzo huffs along beside me, looking left and right. "Dude. This looks like sort of a bad area."

Two guys in low-slung jeans and baseball caps lean against a building on the corner, arms crossed. Another guy joins them, and another. It reminds me of a horror movie I saw once, where these birds start filling up a playground while this lady sits smoking a cigarette, unaware.

"Shit. There's four of them now," Gonzo says.

"Just keep walking and don't act scared."

"Dude, I *am* scared. They could totally kick our asses."

The guys fall in behind us. We pick up speed. So do they. We turn on Rampart Street. They turn on Rampart Street. Maybe they're just headed the same way we are. Or maybe we're about to get our butts handed to us on a platter.

"Oh, man, we are so dead, so dead, so dead."

"Just be cool."

The door opens on a little house. Light and party sounds spill out onto the sidewalk. The tallest woman I have ever seen steps in front of us. She's about six foot seven in heels and dressed like a parade float. Her eyes are made up with sparkly blue eye shadow and false eyelashes, and her hair is red, curled, and piled up on top of her head like a piñata. Big hair. Big jewelry. Big hands. Whoa. Really big hands. She's holding a cigarette between those mammoth fingers.

"Hey, honey, where's the fire?" she asks in a deep voice.

I look behind me, but the guys we thought were after us have set up shop on a different corner. They're practicing dance moves under a streetlight, laughing when one of their crew messes up. They're about as threatening as a boy band, and I feel like a colossal, paranoid tool for getting so worked up.

"Since y'all standing here you might as well make yourselves useful. Y'all got a light?" the lady asks.

"Gonzo," I say. "Matches."

Gonzo hands the matches to the lady, who purses her lips and cocks a hip. "Sugar, you're supposed to light a girl's

147

cigarette, not throw the matches at her. Didn't your mama teach you anything?"

"Sorry," he says.

"That's all right," she says, and lights her own cigarette. Jesus, she's big. Gonzo comes up to her kneecaps, and I only reach her waist. "What're you two lil' scouts doing out here? Baby, this idn't a good neighborhood. I got knifed bad out here one time."

"We're looking for the Horn and Ivory," I tell her, pointing to the matchbook cover. "It's supposed to be here on North Rampart."

"Not for about four million years, it ain't, honey. It moves around. Always has. You have to know where to look." The lady peers down at us through her cigarette-smoke haze, sizing us up. "Now, how come you wanna go to the Horn and Ivory?"

"We want to see where Junior Webster used to play," I say.

The lady's eyes widen. "Junior Webster. I haven't heard that name in a long, long time."

Somebody yells down from the balcony. "Miss D! We need more beer!"

"Get it yourself, honey! I'm busy," she shouts back. "And, uh, how exactly do you think you're gonna get into the Horn and Ivory—*if* you can find it on your own, that is? Y'all not old enough to shave."

"Yes we are," Gonzo insists, his little manly pride deeply wounded.

She rubs a finger across Gonzo's smooth cheek. "Umhmm."

"We don't want to drink. We just want to see the place where Junior played. My friend Eubie told me I had to if I was ever in New Orleans."

"Zat so?" She takes a good long look at us through her exhaled smoke. "Did your friend tell you how to find the Horn and Ivory?"

"No," I concede.

"Uh-hmm, um-hmmm." Miss D says, like it means something. She drops the cigarette to the sidewalk and crushes it daintily with that huge, basketball-player-worthy foot. "Can't have you going back with nothin' to tell, can we? Don'tchoo worry, *cher*. Miss Demeanor's gonna get you in to see Junior."

I don't know what she means by that. Eubie told me Junior Webster's dead. Maybe she means she'll get us in to see the club.

"Well, come on, then, churren." Miss Demeanor sashays down the sidewalk, and we fall into step behind her.

"Man, you sure are tall," Gonzo says.

"Yeah, baby. I surely am." She laughs out loud.

"Gonzo," I whisper a minute later. "I'm pretty sure Miss Demeanor is a guy."

"Right. I knew that." But I can see that he didn't, because now he's trying to steal a look at her, to make sure.

Any other place in the world, we'd be a real spectacle, but I'm coming to realize that the more you stand out in New Orleans, the more you actually blend in. It's like a circus of a town. Within a block or so, we're back in the nonstop party that is Mardi Gras.

A bouncer calls out from a shadowed doorway. "Hey, Miss D, where y'at, dawlin?"

"How I always am, baby—*fiiiine*!" She laughs when she says it, and he laughs, too.

Miss D leads us off the chaotic, crowded street and down a private, narrow alley that dead-ends at an elaborate double gate that's exactly like the one we saw on the Morpheus float, with one side completely white and the other etched with the outline of a trumpet symbol. Just beyond the gate is a red door.

"The Gates of Horn and Ivory," Miss D says. She opens them up and then gives three quick knocks on the red door, followed by a pause, and then a fourth knock. A little window in the door opens. A pair of eyes appears.

"You know me?" she says.

The eyes move up and down, yes.

"So you know I've always been a good friend to this club."

The eyes nod again.

"I need a favor. These here my nephews come all the way from . . ." She looks down at us. "Backwater. They want to see the Horn and Ivory."

The eyes dart over in our direction, take in the state of us for a good long time. They move slowly back to stare at Miss Demeanor.

She sighs, throws her hands in the air, heavenward. "I know. Bless 'em. They're my ugly sister's kids."

The eyes don't even blink.

"The little one's doing that last wish thang. He's got cancer of twelve different organs. Some you ain't never even heard of. We're all just broken up about it."

She purses her glossy lips. The window remains quiet.

Miss D points a finger. "Okay. Okay. But you mess with his last wish and he'll come back to haunt yo' ass." The door doesn't budge. Finally, Miss D holds up the matches. "These boys got business with Junior, *cher*."

The little window closes, and the door opens.

"Thank you, baby," Miss D says, leading the way.

I don't know who let us in, because there is no one

150

standing at the door when we go in. It's like it's opened all by itself.

"Miss D?" I start. "How come you told him we have business with Junior?"

"Well, don't you, *cher*?"

"But isn't Junior Webster . . . dead?"

She smiles. "Not last time I saw him. Course, it's hard to say exactly when that was. Come on, now. Let's catch him while we can."

I'm thoroughly confused, but there's nothing to do but follow Miss D wherever she's leading. We go down a hallway lit with red bulbs. Miss D opens a door that leads to another, smaller door that leads to a little tunnel we have to crawl through on hands and knees. It opens up in a kitchen. Miss D saunters past chefs in stained aprons who take no notice of us. She pushes a button and we step into a small elevator that wriggles up jumpy cables to another floor. This time, the door opens into a big, smoky nightclub. People in fancy clothes and harlequin masks crowd around small tables lit by red Chinese lanterns. The dance floor is crammed with people swaying, spinning, swinging out and back. This place is live. Crazy, wild-man music blares from a jukebox in a corner. Everything about it is fast and unpredictable—the piano runs, the percussion, the guitar riffs, and over all of it is a trumpet swooping up and down and all over like a giant bird in the sky till my heart's beating right along with it. The song makes me want to run and shout, kiss girls and ride motorcycles through the desert. It makes me feel really alive, the way Eubie says music should.

"That's Junior you feel," Miss D says, like she can read my mind. She leads us backstage. A burly bodyguard in a suit and sunglasses, wearing an earpiece, stands guard outside the curtained door.

"Here, baby, you wait with me," she says to Gonzo.

"How come I can't go in?" Gonzo sounds pissed.

"He only sees people one at a time," she says, hands on her hips. "I'll take you up front and get you some nut mix. They got good nut mix."

I hear Gonzo say, "I could be allergic to nuts," as Miss D drags him away.

The bodyguard lets me in and closes the door behind me. I'm in a little vestibule lit by a red lightbulb. On a side table, a dozen of those white candles you see in old churches burn, leaving bubbling trails of wax down their sides. Above the table is the watercolor painting of Junior and the black hole that was on the cover of the "Cypress Grove Blues" LP Eubie showed me in his shop. There's a big white ring in the center of the painting just like on the album. Some Mardi Gras beads hang from a thumbtack. And there's a picture taped to the bottom right corner. I blink when I see it, because I swear it looks like that same picture of Eubie in his harlequin mask on Bourbon Street.

"Somebody there?" a gravelly voice calls out.

I push aside a curtain. The room has nothing in it but two chairs beneath a single lightbulb. Junior Webster sits in one of the chairs, shining his horn. He looks about a hundred years old. His black skin's dark and lined and ashy in spots, like a pair of beautiful leather shoes stained with snow. He wears the same suit as in the poster, with the same straw hat and black sunglasses.

"Come on over and take a seat," he rasps. "I won't bite."

"You're really Junior Webster?" I say, sitting next to him.

Junior chuckles. "All my life."

"Nice to meet you, sir."

"Nice to meet you, too, Cameron."

"How do you know—?"

"In time, in time. Everything's connected, my friend, and we got a lot in common." Junior tucks his horn under his arm. He takes my hands in his. The insides of his wrists are marked by thick scar tissue. "You've seen 'em, haven't you?"

"Seen what?" I say, thinking he means the scars.

"Not what. Who." Junior's lips peel back from his shiny teeth. "Fire giants."

My mouth's gone dry. "You know about them, too?"

Junior nods slowly. He drops my hands and goes back to shining his horn. "Oh yes, my friend. I know 'em. Nasty things. You steal a look at 'em and you 'bout feel you could burn up with your fear. A glimpse of another world beyond this one here. Them fire gods are bad news, all right, but they're not the worst of it. They work for the big guy." He leans close. "The Wizard of Reckoning."

The name and the way he says it raise goose bumps on my arms. "Who's that?"

"You seen him. In your dreams. Maybe on a stretch of road in the middle of the night."

"The guy in the black space-suit armor with the helmet and sword?"

Junior purses his lips. "That's what you see, then that's him. Don't always look the same to ever'body."

"Who is he?"

"Somebody who ain't from around here. Somebody who don't like bein' put off. Somebody you gotta tangle with at some point, whether you want to or not. Him and them fire bullies been trying to get my horn for years and years."

"Why do they want your horn?"

153

"All my passion's wrapped up in the notes. That's not just air I'm blowing through this mouthpiece, sonny. It's my soul. Someday he's gonna come for me, and I'm gonna blow like I never blown before, and we'll see if it's enough. You lookin' for Dr. X, that right?"

"How'd you know that?"

"I met him myself one time. In the hospital, after the war. Yes sir, you and me got a lot in common."

"Wait—how do you know about all this? How could you have already met Dr. X if Dulcie said the wormhole just opened up—"

"Time and space don't always play by the rules you think they do, son, and Dr. X bent a lot of rules," he answers. "I met him then. You looking for him now." He taps the tips of his fingers together. "*All connected.*

"Enough with that talk. I wanna show you a little something. Take my arm."

I help the great Junior Webster from his chair. He may look frail, but there's a lot of strength in that arm. I'll have to tell Eubie about it when I get back.

He drags one leg when he walks. "Got this limp in the war. Went over to play for the troops. Silly songs, mostly. Dance songs. Get-you-some kinds of songs. You feel me?"

I nod.

"I saw things there, such things. Things a man hopes never to see." He shakes his head. "When I got back, I spent a year in the VA hospital. Nerves, you understand? Not right in the head. I didn't play a note for three years. Just couldn't. Some part of me was lying out there on those fields with my friends, dead. Then one day, I picked up my horn, and when I started playing, the sound was all different. Blood on the notes. Heart. Soul. Every bit of me coming out this horn. I didn't hold nothin' back. And that was that."

"That was that?"

"I learned how to live changed."

I don't really understand what he's getting at, but he seems like a nice old man, and I feel sorry that he lived through what he did.

"We goin' over to that corner," Junior says. As we get closer, I can see another pair of gates attached to the wall. They're just like the ones we came in by, like the ones on the Morpheus float, except that these don't go anywhere. They're just art. Smack-dab in the middle of the wall is a big red button. "You gotta open one of them gates to get at the button."

Something about the way he says it makes it sound like a test. "Does it matter which one?"

"It's your choice, son, not mine."

That doesn't do anything to make me feel less anxious. After a quick, silent game of eeny-meeny-miny-mo, I open the white gate.

"Hmmm," Junior says. "All right, then. Go on. Push the button."

As soon as I do, there's a whirring noise that makes me jump. The ceiling opens up. Above us is a plush black night twinkling with stars. It reminds me of a planetarium, one of those optical-illusion skies that you know can't be real, it has to be a projection on a 360-degree screen, but you swear at the time that you could just blast off into space from your chair. It's that real.

"Ain't that a sight? With all the things we know and learn, we still ain't touched the big mysteries—where we come from, where we go next, why we even here. And when something truly miraculous happens, we run and hide in our caves. We deny."

Junior Webster puts the trumpet to his lips, and blows

155

a few bars of "Cypress Grove Blues." He stops and in- clines his head toward the fake sky like he's listening for something.

"The scientists say most galaxies got a black hole at their center. They suck up matter, those black holes. Just gobble ever'thing right on up, don't matter what it is. That's what we *know*. What we can *observe*. But the scientists, they can't observe what happens inside a black hole—not directly, you understand—because the gravitational pull is so strong there ain't a thing that can escape it. Not you. Not me. Not this here horn. Not even light. Only one thing comes out of a black hole, and that, my friend, is *sound*. Music. As things get pulled right on in to it"—he lowers his voice to a whisper— "that black hole *sings*. Do you feel me? It sings in an octave no human being could ever hear, but it does sing."

When he puts the trumpet to mouth this time, the song comes alive. The sound is a force pushing on me; the notes make me dizzy. I could swear the screen-sky is revolving slowly and that we're drifting toward it. And right in the cen- ter is a dark pinpoint getting bigger with every note.

"Mr. Webster?" I say, but he's lost to his playing. I feel like a little kid at the planetarium, like I want to close my eyes and sink down in my seat till it's over. But Junior's angling his face toward it. The solid dark is bearing down on us from above and around. There's no escaping it. I feel like I'm mov- ing toward that black hole, like I'm being pulled right in, and it is freaking me the hell out. Junior's got a strange look on his face; I can't tell if it's terror or awe.

"Sing," he says quietly. "I'm ready. Go on. Lay that note on me."

The hole's so big that the sky's almost completely dark. Stars zip past us into the giant maw of that greedy, cosmic hole and disappear completely, and even though I know it's just an illusion, I'm afraid I'll be next.

But Junior just laughs at the darkness in the sky.

"You hear that?" he asks. "B-flat, I think. B-flat! You a tricky one, but I believe I be catching you later, baby."

He lifts his horn again and blows hard, and even though I don't hear anything, I know he's made some kind of sound. Immediately, the pressure I felt is gone. The sky ceiling fades to a morning blue. It's nothing but a ceiling.

There's a knock at the door. The bodyguard opens it a crack.

"They're ready for you, Mr. Webster."

"Thank you. I be right there."

"You said you met Dr. X once before," I say. "Do you know where he is now? Where I can find him?"

Junior Webster purses his lips. "I might could help you with that. But first I got a show to do. You play any music, Cameron?"

I shake my head.

"Music opens your soul, makes you ready."

"Ready for what?"

He smiles big. "Exactly."

I follow Junior Webster into the completely packed club. As Junior passes, people reach out to touch him. This is what they've been waiting for, a chance to hear the famous Junior Webster and his magic trumpet.

Gonzo manages to squeeze his way through. He falls in beside me. "Dude, I've been waiting, like, twenty minutes next to a bowl of toxic nut mix trying not to breathe in. What happened with Junior Webster?"

"He's gonna tell us where to find Dr. X. But he's got to play his set first."

Junior leads us to a stage beside huge doors that open to a balcony. Down below, it's a surreal sight—throngs of revelers in wild costumes dancing and swaying in the street, waiting for Junior to blow.

Miss Demeanor grabs the mike. "Ladies and gentlemen, the Horn and Ivory Club is proud to introduce the one, the only, Mr. Junior Webster."

The crowd whoops and hollers and chants his name. Junior puts the trumpet to his lips, but before he can blow a note, he staggers, his hand over his heart. A gasp rolls through the crowd. Junior stumbles over and grabs hold of my hand. "You feel 'im, son?"

"Feel what?"

Junior's eyes go wide. "He's here."

Looking out over the gray cigarette haze, all I see is a bunch of people waiting for Junior to give them a good time. The sharp tang of some harsher smoke tickles the back of my throat, though, and cutting through the crowd is a tall figure in black spiked space armor and a shiny helmet. The visor covers his face completely. I feel weak. When I look down at my protective E-ticket wristband, the first of the five listed kingdoms—Adventureland—is starting to lose color.

"The Wizard of Reckoning," Junior gasps. He pats my sleeve. "Get behind me, son."

"You come for this?" Junior waves the trumpet.

The Wizard of Reckoning moves his head slowly from side to side.

"What you come for, then?"

The wizard slides a piece of paper out from behind his armor. It could be just another one of those missing posters plastered to the crumbling walls of New Orleans. I only catch a glimpse, but I could swear it looks like the guy I saw on the Internet. Junior shakes his head hard.

"I cain't let you do that."

The wizard seems to notice me for the first time. He points one gloved finger in my direction.

"No, sir," Junior growls, as if the wizard's spoken. "He ain't ready for you, yet."

A low murmur ripples through the club. Down on the street, revelers shout for Junior. They've come for a show and they're getting pissed off about the delay. The candles on the tables flare suddenly. The Wizard of Reckoning squeezes his hand into a fist, and it's like I can't breathe.

"All right, all right!" Junior shouts, and the breath comes back into my body. The candles die down. "I'll make you a deal. I know you been wantin' my horn for a while now. I'mmo play you for it. I win, you leave in peace and don't come back. You win, you get the horn."

The wizard cocks his head. I don't hear him say anything, but Junior must, because his face falls, his mouth set in a grim line. "All right, then. If that's the way it's gotta be. I accept."

"Accept what?" I ask Junior.

"Never you mind," Junior whispers. "If something happens to me here tonight, you take my horn with you."

"But you just said—"

Junior's voice is as tight as his lips. "I know what I said, son. You take this horn and someday, when you gotta, when there's nothin' else, you play it. You feel me?"

"Okay," I say, not understanding at all.

Next, he hands me his dark glasses. His eyes are cloudy. "Now. You take these glasses and bury 'em under the angel and wait for a message. You need that message to keep on with your trip."

"I don't understand. Is this about Dr. X?" I ask.

"It's about a lot more than that, son." He blows air over his lips, loosens them for playing.

"But what message? What am I looking for?"

"That's for you to figure on out. Now, I'ma school this fool. Back me up." He points to the gleaming upright bass guitar that I swear wasn't there a minute ago.

"I—I don't know how to play."

"Public education," Junior Webster says with a sigh. "No more music, just tests and tests. Well, you be all right. Just slide from here to here to here and repeat," he says, pressing my fingers against the strings in three quick moves.

"But . . ."

"Trust me. You!" He points to Gonzo. "You on drums. I need all the help I can get tonight."

Gonzo scrambles onto the scarred wooden stool behind the drums. He grabs the sticks like he means business.

"You can play drums?" I whisper to him.

"Only on Rock 'N' Roll Simulator," he says, wide-eyed. "But I made it to level five."

"Tonight, I got some special friends helping me out," Junior calls to the crowd.

"It's one of them Last Wish thangs!" Miss D shouts next, and everybody cheers.

"Junior," I call. "I'm serious—I don't know how to play."

"Sure you do, son. Just put your fingers on the strings like I showed you, let go, and keep coming back to one."

He pushes the glasses into the pocket of my Windbreaker, puts the trumpet to his lips, puffs out his cheeks, and lets loose with a furious noise. I've never heard anybody play the trumpet like that ever. It's a crazy, wonderful sound. Hard, soft, sweet, mean, desperate, joyful—a whole life in fierce melody. And I'm backing him up on bass. My fingers slide awkwardly up and down the strings. It sounds a little like a cat being skinned, but it fills in the holes, and I guess people feel too sorry for us to complain. Gonzo's keeping the beat with his entire body, and every once in a while he mutters, "Level five, level five . . ."

Another sound cuts through the club. The Wizard of Reckoning has his own trumpet, and he's matching Junior riff for riff. Notes rise and fall, swoop and soar. Junior's dripping sweat. It slides down his cheeks and wets his collar. But he keeps swinging. I feel like I'm inside this music, and I'm starting to understand the weird, beautiful universe of jazz. It's like that space-sky Junior showed me in his dressing room, a place so vast it seems like it couldn't possibly be governed by any rules, but the more you're floating in it, the more you find that it's got its own strange, secret order to it after all.

Junior's on fire with the music. After one amazing run, the wizard falters. The room goes quiet, and I think we've won. But the wizard comes back hard, and this time, it's Junior who looks like he might go down. He staggers into me.

"You remember what I tole you, now," he says. His feet are slow and unsteady, but he manages to get back to where he was, and the music takes on an extra dimension. It's raw and a little scary. The wizard gives his notes the same intensity. The two of them trade riffs back and forth like fighters in the ring. And then something awful happens.

The wizard takes a deep breath and blows, and nothing comes out. At least, I can't hear anything. But Junior clutches his chest and falls to his knees, still holding tight to his horn. Gonzo's crashing around on the drums, making a lot of noise. I can't play the bass anymore. My fingers have lost their sound.

"Gonzo!" I shout, and he silences the cymbals.

The wizard holds out his hand, wiggles his fingers impatiently, waiting for Junior's golden trumpet, but quick as a whip, Junior tosses the horn to me instead, and I catch it one-handed.

Junior laughs down low in his chest; the laugh mixes with a rattling cough. The Wizard of Reckoning strides across the floor and straddles Junior's body, towering over him. Slowly, he raises his visor. I can't see who he is, but Junior can; his face registers surprise first, then amusement.

"I'll be damned," Junior says, with a weak little laugh. "Don't that beat all?"

He wheezes once. And just like that, the old jazzman hits the floor, dead.

The crowd is stunned into silence, but not for long, because the wizard's not letting anyone off easy. He tilts his head back, lifts his arms, and lets loose with a screeching howl that's part freight train, part missile attack. I feel it in every cell, like a force of gravity times one hundred, pushing down on me. He brings his arms down fast and the walls explode in flame; glass shatters inward. The crowd in the club screams; they crawl over each other in their panic to escape.

The Wizard of Reckoning points his finger at me again, and my body screams in anguish, as if I'm on fire. It brings me to my knees, shutting my eyes against the searing pain.

"Just relax, baby. You be okay." It's Glory's soothing voice. I open my eyes, and she's shooting something into my IV line.

Glory? I hear it in my head, but I don't know if I've said it out loud.

"Try to sleep."

162

"Cameron!" Gonzo's cowering behind the high hat, using the sticks like a cross in a vampire movie.

"Gonzo! We've gotta . . . gotta get out of here," I gasp out.

Gonzo's frozen with fear. He's not leaving the safety of the cymbals. People are pushing and shoving, doing their best to escape the fire. The wizard sees us, and he's coming.

"Gonzo, we've got to go now!" I scream.

Miss Demeanor rushes the stage and pulls Gonzo off the drums forcibly. "This way!"

She runs backstage to Junior's dressing room. "But there's no door here!" I shout.

"Yes there is." She puts the nearly catatonic Gonzo down and flips on the planetarium projector. The sky fills up with tiny moons and planets zooming into the great unknown of the black hole. "Follow me."

She walks straight for it, glittery and bright as a star, and vanishes. I can't see a single spangle of her left.

"Holy *mierda*! Where'd she go?" Gonzo bleats.

"I don't know!"

"This way," she calls, and now I see her perched on a small, rickety ladder that climbs up to the ceiling.

The heat from the fire has reached us. Flames grab at the doorway and bring it down. I'm not sticking around to see what else they can do. I shove Junior Webster's sunglasses and his horn into my bag and race for the hole. It feels like it's pulling me in, but it's Miss D. She grabs my hands and drags me to a hidden door in the shadows. One hard shove of her hip and the door opens. We spill out into the weak light of an alley.

The place is crawling with cops and firefighters now. Blasts of water belch from heavy-duty hoses. Miss D pushes us down the street, away from the fire, till we're far from the crowds and standing by a streetlamp near a storefront for a psychic.

"You boys better clear on out of here," Miss D says. Before we take off running, she grabs my hand. "Whatever Junior told you, you best do, *cher*. He's never been wrong long as I've known him. And Cameron," she adds.

"Yes?"

She flips the matches over in her hand. "Thanks for the light, baby."

We run for blocks until we reach the edge of the Mississippi River. I'm bent over, trying to catch my breath. Gonzo paces, taking in nervous gulps of air.

"What. The fuck. Was that?" He doesn't wait for me to answer. "That guy . . . what was . . ."

"I don't know." I'm not about to divulge that particular info to Gonzo. He'll freak and head back for sure.

"He killed Junior Webster!"

"Maybe Junior was mixed up in something big—gambling debts or, hell, I don't know," I lie. "We just need to focus on finding Dr. X."

Gonzo shakes his head. "This is fucked up, man."

"The sooner we get to Dr. X, the sooner I get cured and you get . . . whatever it is you're getting, and we're done. Agreed?"

Gonzo squints out at the water like he's thinking it over. The dawn's sending out the early team to ready the sky. Gulls dive down for breakfast beside tugboats shining on the river like floating bones.

"I'm hungry," Gonzo says, and I guess we're agreed after all.

The French Quarter's emptying out. The garbage cans

overflow with plastic cups and the streets are a wreck. Horse-drawn carriages clip-clop on the cobblestones, heading home for sleep. A truck idles by a warehouse entrance. Gonzo and I find an all-hours café where they serve crispy, hot beignets and mugs of chicory coffee that taste like it's been made with airplane fuel and stirred with an old stick. But it warms us up and chases away what's left of the night, so we drink it anyway.

"What was that thing he told you about his sunglasses?" Gonzo asks.

"He told me to bury them under the angel." I take them out of my pocket and put them on the table. They're just ordinary sunglasses.

"Which means?"

"I don't know. He said once I did, I'd get a message."

Gonzo eats another beignet. The powdered sugar coats his upper lip like a snowy mustache. "Dude, this is crazy."

He's right. I wish Dulcie would show herself, drop us a hint or two or just give in and tell us where to find Dr. X. The bleary morning light is pressing against the café's windows now, and I get a good look at the desperate crew inhabiting the diner with us at this otherworldly hour: a couple of hospital workers getting off the night shift, trying to laugh off the stab wounds and gunshot wounds they saw but not really shaking the lines that have settled around their mouths like parentheses closing off all the relevant things that could be said. A couple of homeless schizophrenics talking to themselves and drinking coffee with their few panhandled coins, though coffee seems like the last thing they need. A group of still-drunk college kids in wilting costumes trying to sober up over pancakes and toast. It's a long way from the stupid, choreographed riding mowers of my safe little suburb, and something about it makes me feel both sad and exhilarated all at the same time, like now I know a secret the sleeping citizens back home don't, even if the secret is basically how alone we can be out here in the dead-honest haze of six a.m.

Gonzo's going on about Captain Carnage and the time he beat a flock of Teddy Vamps. His voice is white noise. My body aches, and my arm's shaking. I just want to sleep. My eyelids fall, closing out the world.

I'm dreaming of Disney World, but it's like a herky-jerky, grainy home movie with the sound turned down. Hotel bathroom, Mom smiling, rubbing my wet head with a white towel. Dad and me waving from the line to the Peter Pan ride. Mom holding Jenna, who blinks at the sun. A random shot of Tomorrowland looking like another planet made of colorful balls and gears. The dark of the Small World ride. Mechanical kids going around and up and down. A splash. Me underwater, sinking, opening my mouth wide.

I wake with a gasp. Gonzo's not talking anymore, and there's a face inches from mine.

"Buy me a cup of coffee?" One of the schizo dudes hovers over me. He's as matted as a feral cat and smells like he rolled in his own piss. He's got about four teeth left, and they don't look long for this world.

"Buy me a cup of coffee, please? I'm a homeless vet. Me and my wife got burned out of our home and I gotta support five kids and the littlest one needs an operation on her eyes and I wouldn't do this, man, I wouldn't be out here if it wasn't for them, and a guy's gotta live, you know, gotta make his way and find his meaning in life and love, and to do that he needs coffee, he needs coffee and coffee and coffee."

Gonzo's shrinking down into his chair till I can only see his eyes and that huge 'fro, but I can tell by the redness in his cheeks that he's holding his breath. The smell is pretty harsh, but I know Gonzo's probably more afraid that he could catch some rare, untreatable disease just by sharing the same air-space as this guy.

"Here you go, man." I leave a dollar on the table and he snatches it up.

"Thank you. Thank you. I got burned out of my house-boat and my kid needs an operation on her lungs so I need to get me some coffee and head out to the cemeteries to take care of things. To the cemeteries you just take the Canal Street cable car to the end, all the way to the end of the line, to the end where the angels live, and that's where you go to bury things."

My skin's tingling now, but it has nothing to do with my disease. "What did you say?" I ask the homeless guy, but the cook's shooing him away.

"Come on, Spanky, leave these people alone, now," the cook says. He yanks the string to the front window shades and the café is flooded with light.

CHAPTER TWENTY

**In Which We Visit a Cemetery
and I Receive a Message. Sort of. I Hope.**

We take the Canal Street car out to the cemeteries near the
interstate. It's a depressing ride. Sandwiched between the re-
furbished law offices, used-car lots, and prisonlike schools are
tiny little houses that look like they could fall down any
minute, all peeling paint and chipped shutters. Some of the
wounded doors have red X's drawn on them like animals
marked for slaughter. Abandoned cars peek out from coats of
dirt, rust, and leaves. On the corner, there's a bent ONE-WAY
street sign pointing to the ground.

"End of the line," the guy says, which is pretty funny, considering. All around us are cemeteries—left, right, center.

"Now what?" Gonzo asks as we get off the cable car and
cross over the tracks.

"He said I'd know the one," I say, eyes scanning the miles
and miles of gravestones.

Gonzo snorts. "Well, that's helpful." He calls out the names of the cemeteries around us. "The Odd Fellow's Rest? That sounds like your speed, amigo. The Greenwood?"

Gonzo's waiting for some direction from me, but hell if I know what we're looking for. Junior Webster's sunglasses feel heavy in my hands.

"Cypress Grove," Gonzo says. "Or the . . ."

"There's one called Cypress Grove?"

"Yeah. Over there. The small one."

"This way," I say. We pass under the wrought-iron arch that spells out Cypress Grove and into the cemetery. A grass and gravel path leads us past limestone mausoleums, pretty little houses for the dead. Set into the ground are raised stone platforms with inscriptions that read OUR BELOVED BROTHER or OUR DARLING BABIES.

"What are we looking for?" Gonzo asks.

"An angel."

We scan the mausoleums and headstones. In this row alone, I count twenty-seven angel statues.

"Could you be more specific?" Gonzo asks.

"He said I'd know it. Let's keep looking."

"Hey, check this out!" Gonzo yells, climbing up onto the platform of a coffee-colored mausoleum. "It's like a fucking castle. Oh shit. Can you say 'fuck' in a graveyard or will that jinx you with the undead?"

I suck in my breath. "Well, it's too late now."

Gonzo's eyes get huge and I can tell he's heading for a full-on feardown. "Seriously. You don't think there's some voodoo action on this place, like hands sticking up through graves and stuff? Dude. For real?"

"Gonzo, no hand is going to break up through a stone mausoleum, okay? Chill out."

"Yeah, okay," he says, letting out a deep breath. "This could be zombie heaven, man. Dude, I wish we were making a horror film. That would be mad awesome!"

Gonz snaps a few pics with his cell phone. Weird shit like his hand resting clawlike against a headstone so that it looks like he's rising from the dead, horror-movie-poster style. These are accompanied by "aargghs" and "aaaahhhs" and various zombie-esque grunts made deep in his throat.

"Funny. Can you stop playing Dawn of the Living Ass-Hat long enough to help me find Junior's message?"

A few feet away, three blond girls jabber on in German as they snap photos of the decaying headstones. One of the girls asks me in halting English if I'll take a picture of them together.

"No-a speak English," I say, turning away.

"Here, I'll do it," Gonzo says.

I start to remind him we're here for a purpose, but he's already got their camera and is using a mix of Spanish, English, and hand gestures to direct them while they bump into one another in confusion and laugh.

"Copenhagen Interpretation?" one girl says. She plays a snippet of song from her phone, and Gonzo nods, smiling, and they all nod, smiling.

I wander off down the narrow lanes till I'm alone. The air is heavy with the rain that won't come. It presses down on me, making my legs heavy and my chest tight. I find a place to sit on the stone steps of a gravestone hidden by a weeping willow. The moss hangs so low it tickles my cheek and nose. It smells like sorrow.

"Hey, cowboy."

At the sound of Dulcie's voice, I whip around, left and right, searching.

"Up here," she calls.

"Ah. Very cute." She's posed on the top of a white, churchlike mausoleum, her wings folded, her chin resting on her hands like the Thinker Angel. She could blend right in, except for the boots and the bright pink hair.

She hops to the ground with an impressive thud, her boots sending puffs of ancient Southern dust onto my jeans, and settles onto the new grave of a soldier. "So what do you think of the Big Easy?"

"I don't know," I say, sitting next to her. "It's kind of depressing."

Dulcie puts a hand on my shoulder. "Cam, you're in a graveyard."

"Funny."

Dulcie nods at the sunglasses in my hands. "What are those?"

"Sunglasses."

"Going for the literal. Okay. I'm game. Where'd you get them?"

She could be putting me on. For all I know, she's been watching the whole time and has seen everything. "This guy named Junior Webster," I say, waiting for a reaction. But her expression doesn't change and I figure she really doesn't know anything, which means she's the lamest angel ever. I go ahead and tell her about our night, the Wizard of Reckoning and his Fire Giants—the dark energy—showing up to our little party, Junior's death. The only thing I don't tell her is how scared I am. In the distance, I can hear a smattering of German and laughing. I can make out Gonzo playing director. He's telling one of the German girls to act like a zombie.

"Junior told me I'm supposed to bury these under the angel and wait for a message. Thing is, there are, like, four billion angels in this cemetery."

Dulcie nods. "That's a toughie."

"I thought maybe you would know where? Like maybe that might fall under the category of special angel-privy info you could share?"

She leans back, crosses her legs and swings one out, touching me lightly each time with her boot. "I told you, Cameron, I'm just a messenger."

I put my hands up. "Fine. Junior Webster wanted me to bury these sunglasses under the angel? I'm on it. If this doesn't work, I really don't give a shit anymore. Move your feet."

Dulcie sweeps her boots to one side. I make a small hole in the fresh dirt of the soldier's grave, drop in the sunglasses, and cover them up. I wipe my hands on my jeans and sit beside Dulcie to wait. Gulls circle overhead, crying. After five minutes, I check the ground, but there's nothing.

"So where's this secret message?"

"Beats me," she says, dipping into a secret stash of ChocoYums. "But I love the not knowing. The sense of mystery. Don't you?"

"No. I really, really don't." We sit quietly for another minute or two. My butt hurts and all I want to do is leave. "Should we say something? Are there some, like, magic words that could speed this along?"

Dulcie puts her hands out like a magician about to levitate a rabbit. *"Domo arigato, Mr. Roboto."* She shrugs. "I heard that on the radio once."

"That's it. I'm out of here." I stand up and promptly trip over a large rock on the path. Under the rock is a scrap from today's newspaper, the classified section.

"Did you find it?" Dulcie asks, peering down at me from her new perch at the top of the willow tree. She's totally showing off.

"Could you let me read this, please?"

She mimes a zipper over her lips, and I scan the section of newspaper. It's all a random jumble:

HERE AND THEN NOT—MYSTERY OF THE
COPENHAGEN INTERPRETATION SOLVED! NEW PHOTOS
OF LONG-LOST INUIT BAND FISHING IN SNOW.

BUY NOW. VALHALLA YARD GNOMES—
LAWN ORNAMENTS FIT FOR A GOD.

DEAR TOBIAS, I FORGIVE YOU. TO ERR IS HUMAN; TO LIVE,
DIVINE. LET US LIVE TOGETHER FOR THE REST OF OUR DAYS.
I WISH IT TO BE.

NEED A RIDE TO THE YA! PARTY HOUSE?
WE'VE GOT SPACE IN OUR CAR.

THE PURSUIT OF HAPPINESS CORPORATION'S
TRAVEL OFFICE IS NOW OPEN.

LOOKING FOR WORK?
OUR OPERATIONS ARE EXPANDING!
CALL UNITED SNOW GLOBE WHOLESALERS
AT 1-800-555-1212.

There are at least twenty different classifieds here, none of them particularly meaningful or helpful.

"This is hopeless," I say.

Dulcie's voice floats down from the tree. "Keep looking. You'll find it."

"Yeah? How do you know?"

"Because I believe in you, Cameron," she says without a hint of sarcasm.

I look again, and this time, way down in the right-hand

corner, I see a tiny, illustrated ad for the Roadrunner Bus Company with their tagline: *Follow the feather.*

"Hey, is that it? Is this what Junior meant?" I start, but the willow tree's empty. Dulcie is already gone. A sudden gust of wind tears the paper from my hand and blows it far away. I'm left with just a scrap. Two words: *to live.*

CHAPTER TWENTY-ONE

In Which Junior Webster's Cryptic Message Does Not Become Any More Uncryptic, and the Worst Pictures Ever Taken of Us Are Circulated

We're at the bus station, feeding my dad's credit card into the ticket machine. Our bus to Daytona is scheduled to leave in five minutes. I don't know if that's the bus we need to be on; I'm just going off what I saw on the classifieds page. It mentioned the YA! Party House. The Party House is in Florida. There are three buses leaving this evening and one of them is headed to Daytona; ergo, we are headed to Daytona. I am divining my future based on a classified ad I found in a graveyard.

"So, you think this is part of the secret message?" Gonzo asks, looking at the newspaper scrap.

"Don't know, don't care right now," I say. The ticket machine wheezes like an old man, coughing out two tickets to Florida in a painfully slow fashion.

"*To live.* Maybe he means *too live,*" Gonzo says, making a long "i" sound. "You know, like, like, hey, cats and kittens, it's all too live," he says, adopting a hipster voice.

"Or maybe it's just bullshit. *To live?* That's not a secret message. That's a fortune cookie."

"Maybe he meant you needed to live. Maybe he's telling you Dr. X will cure you and everything will be okay. Dude, I'll bet that's it!"

Gonzo's face lights up now that he thinks he's solved the puzzle, but I just feel like some kind of jerk who's having a cosmic prank played on him. I wanted something concrete—turn left at the Auto Mart. Dr. X's office is on the corner of Fifth and Main and you have an appointment at eleven o'clock next Tuesday.

Just as they're making the announcement for our bus, a couple of cops enter the station. At the sight of them, we automatically go low-profile, hiding at the back of a pack of people heading for the buses. They've got a flyer they show to people in the station.

"Keep your head down," I whisper to Gonzo. The cop stops to ask a lady with three small kids if she's ever seen these two guys, and I get a look over his shoulder. The flyer shows two very bad school photos of Gonzo and me under the word MISSING. I hate that picture of me. I look like a complete putz. But at least I'm not sporting the ridiculous upper-lip peach fuzz Gonzo's got in his.

"Gonzo," I say. "Be cool. Those cops are looking for us. Blend in."

"Blend in? Easy for you to say!"

The line presses forward toward the bus. The driver opens up the metal jaw on the side and passengers hand over their suitcases for storage. Why do people have to travel with so much stuff? The cops are out here now, scouring the buses for two teens—one a dwarf—who escaped from a hospital in Texas. I position Gonz in front of me so I can block his body with mine. Trouble is, he's wider than I am, and it makes it look like we're one of those Indian goddesses with lots of limbs. After what seems like forever, the driver opens the doors, and Gonzo and I nearly kill each other in our rush to reach the back of the bus, where we pile into our seats and slink down.

"Cover your face with your jacket. Pretend you're asleep," I say.

We bury ourselves under Windbreakers and backpacks so that only the tops of our heads show. People lumber on now, looking for seats. I peek over the top of my jacket to see the cop stepping into the aisle. He cranes his neck, looking for us, but there are too many people moving around to really see.

The driver climbs on. "Excuse me, Officer. If you're done, I got a schedule to get to."

The cop gives a last hard look, and I duck under the safety of my jacket. After a few seconds, I hear him thank the driver. The doors close with a hiss, sealing us in. The bus rolls out of the station, but my heartbeat doesn't get back to normal till we're far from the city limits of New Orleans.

When he's ready to take a nap, the guy next to us lets us borrow his deck of cards. We eat RealFruit Lassos and play Texas Hold 'Em and Jacks Are Wild. The bus bumps along the coast. Oil refineries send up plumes of toxic smoke. The smell, like rotten eggs mixed with cleaning fluid, makes me want to gag. A couple of shrimp boats bob on the water, the fishermen pulling up the soul of the sea in their heavy nets.

I like watching the country roll by my window. I wish we'd taken more vacations. I try to remember why we stopped. Dad got busy with work and Mom got busy looking busy and Jen and I started hating each other and next thing you know, we're a bunch of strangers totally uncomfortable being around each other. And who wants to go on vacation with a bunch of strangers?

Gonzo deals out a new hand. The sky's getting darker. The lights in the bus kick on. Little cones of yellow-white shine down on our cards, making our hands look bleached out.

"You get a phone number from that German girl back in the graveyard?" I ask. "I think she was hot for you."

Gonzo shakes his head. "Not my type."

"What? German? Tourist? Girl?"

Gonzo flashes me a Don't Go There look.

"So what is your type?"

He thinks for a minute. "Sweet, but dangerous-looking. I like Southern accents. And tattoos."

I let out a sharp laugh. "Tattoos? Whoa! Who'da thunk it? The Gonzman likes 'em a little tough."

He grins. "You don't know everything about me, *pendejo*. I'm a pretty complicated dude."

"You're, like, a totally open book, Gonz," I say, laughing. "I've never met anybody more transparent in my life."

"You don't know me, dude," he says, not smiling this time. Gonzo examines his cards, prepping for his next move. "People always think they know other people, but they don't. Not really. I mean, maybe they know things about them, like they won't eat doughnuts or they like action movies or whatever. But they don't know what their friends do in their rooms alone at night or what happened to them when they were kids or if they feel fucked up and sad for no reason at all."

I've got an image of Gonzo sitting in his room alone

feeling fucked up and sad and I hate it, because now I feel responsible for him in a way I didn't want to.

"You're not going to say something cheesy like 'people are like onions; they have lots of layers,' are you?"

"Just trying to have a conversation. Forget it, dude. Whatever. Just play."

He discards a two and I pick it up. I've got a pair of twos and that's it. My cards suck.

"So, what's your type?" Gonzo asks a few minutes later.

"Wow, let me think. Um, anyone who would have me." I put another card on the pile. What is my type? A brief image of Dulcie with her armor and pink hair comes unbidden to mind. I push it away. "You know Staci Johnson?"

"Staci Johnson!" Gonzo snarls. "Say it ain't so, dude! Staci Johnson is the devil's spawn!"

"I know, I know. She has no working brain cells, a subpar personality, and nothing interesting to say ever, unless you're into what happened last night on YA! TV. But once you make it past that, she's seriously fine. Yo, I discarded."

He ignores my card and draws from the stack. "Staci Johnson. Dude. I feel like I need to shave my insides when you say that." Gonzo organizes his cards, moving one from the end to the center of his hand. "Well, maybe when you get back from Florida, you know? You'll have that whole road-trip mystique working for you. Plus you will have saved the world. That's gotta count."

"And a tan," I add, glancing at my flounder-belly-white arms.

"Tan works."

"Also, I won't be dying. Hopefully."

"Always helpful." He fans his cards out on the table. "Royal flush, Señor Pajero. You owe me four bags of chips."

We've been on the road for six hours when my right leg

starts to twitch uncontrollably. The E-ticket's lost a little more color; Adventureland's totally gone, and the second line, Frontierland, is a hazy green. I cross my left leg over my right and put my backpack on top, hoping no one will notice, hoping the twitching will pass soon. The tremor travels. My right arm goes tight. I can't lift the sucker; it's like lead. *Please don't let me have a seizure here. Please. Just let me make it to Florida.* Out on the dark horizon, little bursts of flame pop up. They look just like the fire balls on top of the refineries. I even try to convince myself that that's what they are. But my gut says it's the fire giants out there. Getting stronger. Bigger. Waiting for me. My eyes get heavy watching them. The rhythm of the road lulls me to sleep.

"Cameron? I thought I'd read some more of *Don Quixote* to you." Mom's sitting beside me in my hospital bed, bathed in a pool of light. The curtains have been drawn sealing us into a little drapery cocoon. "Would you like that?"

Her voice wraps around me like a dryer-fresh blanket, and I drift in and out of the crazy knight's amusing adventures with Sancho Panza. "'Take my advice and live for a long, long time,'" Mom reads. "'Because the maddest thing a man can do in this life is to let himself die.'"

After a while, Mom closes the book and strokes my hair. "It's kind of nice, reading to you again," she says. "Do you remember when you were a kid and in the summers we would go to the library? I'd let you pick out five books, and you could never wait till we got home. We'd have to find a corner and sit and read them all before we left the library."

Why don't I remember that? How could my mom and I have shared the same experience but I don't remember it?

"Why did we stop doing that?" Mom wonders aloud. "We just stopped going. You didn't want to, I think. And I was afraid of pushing you. I was always afraid of saying the wrong thing, so I stopped talking."

Mom's crying a little bit, quietly, the way she always does. She never utters a sound even when she's crying, and that makes me a little sad. Doesn't seem right. When you cry, people should hear you. The world should stop. I squeeze Mom's hand and she squeezes back. I don't say anything, but at least she knows I've heard her.

People drift in and out in my dream like actors in a play. Eubie comes to visit. He slips headphones on my ears so I can hear "Cypress Grove Blues," and I want to tell him that I've been to New Orleans, that I've seen Junior Webster, that I played bass for him, but it's a dream, and the words won't come. At one point, Dad sits on my bed, reading to me from a physics paper he's grading that's about supercolliders.

In the corner, the muted TV plays the same cartoon of the roadrunner and coyote chasing each other in and out of doors. The last thing I see is the old lady from across the hall standing at the foot of my bed. She's dressed in a coat and hat and has a little suitcase with her.

"A house by the sea. Don't forget."

"I won't," I say, but I'm not sure anyone hears me.

And on TV, the coyote waits for the anvil to fall.

CHAPTER TWENTY-TWO

Wherein the Angel Discusses the Wonders of Microwave Popcorn and Gonzo Gets Our Asses Stranded in the Middle of Nowhere

When I wake up, it's morning, early. The light hasn't been up much longer than I have. People are asleep. Their heads rest against the windows and seat backs, their jaws spread wide, like the arms of a can opener left on a counter. Through the thin, wet layer of dew on my own window, the countryside rolls past. We're in Mississippi or maybe Alabama.

A gray mist sits on the rooftops of little tar-paper shacks where clotheslines are strung across the front yards. The shirts catch the breeze like they wish they could sail on out of there, out of those small, junky yards with their rusted car shells and broken-down plastic toys. I breathe on the window a few times, watch it fog over and retreat, fog over and retreat.

I like the feel of the road under me. The solid *thumpthumpthumpthump-thump* drum cadence of those big tires.

Gonzo's out cold next to me, that big head of his resting on my shoulder. He mumbles in his sleep, and I wonder what dreams he has.

"Peekaboo." Dulcie's face peers over the seat in front of me.

"What are you doing here?" I ask, looking around.

"There's some welcome."

"Look, it's just . . ." I lower my voice. "I don't want people to think I'm opening up a six-pack of crazy here on the bus. I'll get kicked off."

"Looks like everybody's sleeping."

"Can anybody else see you besides me?" I ask.

"I suppose they could if they wanted to, but maybe what they see isn't what you see," Dulcie answers in her typically cryptic fashion. "Hey, check it out." She unfurls her wings slightly. *Cameron rock*, they read.

"Shouldn't there be an 's' at the end? Cameron *rocks*?"

"Yeah. I ran out of spray paint. But the sentiment is one hundred percent there." She rests her chin on the seat top and grips the sides with her hands. It makes her look like she's been beheaded. "You seem a little tired, cowboy."

"Weird dreams," I say.

"Want to tell me about it? The doctor is in."

"Just stuff about my mom. She was talking about how she used to take me to the library when I was a kid, and I didn't remember that at all. But just as I woke up, I *did* remember it. Crystal clear I could see myself sitting in my mom's lap over near the water fountain, and she was reading some rhyming book about monsters to me. She had on sandals and she smelled good, like shampoo. And I was happy. How did I manage to forget that?"

"That's a nice memory," Dulcie says.

We listen to the road *thumpity-thump*ing beneath us, and for a few minutes it feels like we're the only two beings in the entire universe.

"Do you have some nice memories?" I ask, offering her some Cheesy Puff Fingers from our open bag. "You know, from before you were . . ." I gesture to her wings in a completely ineffectual way. "You know."

Dulcie gets a funny little smile. "I'm making a nice memory right now."

"Now?"

"Here. With you." She downs two Cheesy Puff Fingers.

"But what were you before you were an angel?" I press.

She takes a sip of my warm soda, makes a face. "Does it matter?"

"Yeah. I think it does."

"Okay, then," she says, taking another drink from the can. "I was somebody else."

"What does that mean?" I say, getting pissed off. "Did you have parents? A dog? A parakeet? A Social Security number? Can you remember? How do you feel? Is there a God? What happens when we die? Will I be like you, spray-painting my wings with misspelled messages and guiding people on stupid, insane missions?"

"It's not stupid, Cameron," she says softly.

"I'm out here on the road looking for some renegade miracle man, totally sticking my neck out for you, and you can't even answer one single fucking question!"

The guy across the aisle opens one eye for half a second, then turns over, and I lower my voice. "I think you owe me that."

Dulcie wipes her mouth, but some of the Day-Glo cheese powder clings to her lip. "All right. I'll answer one of your questions."

184

"Thank you."

"I feel like I swallowed a Magritte."

"What?"

Dulcie reaches in for another Cheesy Puff Finger. "You asked me how I feel. And my answer is: I feel like I swallowed a Magritte. Like on the inside, I'm made of clouds and floating eyes, green apples, and slowly rising men in bowler hats."

"You are officially the most annoying unreal creature ever."

"Meet a lot of us, do you?"

"Lately it's gotten very weird."

"Cameron." She puts her hand on my arm. "The point is, you're alive right now. Look around." She widens her arms to include the sleeping passengers. "Half the people I see aren't really aware. They aren't in the game at all. They never notice how fabulous stuff here is."

"Like what?"

"Like . . ." She thinks for a few seconds. "Microwave popcorn."

"You're kidding."

"Think about it. You put this flat bag of kernels in the hopper, wait four minutes . . ." She opens her mouth and taps her fingers against her taut cheeks, making a popping sound. "And voila! You've got a steaming bag of buttery goodness right there."

"This is your miracle of human existence?"

"No. But it doesn't *suck*. It's a simple pleasure, okay? You got any of those?"

"Sure," I say.

She folds her arms over her armored chest. "Such as?"

"Masturbation."

"Yeah? What else?"

I think about it for a good, long minute. "Eubie's."

Dulcie sits, waiting. *"And?"*

"Can't think of anything else."

"Well, how about pizza—in-restaurant, not delivery. Water fountains. That chill on your arms when you go from an air-conditioned movie theater into the heat. The smell of Laundromats. Snow. CDs . . ."

"No, not CDs, records. Gotta be vinyl."

"Vinyl, then. What else?"

"You know I hate that you've drawn me into this, don't you?" The morning light's falling on Dulcie in a way that makes her glow, and I have the impulse to say, *This. Right here. Right now.*

I shrug. "That's all I got."

She shakes her head. "We've got work to do, Bucko."

The bus driver's got his signal on. We're exiting.

Dulcie gets up. "That's my cue."

"So, like . . . when will I see you again?"

"Soon," she says, ducking into the john. "Get out there and make some memories, cowboy. Oh, and don't forget to save the universe."

Five minutes later, the bus pulls into a rest-stop area. The sign welcomes us to the fine state of Mississippi. A bunch of eighteen-wheelers are parked near the gas pumps. The bus comes to a stop and the driver opens the doors. "Y'all wanna stretch your legs, get some air, go 'head. Just be back on this bus in ten minutes. I got a schedule to keep."

Gonzo and I pile out with the rest of the road-weary passengers and head for the big green MegaMart across the parking lot.

"Awww, dude! They've got the Mega XL Death Captain Carnage!" He runs for the bank of video games beside the tiny ATM machine. "This is just the most awesome game ever! If you get to level three, you get a special battleax that

186

lets you slice-and-dice your way through nursery rhyme characters. Sweet! Hey, you got a buck?"

I give Gonz the dollar and in another minute I hear him killing beloved storybook characters with glee. There's an explosion, and the dish yells, "Run away, Spoon! Save yourself!" I use the ATM. Buy a few more snacks. Get some change.

"Gonzo—" I start to ask if I can use his phone, but I know he's terrified of using up his minutes. "Listen, I gotta make a call. Keep an eye on the bus, okay?"

"Sure," he says, eyes glazed.

Around the back is a pay phone. I drop in my coins and punch in the digits I know best. On the fourth ring, Jenna's sleepy voice answers.

"Hello?"

"Jenna?"

"Cameron? Oh my God, is that you? Where are you?"

"Shhh, don't wake up Mom and Dad."

"Okay," she says. And I know how hard it is for her to break the good-girl code for me. The line buzzes with static and the occasional click. "How are you?"

"I'm okay. How is everybody there?"

"Mom and Dad are completely freaked. They put posters up all over town. And people have these brown and white ribbons on their trees that they say they're not taking down till you come home again."

"Brown and white?"

"Like a cow." She sucks in her breath. "The cops are looking for you, Cameron. They traced your credit card to New Orleans. Cameron, why don't you just come home? Please?"

"I can't do that, Jenna. Not until I find the guy who can cure me."

"What are you talking about? What guy?" She sounds like she's about to cry.

"It's . . . complicated. But I promise I'm okay. Listen, Jenna, I need you to do me a favor."

There's a pause. The line is really bad. "Okay."

"Just let Mom and Dad know I'm okay. I'll call back as soon as I can. I promise. I . . ."

Another phone picks up.

"Cameron? Cameron! Is that you? Where are you?" It's Dad's voice. In the background, I hear Mom telling him to let her talk. "Cameron, just tell us where you are and we'll come pick you up. We love you. We—"

More clicks. A finger comes down on the clicker. "They're tracing the call." Dulcie's standing there. Something serious in her eyes makes me obey. Slowly, I put the receiver back into its cradle.

"You have to let them go, Cam. You have to move forward. You've got a mission."

"I know that, okay?" I explode. "Just leave me alone, would you?"

"Leave you alone?"

"Yes."

"Totally alone?"

"Yes! God."

She bites her bottom lip. "Okay. See you around, cowboy."

"Yeah. See you."

I run across the parking lot to the bathroom island and push my way into the filthy hole of a men's room. The E-ticket scratches against my arm. Frontierland's gone even lighter, the lettering getting hard to read. How much time do I have left? In the cracked mirror, I look like Grade-D crap—pale and stubbly.

"What the fuck are you doing?" I ask my fractured reflection. Tears sting at my eyes. A big guy in cowboy boots comes in and I splash water on my face.

Out in the parking lot, two trucks gas up at the pumps. A family eats their fast-food meals in their station wagon with the windows rolled down. Two guys stand by a stack of tires, away from the pumps, smoking like a couple of idiots. And over where the bus was parked earlier, I see nothing but a big empty space.

No. No, no, no, no, no.

I push through the MegaMart doors so hard, the bell jangles like it's caffeinated. Gonzo's still at the Captain Carnage game.

"Gonzo!" I snarl.

"Dude, not now! The Teddy Vamps are on me."

"I thought you were watching the bus!"

"The bus?" He doesn't take his eyes off the game.

"Yeah. You know, that long, rectangular vehicle that gets our asses out of here and is nowhere to be seen?"

Gonzo finally looks up, wide-eyed.

"Yeah, exactly," I say.

We race outside to the parking lot and stand in the empty space where there used to be a bus to Florida.

Gonzo swallows hard. "It's . . ."

". . . gone," I finish. "Congratulations. We are officially fucked."

CHAPTER TWENTY-THREE

Wherein We Take a Van Ride with Possible Serial Killers

"I don't understand. I looked outside, like, maybe *two seconds* before and it was there, dude. I swear."

"Two seconds," I repeat.

"I swear!"

"Let's go to the replay. Hmmm, oh, looks like maybe Gonzo was so busy smoking Little Miss Muffet he *forgot. To watch. For the damn. Bus!*"

"I'm sorry," he says, hanging his head like a little kid who just peed on your carpet by mistake.

"Just keep looking for signs of civilization."

We're on a dirt road in the middle of freakin' nowhere. So far, we've passed a farm that stank to high heaven, some cotton fields, and four ancient husks of tractors getting their rust tans in the sun. It's bright and the heat's beating hard on the back of my neck.

"Try calling her again," Gonzo says.

"I've tried. She's not coming." I started yelling for Dulcie the minute we realized the bus was truly gone and we were on our own. But I guess she's taking that "leave me alone" edict seriously.

"Where are we, anyway?"

"I don't know," I say, wiping the sweat from my forehead with my arm. "Somewhere in Mississippi. Fuck!" I kick at a stone in the road, sending it skittering away through a cloud of dust.

Gonzo starts coughing. "Dude, I can't breathe right."

"Don't you dare panic on me," I warn.

"I'm not," Gonzo squeaks, holding back a cough that barrels out anyway. "Look, I'll just call my mom," he says, whipping out his cell.

"Yeah. Absolutely. Wouldn't want to go another step without input from Mom."

Gonzo ignores my snarkiness. "You said if there was an emergency, amigo. This counts as an emergency, right?" Before I can stop him, he pushes number one on his speed dial and in a second I hear him saying, "Mom? *¿Mamí? Sí. Es Gonzo.* Jeez, don't cry, Mom. I'm fine. I promise."

"Yeah, Mom," I say to the air. "We're just stuck on a dirt road in the middle of nowhere with no idea where we are or how to get out of here. Everything's great! Wish you were here!"

Gonzo peels away from me. "Listen, Mom, we need a little money. . . . I what? I sound sick? No. I feel fine. *Sí.*" He coughs. "It's just dry. No, it's not pneumonia, Mom. No, I . . . yeah, I've got my inhaler. The prescription's not more than three months old. Do you think I should get it refilled?"

"We're all gonna die! *Die! Die!*" For Gonzo's benefit, I

put my hands to my throat, stick out my tongue, and fall to the ground, spazzing.

He covers the mouthpiece of the phone with his hand. "Dude, that shit is so not funny. Mom? What do you mean the tests were inconclusive?"

I can't deal. I wander off the road into the cool grass and let the long, tall blades skim my fingertips. There are a few cows out grazing. They look up, chewing, but I'm not grass, so they ignore me. I inch closer to one. It's got big wet nostrils that sniff the air around me. Its tail flicks at the flies. We're nose to nose. She seems soft, and I reach out a hand to stroke her fur, which is warm from the sun. She lets me do it, just goes on munching grass while I smooth my hand across her wide back.

"How now, mad cow?" I say.

"Cameron!" Gonzo calls out.

"Catch you later, Bessie," I say to the cow, who eats another mouthful of grass in response.

When I reach Gonzo, he's pacing, and his face is sweaty. "I knew I shouldn't have come on this trip," he says, and he looks like he could cry. "My mom said they found this spot on my lung on the chest X-ray. It could just be a blip on the film or a cyst—or it could be something really bad, like cancer or a mutant virus or bacteria."

"Or it could be your mom freaking out over nothing."

I offer him my hand, but he crawls over to his backpack in the grass and fishes out his inhaler. He pulls deep on it, but he's having a hard time calming down. He stands, trying to shake it off. "A spot! That doesn't sound good. What do you think that could mean?"

I grab Gonzo's shoulders a little too hard because he is annoying the crap out of me. "I have bad news, man. You're going to live. Deal with it."

He twists out of my grip. "I think we should go back, Cameron."

"No way. I'm not going back."

"I can't go back by myself, dude. I could be dying." He pulls deep on his inhaler again.

"*You're* not the one who's dying, Gonzo!" I'd like to kick his ass all the way to Florida. He gives me that wounded-puppy look, effectively killing my karate fantasy. "Doesn't she do this to you all the time?"

"What do you mean?"

"Scare the bejesus out of you?"

"She's looking out for me, okay? You don't know her, Cameron. I shouldn'ta left like that. Like my dad."

"You ever think there was a reason your dad left?"

He kicks at a pebble in the road. It skitters sideways into the long grass and disappears. "Me."

"Maybe it wasn't you."

"She's the best thing in my life. I know that."

I should just shut up. But I'm so pissed off—about the bus, about the cows, about Gonzo's crazy mom, about everything—that I just want to slice and dice. "Well, that's pretty damn sad, then. You ever think that maybe the best thing in your life would be to get the hell away from her before she turns you into a complete emotional cripple?"

Gonzo's left eye twitches. His mouth goes slack. And then he comes running at me full speed, swinging hard. "Just shut up, man, shut the hell up! You don't know what you're talking about!"

He lands a solid punch to my stomach, and that sucker hurts. I'm doubled over, hoping my breath will have a return engagement with my lungs.

"Say you're sorry, *pendejo*!"

"Sorry," I squeak out.

193

He backs off, but he's still way pissed. "My mom has given up a lot to raise me. She was supposed to be a singer."

"Okay. I believe you." When I'm able to stand, I hand him his backpack. He stuffs his arms angrily through the straps. "Did you ask her to do that?"

"Ask her to do what?" he says, giving a little hop to secure his pack.

"Give up her life for you."

He looks confused for a second. "That's not the point. Look, just drop it, dude."

"It's dropped."

We start walking. In the field, I see the old lady, Mrs. Morae, from the hospital. She's sitting in a chair, holding on to her IV pole, like she's at a bus stop, waiting. Her face is grave. "Watch out," she warns.

"I will," I say.

She smiles at me. "In a house by the sea with the air scented of lilies."

"Dude, who are you talking to?" Gonzo's face is right in mine. I slide my eyes to the right, but the old lady is gone.

The pins-and-needles sensation burns in my legs. "No one," I say. "Just keep your eyes peeled for a car or a bus. Something other than gravel and dust."

We amble down the dirt road till we hit an old paved road that at least has a route sign. There's nothing coming in either direction yet.

Gonzo's still riled up. "I had appendicitis when I was eight, and she had to leave an audition to rush me to the ER. Okay?"

"I'm sure she's a good mom."

"She's great. A great mom. When we get to a town, I'm out of here. I'm going back, dude. If the world ends, it ends. You're on your own."

194

"Whatever. Just keeping looking, all right?" I walk left and Gonzo goes right.

I feel like I've been swallowing stones. My muscles ache and my legs are heavy. The air is thick with the smells of cow dung, tractor exhaust, road dust, flowers, and something else. My eyes sting and my throat's irritated. Smoke. Could be crops burning. Small brush fire, maybe. So why is the hair on the back of my neck creeping to attention?

I whirl around, searching for the source. In the distance, Gonzo's silhouette flickers around the edges, distorted by the squiggles of heat rising from the road. I start to call out, but my feet are summer-sidewalk hot. I hop back just as small puncture holes pop up along the ground. There's a hiss from below, and before I can shout a warning, the asphalt splits open with the force of a geyser. Steam, smoke, and flames shoot into the sky. The force of it knocks me back a few feet. I land hard, feeling the sting as my shirt is torn and my back is bloodied by gravel. One by one, the fire giants crawl out of the broken road and push themselves up. In the time it takes me to gasp, they zoom up to about eight feet and fan out into positions like loyal soldiers. The way ahead is consumed by an orange wall of heat.

"Gonzo!" I yell, but I can't see him. It's too bright.

The fire giants stare down at me with their baleful eyes, and I feel myself sinking. I don't even know how to fight these guys. There's a stick on the road. I grab it and start swinging, *Star Fighter* style. The fire gods seem to find it amusing. They throw their heads back in a laughing howl that makes me shiver. One of them darts his head forward and flicks a serpentlike tongue around the stick. A red glow shoots up the wood. With a hiss, I drop it fast and it disintegrates.

Several slink forward on all fours and sniff me. One growls.

They're through fucking around. Their breath heats my skin. Suddenly, they pull up short. A van's cruising down the road. The sun's reflecting off the windshield. I have to put my hand to my eyes to block the glare.

"Hey!" I shout, waving my arms. "Over here! Help!"

I try to crawl toward it, but a fire giant blows me back. My body screams in pain as I tumble along the pavement. I try to get up but I can't.

"Gonzo!" I croak.

The fire god pries open my mouth and covers it with his. He breathes out, filling my lungs with choking smoke. My body shakes. Somebody's pushing against my chest in a hard rhythm.

"Page Dr. Xavier!" Glory shouts. I'm on a gurney, watching the fluorescent ceiling lights strobe over me fast. Mom's running alongside, trying to keep one hand on the metal rail. She looks worried. I'm pushed through wide doors. More lights. Hard on my eyes. God, my body hurts so bad. Like I'm being burned with lit matches.

I fight to clear my head.

"Give me suction now!" somebody calls. And then I hear my name again and again.

"Cameron!" It's Gonzo's yelling. He's running up the road. "Dude—watch out!"

The next thing I know, I'm on the pavement of Farm Route 44 with a van headed right for me. I shut my eyes tight. There's a screech of braking tires. I can smell the scorched rubber and the pungent mix of hot gasoline and motor oil. When I open my eyes, my head is an inch from the front bumper. I see feet running toward me.

"Is he okay?" A girl crouches next to me. She's pretty in a neohippie sort of way. Her T-shirt reads CESSNAB CRUSADERS.

A guy in a baseball cap comes over and checks me out, shining a little flashlight in my eyes, checking my pupils. He's got the same CESSNAB shirt on. They all do. "You're lucky you weren't killed, friend. Can you stand up?"

The guy helps me to my feet, but I'm shaking all over and I have to lean against him to walk.

"Easy there, friend. Do you live around here? Where are your parents?"

"Holy shit!" Gonzo says, running up. "Dude, you okay?"

The guy in the baseball cap frowns. "Friend, could I ask you to watch your language? There are ladies present."

Gonzo looks like somebody just took the pudding snack out of his lunch box. "Uh, sure. Sorry."

"I think you should come back with us," the guy says, turning back to me. "We've got a doctor at our compound who can make sure you don't have a concussion or something else nasty, okay?"

I nod and it's like a tiny revolver has fired inside my skull, pinging every part of my head with pain bullets.

"What's your name, friend?"

"Why do you want to know?" Gonzo asks.

The guy holds up his hands. "I only want to help, friend."

"I'm Cameron," I say. "And this is Gonzo."

"I'm Daniel." The guy shakes my hand, which also hurts. He introduces the others, including the hippie girl, whose name is Ruth. "I'm just gonna move stuff around, get the van ready. Be right back."

Gonzo grabs hold of my arm and my skin screams in protest. "Cam, dude, I don't think we should get in the van. We don't know these guys. They could be serial killers."

"They're not serial killers. They have matching shirts."

"Think: who has vans, huh? Soccer moms and serial killers.

197

They mentioned a compound. And 'getting the van ready.' Ready for what?"

"You're tripping."

"Dude. I'm not getting in that van."

The dust on the road stings my eyes. I'm hungry and tired and scared. "Then stay here. I'm going with them."

A smiling Daniel ambles over and puts his arm around me. "Don't worry. We'll take good care of you, Cameron."

"We've got snacks in the van," Ruth says. "I'll bet you could use a snack."

They belt me into a seat in back. Gonzo's still on the side of the road, looking panicked. "Cameron, don't you think we should wait here till your aunt and uncle come to pick us up? You know, your *aunt* and *uncle,* who are supposed to meet us out here *any minute?*"

"We can have them pick you up at the CESSNAB," Daniel says. I don't know what a CESSNAB is and I don't care. Right now, I just want to drink a vat of water and lie down for about two days. I can barely hold my head up.

Daniel extends a hand to Gonzo. "You coming, friend?"

Ruth smiles. "We'll take you bowling."

Gonzo's revving as hard as the engine, like he doesn't know whether to be more freaked out about getting in the van with a bunch of possible serial killers or to take his chances alone by the side of a road in Godonlyknowswhere, Mississippi. I decide that Possible Serial Killers would make a good band name. I promise myself if I'm cured, I'll start that band.

"Okay," Gonzo says, climbing in at last. "But I want to sit by the door."

CHAPTER TWENTY-FOUR

Of What Happens When I Bowl a Perfect Strike and Learn Not to Hurt My Happiness

Once we hit the road, the Possible Serial Killers start to sing a song I don't know. Something about showing your happiness and loving your happiness and defending your happiness. One of the guys tries to ad-lib some "oh yeah's" until Ruth frowns and tells him it's "a little competitive" and "off message" and he stops.

I polish off a huge bag of pretzels and a big bottle of water, then fall asleep. When I wake up, we're driving up to a sprawling, glass-and-stone building on about a gazillion acres of land. At the far end is a bank with three drive-thru lanes. Everything is new. You can practically smell the paint. And out on the lawn is a big sign that reads CHURCH OF EVER-LASTING SATISFACTION AND SNACK-'N'-BOWL.

The van pulls into a freshly paved parking lot. The white lines are sharp. The whole place seems to sparkle. Gonzo's the first one out when the doors slide open. He's still in serial killer mode. Daniel gives me a hand getting to the door of the building. He punches in an elaborate alarm code and we walk in past two uniformed security guards. Daniel calls to them by name.

"Hey, Peter. Hey, Matthew."

They wave and get back to their heavy task of watching the mostly empty parking lot.

"How are you feeling?" Daniel asks.

"Better. Tired."

Daniel smiles, pats my back. "You've come to the right spot for healing. You'll see."

At first, I think we're in a mall. There's a food court with about six different kinds of cuisine. Fake ferns. A water fountain. And a bunch of stores. They all have CESSNAB in the name. CESSNAB Shirts. CESSNAB Tunes. CESSNAB Sports. CESSNAB Kids. CESSNAB Tech. There's even a CESSNAB Tattoo, where you can get forty-two variations on CESSNAB in different fonts or a bowling ball with wings on the side.

"What's CESSNAB?" I ask.

"It's this place." Daniel spreads his arms wide. "It stands for Church of Everlasting Satisfaction and Snack 'N' Bowl."

"So it's a church?" I say quickly.

"It's everything. Stores. School. Bowling alley. We've got everything we need right here. Cool, huh?"

Ruth falls in beside us. "Do you want a CESSNAB smoothie? They're so good!"

"Great idea, Ruth. Cameron—what flavor do you want? Strawberry?"

"Banana?" Ruth interjects.

"Uh, you know. Whatever."

Daniel and Ruth smile. "Strawberry-banana!" they say at the same time. Daniel goes off to the CESSNAB Smoothies stand and comes back with four tall take-out cups. "Strawberry-banana."

Daniel offers a cup to Gonzo. "Gonzo?"

Gonzo glares at them. "No thanks. I'm, uh, allergic to strawberries," he says, which is total bullshit, I'm sure.

"Gonz, they're not serial killers. And this is not going to kill you. It's a smoothie, okay?"

"I'm *allergic*," he says emphatically.

"Thanks," I say, taking mine. I drink about half. "Huh. Weird."

"What's that?" Ruth asks.

"It tastes just like vanilla."

"Oh, they're all vanilla," Ruth says. "At first, we gave people a choice. But then we found they didn't like the blueberry as much as they thought they would or they wished they had gotten the strawberry instead, just like their best friends did. It was a big bummer. So we simplified things for them. Now, they can order whatever they want, but in the end, it's all the same flavor. You're guaranteed the same experience every single time. And you're having the same experience as everybody else. Cuts down on things like dissatisfaction, envy, competitiveness, longing, regret. All that bad stuff."

"Oh. Huh." I take another sip. The vanilla's good, actually. Thick and creamy. I don't really miss the strawberry and banana that much, I guess. I offer a sip to Gonzo, who glares at me.

"If you want more, it's no problem," Daniel says. "There's

201

plenty for everybody. Part of the philosophy—no wanting or waiting. No one has to feel dissatisfied. Here, everybody is gratified all the time."

Ruth's face goes dark. "Except for some people."

Daniel sighs but it turns into yet another smile. "Some people have a hard time with our beliefs. They have a hard time letting go of the negative." He makes a pushing away motion with his hands, and Ruth follows suit. "And embracing the positive." They cross their arms over their chests like they're hugging themselves. "So they leave and go out there again."

"So stupid," Ruth says.

"Troubled," Daniel corrects. "They're our troubled friends, Ruth, remember."

Ruth nods. "Troubled."

"No negative thoughts here."

"None," Ruth says, beaming. "We are happy 24/7. Don't hurt your happiness."

"Don't hurt your happiness," Daniel echoes. "Here, it's on our key chains. Have one."

He hands me a bright yellow key chain with DON'T HURT YOUR HAPPINESS in flowing, white script.

"Thanks," I say. I'm feeling better.

An alarm sounds. On the walls, domed lights flare red. Gonzo drops to the ground and covers his head with his hands. "I told you, Cameron! Didn't I tell you?"

Suddenly, the room is flooded by guys in commando gear. "Move, move, move!" they shout. They pass us by and surround a yellow sofa, where a young guy sits in his pajamas.

"Team leader! We've got a situation!" one of the commandos shouts.

"Excuse me, Cameron," Daniel says. He goes over to the kid on the couch. "Thomas, what's wrong, friend?"

"Uh, I don't know. I just started feeling . . ." He searches for the word. "Sad."

Daniel gives Thomas's shoulders a squeeze and the kid winces. "We don't feel sad, here, Thomas. Why do you want to hurt your happiness?"

"I totally don't! I don't know what happened. It's like I just couldn't help it. I was thinking about the time my dog, Snuffy, got hit by a car when I was six and how I still miss him, and it . . . the *sad* just snuck up on me."

"Smoothie," Daniel says to a commando, who opens the right side of his coat, displaying a dazzling array of cups.

"What flavor?" Daniel asks.

"Uh . . . mango?" Thomas answers. The commando hands off the cup and Daniel puts the straw to Thomas's lips.

"Here drink this."

Thomas takes a few sips like he's not really thirsty; he's just being polite. "It tastes like vanilla."

Daniel's really concentrating. "Just tell us what you want, friend. Tell us."

Thomas buries his head in his hands. "I don't know. That's the problem."

"Here. We'll help you." The commando opens the left side of his coat. It's like a magazine rack of catalogs. Daniel calls them off. "CESSNAB Jeans? CESSNAB Music? CESSNAB Golf? CESSNAB Games?"

"Games?" Gonzo comes out of his safety crouch.

"I'm telling you, I don't know!" The poor guy's in a panic. Like he's lost his happiness and can't remember where he put it.

Daniel puts a hand on his shoulder. "Thomas. You know what you need? You need to go bowling."

This is greeted by a chorus of "Amen's."

"I don't think . . ." Thomas starts, but he's cut off by the choir.

You're special.
I'm special.
They're special.
The whole world's special, so don't you forget it.

The Universe wants us
All to be happy,
Full of smiles and all that stuff,
All that stuff
That's happy and smiley.
So get happy, happy, happy right now!
Get happy, happy, happy right now!
Get happy, happy, happy right now!

"Come with us," Ruth says, taking Gonzo and me by the hand as Daniel and Thomas lead the way to a set of wide double doors with the winged bowling ball insignia in the middle. Everyone gets quiet.

"What is this place?" I whisper to Ruth.

"This is our church. The Church of Everlasting Satisfaction. And Snack 'N' Bowl."

"Amen," everyone intones, and the doors are opened wide.

"Get the fuck out," Gonzo says under his breath.

This has to be the biggest friggin' bowling alley I have ever seen in my life. Just row after gleaming row of well-maintained lanes bordered by litter-free gutters. There's not a scuff on the floor. An enormous TV screen encased in theater-worthy lightbulbs is suspended from the ceiling.

"Every single one of us knows what it's like out there," Daniel says. "The stress. The worrying—am I good enough, strong enough, smart enough, pretty enough? How come Johnny got an A-plus on his paper but I only got a C? Is he better than me?"

"Why does only the winning athlete get a first-place medal?" another kid says, putting "winning" in air quotes.

"Why do bad things happen? There must be a reason for it—something you can avoid doing so you'll never, ever be sad," a girl in saddle shoes says.

A kid with a bowling ball tattoo on his arm speaks up. "Why shouldn't we all just be happy all the time?"

"Amen," Daniel says. "No questions. No fears. No unhappiness. That's why there's CESSNAB. Our friend Thomas had doubts. But we'll help him embrace the positive."

They all make the hugging motion. Daniel sets Thomas up in lane one. Ruth rubs his back. "Think of something happy, Thomas, like getting new jeans."

Everyone makes a circle around Thomas, arms linked. They chant, "Thomas is special. Thomas is special. Thomas is special."

Thomas takes a deep breath and lets the ball roll, shooting it straight down the middle. The pins smash to the ground in one stroke, and the TV lights up slot-machine style. An image of an angelic pin floats on screen. It makes an Okay sign with its fingers. An automated voice purrs, "Way to go, friend!" Everybody whoops and hollers.

205

Daniel smiles. "See, Thomas? You can do anything. You can be anything you want!"

The choir launches into another song: *"I can be whatever. You can be whatever. We can be whatever. Whatever, together."* They put their arms around Thomas and soon he starts singing along even though he's still not smiling.

Daniel slaps me on the back. "Hey, Cameron, why don't you give it a try?"

I've only been bowling twice and both times I sucked ass. I think I managed to hit one pin. "I'm a pretty lousy bowler."

"You've never bowled at the Church of Everlasting Satisfaction and Snack 'N' Bowl before," Daniel says.

"It's the bad thoughts that stop us. If you embrace the positive"—Ruth makes the hugging motion again and the other CESSNABers follow suit—"you'll be fine."

The ball pops up from its dark cave and glides around the silver tracks, stopping right beside me.

"You have to believe you can do it, Cameron," Ruth says. "That you're entitled to happiness—by any means necessary."

Believe I can bowl. Right. I can bowl. I step up to the line, pull my arm back, and let it fly. Right away it starts heading for the gutter. But then, something miraculous happens: it corrects itself. The ball rolls straight down the center, and the next thing I know I'm listening to the crash of pins hitting the deck in a perfect strike, my first ever.

Ruth jumps up and down. "That was amazing, Cameron! See? See what happens when you embrace the positive? Go again."

"Beginner's luck," I say. "Won't happen again."

"We're all winners here in the Church of Everlasting Satisfaction," she says softly, and I want to believe her.

"Okay, thanks for taking care of my amigo here. This looks like fun, and we wish you well and shit," Gonzo explains to the crowd. "But we got, like, a mission of our own to get to. So if somebody could just give us a ride to the bus station—"

I pick up a second ball and let her rip. Bam! Right down the middle.

"That was awesome!" I shout, pumping my fist in the air.

Ruth throws her arms around my neck. "See? The universe doesn't want us to be unhappy, Cameron. The universe wants you to be happy all the time!"

"Yeah," I say. Yeah, why not? Why shouldn't I have whatever I want when I want it? And what I want is to be happy and safe like these guys. I don't want to think about prions and fire giants and Dr. X and saving the universe. I just want a smoothie.

"Cameron, we gotta motor," Gonzo says.

"I don't want to go yet."

I march over to the next lane and roll another perfect strike followed by another. Everybody claps and makes some noise. They tell me *I'm wonderful just for being,* and that I'm *increasing their happiness with my happiness.*

Four lanes over, Thomas bowls another flawless game, but he doesn't seem happy about it. At one point, he purposely throws the ball out of the lane and into the next one, where it sails down the center and knocks down every pin. Thomas stares at his feet. There's a small, muscular, ebony-skinned girl with a shaved head standing next to him. Besides Thomas, she's the only one who's not smiling. Suddenly, Thomas starts to bawl, and the alarms go off again. Ropes drop from the ceiling, and the commandos shinny their way down. They make a beeline for Thomas and

207

usher him toward the door. Someone wraps him in a big yellow CESSNAB blanket, covering every part of him but his head.

After my rousing victory in the Church of Everlasting Satisfaction, Daniel and Ruth take me to the CESSNAB Snackateria. They ask Gonzo if he wants to come, but he says he's going to kill things in the arcade to "get the slime of happiness off."

The Snackateria has everything you could ever want—chips, soda, candy, pizza, burgers, fries. Every table has ordering stations where you can look through catalogs of stuff and order whatever you want. The shipping times have been crossed out and now there's an Instant button. When you push it, somebody rushes in from a back room and brings it right to you.

"Having to wait for things hurts your happiness," Ruth explains. "Want some more fries?"

I say yes, and she gets me a new batch. They're perfectly hot and crisp, like the first batch.

"I'm sorry you had to see that with Thomas earlier," Daniel says, shaking his head. "Some people just can't adjust to being happy all the time."

"Omigosh," Ruth says, midfry, her eyes wide. "When I first got here, I was a mess. Just a total and complete mess. Remember, Daniel?"

"Hmmm," Daniel says meaningfully, though he seems way more into his fries than what Ruth is saying. He's arranging them in straight lines and putting a thin string of ketchup directly over the middle.

"I used to do pageants and stuff, but then I developed

an allergy to spray tanner and I couldn't compete any-more? My whole world crumbled. I totally went into a depression, got all messed up on drugs and stuff," Ruth explains. "I was hurting my happiness. So they sent me to CESSNAB."

"Whoa," I say.

"Oh, not because they didn't want to deal, but because they loved me so much. I see that now," she says, biting her already ragged nails. "The first time I bowled and hit all those strikes, it was like I'd won the evening gown competition and finished it off with a speedball! I totally cried. Everybody was so happy for me. And I just wanted to keep doing that, you know? To keep being all happy."

Daniel lays out another line of fries and does the ketchup art on them again.

Ruth claps. "Oooh! Tell him your story, Daniel."

"I had major control issues," he says, eating his fries one at a time. "I grew up playing sports and being in honors classes, which was cool when I was on top. But by the time I hit sixth grade, I wasn't getting the top grade in math or pitching the best game. They'd built another school in my town and these other kids were really good. I couldn't handle it. I cracked under the pressure. One day, I crawled into a locker at school and wouldn't leave it. They had to use the jaws of life to get me out. That's when I had my awakening. All that competi-tion and winning and people being better at things than other people? It hurts your happiness."

I squirt a whole bunch of ketchup on my plate. It splatters my fries. Daniel looks a little sick. "But doesn't it also make you want to try harder? That sense of competition?" I can't believe I'm saying this. I've never tried hard at anything in my life.

"That's where you're wrong, my friend," Daniel says, smiling. "It's our culture that teaches that. Not our nature."

Ruth looks me right in the eyes. "Don't you just wish you could let that stuff go? All that worry?"

"Yeah," I hear myself say. "I do."

Daniel puts his arm around me like we're best buds. "That's the great thing, Cameron. You can! Being happy is a choice totally within your control. The universe has arranged for you to be happy. You just have to accept it."

"And here at CESSNAB, we've got a lot of products to back that up, to keep the happiness going, so you never have to feel unhappy. Not for one, single second." Ruth smiles at me in a flirty way. "You seem happier since you bowled, Cameron. Am I right?"

"Yeah. I guess so," I say.

"See?" Daniel pats me on the back. "That's the power of this place."

"We like to think of CESSNAB as a gated community for the mind, and the stuff that doesn't increase our happiness we just keep out," Ruth chirps. "Like your friend, Gonzo. He's . . . troubled," she says, using the word Daniel supplied earlier. "Full of fear. Fear is such a negative emotion, you know?"

"We find we don't need that here," Daniel says. "That's why we have the commandos, why we work to keep out the bad things. So we're always safe all the time. And if we're safe all the time—no rejection, no bad news, no negative thoughts, no failure—we stay happy, and then our parents are happy that we're happy, and, you know, it's all good. It's a pretty simple philosophy, but it works."

"How do you pay for all of this?" I ask.

"We put together SPEW tests for the entire nation, plus

all the prep materials, 'Everything you need to SPEW without a second thought,'" Daniel says.

"So, what were you doing out on the road?" Ruth asks. When I don't answer, she puts her hand on mine. "Hey. It's okay. We've all been there."

Everybody's been so nice to me here. It's the first time since my diagnosis that I've felt sort of normal, and I'm afraid of fucking it all up. "You wouldn't believe me," I say.

Ruth and Daniel stop eating and give me their full attention. "It's okay," Daniel echoes. "There are no secrets here. Secrets hurt your happiness."

I'm too tired to keep hiding, so I tell them everything about my mad cow disease, our mission to try to find Dr. X and save the universe, the Wizard of Reckoning, and the fire gods on my ass. I half expect them to kick me out, but they don't.

Daniel takes hold of my shoulder in a protective way. "No one's gonna get you here, Cameron. The world is not going to end. I promise you that. You're one hundred percent safe. As for your disease, doctors are wrong all the time. They need sick people in order to make money."

"Only people who want to get sick actually get sick. They do it to themselves," Ruth adds. "You can even think yourself well if you want to."

"Yeah? You think so?"

"I know so!" Daniel says. "I've seen it happen. You can beat it."

I think how easy it would be to stay here, but Dulcie told me that I need Dr. X to be cured. Then again, where the hell is she?

"Cameron? You're making a frowny face," Ruth says.

Just thinking about Dulcie has soured my happiness, and

I am pretty happy here. I could stay at CESSNAB and bowl and have a big smoothie and take it easy.

"Are you okay?" Ruth says, her hand hovering near the commando alarm.

I give her a big smile. "Yeah, I'm good. Really good. In fact, I'd like to stay for a while, if that's okay."

Ruth gives a little shriek and hugs me. Daniel claps me on the back. "That totally increases my happiness, friend."

CHAPTER TWENTY-FIVE

**About What Happens When I Learn
the Secret of Perfect Bowling and
the Revolution Goes Down Big-time**

For five days, I've been learning how to become a part of the
CESSNAB Crusaders family. In choir group, I picked up four
new songs—"Who Wants to Be Happy," "Happy Time Starts
Right Now," "Everything About You Is Totally Perfect," and
"Your Name Is Spelled Like 'Special' (Only with Different
Letters)"—and got to do a big tambourine solo, which I
rocked. Daniel and Ruth took me to the CESSNAB video
gaming center where we played Extreme Self-esteem Builder!
and How Awesome Are You? And of course, there's church.
Every day, we congregate in the huge, gleaming bowling
alley, think our most positive I-am-special thoughts, and
bowl perfect game after perfect game, which Daniel says is
proof that we're doing everything right. The only blip on the
happiness road came on day one, when I had a small seizure
and woke up surrounded by five hulking commandos with

giant smoothie cups at the ready. So I had some vanilla yum through a straw while Daniel explained that it was not the prions attacking my brain, I just needed to say my mantra over and over—*I am special; special people don't die*—and maybe order more stuff. And it's been great ever since.

"Dude, you are living in a dreamworld," Gonzo says as I ponder ordering a pair of Extra-Cushion-Action CESSNAB Bowling Shoes from the Instant Satisfaction station in the Snackateria. He is definitely not increasing my happiness. "They don't even have any killing games."

"Mmmm-hmmm."

"Five days, dude. Five fucking days of Smiling Zombie Nation. I can't bowl or make CESSNAB T-shirts or smoothie it for one more minute. I'm telling you, these guys are freaky. Don't you think they're freaky?"

"No, I don't. And don't forget you thought they were serial killers."

"They totally still could be, dude. They're fattening us up for the kill."

"No, they're helping me get well." I'm not going to let him defrost my happy chill. "Why don't you order something, friend? A new jacket or some tunes? You like music."

Gonzo snorts. "Yeah, *real* music. Not this hideous, bowling-for-God CESSNAB shit that's been raping my eardrums all week."

I take a deep breath; in my head, I list five things I love about myself. "You know what, Gonzo? I want to help you find what I've found. Here, have a key chain," I say, handing him one of the sunny yellow giveaways they hand out whenever you do something even remotely good, like remember to put the toilet seat down. Sometimes they give you a key chain just for showing up.

Gonzo drops my key chain present into a trash can. "Yo, *cabrón*, aren't we supposed to be on the road to Dr. X?"

"Aren't you supposed to have a spot on your lung?" I snap, and then I remember myself. "Look, Gonzo, I'm sorry. I don't want to hurt your happiness."

"Dude, you're not hurting my happiness. You're just totally freaking me out." He waves his hands in front of my face. "Look at this place, man. It's some kind of happiness cult. It's not real. You don't want to stay here."

"But I do. I feel great. No symptoms. No weird dreams. No sign of the fire giants. Gonzo, I think this might be the cure. There's no need to save the universe, because nothing bad can happen to me at CESSNAB."

"Bad things can happen anywhere. That's life, amigo."

"Well, I've got a new life now, friend, and I'd appreciate it if you'd stop messing with it."

I don't want to get all worked up, so I leave Gonzo there by the Instant Satisfaction station and head for the library. I recognize the girl with the shaved head who's behind the counter. It's Thomas's bowling friend. Her CESSNAB shirt has a faint line through NAB and the word POOL has been scrawled just above it.

"Can I help you?"

"Hello, friend," I say with a big smile. She doesn't return it, which is weird, because everybody smiles at CESSNAB. "Um, I wanted to check out a book?"

She points to the floor-to-ceiling stacks. "Help yourself. Be happy."

"Okay, thanks. Hope the day is as special as you are," I say, quoting the line I saw on a T-shirt here.

She snorts. "Yeah. Me too."

The library is packed with more books than I have ever

seen. I'm hoping they have *Don Quixote* so I can finish my reading for Spanglish class—not that I'm going back, but I would like to know how it all ends. The bottom two rows only seem to be filled with copies of *Don't Hurt Your Happiness,* so I go through the next two rows and the next. It's just more of the same, in hardcover and paperback. The whole library is stocked with copies of just that one book.

"Excuse me," I say, hopping off the rolling ladder. "But where are the other books?"

"We don't have any other books," Library Girl says. She's using a highlighter on her copy, underlining random words to make new, slightly naughty sentences. I wonder if she should be doing that but decide not to say anything.

"But . . . it's a library. Right?"

She speaks slowly, like she's talking to a little kid. "We found that a lot of the stories or words or even ideas contained in most books could be negative or hurtful or make you question your happiness or even question the concept of happiness as an ideal, and that just wasn't working for us." Now she gives me a big smile that reminds me of Dulcie.

"Well, isn't that the point of books? To make you think about things? Come on. You have to have a copy of *Don Quixote* back there. It's a classic."

She whips open a drawer and pulls out a stack of papers stapled together, which she runs through until she finds what she's looking for. "Ah. Sorry. *Don Quixote.* Complicated ideas and language. Some people found it hysterical, but others felt inadequate about not understanding it right away. We don't like to induce *nonpositive experience* feelings in people, so it had to go."

"*Catcher in the Rye?*"

"One Holden Caulfield, sixteen, very angry, very negative, visits prostitutes and says bad words."

216

"*Lord of the Flies?*"

"Too violent."

"Comic books."

"Wow—out on all counts." She ticks off the points on her fingers. "Too dark. Too scary. Superheroes have unattainable powers, and are therefore not relatable and might make kids feel bad about themselves. Also, some suggestible kids might get ideas about jumping off buildings or trying to mind-meld the weather."

"Ha—got one," I say. "*Winnie-the-Pooh!*"

She shakes her head. "Bears don't really talk. Might confuse the little ones."

"Fine. I'll take a copy of *Don't Hurt Your Happiness.*"

She stamps the card and hands me the book. "You can turn it in at the end of the week. Or whenever, really. It's just a formality. We find that *requiring* things of people and making them *responsible* is a big drag, and that is *so* not happy. Enjoy!"

Grumpy thoughts threaten to invade my new sunny-day brain. I push them away and settle into one of the ergonomically correct Day-Glo yellow chairs and open to page one. *You are special,* it says in big block letters. *Everybody is.*

"Hey," I say to the guy sitting next to me. He's totally into his CESSNAB electronic bowling game. The beeping digital score card shows three hundred perfect strikes in a row. "Have you read this?"

"Some of it," he says, without looking up. "But I have friends who know other people who've read it and they told me everything."

"Well, I was just wondering about this thing on page one: *You're special. Everybody is.*"

"Yeah?"

"How can you be special if everybody is?"

217

"You're just part of the specialness, I guess." He makes another strike and the game congratulates him with an electronic *"That is awesome, friend. Way to go!"*

"Oh," I say. "Thanks."

"No problem."

Page two: *Happiness is the new Manifest Destiny. Go stake your claim on it!*

Page three: *If you start to feel unhappy, buy something.*

Page four: *Embrace the positive!*

I look up for a second. Library Girl is staring a hole through me. I start toward her, and she quickly opens the books on the return desk, stamping them a little forcefully.

"Finished already?" she asks in a fake-happy voice.

"Yeah."

"Was it enlightening? Life-changing? Mood-altering? Did it increase your happiness?" She fiddles with one of the ten earrings along her left ear.

There's no doubt she's playing me. There's also no doubt that she's pretty hot.

"I'm a-tingling with joy," I say, matching her smile and wiggling my fingers like I'm on some highly caffeinated drill team. It's sarcastic, and I know sarcasm hurts your happiness, but it feels kind of good to do it, like stretching a muscle I haven't used in a while. The corners of Library Girl's lips twitch into something resembling a smirk, an expression that feels one hundred percent real.

"Meet me in the bowling alley," she whispers. "Five minutes."

When I get there, the church is empty except for Library Girl. She's perched on my favorite ball return, chewing a huge wad of pink gum and blowing bubbles she pops with loud smacks.

"So, tell me," she says, sucking a dead bubble back into her mouth. "How do you like it here?"

"It's great."

"Yeah," she says, staring at the ceiling and swinging one leg. "Great. Special. We're all special."

"Exactly."

"Wanna put that to the test?" she says.

"What do you mean?"

"A little scientific experimentation. Go ahead. Bowl a perfect game. You can't lose. If you believe you can do it . . ."

". . . Then you can!" I finish.

"So why don't you test it. Think the worst thing you could possibly think and let the ball roll. See if the universe gets mad."

"If I get sad, the alarm will go off and the commandos will come in. So you can't really test it," I say.

"Huh." She pushes up her sleeves, revealing a pair of kick-ass biceps. "Here's a secret," she says, looking around. "Sometimes, they're busy ordering stuff and don't watch. Like now."

She flips a switch and the balls come to life, bouncing along on their well-oiled, shiny grooves. My favorite purple ball is within reach. I haven't had any unhappy thoughts for days. I'm out of practice. I'm sort of annoyed at Gonzo for what he said earlier but not enough to really work myself up about it. Dulcie pops into my mind, the way she just left. And then a thought I have no control over works its way into my brain: *What if I never see her again?*

"Oooh, you look pretty bummed. Let her rip."

I throw the ball at the lane. It bounces and skitters across the smooth, polished wood, careening unpredictably. By all rights, it should hit the gutter, but it doesn't. Instead, it scoots right back to the center and delivers a perfect strike.

"Try again," Library Girl urges.

I imagine all sorts of things this time: Mom and Dad and Jenna back at the hospital. Kids too poor to have Christmas. Beloved pets being put to sleep. Losing all my Great Tremolo CDs. Pep rallies. Still I hit strike after strike after strike. I couldn't lose if I tried, and I am definitely trying.

"Not so fun anymore, is it? Now for the rest of our experiment . . ." Library Girl pulls a magnet from her pocket and does something to the console with it. Then she uses the magnet on the other lanes. "This time, do what they say: embrace the positive."

I close my eyes and say my mantra: *You can do it if you think you can. You deserve to win.*

When I launch the ball, it rolls down the center and drifts off to the side, sliding into the gutter and out of sight without knocking down a single pin. "Whoa. What just happened?"

Library Girl holds up her magnet. "They're magnetized. There's a little magnet in the ball and another in the gutters. They repel the ball. Like I said, you can't lose. You achieve every time."

"But it's not an achievement if the game's rigged."

Library Girl holds up two fingers on each hand, making quote marks in the air. "Failure doesn't increase your happiness."

I give it six, seven more tries, and the best I can do is take out four pins. "Maybe you made the game too hard now," I say.

"Or maybe you're just not that awesome, special, and perfect all the time."

"That's harsh," I say, even though my gut says she's right; I've sort of gotten used to hearing only the good stuff. "But

220

what about what they say here, that competition hurts your happiness. We have to get rid of our bad feelings to be happy."

She rolls her eyes and lets out a growl. "You can't 'get rid' of any of your feelings! We're human beings! When some jerk pisses me off, I have the urge to kick the living shit out of him. But I can't, because if we went around kicking people all the time, we'd never be able to buy groceries or take the dog for a walk or eat out. It would be complete chaos. That's why we have civilization. And table manners."

"Exactly! But that's why this church exists. To make us better people. And to be better people, we have to get rid of all our negative feelings."

"No. We have to learn to live with them. What if those so-called negative feelings are useful?" Library Girl spins the shiny pink ball that's sitting on the metal grid waiting for a game. It wobbles like the Earth on its axis. "I mean, suppose you take your anger and you channel it into a painting. Pretty soon, you don't care about getting back at that idiot who pissed you off anymore because you're totally into your painting. And then maybe that painting hangs in a gallery someday and it inspires other people to find their thing, whatever it is. You've influenced the world not because you wanted to hug it and cuddle it and call it sweet thing but because one day you wanted to beat the crap out of somebody but you didn't. You made a painting instead. And you couldn't have made that painting without that feeling, without something to push off against. We human beings can't evolve without the pain."

"What do you mean?"

"Bad stuff happens." She flicks out a switchblade and cuts through one of the commando ropes that's been left

221

hanging after an earlier sadness incident and wraps the length around her wrist. "People fail. They get dumped. They bomb tests. They lose the big game or screw up in a hundred small ways or get rejected or have to start over. They feel confused and scared. Or sometimes they just don't feel like they fit in. They're part of some kind of primal, universal loneliness and that's just the way it is and you have to learn to deal and a big vanilla smoothie is not the answer, you know?"

"But what if we didn't have to feel that?"

"But we do! It's what makes us human."

"So you don't think human beings can be made happy."

"I didn't say that," she says, fashioning the rope into a sort of double bracelet with a sliding knot. "I just don't think happiness is a sustainable state. You can't have it all the time. That much happiness makes people *un*happy. And then they start looking for trouble. They start looking for the next thing that's going to make them happy—a happiness fix."

I feel like a balloon slowly settling to earth, slightly deflated but kind of glad the trip is over. It's weird, but it's sort of a relief not to have to be happy all the time.

"So if you don't believe any of this, why are you still here?"

"To do what needs to be done." Library Girl strokes the side of my face. "Cameron, you are a really nice guy. And that's why I'm sorry about this."

"Sorry about what?"

Superquick, she slips the rope bracelet over my wrists and tightens the knot so I can't move my hands.

"Hey!" I tug but it only tightens the knot.

"Don't struggle, Cameron. It'll be easier."

"What the f—"

Alarms go off at an earsplitting volume, louder than I've ever heard them.

"What's that?" I say, wishing I could cover my ears.

"That, *friend*, is the beautiful sound of revolution." Library Girl tugs on the rope, and all I can do is follow her.

Pandemonium has erupted in the rest of the Church of Everlasting Satisfaction and Snack 'N' Bowl. People in varying degrees of CESSNAB dress run through the halls, screaming that we are under attack. The walls are crawling with commandos. It's like some kind of extreme soap-on-a-rope. Five teens with a shopping cart pass us by. At first, I think they're from CESSNAB because they're wearing the big yellow happy face shirts, but then I see it's really a sad face, a mad face, a stoned face, and a face with a raised middle finger under the chin. The shopping cart is full of books and newspapers, which they toss at anyone they see.

A guy brandishing an open newspaper screams, "The world's fucked up! Stop ordering jeans and pull your heads out!"

"Happiness is a fascist state!" one of the hurlers yells. It's Thomas. "What if I don't want to chill, huh? What if I miss my dog, Snuffy?"

A guy in a CESSNAB sweatshirt zigzags by, hugging himself frantically. "Embrace the positive! Embrace the positive!"

Library Girl looks up into the ceiling camera. With a wicked grin, she leans over and kisses me hard on the lips.

"Whoa," I gasp.

"Come on," she says, dragging me into the radio station's recording booth. She bolts the door behind us, and for a split second, I have the crazy idea I'm about to pop my cherry under the weirdest of circumstances—a total coup de virginity. But Library Girl cuts my hands free of the rope handcuffs and abandons me for the console. Switches are flipped, knobs are turned, the volume is set at ten.

"Hand me that backpack that's under the CESSNAB locker," she says.

Still kiss-dazed, I bring it to her and she pulls out a well-worn copy of *Anderson's Anthology of English Literature* and opens to a bookmarked page. Her voice zips into the microphone and floats out into the compound.

"Shakespeare, people. Complicated. Beautiful. Sad and violent. And the language is a bitch. Let me blow ya minds with a little *Hamlet*:

> *"To be, or not to be—that is the question:*
> *Whether 'tis nobler in the mind to suffer*
> *The slings and arrows of outrageous fortune,*
> *Or to take arms against a sea of troubles,*
> *And by opposing end them? To die, to sleep—*
> *No more; and by a sleep to say we end*
> *The heartache, and the thousand natural shocks*
> *That flesh is heir to? 'Tis a consummation*
> *Devoutly to be wish'd. To die, to sleep;*
> *To sleep, perchance, to dream, ay, there's the rub;*
> *For in that sleep of death what dreams may come—"*

The door shakes with pounding. An ax bites into the wood, scaring the shit out of me, but Library Girl keeps her lips pressed to the mike:

> *". . . who would fardels bear,*
> *To grunt and sweat under a weary life,*
> *But that the dread of something after death—*
> *The undiscover'd country from whose bourn*
> *No traveller returns—puzzles the will,*
> *And makes us rather bear those ills we have*
> *Than fly to others that we know not of?"*

The door bursts open with a sick splintering sound, and Ruth stumbles in. She takes one look at me there with Library Girl and her lower lip starts to quiver. "Cameron. You are so hurting my happiness right now."

Daniel's right behind her, brandishing a torch. He speaks into his bracelet. "Roger one-niner, we have a situation in the radio room."

"Roger one-niner? Isn't that airplane code?" I ask.

His lips go tight. "It makes me happy to say it."

A commando squad, all wide shoulders and, holy crap, honest-to-God guns this time, arrives on the scene. They grab Library Girl, who tries to hold on to the microphone. The commando picks up the mammoth anthology and brings it down hard three times on her hands, making her scream in pain till she's forced to let go.

"What are you doing?" I shout, running toward them.

Daniel grabs a gun from the commando's holster, points it at me. "Happiness. By any means necessary."

He lifts the gun by the nose and brings the butt down hard on my head, and the room slips away.

CHAPTER TWENTY-SIX

In Which Some People's Happiness Gets Its Butt Kicked and Gonzo and I Make Our Escape

Blacking out isn't so bad, really. All in all, it's a lot more pleasant than, say, celebrating a family birthday at a medieval theme restaurant or pretending you care about your GPA. Unconscious, I float out into a black universe where stars are winking electric Christmas candles, past the Buddha Cow raising one hoof in a Zen salute. It's like I'm on some cool ride, chugging past automated exhibits: Mom and Dad are sitting in the hospital cafeteria, not talking over cups of luke-warm coffee. They look like shit, like a couple of toothpaste tubes that have been grabbed in the middle one too many times till whatever's left is too hard to get out. Raina walks through the doors. She doesn't look like shit. She looks fresh and alive and full of promise. Dad sees her and stands up, gives a little smile. Mom watches him like he's a stranger she's seeing for the first time. Raina hands Dad some papers and says "I'm sorry" and "If there's anything I can do," and Dad answers, "You're doing so much already, Raina." In the way she blushes and tucks her hair behind her ear, in the way Dad pays attention to that one small gesture, Mom's face changes. She knows.

The ride loops around. To my right, the roadrunner keeps pace with me. It zips into a cave, and when it comes out, it's the Wizard of Reckoning, the fire giants burning a giant black hole into the sky behind him. He reaches out, but the ride drops, making my stomach tingle. It creeps up the invisible mechanical hill toward a brightly lit room, where Glory's taking the empty bag off the IV pole. "Just need to switch you out, honey." She hooks the new fat pouch on the pole. The ride slows till I'm even with her. Her face is like one of those carved totems I saw once in a book about Easter Island—dark, beautiful, forever.

She strokes my cheek, and I swear I can feel the warmth of her skin. Her big brown eyes look into mine. "Cameron, child, are you awake in there?"

"I said, are you awake?"

My aching eyes open to see Daniel sitting across from me in a chair with his arms crossed. He looks like his happiness is more than hurt; it's pissed and coming out swinging. I'm tied to my chair and Library Girl is nowhere to be seen. At least the gun's gone. The bright lights of the Snackateria are little needles of pain slipping into my head.

"Yo! Cameron."

"Yeah," I croak. "Where's Library Girl?"

"Who?" Ruth asks.

"Never mind," I say. "Where's Gonzo?"

Daniel sneers. "The midget freak? Maybe you can tell us. We haven't found him yet."

I'd like to beat the crap out of him for calling Gonzo a midget freak, but I'm tied to a chair and the lizard part of my brain has been activated and is now occupied with survival. Daniel gets right in my face. "So, tell us: how long have you and your spies been planning this little attack?"

"Me? I couldn't even plan dinner. I didn't have anything to do with this—"

Ruth cracks me on the knuckles with the anthology.

"Ow!" I screech.

"That's for reading this depressing, hard stuff over the loudspeakers."

"Wait, it wasn't me. I—"

She cracks my knuckles a second time.

"And that's for breaking the smoothie machine! They say it might take twenty-four hours to fix it. Twenty-four hours! That's like a lifetime!"

Daniel paces the room. He's a little scary. In fact, I'd give him just about anything that would increase his happiness right now before he goes commando on me. "We saw the security camera footage—she kissed you! And you handed her the backpack. We know you're in this together. All the order stations have been hacked into so when you try to order a CESSNAB product you get rerouted to a book called *My Happiness Wants Your Happiness to Go to Hell* with quotes like 'Read a damn book already. It won't kill you.' 'People screw up all the time. Deal with it.' 'Not everybody gets to be famous.' 'If you're so special, why am I so annoyed?'"

"Read that really bad one, Daniel!" Ruth says.

Daniel flips on a screen and reads the word flashing there. "No."

"I want a smoothie," Ruth says quietly.

Daniel's face is so close to mine I can see the acne cream on his chin. "You've hurt a lot of people today, Cameron. And now you're going to have to pay."

"What if that hurts my happiness?"

"Little late for that. Friend."

"Okay. I'll leave. You know? I'll just leave and never come back."

Ruth hits me with the book again so hard I swear *Beowulf* is lodged in my cheek. "Ow! Quit it!"

"No, Cameron," Daniel says, stepping back. "Your lack of complete happiness is a threat to our happiness. It's like a cancer. And you know what you have to do with a cancer?"

"Hope it goes away?"

Ruth drifts closer and I flinch, but five hundred years of the world's least exciting literature does not come near my flesh.

"No. We have to cut it out so the good cells can continue to grow." Daniel turns to the commandos. "Get him on his feet and meet me in the church. We're going bowling."

Ten minutes later, with two CESSNAB camo'd goons on either side of me, I'm half dragged into the packed Church of Everlasting Satisfaction and Snack 'N' Bowl to face my doom. The church band is plugged in; they're playing an uptempo tune with a vaguely rock-pop beat. My head still hurts from where Daniel smacked me with the gun, but I think the words say something about happiness only belonging to the right kind of people.

Daniel cuts a path through the throng and the band fades into a little feedback and then nothing. He stands in Lane

#7, right under the big-screen TV that shows the dancing pins when you make a strike. The pins usually say things like *Wow, you're awesome* and *The universe loves a winner, so the universe must really love you!* The screen's off today. I imagine the pins have heard all about me and Library Girl and the supposed revolution and they're scowling and flipping me the bird and gathering implements of torture.

Daniel holds out his hands like a preacher. "Friends, I want you to know that the smoothie machine is being fixed."

The walls of the church shake with the sound of applause, wolf whistles, and whoo-hoos.

"I also want you to know that even though Cameron has hurt our happiness, he's really hurt his own happiness more. This is what happens when people don't embrace the positive. But are we going to let Cameron disappoint himself?"

"No!" the CESSNABers shout.

"That's right. Cameron is part of our specialness, and we're going to prove that our way is the right way, the only way. The universe wants Cameron to be happy, and all he has to do to be forgiven is to bowl."

Daniel flicks the switch, and the ball machine thunks and rolls into action. My favorite, the purple one with a really high shine, shimmies up to my hand and waits.

"Daniel . . . ," I start, but he forces my hand onto the ball, his smile like a rictus grin. "Pick it up, Cameron. Crusaders, let's give our troubled friend a little inspiration."

The band kicks in. Ruth's shaking a tambourine, and I don't mean to brag, but my tambourine solo totally kicks her to the curb. For half a second, I consider staying. Maybe I could find that bliss state again. Maybe I could stay here, follow all the rules, be safe always. But as soon as the thought enters my mind, another one swims in and eats the first one like a shark. *Fuck that*, it burps.

230

"Here goes nothing." My fingers sink into the holes of that purple beauty; I pull back and throw the ball into the lane, where it sails down the slick middle like it's always done, heading for a perfect strike. But the ball veers off course. It drifts toward the gutter like it has every time I've ever bowled here, but instead of popping back out, it slinks into the loser trough with a loud rumble and disappears. Not a single pin falls. There is complete shock and silence.

"That can't happen," Daniel says, eyes wide. "Everybody's a winner here."

"Do it again!" someone challenges.

"Great idea," Daniel agrees, but his face is a little pale. "Come on, Cameron. Embrace the positive."

I shrug. "Your funeral."

Once again, the ball wobbles off course. It manages to knock off one measly pin before vanishing.

"Let me try it." Daniel pushes me out of the way. "Embrace. The. Positive!" he shouts, letting the ball fly, then watching in horror as his ball slips sideways, taking out only two pins at the far end. "But . . . I'm special."

"Holy shit," a kid named Luke shouts. "No way!" He races for a ball at the same time his friend John does.

"Dude, I'm so going first," Luke says.

"The hell you are," John protests. They run out to the lanes, where Luke knocks down six pins to John's three.

"Ha! I beat you by three pins! In your face!"

Ruth climbs on top of the Snackateria's Holy Cheese Fry machine. "Luke, we're not competitive here. Everybody's a winner. Everybody is part of the team."

John doesn't hear her. He's too busy lining up his next shot. "Think you can do it again, shithead?"

Luke breaks into a grin. "Dude, I will totally smoke your ass."

Daniel's practically screaming now. He's running across

231

the lanes, dodging balls as they fly. "Guys, we're all part of the specialness. Don't forget that."

Luke and John stop and stand there, looking at their feet. Luke takes a ball from the carousel and hands it to John, which makes Daniel smile.

"Ten bucks says I win."

"You're on."

The balls clatter into action. People start taking sides, cheering on either Luke or John. John makes a strike, a real one, and Luke yells, "You *suck*!" and they both start laughing.

The doors fly open. I can't see Gonzo in the crowd but I can hear him saying, "Excuse me, excuse me, could you get out of the way you smoothie-loving happy freaks?"

"Gonz!" I say, picking his little man body up for a full-on hug.

"Can we go now?" he says. " 'Cause after five days in this joint, I need to eat a bag of Cheesy Puff Fingers and listen to some hardcore face-melting music to get my synapses back to normal. If I never see a smoothie again, it'll be too soon."

A huge brawl breaks out in the bowling alley—people trying to best each other, idiots throwing balls into each other's lanes, arm-wrestling matches, a few choir members playing air guitar—while other CESSNAB Crusaders try to drown them out with happiness songs and chase them down for group hugs. They're so busy going crazy, they don't see Gonzo and me slip away. Even Peter and Matthew aren't at their stations in the parking lot. Just as we turn onto the road, I think I see Library Girl standing in a patch of trees, two streaks of white behind her back, but then she's gone, and I'm pretty sure I imagined the whole thing.

We walk the five miles to the nearest town, and just to

torture me, Gonzo starts making up his own CESSNAB song about making your happiness cry uncle and feeding happiness to your dog so he has wicked happiness gas, and we laugh. It's a pretty long walk, but my body's cooperating and the Wizard of Reckoning feels a long way off, so far off he's not even a sound you can pick up with the sonar of your soul. And it's only when we get close to the highway and the constant hum of cars taking people to and away from places that could be home or a new start or nowhere in particular, just a spot on the endless road, that I see the Buddha Cows floating gently to earth like a surreal snow.

But it doesn't seem worth mentioning, so I don't.

CHAPTER TWENTY-SEVEN

**Wherein We Crash at the Mister Motel
and I Learn Some Stuff About the Ayatollah of Harsh**

We take a crappy room in an even shittier motel, the Mister Motel right off the interstate. The blinking neon sign shows a winking guy tipping his hat, the Mister of Mister Motel fame, I assume. He looks like he should have a speech balloon coming out of his mouth: *Rent rooms by the hour, real cheap.* The room we get is a dark hole that looks like it hasn't been changed in at least thirty years. Butt-ugly brown bedspreads and yellow paint on the walls. Dark, fake wood headboards. Threadbare carpet in a color that's best described as "indiscriminately green"—great at hiding stains. The only new addition, for some crazy reason, is a bright orange balloon tied to a chair. The balloon advertises a used car lot, Arthur Limbaud's Resale Beauties.

Gonzo, of course, is freaked about hygiene issues.

"Do you suppose they use bleach on the sheets?" he says,

sitting tentatively on the bed and hugging his backpack to his chest. "I mean, really, you have to use bleach and the hot cycle to kill all the dust mites. And anything else."

I don't ask what "anything else" means and I don't intend to. I'm tired. I want to go to sleep and not wake up till morning, when I'll have to figure out how we get back on the road to Florida with no bus tickets and about three dollars to our names.

"I'm just gonna call my mom," Gonzo says. He uses a tissue to pick up the receiver of the Mister Motel phone, which looks as ancient as everything else.

"What are you doing?" I say, putting my finger over the clicker to disconnect him.

"I told you, calling my mom. My cell's dead and I don't have the charger."

"We can't afford a phone call to your mom."

"I don't like this place, man." Gonzo starts to wheeze.

"Calm down, Gonz. You're okay. It'll all be fine, I promise. Just breathe, okay?" I say, talking to him like I would if *I* were his mom. If I can keep him from panicking, he'll be okay. I'm not even sure he has asthma. I think he just has Freak Out lungs. Gonzo's not having any of my Zen master shit. He's tearing through his bag frantically, like a squirrel desperate for its nut.

"My inhaler. Dude, it's gone! Oh my God!" His face is really pale, and even I'm getting a little wigged about him.

"Be cool, be cool. Don't freak on me. It's here, okay?"

Gonzo's nodding, but he's saying "Shit, shit, shit" under his breath. I'm grabbing around in the bag, but I don't feel the inhaler.

"What if it's lost for real?" he wheezes. "Or stolen. Shit. Call nine-one-one, man. Call nine-one-one!"

I keep pawing through his bag. "I'm not calling nine-one-one. Calm down."

"Dude, I can't breathe!"

"You're yelling! If you can yell, you can breathe, all right? We call 911 and it's game over. We go back and I die in a diaper listening to instrumental light rock and the world goes poof and that is not gonna happen, so just get a grip."

The neon light from the parking lot falls across Gonzo's face like a strobe effect. His eyes are wide and he's clutching his chest.

"Please. Dude. This could be game over. Call nine-one-one stat! Tell them to bring a nebulizer!"

I grab his shoulders hard and shake him. "Gonzo! I am not going to let you die. Okay? I'm not your mom! I am not rushing you into an early grave so I can get on with my life. Okay? Okay?"

I'm waiting for him to go medieval on my ass for talking about his mom that way, but surprisingly, he just nods, letting me get back to his bag. This time, I find the L-shaped metal canister. "Here," I say.

Gonzo grabs it with both hands, shakes it hard, then positions it at his mouth like a tiny pistol and fires away. His eyes close as he holds his breath, waiting for the medicine to do its work. Exactly thirty seconds later, he takes another hit, holds his breath again until he can't anymore, and it all comes rushing out of him in a whoosh. There's a lot of coughing. In another minute, the color returns to his face. The air conditioner clicks on. It pushes the orange balloon back and forth in the artificial breeze.

"You okay?" I ask.

He shrugs. He can't really commit to being okay. It might kill him.

"That wasn't cool, what you said about my mom," he says quietly.

"Okay, sorry," I say, because I don't have any fight left in me. "Let's just crash."

I turn off the lamp and lie down. The room is tomb dark. Only hotel rooms ever get this dark, like they know it's their function to close you off from the world. When my eyes adjust to the lack of light, though, I can still make out Gonzo sitting on the edge of his bed, not moving.

I sigh. "Gonz, you're not, like, having heart palpitations over there or anything, are you?"

"No. I was just thinking." His voice sounds weird in the dark. Hollow and detached, like he's as full of air as the orange balloon. "You ever have, like, these totally random memories sometimes?"

"I guess."

"I was thinking about this one time when I was a kid. I was, like, I don't know, five? Six, maybe? It wasn't too long after my old man took off. The kids next door had this new swing set. It was ridiculously tricked out: swings, clubhouse, slide, monkey bars. The whole *bolo*, man. Way cool. To a little kid, anyway."

He pauses, and I wonder where this little trip down memory lane is taking us. My pillow's heating up under my head. I flip it over, settle my head against the cool cotton.

"Anyway, they told me if I wanted to be in the club, I had to be able to cross the monkey bars without falling. Dude, those bars looked like they were about four thousand feet high. But it was the first time they'd asked me over, so I didn't want to mess it up. One of the boys gave me a boost and I started making my way across. I was totally sweating it. But I got to the second one and then the third one. By the time I got to the fourth rung, they started cheering for me, telling me to keep going. It was this freakin' amazing feeling, like . . . I don't know how to describe it. I was doing it, you know? I was *making it, muchacho.* Two more to go and I'd be home free."

I can hear him playing with his inhaler; it makes a soft rattle.

"I was about to reach for the next one when I heard my mom scream my name. She was standing in our yard with this look of terror on her face. I could tell she was ready to run for me—she didn't *trust,* you know what I'm saying? When I looked back at that next rung, it seemed about a million miles away. I didn't feel so sure anymore. I reached for it, but sorta half-assed, you know? And I missed. Fell down and broke my arm and a rib and started crying. The kids thought I was a weenie, and their moms said I couldn't come over anymore because they didn't want me getting hurt in their yards. I spent a few days in the hospital and my mom bought me a bunch of Fast Wheels cars that I told her I loved and then I buried them in the backyard later and told her I lost them and she acted all hurt and said I took things for granted just like my dad."

He makes a funny sound that at first I think is a hiccup. But then I realize he's crying. "That was the first time . . . the first time I got that feeling . . . that . . . the only thing keeping me alive . . . was my mom. And I hated her for it."

Outside, somebody's getting ice. The machine thunks against the wall like a dying man's cough. It mixes with Gonzo's strangled, silent crying.

"So . . . ," I start. "So, you know, what did you have against the Fast Wheels?"

The sniffling slows down. Gonzo shifts on the bed in the deep motel black. "Huh?"

"I know you hated your mom. Shit, I don't blame you. But what did those little toy cars ever do to you to deserve such a fate? Buried alive. Dude, that's harsh."

Gonzo goes totally silent—not even a sniffle. For all I know, I've pissed him off so completely, he's about to risk another asthma attack just to kick my ass. I position my pillow as a shield just in case I have to ward off forty-two inches of the Gonzman pounding at me in Little People fury. And then I hear it in the dark—a bubbling laugh through tears.

"My friend," he says with a snort. "I am the Ayatollah of Harsh. Do not fuck with the little people. We will lay waste to your souls!"

"Oooh," I say. "Now you got me scared, dude. Terrified."

"I put a freakin' fatwa out on those cars." He's laughing so hard he sounds totally manic, but hey, whatever it takes to keep him up.

I put the pillow back behind my head. "Well, they didn't deserve to live. They were tools of the infidels."

"Goddamn right," he says, his voice less tight. He flops down on the bed.

It's quiet for another minute, and I try to get my body to relax. My legs really ache, and I hope it's just regular, tired aching from the long walk.

"Cameron?"

"Yeah?"

Gonzo turns on his side, facing me. I can make out the silhouette of him, my shadow friend. "You ever think about it?"

"Think about what?" I say.

"Dying."

Do I ever think about it? What does he want to hear? That lately I think about how my mom's face looks when she's drinking her coffee in the morning, staring at her crossword puzzle like she just might beat it today. I think about driving with my dad to the lake the day before he and Mom bought the new house when I was eleven, him singing along to the radio and looking like all he wanted to do was keep driving and singing. I think about the Jenna who made me a Christmas ornament out of macaroni when she was six, and the current Jenna, Jenna of the dance team, Jenna who can't stand me, Jenna who will miss me when I'm gone, even if it's just because I'm not there to make her look so much better to the world. I think about the fact that I will probably never bone Staci Johnson, and there's not a damn thing I can do about it. I think about dying every day, because I can't stop thinking about the living.

I fake a yawn. "Oh, man, I'm wiped out, okay?"

Gonzo shifts onto his back. "Oh, sure. No prob. Good night."

"Yeah. Night."

CHAPTER TWENTY-EIGHT

**Which Treats of My Visit to a Keg Party
and of My Chance Encounter with the
World's Grumpiest Yard Gnome**

Within thirty seconds, Gonz is snoring lightly. It's 12:20, and I'm wired. I can't turn on the TV, so I put on my shoes and pad out to the Mister Motel's parking lot with its magnificent view of I-10. A big semi roars past, followed by another. All those trucks carrying things that people think they can't live without—new sofas and light-up sneakers, ponchos and twelve different kinds of processed cheese in cubes, strings, squares, or shred pouches.

I trip along the access road to the blinking yellow lights of the underpass. On the other side of the freeway, there's a Gas-It-N-Git all lit up like a fluorescent mirage.

There's only one car in the lot and no people except the guy behind the counter, who's watching a little TV he's got by the register. I've got three dollars in change in my pocket and I slide it all into the pay phone. My fingers are stiff. I keep dropping coins that I have to pry off the pavement.

The phone rings a few times. Dad picks up. "Hello?" he says in a barely awake voice. For a second, I don't say anything. I just listen to his sleep-heavy breathing on the other end of the line.

"Dad?"

"Cameron? Is that you? Are you . . . Say something. Please."

His voice sounds different to me coming from so far away over thousands of miles of thin wire. It doesn't sound pissed off and controlled. I hear other notes in it. Fatigue. Hope. Sadness.

"Cameron?" he whispers. "I know you can hear me. I don't care where you are right this second. I just want you to know you are my boy. You're a part of me and I'm a part of you. Always."

"Dad?"

"Cameron?"

"Love you," I say, just as a big semi roars past on the highway, taking more stuff to more people to pack around the empty spaces of their lives.

Mom's waking up. I hear her asking Dad what's going on, who's he talking to, did the doctor come in? Dad tells her it's nothing, go back to sleep.

"Cameron?" Dad whispers. "Can you hear me, pal?"

A recorded operator voice politely asks me to deposit more change, but I don't have any more, so I hang up. It feels like there's a walrus sitting on my chest, and my eyes sting. I'd give anything to get high right now, to get good and numb.

There's a girl at the other end of the Gas-It-N-Git standing around like she's waiting for something. She's got on shorts and a fake fur jacket, even though it's muggy and my

T-shirt's sticking to my chest in places, leaving those little pellets of sweat, like a giant connect-the-dots. I nod to her on the way in, and she ignores me, which is fine, really.

The unnaturally bright lights hit me like a punch. That and the rancid nacho cheese smell from the big dripper beside the counter is working me over pretty good. The speakers administer a muzak dosage of a Copenhagen Interpretation song. The DJ's soporific voice follows the end notes. "And that was 'Words for Snow' by the Copenhagen Interpretation, from the *Wonder Whatever Happened to Them* files. . . ."

I move toward the back, stopping to pull the porn magazines out of their protective plastic coverings. The guy behind the counter's watching me in the convex We See You So Don't Even Think of Shoplifting Here mirror. Shit, there's no way this guy's gonna let me buy beer. I waste time picking up stuff I have no intention of purchasing: Cheap toy guns. Disposable razors. Cans of beans. Couple of snow globes. Jumbo packs of AlmostReal Fruit Leathers. Finally, I open the cooler, letting the frigid air wash over me, and grab a Rad Xtra Energy drink. If I'm going to be wired, I might as well go all the way. When I go for a bag of Corny Doodles, my coordination goes haywire. My muscles stiffen up; I grab hold of the wire display for support and send the whole row of chips to the ground.

"What do you think you are doing?" the clerk shouts in very precise English, like he's been practicing. His name tag reads EMPLOYEE #12, and I wonder if he's got a name or if his bosses just don't give a shit what it is.

He's yelling at me. "You think this is funny? You think this is a funny joke? Go on. Get out of here!" he shouts, pushing me through the front doors. "You are on drugs. Get going before I call the cops."

Back in the parking lot under the hazy lights, I gulp in the air, trying to calm my body. My E-ticket meter flares, then fades, and when I look, Frontierland has been completely erased. I'm down two health bars, as Gonzo would say. I wish I had my soda. The chick in the fur vest is still standing there, a lollipop in her mouth. Underneath all that makeup, she's not so old. Maybe fifteen. Sixteen. It's hard to tell with girls.

"Whadjoodo?" she asks.

"I beat his high score on Captain Carnage. He's pissed."

She doesn't laugh, and it depresses me.

She takes the lollipop out of her mouth. "If you wanna take something you have to put something on the counter first. Like you put a few candy bars there and ask if you can keep them on the counter while you get the rest of your stuff. They always say sure and then they think you won't rip them off. They stop watching you."

I'm not real sure on the etiquette for advice on shoplifting so I just say, "Cool. Thanks."

Some guy drives up in a tricked-out SUV. "Tara, where the hell you been?" he shouts through the open passenger window.

Taking the lollipop out of her mouth, she yells back, "None of your fucking business!"

"Why you gotta talk that way? Let's go to the party."

Tara tosses the lollipop into the parking lot. "I'm out of cigarettes."

"I got cigs. Who's this?" he asks, nodding in my direction.

Great. Just what I need.

"Whaddyou care," she says. "Maybe he's my new boyfriend."

"I just came here for a soda," I say.

"Yeah? Where is it, then?" the guy in the SUV taunts.

If this were a movie, I would bust a secret move so fierce the entire place would be razed to the ground. I'd finish with something snappy like "And don't forget my soda, punk" while I strolled off into the night. But it's not a movie, and I just stuff my twitching hands into my pockets like the big mad-cow-disease-afflicted chickenshit that I am.

"You're not the boss of me!" Tara shouts to the guy in the SUV. "I can do whatever I want. In case you forgot, we are broken up, *Jus-tin*!" She gives it a head swivel for added effect and puts her arm around my waist, which is basically like painting a target on my chest.

"I should be getting back," I say, stepping away from her.

Jus-tin! turns on his inside car light. I can see he's wearing a blue trucker hat and an oversized football jersey, and a huge diamond stud in his right ear. He's got a scruffy brown beard. "Aw, come on, Tara. You don't mean that, baby."

She turns to me. "Do you have any cigarettes?"

"Sorry. No."

"Can you get some?" she asks, sidling up to me. I notice with no small percentage of fear that the Justin guy looks like he could seriously kick my ass.

"That guy won't let me back in," I say, holding out my hands in a "sorry" pose. They've stopped spazzing, so there's that, at least.

Employee #12 stands near the doors with his arms folded across his chest, letting us know we are not welcome in his Gas-It-N-Git lot. It's a cops-will-be-called stance. An I-am-an-action-hero-of-the-all-night-mart stance. I wonder how he would sound saying "Don't forget my soda, punk"?

"Dammit," Tara says, chewing at a ragged nail. She saunters over to the open passenger window on the SUV. "Gimme a smoke."

245

A lighted cigarette is passed through the window. She takes a deep puff, blows out some smoke, and just like that, opens the door and crawls in. There's some intense kissing. Justin turns off the interior light.

"Okay, later," I say, walking back toward the hulking shadow of the interstate.

"Wait!" Tara calls. She's hanging out the window, her arms dangling, the cigarette stuck between her first and second fingers. "You wanna go to a party?"

We drive through the sleeping town. The traffic lights have gone to blinking yellows, and the streets glisten from an earlier rain. Tara tells me her five-minute life story. She's fifteen. She lives with her mom, who works as a nail technician and brings home free polish and cucumber lotion to the trailer they share with four cats. "The whole dang bathroom smells like cucumber and cat poop, I swear," she says, offering me a cigarette, which I decline. Tara *hates* school but *loves* a show about supermodels and wants to be one.

"She just did a boat show," Justin tells me with a mix of pride and wariness. Like he only wants other guys to notice that he's with a hot girl, not actually notice the hot girl herself. Justin's eighteen but still a junior. He also lives with his mom and her "sorry-assed retard of a boyfriend" in a "crappy, two-bedroom apartment near Enormo-Mart." For money, he bags groceries and sells the odd bit of pot, which is why hitting Brian Kinner's party is "so vital."

They finally ask me about myself. Usually I would edit my story, say as little as possible so I could stay in hiding mode. It's been my M.O. my entire life—living just below the radar. But tonight, I'm so tired I just tell them everything. It feels good not to hold myself in check.

"Mad cow disease?" Tara says, exhaling smoke. "Is that something you get from sex?"

"No," I say. "It's not contagious."

"Wow," Tara says. "That's so sad. Justin, don't you think that's so sad?"

"Yeah. Real sad. Hey, you wanna get high?"

Justin pulls the SUV over into the post office parking lot under a sign advertising that THE NEW CANCER STAMPS ARE HERE! and we smoke a joint. After the third or fourth toke, my head's bobbing on my neck like one of those bobblehead toys you see on dashboards. Welcome back to Numbsville, population: one.

"Can't wait to get out of this town," Tara mutters, eyes closed, head lolling against her seat back.

Justin scratches at his scruffy attempt at a beard. His hair sticks out from under his trucker hat in long, scraggly wisps. "'S not so bad."

Tara looks at him like he's just said all babies should be euthanized. "Yes it is. It sucks."

"I'm here," he says quietly.

Tara snuffs out the joint. "I'm baked."

"You cool back there?" Justin asks me.

"Ummn" is all I can manage in my semiconscious state.

"Time for a little fun," Justin says.

He fires up the SUV and we drive through a neighborhood of insta-mansions—huge, sprawling houses, some with their own turrets. The walkways are lit up with in-ground electric torches. Alarm signs dot the edges of the lawns.

"Tara, take the wheel."

Tara puts her left hand on it and we inch toward the curb. Justin pulls a baseball bat out from under his seat and leans his body out the side window. He swings the bat hard, knocking a mailbox off its stand.

"Whoa," I say. Or at least, I think that's what I say. I'm stoned. For all I know I could have said, "Board the cows! We've come to enslave your marigolds." This makes me laugh, chuckling all to myself in the back.

Justin bangs away at the mailboxes. He misses one or two, which he blames on Tara's driving.

"Fine. Drive yourself," she says, pouting. But she doesn't give up the wheel, and on the next one, he hits pay dirt. The mailbox is knocked completely clear of its post. It skips across the street with a grating clank, making little sparks on the asphalt. Lights flip on in the house. A dog barks with intent. Tara giggles high and loud. A stoner laugh. Justin tucks the baseball bat back under the seat and drives off fast. We run aimlessly up and down streets with names like High Court, Royal Acres, Imperial Lane, King's Row, every street striving to be more important sounding than the last. Even the roads have aspirations here.

Justin rolls onto Westminster Lane. He cuts the SUV's lights and slinks into the driveway of a dark house.

"Isn't this the McNultys'?" Tara asks.

"Yeah," Justin answers. "They're away."

"How d'you know?" she teases.

"My mom's retard boyfriend cleans their pool. He said they're in Spain or Portugal or some city like that."

"Charlie McNulty is president of the student council at our school. He's supersmart," Tara explains, like a tour guide. It strikes me as funny and I laugh to myself.

"This way," Justin says, taking us to the back. Around the side of the house is a wooden fence. Justin opens the gate into the backyard. The place is freaking huge. It's got a nice stone patio with a huge gas grill, teak patio furniture, and a glass table with an umbrella shooting out of the middle. And there's the pool Justin mentioned. It's a clear blue that lets you see the pattern of red and yellow Mexican tiles around the sides. I can smell the chlorine coming off it.

Justin shucks his pants and shirt, getting down to his skivs. I'm afraid he's going to take those off, too, but he doesn't. He slips into the water in his underwear and pushes away from the side on his back. Tara's having trouble with her clothes, but soon she's down to her bra and underwear. I can see the outline of her dark hair against the thin pink fabric of her panties. It gives me a hard-on. No way I'm stripping down now.

"What's the matter, Cameron? You shy?" She takes my hands in hers and starts pulling.

"No," I protest, hoping she doesn't steal a look below. "It's my disease. I can't swim. It's not good for me."

"Bummer," she says before taking a flying leap into the pool. Water sluices up the sides for a good five seconds after. "I like making an entrance," she says. "Otherwise no one notices you."

In the end, I take my shoes off and stick my feet in, letting the lukewarm water lick at my ankles. It feels good, and not just because I'm stoned. I make a mental note to add this to Dulcie's list of things worth living for. For some reason, I keep seeing her rolling her eyes at me, that big, goofy grin stretching her face like Silly Putty. On my private list, I add her smile. She doesn't have to know.

"This is great," Tara says. "When I'm a model, I'm buying a house just like this one. Maybe I'll even buy this one from the McNultys and everybody who was ever mean to me can just eat shit when I'm all famous and everything."

"Baby, you can build your own house," Justin says.

"Yeah, I can, can't I? Better than this one," Tara giggles.

She swims over to Justin and wraps herself around him, spider style. They float together like that, kissing. I look around the yard like I'm interested in the landscaping.

Tara laughs. "I think we're embarrassing Cameron," she says in a little singsong voice.

Justin gently pushes away from Tara and stretches for the side of the pool.

"Hey!" Tara says, treading water. "Where you going?"

"I gotta take care of business."

Just like that, they climb out and dry off with some towels they take from a neat stack in a cabinet by the back door. They peel off their wet underwear. I look away and pretend I'm not getting another hard-on thinking about riding in an SUV with a girl who's not wearing any panties.

"Let's go," Tara says once they've got their clothes on again.

"Hold up a sec." Justin's riffling through the sideboard of the grill. He pockets some BBQ sauce and a bottle opener.

"Should you take that?" I ask. My head's starting to clear a little. It's not as cottony.

"They have everything. They won't miss it."

When we get back into the SUV, Justin opens the glove compartment and tosses the bottle opener in there. It joins three more bottle openers, a cigarette case, some photographs of other people's families, keys, and a dog collar.

"You take all that?"

"Yeah."

"Why?"

"I like having their stuff. I like knowing they don't win all the time."

"Justin," Tara whines. "We're gonna miss the party."

"Don't tell me what to do," he says, real low and quiet.

Tara rolls her eyes and squeezes the water out of her pony-tail. "Gimme a cigarette."

We drive out of the mansion neighborhood through a good-but-not-as-expensive one into an okay one, falling through the pecking order of neighborhoods till we're in a run-down section with a bunch of ranch houses guarded by crappy, American-made cars and trucks.

Justin parks the SUV at the end of a long line of cars. We follow him down the street to the house where all the lights are blazing and party sounds blurp from the backyard. Two kegs are the only furniture in the back. Some kind of metal-rap mix blares from stereo speakers pulled out through the sliding glass doors and parked precariously on the uneven concrete patio.

A heavy guy in a black wrestling T-shirt greets Justin with a complicated handshake that ends with them both bump-ing chests. "Justin. Whassup?"

Justin shrugs, hands in his pockets. "Not much, bro. How's the action?"

The big guy looks around. "So-so. Too many guys, not enough girls. Hey, Tara."

"Hey, Carbine," Tara says, taking a drag off a new ciga-rette. "This is Cameron. He's dying of mad cow disease."

Carbine nods at me. "Cool. Want a beer?"

"No, that's okay."

He hands me a full cup. "Here you go."

"Thanks," I say, taking it.

Carbine throws some playful punches to Justin, who fake wrestles him back, and I wonder who decided this was supposed to be the okay male greeting. Hi, good to see you. Let me show you how glad I am by beating the crap out of you.

They stop hitting each other and Carbine says, "Yo, Justin. Can we do a little bidness?"

"Lead the way, bro," Justin says, and they disappear.

A guy walks up and takes the beer out of my hand, drinking it and handing me back the empty cup. Tara sees some girls she knows and runs over to whisper with them in a huddle like girls do. It's in their DNA.

I wander through the house. A strip poker game has taken over the kitchen. One girl's down to her bra and jeans. A guy's sitting there in his tighty-whities. I grab a handful of chips and head into the living room. The guys stand around in clumps, eyeing the girls who sit on the couches, drinking and talking and waiting for the guys to make a move so they can hook up. The ones who do hook up walk to the back rooms and don't come out. Some poor dude's out cold on the couch and his friends are writing ASSWIPE across his forehead in permanent marker. The news is on TV. I'm transfixed by pictures of flames tearing through some town. I wish I could hear what the anchorwoman was saying. There's only the crappy closed captioning, which says something about *poasssble asson,* which I think means "possible arson." On the scene, mustachioed guys in mirrored sunglasses and baseball caps stand around taking notes. Somebody switches the channel to wrestling.

I push through the screen door and walk out into the yard, where it's mostly quiet. You can see stars here. A smiling yard gnome like the one from Dad's photos keeps watch over a rock garden. This one's about three feet tall, with white hair and beard, red cheeks, a Viking helmet, brown pants, and a chain-mail tunic.

I have no idea where I am or how the hell I'm going to get back to the motel. It's a good thing Gonzo's a heavy-duty sleeper, because if he woke up and found himself alone, he'd have a full-blown panic attack. I step back, accidentally toppling the yard gnome.

"Sorry, little guy," I say, righting him.

"I'd prefer that you not refer to me as 'little guy.'"

That pot must have been better than I thought, because I could swear the yard gnome just said something. "Excuse me? Did you just t—"

"It's derogatory. I don't refer to you as skinny guy, now, do I?"

Holy shit. I'm talking to a yard gnome.

Somebody barrels down the street too fast, taking off the side mirror on a sedan. I look around but there's no one I can turn to for verification.

"Did you see that? He didn't even stop," the yard gnome says without losing his cheery smile. "This neighborhood is going to hell."

"Who . . . who are you?" I croak.

"My captor—the man who stole me from a fraternity house—calls me Grumpy. Of course, he's also the sort of educated gentleman who pisses on me when he comes home drunk, so there you are."

"Okay. Not loving the name Grumpy. What do you want to be called, then?" I ask.

"Ah, a question of identity, *ágætr*. Who would you be if you didn't know who you are? How do you put a name to your soul, your essential *sjálfr*?"

"Don't look at me. My parents named me Cameron after some actor they liked."

"Exactly. You've been assigned an identity since birth. Then you spend the rest of your life walking around in it to see if it really fits. You try on all these different selves and

253

abandon just as many. But really, it's about dismantling all that false armor, getting down to what's real."

"And what's that?"

"I don't know," he says, sounding weary. "But I can tell you what it isn't. It isn't standing in somebody else's yard, smiling and rosy-cheeked while the dogs sniff you for a crap post. It isn't having teenagers steal you in the night and take you on vacations where they snap your photo in front of the Matterhorn or Old Faithful or a KOA campground just for grins. It isn't the mailman giving you a kick for fun. It isn't this."

"I'm sorry. I've never spent a party talking to a yard gnome. In fact, I'm not convinced you're not a hallucination."

"I give you my word that I am as real as you are. You asked my name." His voice gets deeper, majestic. "I am Balder, son of Odin, brother of Höðr, friend to all."

"Balder, wasn't he a Norse god?" I say, remembering all my mother's bedtime stories.

"Indeed." He sounds pleased. "I am. Or I was. Once, in another time, another world. But Loki, the trickster, cursed me," he growls. "And I found myself in this false form, forced to travel endlessly the nine worlds of Yggdrasil in the possession of others until I could find one who could understand, who had the sight to see through to my true nature. You are that soul, and now you will guide me to *Ringhorn*."

This whole thing is starting to make me wonder if maybe I should get on some serious meds pronto.

"*Ringhorn* is my ship, which waits for me. If I can make it to the sea, to *Ringhorn*, the curse shall be lifted and I shall be free. At last, I feel the winds of luck have shifted—thank the gods."

A dog comes sniffing through the grass. It gives Balder a quick once-over, lifts its leg, and lets go all over him before trotting away.

"Could you turn on the hose, please?" he asks with a heavy sigh.

I find the knob for the hose, crank it to medium flow, and follow the green rubber snake of it back to Balder. With my finger over the nozzle so it sprays like a real shower, I give him a good dousing. Finally, he sputters that it's enough and I turn it off.

"Hold on," I say, running toward the house. "Don't go anywhere."

"You're quite the wit," he grumbles.

In the kitchen, a couple of guys are fighting near some half-dressed girls. Carbine's shouting, "Break it up! Break it up, dudes!" and pulling them off each other. No one sees me as I grab the roll of paper towels and sprint back outside.

"Here," I say, blotting him dry. I can't believe I'm toweling off a yard gnome. He's still damp but better than he was.

"Thank you," he says. "You're most kind."

No one has ever called me kind. Selfish. Weird. Unreliable. Frustrating. But not kind. I'm not sure what to say.

"You're welcome."

A handful of guys push through the screen door and congregate by the window air conditioner unit, where I know they can't hear us.

"How have you come to be here in this place? What trick of fate has allowed our meeting?" Balder asks.

I shrug. "Somebody invited me to a party. Now I don't know how to get back to the motel."

"You have money?"

"Not much," I say.

"Hmmm. Well, I wouldn't ordinarily advocate stealing," he muses. "But the idiot who lives here keeps his drug money in a jar under his bed."

"I don't know. Carbine looks like he could kill me without even breathing heavy. I don't think I want to tangle with him."

"I'll do it," the gnome says.

"I'm not trying to insult you, but how exactly can you do that?"

"I am bound to the one who owns me, taking whatever form they deem necessary. If you take ownership, I am pledged to you. You can grant me the use of all my faculties."

"Okay," I say. "What do I do?"

"Place your hand over my heart, and say what words form in your own."

I put my hand on his chest. It's cold, wet, and ceramic, and I feel like an A-1 asshole. "I, Cameron Smith, do grant this yard gnome slash possible misplaced Viking god, Balder, use of all his faculties to use as he sees fit. And stuff."

Immediately, there's a thump against my hand, followed by another, a clear heartbeat growing stronger, and Balder's chest warms. The painted coating bubbles up, dissolves, and is sucked into his pores. Sun-bronzed flesh emerges in its place. His beard softens; tendrils of it touch the collar of his chain mail, making him look like an eccentric guitarist for some Texas blues band. His cheeks blaze red, and his painted-on smile morphs into a very real, very wide smile. Those gray-blue eyes twinkle with wonder, and two thin streams of tears trickle down his red cheeks and disappear into his thick beard. The yard gnome is as alive as I am.

"Holy freakin' Ragnarok!" I gasp.

"Noble Cameron, I am forever indebted to you," he says with a little stiff bow. He wipes his face dry. Mischief glints in his eyes. "Now, to help you. Carbine's bedroom window is around the side of the house to my right. If you will give me what you call a boost, I shall crawl in, plunder, and return with the money. It would be best if you were to carry me past the others, allowing me to 'play dead,' so as not to arouse their suspicions. Let us make haste."

As a kid, I imagined lots of different scenarios for my life. I would be an astronaut. Maybe a cartoonist. A famous explorer or rock star. Never once did I see myself standing under the window of a house belonging to some druggie named Carbine, waiting for his yard gnome to steal his stash so I could get a cab back to a cheap motel where my friend, a neurotic, death-obsessed dwarf, was waiting for me so we could get on the road to an undefined place and a mysterious Dr. X, who would cure me of mad cow disease and stop a band of dark energy from destroying the universe.

Five minutes after I've helped him in, the gnome appears at the window again, a big wad of crumpled bills in his hand. "I'm afraid I'm a bit rusty yet. Grab my legs!" he whisper-shouts. I pull him to safety and he presses the bills into my hand. "I took the whole of it, three thousand dollars, just to be sure."

"Whoa." I can't stop staring at all that green.

"Quickly," Balder admonishes.

I shove the bills deep into my pockets. "I feel kind of bad taking this."

"Don't," the gnome says. He wobbles on shaky legs toward the yard. "His wealth is ill-gotten. And once he dressed me as a 'Hootchie Mama' and posted Internet pictures on a fetish site called Naughty Gnomes. I cannot adequately convey the trauma of it. Now. The telephone is in the living room by the TV. I've seen cabs here before—County Cab, 1-800-333-1111. When you've been taken hostage as much as I have, it helps to pay attention."

"Thanks," I say.

"You're welcome."

After I make the call, I come out to find the guys who were smoking the J now crowded around Balder. "Hey, man, I'll bet this little guy would make a good football or target practice."

Balder's face is a mix of terror and sheer pissed-off-ness. Given the chance, he'd run these guys through, I bet.

"I wouldn't do that," I warn.

The guy closest to Balder shouts, "Yeah? Why not? You gonna kick my ass?"

Lovely. Gee, I hope we'll be friends forever. "Naw, man. I just saw this big dog come and take a piss on him."

He jumps back fast, and the other guys laugh and high-five each other. "Awwww, dude! Close one. Dog piss!"

Somebody sticks a head out the door. "Yo! They're showing *Chainsaw Motel* on the late show! Get your sorry asses inside."

"All right! Cannibals!" the guys yell, and stumble-run to the house.

Balder lets out the breath he was holding. He bows. "That was a nice thing you did. You are indeed noble." With his chain mail and domed helmet, he reminds me of some weird, courtly little knight. "Please allow me to read your fortune in the runes."

"What?"

"The runes," he says, drawing a small leather pouch from his pocket. "We from the North use them as tools of protection and divination. Here." He offers the pouch. "Draw one."

I pull out a smooth stone with a weird "R" etched into it.

"Ah," Balder says, lighting up. "Raido. The rune of travelers, for it means a journey will be undertaken. The journey will be important and there will be no getting around it." He puts the pouch back. "You might need the services of a warrior. I would be happy to ride into battle with you, if you chose to take me with you on your journey." He shoots me a hopeful look.

How the hell am I going to explain this to Gonzo? My cab pulls up to the curb. The driver honks once. I stand up and brush the grass from my jeans. "Okay, here's the deal: I'm traveling with a friend, Gonzo. You have to talk to him, too, because he already thinks I'm going insane, and I don't need any more help on that front. Got it?"

"Indeed."

"We're going to Florida. There's a beach there. I don't know if your ship will be waiting for you or not—I mean, I can't promise anything—but it's a shot."

He bows deeper this time. "The gods have truly sent a wise one to me. I shall honor your wishes, and I shall make one condition of my own."

"What's that?"

"You and your friends are not to take any unauthorized pictures of me. I do not wish to show up on your Internet page posed in front of any national monuments or next to dubious signage with some obnoxious caption underneath. I've had quite enough of that." His expression is as no-fooling as they come.

"Got it," I say.

I lift him in my arms like a baby. On the way to the cab, Balder gives one last look at the cul-de-sac—the weedy yard, the rock garden littered with butts, the cars lining the block like conformity guards. He gives a small wave, and I think maybe he'll miss this place after all, but then his fingers slowly bend till only the middle one's left standing.

CHAPTER TWENTY-NINE

In Which I Learn That Two Very Small People Can Add Up to a Major Pain in the Ass and We Nearly Bite It at the Konstant Kettle

Gonzo's gotten up in a bad mood. He's not happy that I went to a party without him. He's not happy that I don't have exact change for the soda machine. He's not happy about getting his lazy ass up before noon, even though the Mister Motel—while being lax about the sort of cretins who rent their rooms—is pretty serious about their eleven o'clock checkout policy, and I am not about to be charged another full day rate so Gonzo can sleep in. But once I introduce Balder, the talking Viking yard gnome, Gonzo is unhappy for a whole new set of reasons.

"I'm just gonna verify this one more time, dude: I'm having breakfast with a yard gnome," he says, once we're established in a booth at the Konstant Kettle, located conveniently to the right of Mister Motel. He hasn't touched his breakfast.

"I am Balder, god of wisdom, second son of Odin," Balder

explains between sips of tea. He's wedged in the corner, where no one else can see him eating.

"Okay, you're a *delusional* yard gnome," Gonzo says.

"Let's not talk about delusional," I warn, looking around the place. I'm sure everyone's noticed us—the twitchy teen, cranky dwarf, and talking yard gnome—but no, people are just going about their business here, digging into their corned-beef hash and eggs. It's kind of funny and sad how people never really notice what's going on, just like Dulcie said once. I wonder if I'll ever see her again.

Balder's eyes narrow. "You don't believe me."

Gonzo finally spears a slimy egg. "Uh, let me see. Hmmm . . . no. No, I don't believe the yard gnome is a Viking god. Call me crazy."

"Gonzo," I start, but he holds his hands in a time-out "T" and turns to Balder.

"Let's stop talking shit and be honest here. You're a *dwarf.* I know it. You know it. Just own it, man. Stop the self-hate."

"Very well. I shall prove that I am Balder." He hands Gonzo a table knife. "Run me through with this smallish but worthy sword."

Gonzo stops midchew. He opens his mouth full of gnarly egg-toast mash. "You want me to shiv you with a dull butter knife?"

"I want you to try to kill me," Balder explains. "To make my blood flow like the Leiptr."

"Dude, I'm eating," Gonzo whines.

Balder smiles. "Don't worry, I cannot be harmed. That is the power of Balder the great."

"Listen—" Gonzo starts. Without warning, Balder pushes himself onto the knife in Gonzo's hand. The blade disappears in his rounded belly.

"Aaahh!" Gonzo cries. A few heads pop up in our direction. I use my body to block any view of Balder.

"Would you guys chill?" I whisper through tight lips.

Balder pulls the knife neatly from his skin and lays it on the table. It's completely clean.

Gonzo's face is white. "Dude, you are freaking me out."

I put my hand on Balder's stomach. There's no wound. "How did you do that?"

"I am immortal." Balder takes a sip of his tea. "You see, I had a fearsome dream that I would be killed, and so my mother, Frigg, traveled to the underworld to beg for protection. She went to everyone in the realm and made each one promise not to hurt me. All swore an oath, save the tiny mistletoe bush, who was too young to make such a promise. Thus, I was protected."

I vaguely remember my mom telling me this story. It seemed different when she told it, but I can't remember—all that stuff is disappearing from my head, misplaced files I can't always find. Mom. If she were here right now, she'd be pitching a fit about Konstant Kettle. She'd probably tell the poor waitress that Constant shouldn't be spelled with a "K" and that they're contributing to "education erosion." That's the sort of stuff that always embarrassed me about my mom. I feel bad about not calling. She's probably going nuts. I use the complimentary pack of crayons to draw on my napkin.

"For sport, the others would try to kill me—they'd throw stones and darts, even spears," Balder chuckles. "I remained unharmed."

Gonzo smears an inch of butter on his toast. "And I thought dodgeball was sadistic. I'd hate to take a Viking gym class: 'Hey, Timmy, dodge the spear and . . . oh, sorry,

Timmy. Listen, you don't need more than one arm, not really.'"

"May I finish?" Balder says, clearly annoyed.

Gonzo reaches over him for the jelly. "I thought you *were* finished."

"When a Viking warrior dies, they make a pyre upon a mighty vessel, set him on it, and send him off to Valhalla, the hall of the gods in the afterlife. It's a very noble death."

Gonzo rolls his eyes. "Set on fire? Yeah, sounds like big fun. Can you pass the ketchup?"

"I don't expect you to understand," Balder says. "You are not noble."

"I came on this trip, didn't I? I didn't have to do that? Cameron, tell him I didn't have to do that."

"You didn't have to do that," I say.

Gonzo points at me with his fork as if to say, *See, you asshole?*

Balder sizes Gonzo up. "You're quite small, aren't you?"

Gonzo narrows his eyes and tightens his grip on the fork. "I don't really think you're in a position to be talking about somebody's size, are you, dude?"

"It's not a question of size. It's a question of stature. In my travels, I've learned to speak five languages. I'm versed in science, the arts, music."

Gonzo stares at him. "You're a freakin' yard gnome. Dude."

"Dwarf," Balder grumbles.

"Piss post!"

"Ignoble."

"For Chrissakes, can we just get along and eat in peace?" I say with a sigh. I don't feel so great. My head's throbbing and my stomach hurts. I don't think it's my CJ, just an old-fashioned hangover. I look down at the napkin, where I've crossed out the "K" in Konstant and replaced it with the proper "C."

"I'll be right back," I say.

"Where you going?" Gonzo sounds panicked.

"I'll be right back. You guys just . . . get to know each other. Bond," I say.

Balder offers Gonzo the butter knife. "Perhaps you would like to stab me again?"

"Cameron, don't leave me with the freaky yard gnome!" Gonzo pleads, but I'm already up.

There's a pay phone in the way back next to the men's bathroom. I drop in all the change I've got and make the call. It rings four times and goes to voicemail. I hear my mom's familiar message—"Hi, this is Mary Smith. I can't come to the phone right now because I've probably been carried away by griffins. But if you leave your name and number, I'll get back to you just as quickly as Hermes would." There's a pause, and then she says to me, "Cameron, did I do that right? Oh! We're still recording! Oh my goodness . . . ," and her laugh is cut off. That message used to annoy the crap out of me— my mom being all spacey and mom-ish. But right now, hearing her voice is the best thing in the world, like waking up and realizing there's no school. There's a beep, and my stomach tightens.

"Um, hi, Mom. It's me. Cameron. Well, you probably figured that part out," I say, sounding like the biggest dork. "Anyway, I'm okay. I want you to know that first. And, you know what? Keep grading those moronic English Comp 101 papers, because otherwise, we're all gonna be getting our gas at the K-W-I-K S-E-R-V and drinking our E-X-P-R-E-S-S-Os at the *Konstant Kettle,* two K's. Seriously, the world needs you. You matter. A lot. Okay, I gotta go, 'cause the griffins are here and you know how much they hate to wait. Love you," I add quickly, and hang up.

I turn and bump into somebody reading a newspaper. "Sorry," I mumble.

"No problemo," comes a familiar voice. Dulcie lowers her newspaper. Her bright pink hair has been twisted into short, corkscrew curls that wiggle when she shakes her head. "You would not believe the things people put in the personals these days."

"Dulcie! Where've you been?"

"You said you wanted to be left alone."

"Yeah." I trace a crack in the tile with my foot. "Sorry. I promise not to be an asshole from now on."

"Don't make promises you can't keep," Dulcie says, laughing. Like a pair of excited puppies, her wings perk up and spread out till they touch the walls of the narrow hallway. I glance nervously toward the restaurant. "You might wanna ix-nay on the ings-way?"

"What? These?" She fluffs them so I can see today's artwork, a mural of rainbows. "Don't worry—people only see what they want to see."

Right on cue, a lady barrels into the narrow hallway and asks if Dulcie is in line for the bathroom. Dulcie shakes her head, and the lady goes right on in without so much as an extra blink.

"I'm just curious, what did she see?"

Dulcie shrugs. "Who knows? Everything hunky-dory in Camland? It's been a while."

"Yeah. It's been a weird couple of days." I tell her about missing the bus, CESSNAB, the party, and Balder.

"I'm special, you're special," Dulcie sings.

"How do you know—"

"Must've been on a greatest hits CD. Great and special," she says quickly. "Anyway, I've been thinking—I know you said to leave you alone, but I don't think that's such a good idea, Cameron. You need me."

"I need you?" I try to think of a comeback, but the truth is, I'm just happy to see her.

"You've got grape jelly on your cheek," she says, brushing it off. "Oh, also? Something just came in."

"Came in where? Angel Central?" Dulcie doesn't answer me. "Wow, do you have cubicles? Is there middle management and one annoying angel who drinks all the coffee but never remembers to make a fresh pot?"

Dulcie gives me a playful punch in the arm. "Very funny, Cameron. You know, I'd love to tell you all about it, but, sadly, then I'd have to kill you. *Anyway* . . . this just showed up. It's recent footage of Dr. X."

She pulls out an MP7 player and presses Play. Grainy video rolls. A guy in a lab coat in a white room. It's vaguely familiar. "Wait—I've seen this guy before! The night the fire giants showed up, I did an Internet search and it led me to him. It led me to Dr. X."

"Everything's connected," Dulcie says softly, and ups the volume.

The quality's crap, and every few words are replaced by a mumbly hiss. ". . . So close to finding the answer . . . *pssssttttt* . . . The passage of time is an illusion; time . . . *pssstttt* . . . does not exist, or rather, we live in all time, always . . . *pssssttttt* . . . as if we could reach out and touch what has come before, what is yet to be . . . *pssstttt* . . . and here is the most important thing of all . . . *pssssstttttttt* . . ."

Suddenly, the video jumps to something else. It's like the

267

channel's been turned and we're smack-dab in the middle of somebody's vacation footage—jumpy shots of people in shorts walking around, crowd sounds, chirpy music, furry cartoon characters waving. The camera pans over a gate studded with colorful planets and gears. A sign reads: TOMORROWLAND— THE FUTURE THAT NEVER WAS. The video freezes and a little Play Again triangle pops up.

"What the hell happened?" I ask.

Dulcie sighs. "Sorry. I was lucky to even get this."

"What does he mean by all that 'time doesn't exist' stuff? I mean, how about, 'Hey, here's the cure you need. Oh, and let me tell you how to close the wormhole and save the universe. Just turn left in Alabama and you'll be fine.'"

"I'm sorry, Cameron. I know this is frustrating."

"You think?"

"And I don't mean to make it harder, but I think our clock is ticking a little faster now. If the wizard gets to Dr. X first, they'll pull him back through the wormhole, and then it's all over."

"Great," I say.

She bites her bottom lip. "Did you get a sense from that? Anything at all?"

I shake my head. "Nothing."

Dulcie's expression is unreadable. "Okay. Well, I'm going to see what else I can find out about Dr. X. You keep pushing on, following whatever signs you find."

"So you're going again?"

"I'm here whenever you need me." She breaks into a goofy grin, and I want to tell her not to go, to stick around and meet the gang, have some pancakes. I want to say something cool, something to keep her smiling, but I can't think of anything. *"Você é a vaca do meu contentamento,"* I say, quoting a Great Tremolo song.

Dulcie gives me a weird look and bursts out laughing. "You are the cow of my contentment? Wow. I'm speechless."

"Is that what it says?"

" 'Fraid so."

"I knew that."

"Course you did." Her laugh dies. She shrinks back, her eyes wide.

"What's the matter?" I say, following her gaze to the front of the restaurant, but I don't see anything unusual. A hostess behind the cash register next to a stack of menus. People paying. A guy in a United Snow Globe Wholesalers shirt wheeling in a dolly full of boxes. A man picking his teeth with a toothpick. Bus boys and waitresses running back and forth with trays and loaded bus tubs. The guy delivers the box, and the hostess opens it up. She pulls out a snow globe, which she shakes vigorously before mounting it on a high shelf above the cash register.

"Dulcie?"

"It's nothing," she says weakly. "See you down the road, cowboy. Here's the paper. And Cameron? Be careful." And just like that she's gone.

"Hey, you forgot your player!" I say, but she doesn't materialize.

I give Dulcie's paper a quick scan. There's the usual mess of the incomprehensible mixed in with the ridiculous, but I do see an ad for cheap tickets to Daytona Beach. I take that as a sign we're on the right path, though truthfully, it's as right as any other random thing I want to assign meaning to—cartoons, the Great Tremolo, the way Staci Johnson flicks her ponytail. I smooth out Junior Webster's scrap of a compass—*to live*—fold it neatly, and tuck it back into my pocket along with the MP7.

When I get to the dining room, some kind of fight has

broken out. People are clumped together in spectator fashion, cheering.

"What's going on?" I ask the guy next to me.

"Some kinda wrestlin' promo, I think. It's entertainin', I'll say that much. Them little guys got lots of spunk, I tell you what."

"Little guys?" I croak. Oh no they di-in't. "Excuse me, excuse me!" I say, pushing through. Balder's on the table, and people are lined up, throwing whatever they've got at him—knives, forks, coffee cups, rocks. One little girl hurls her waffle and it bounces off his round belly like a spongy boomerang.

"Two dollars a shot! All comers welcome!" Gonzo shouts. He's running between everyone, gathering money in Balder's Viking helmet.

"I cannot be injured, for I am Balder. . . ." A knife sticks into his arm, but he keeps going. "Son of Odin . . ." A fork lodges into his skull. "Brother of Hoor," he says, pulling them both out. "Immortal."

"Yeah? Let's just see about that." A guy in a mall security guard uniform pulls out his piece and shoots Balder in the chest. There's a gasp from the crowd. Instead of going down, Balder does a little dance.

"Boo-ya!" he says, and I'm pretty sure that's the original Norse.

"Well, I'll be," the mall guard says. Everyone claps and cheers.

"Two bucks!" Gonzo insists, pocketing greenbacks from the shooter.

"Okay, show's over!" I announce, running up and yanking Balder off the table. "You've been great. Be sure to come out and see our show at the monster wrestling truck arena this weekend. Thank you. Thanks so much. Thank. You." As the breakfasters settle back at their tables, I level a sharp gaze at both Gonzo and Balder. "Way to keep a low profile, guys."

"He started it," Gonzo grumbles.

Balder gives me one of his courtly bows. "I did not mean to cause trouble, Cameron the Noble."

"When I said 'bond,' I meant, like, tell some stories, trade a few fart jokes, draw pictures of the waitress with a mustache. Not cause a scene."

"Look how much cash we got, though." Gonzo shows me Balder's helmet full of green. They're both so excited, it's impossible to be mad at them anymore.

"All right. Okay. But don't do that again. Look, let's just pay the check and—" I smell an acrid stench that makes my eyes water. There's something familiar about it. "Do you smell that?" I ask, goose bumps rising on my arms.

"Smell what?" Gonzo asks.

Wispy black smoke slithers across the floor and coils around my legs, and they start trembling. My body feels as if it's on fire. My throat muscles clench.

"Guys . . . ," I croak.

"Cameron?" Gonzo asks, his eyes full of concern.

"It's them," I manage, just as the kitchen doors are blasted off their hinges with the force of an explosion. The fire giants have found us.

"This part of the wrestlin' show?" a man at the next table asks his friends.

A second explosion rocks the Konstant Kettle. People scream as debris rains down and flames pop from the walls. But I can see they're more than flames; they're ginormous, burning men with black holes for eyes and mouths made of sharp, flickering teeth. They're fast and determined and

271

merciless, and they bring chaos in their wake. With glee, the fire giants leap from the walls and land wherever they like, smashing tables, kicking chairs, ripping up flooring; everything they touch burns down to ash. Two of the creatures crawl along the ceiling, biting into it with their teeth, tearing huge holes in the cheap white acoustic tiles. The place fills with choking smoke. Mothers grab children; truckers leave their All-U-Can-Eat Freedom Pancake Towers untouched; the waiters and busboys abandon the kitchen and coffee stations and run for the safety of the exits, screaming in panic.

"Cameron! Dude! We gotta get out of here!" Gonzo's offering me his hand, but I can't move. My legs won't work.

The smoke parts, and the Wizard of Reckoning gleams in the firelight like some cyborg knight, a black cape fluttering behind him. He's added a cape, cheeky bastard. He seems taller and stronger than the last time we met. My brain's saying run but my body won't translate the command. The wizard points right at me, and my stomach goes into free fall. Leg muscles jerk and twitch and tighten up completely, and I crumple to the floor.

"Cameron! Get up, dude!" Gonzo shouts.

Using my arms, I drag myself under the table and hug my knees to my chest, struggling for breath. Across the restaurant, the Wizard of Reckoning peels his space suit from his chest. In the center is a big black abyss, and I feel like I'm being pulled in.

"No," I croak. "Not yet." I close my eyes tight, trying to resist the pressure squeezing me on all sides.

And then, I feel nothing.

Open my eyes, and I'm lying in the grass blinking against the light of the sun. The choking smoke is gone. In fact, the air smells sweet. Really sweet. Like flowers. I sniff in a big noseful of it.

"That's lily of the valley you smell. Delightful, isn't it?"

"Ahhhhh!" I scream. I sit up quickly and scramble backward on my hands, spider style. My eyes do a quick inventory: flowers, grass, paper lanterns, bright sun overhead. And a few feet away is the old lady from the hospital. She's still in her gown with her tags around her wrist, but now she's also wearing a wide-brimmed sun hat and a cow-hide-patterned apron. She snips at things in her garden with a pair of long, thin shears.

"What's going on? Where am I?" I gasp.

The old lady smiles and opens her arms wide. "This is the place I told you about—my house by the sea."

"What? This is crazy—two seconds ago, I was in a restaurant and it was burning and . . ." I hear it. The sea. I turn around. Behind me is a two-story farmhouse overlooking a calm ocean. The waves lap the rocky shore, back and forth, back and forth, making me sleepy. Peaceful.

"For lo, the winter is past, the rain is over and gone; the flowers appear on the earth." The old lady scrutinizes me. "You've got a spot of jelly on your cheek, dear."

I wipe at my face. "Okay, seriously? I'm starting to freak out."

"No need for that," she says, and hums to herself. "The Copenhagen Interpretation. I just love them! I hear they're Inuits?"

"I . . . I left my friends in the diner with the fire giants and the freaking wizard."

"Agents of chaos," she snaps. "Oh, these are frightening times. Are you sure you're all right, dear?"

"I'm so tired. Just want to sleep."

The old lady purses her lips as she flattens out the long stem of one weed, trying to figure out where to make the cut. "You could do that. There is a bed right upstairs with a window that looks out on the sea. Very good for sleeping. But I thought you were searching for that doctor, the one with the cure for what ails you."

"Dr. X?" I murmur. Sleep sounds so nice right now. "Yeah. I'm supposed to find him. That's what Dulcie told me."

The old lady cuts the stem and the weed shrivels up and dies. Something else comes up right away, a blue flower. "Well, you could stay here, if you like. Get off the road. Go to the beach. Or we could make waffles. I adore waffles, do you?"

"Waffles are good," I say.

"They didn't have waffles in that wretched hospital. Just that damn gluey oatmeal," she snipes.

"The thing is, I'm supposed to save the universe, 'cause it . . . it needs saving," I say, but I'm so exhausted. "Maybe just a quick . . . nap."

I lay my head down in the soft grass and go to sleep. At one point, I open my eyes, and I'm back in my bed at St. Jude's, the TV showing the coyote chasing the roadrunner, the numbing hum of the respirator and feet padding down corridors filling my ears. I drift back into sleep. But in my dream, I see Gonzo and Balder back in the diner, trying to fight off the fire giants and the Wizard of Reckoning by themselves, and I think, *I'm the one who got them into this mess. I can't sleep; I have to go back.*

I wake with a start. The old lady's still tending her garden. "Feeling better, dear?"

"Yeah," I say.

"Did you make up your mind about those waffles?" she asks, examining another long vine, her scissors paused above it.

"I can't," I say. "I have to get back to my friends."

The old lady lets the vine spring back and moves on to another. "Very well. Another time. Oh, my dear, I left my watering can over there. Could you bring it to me?"

"Where?"

She waves in the direction of the green fields. "Out there. You'll find it."

Tromping through the tall grass, I'm stopped in my tracks by the sight of a roadrunner. It's standing there calmly, just watching me.

"Hey," I say, inching closer. "Hey there, little fella."

The minute I get close enough to touch it, the roadrunner takes off. It stops about a hundred yards away and looks back at me, like it's waiting for me to come after it.

"I'll be right back with that can!" I yell.

The old lady keeps singing her song, something about sand castles and ninjas. I chase after the roadrunner, going faster and faster, reaching my hand out to touch its feathers. My fingers close around air, and I hit the ground hard, coughing and hacking as the dirt fills my mouth like smoke.

"Cameron! Cameron!" Gonzo's holding a wet napkin to his mouth with one hand and trying to pull me out from under the table with the other. "Come on, *cabrón*—move your bony ass!"

I give one good cough. My legs finally get the command and I push out of there with enough force to take Gonzo with me.

"Where's Balder?" I scream.

"I don't know!"

"I am here!" The world's most badass Viking yard gnome is on the counter by the cash register using a dinner plate as a shield and a steak knife as a sword. "No doubt Loki has sent this treacherous wizard and his dragons to test me," he shouts. "Fear not! I will slay them all and use their bones to adorn my table at Breidablik before I would allow them to harm you, noble Cameron!"

"I'm here, too, you know!" Gonzo shouts.

"Live to fight another day, my friend," I say, grabbing him and pushing through the door into the smoky parking lot. People race away from the burning restaurant, searching for a safe spot in the madness. The sky's unnaturally dark. Lightning boxes the clouds with quick uppercuts of electricity. Howling, the fire giants stretch over the top of the restaurant and beat their chests in triumph.

Just then, an enormous boom rattles the entire parking lot, and everything—the Konstant Kettle, the Mister Motel, the cars and trucks—is sucked into the swirling black hole above. The sky closes. There's nothing left but flames and smoke and bystanders, and curiously, the restaurant's collection of snow globes.

Across the freeway, the freaked-out patrons of the Konstant Kettle wave down cars, yelling for help. We run as fast and as far as we can, until we're about a mile down the road. In the distance, a fleet of fire trucks screams toward the big orange fireball that used to be a restaurant. The Kettle is Konstant no more.

Gonzo comes toward me, wild-eyed. He makes a time-out T with his hands. "Okay. Pause game: what the hell just happened?" He's panting.

"From the depths of Hel," Balder whispers.

"That guy was the same one we saw in New Orleans," Gonzo continues. "What's he doing here with those creepy fire acrobats? And don't tell me this is about some old dead jazzman's gambling debts, 'cause I ain't buying that *mierda* anymore."

"I—I think they're following us." I'd cry, but I'm too scared.

Gonzo puts his inhaler so far into his mouth I think he's going to eat it. "Holy Shithenge," he says when he can talk again. "Why? What did you do to piss them off? Whatever it was, tell them you're sorry!"

Balder strokes his beard. "This is some treachery brought about by Loki, I've no doubt. The trickster god is ever in play and will do his part to bring about the twilight of the gods."

"You are freaking me out, gnome man!" Gonzo screeches.

"Chill, both of you." Another siren wails past us on its way to the fire. I take a deep breath, try to calm myself. "He's called the Wizard of Reckoning, and those guys with him are the fire giants. They're not from this world. They got here through the wormhole Dr. X opened up. They are the dark energy that's going to destroy the world. I think they're following us to Dr. X's secret location, because he's the only one who can close the portal. They take him out first, it's game over for everybody."

Gonzo takes another puff on his inhaler.

"That's why we have to find Dr. X as soon as possible," I explain.

"This Dr. X will heal the rift and make it all better, as you say?" Balder asks.

"Absolutely," I promise.

Gonzo reaches into his pack and comes up with a bottle of SPF-to-the-tenth-power lotion. He rubs a big dollop on his face; it leaves big white streaks under his eyes. "Hold up—how do you know all of this is true?"

"Dulcie told me."

Gonzo laughs. "Oh sure, right. It must be true because you heard it from the hot angel who *lives in your head*! For all we know, she's the one bringing the end of the world," Gonzo says.

"She's not."

"Ha!" Gonzo starts throwing stuff into his pack. "You know what? Forget this, yo. I'm-a call my mom as soon as I can get to a working phone."

"She doesn't live in my head. She's real," I say, but I don't know if I'm trying to convince Gonzo or myself.

"Yeah? So how come she doesn't come around?" Gonzo puts his hands on either side of his mouth and calls out, "Paging all supernatural chicks with wings! Conference on the side of the road near the burning pancake palace!"

"Fuck you."

"Whatever," Gonzo snaps right back. "I'm just saying, it's hard to believe in all this crazy without a little proof."

Proof. The MP7 player in my pocket.

"You want proof? You got it." I pull it out, find the link, and press Play. But where Dr. X used to be is just white noise, followed by the vacation footage of Disney World. Gonzo makes a disgusted laugh deep in his throat. Even Balder's looking at me with a mix of wariness and pity.

"It was here. I swear it." I press Play again and again, but it's gone.

Gonzo's gaze is steely. "I didn't have to come, but I did. But you told me there was something in it for me, too, and so far, amigo, I got a lot of trouble and no payoff. Tell me why I should stick this out."

"Because Cameron is our brother, our friend, and we do not abandon our friends," Balder chides.

"Thanks, man," I say.

"No matter if he has lost his wits completely and speaks like one whom the dogs should tear asunder in a mercy killing," Balder continues. "This is a quest. I pledged my loyalty to Cameron back on the cul-de-sac. I shall see it through till the end."

The way he says "end" makes me feel all wonky inside.

Gonzo just stands there, staring at the burning diner in the distance. He has every right to call his mom and head back to Texas, but I hope he won't. The truth is, I've kind of gotten used to his neurotic weirdness, and I'd miss it if he left. Maybe that's what real friendship is—getting so used to people that you need to be annoyed by them.

"I'll tell you what, *pendejo*," Gonzo says. "We better invest in some adult diapers, 'cause if those freaks show up again, I'm gonna need 'em."

I could almost hug him.

"Yeah, so, you know, let's kick some parallel-universe dark-energy ass and shit," he adds, trying not to look scared.

"A wise choice. But we must gain some protection against these travelers from Muspelheim and Niflheim. I shall cast the runes and seek their prophecy." Balder reaches beneath his tunic and pulls out the leather pouch.

Gonzo makes a face. "Dude, you weren't, like, keeping those in your pants this whole time, were you? I mean, use a wipe or something first. Damn."

Balder shakes the pouch till it clacks. Eyes closed, he grabs a rune, places it on the patchy ground. It's just a piece of rock etched with a symbol that reminds me of an "M" wearing a bra.

"Hmmmm." Balder strokes his beard. "Mannaz."

"What's that?" Gonzo says, his inhaler hovering near his

mouth again. "Is that some bad juju? Are we marked for death? Give it to me straight, Gnome-Man!"

"Man is the augmentation of the dust," Balder intones. "So says the rune."

"What the hell does that mean?" Gonzo asks.

"I cannot know, but I will invoke a prayer of protection for our journey. It is all I can do."

Balder chants something in a language I don't understand. The wind changes direction, bringing the smell of scorched earth mixed with spring flowers. Ragged streaks of smoke cut across the blue sky like the claw marks of some great beast. I don't see how we can possibly protect ourselves from something so totally random. There's no plan for something like that. "Shit happens" is more than just a T-shirt slogan.

"So . . . you think that'll help us out?" I ask hopefully.

Balder gathers his runes, hides the pouch again. "I believe as surely as I believe that *Ringhorn* is waiting for me and that I shall return to my home and the hall of the gods."

I sigh. "Your runes have any prophecy about how we get out of here?"

"I can't do another bus, dude. I'm nauseated just thinking about it," Gonzo says.

"Yeah, well, since we are currently wanted men, I think buses are a bad idea." I take a look around, trying to get our bearings, but there's not much help—highways, faceless industrial complexes, gas stations. A green and white road marker points the way to Bifrost Road under the overpass. "Gonzo, how much money do you have?"

He pulls out wads of crumpled bills he collected from the patrons of the Konstant Kettle and adds them to what he's got in his pocket. "Forty-eight dollars and . . . twenty-five"—he drops a penny—"twenty-four cents."

Adding that to my leftover two thousand nine hundred and ninety dollars of stolen drug money, we've got enough for plane tickets for sure. But Gonzo doesn't have a driver's license. No ID, no flying. And since Balder's too bulky to fit in the overhead bin, we'd have to check him as luggage. Crap.

High above the crisscross of highway, a murky rainbow shines under the wisps of smoke, staining the sky like an oil slick. It dead-ends in the distance near the rippling pennants of a car dealership. And then I remember the orange balloon in our room.

"Come on," I say, shouldering my backpack. "Screw mass transit. It's time we got ourselves some wheels."

CHAPTER THIRTY

In Which We Buy a Car and the Gnome Gets a New Outfit

We have to use fifteen dollars of our precious cash to cab it across those highways to Arthur Limbaud's lot. The place is huge—acres of cars with prices shoe-polished across the windshields. Nothing as low as what we need, though. It's looking grim. We make our way to the low concrete building in the center. It's decorated with colorful plastic flags that flap in the breeze, going round and round like the blades of windmills. Inside the showroom, beautiful shining cars sit on raised, revolving platforms. These are the Don't Even Look Because You Can't Afford Us cars. A tall man in a Western-cut suit, cowboy boots, and a cowboy hat strides over. His face is weathered as an old map, lines everywhere. He's got a solid black mustache and a toothpick poking out of the side of his mouth, which he works with his tongue, rolling it back and forth. "Hi-dee," he says, shaking my hand hard. "Arthur

Limbaud—that's an 'O,' not an 'aw' by the way. Welcome to Limbaud's Resale Beauties: Every Car a Beauty. That's our motto. What kin I do fer you, gen'lemen?"

"Well," I start.

"You two boys going somewheres special? Let me guess, you just gradjeeated high school and now you wanna see this fine country of our'n? Am I right?"

"Yes, sir," I say, copping my best Eagle Scout imitation. "You are right."

"Well, ain't that grand. Where you headed first?"

I say "Montana" at the same time that Gonzo says "Florida."

"It's a long trip," I say.

"Well, that's mighty fine, mighty fine." Arthur smiles with the toothpick between his teeth, which are the color of nicotine stains. "What kind of beauty did you have in mind?"

"We're sort of on a budget," I say, hoping he doesn't laugh and throw us out when he hears what we've got to spend.

"We work with all kinds here, son. No budget too small."

"We need something for under three thousand dollars . . . ," I say, watching Arthur's smile fade. "Or so."

"Three thousand, huh?" he says, letting out a long whistle that vibrates the toothpick in his mouth.

"Or so," Gonzo adds.

"That do put me in a bit of a pickle," Arthur says, shaking his head sadly. "But seein' as you boys got your hearts set on seein' the country, and since I were a young man myself once, lemme see what I kin do fer ya. Hold on."

"Why don't you just fax our itinerary to the police?" I say to Gonzo as Arthur disappears into the office.

"Sorry," he says.

"Could you get me one of those free Danish?" Balder asks.

He's propped up on the hood of a shiny pick-up truck like a bizarre cross between a hood ornament and a traffic-accident victim. I bring him a Danish and some strong black coffee with nondairy creamer that freckles the surface with little white marks. It looks diseased, but Balder drinks it anyway.

"I hope you can hold your coffee, yard gnome, because we're not stopping," Gonzo says.

"I'm the one who's clever enough to eat the free food before we get on the road."

"You don't know how long those things have been sitting there," Gonzo says with a shudder. "Or who's been touching them. They're like little pastries of salmonella."

Balder licks a big dollop of cream cheese out of the middle. "Ummm."

Gonzo pales. "You're one sick dude."

Arthur returns. I grab Balder and shove the rest of the Danish in my own mouth. I feel him sigh under my arm.

"Weeeell now, boys, never let it be said that Arthur Limbaud wouldn't work for his money. I looked at my records and it jes' so happens that I got a car might work out, a very special ve-hicle. It's a rehabbed Caddy called the Cadillac Rocinante. Boys, they do not make cars like this anymore. I mean that—they stopped production on 'em back in 'sixty-eight. She's a special car, yessir. And she can be all yourn for . . . what'd you say you had? Four thousand dollars?"

"Three thousand," I remind him.

Arthur points his toothpick at me. "A smart bidnessman. I like that. Three thousand dollars it is." Arthur M. Limbaud's dry, cracked face spreads into a grin that makes the short black hairs of his mustache stand at attention. "Son, you have got yourself a deal."

This means for sure we are buying a piece of shit that no

one else would touch. I don't care if it's held together by spit and rubber bands. I just need something that costs less than three thousand dollars and can get us to Florida in one piece.

"Sounds great," I say. "Uh, can we see it?"

"Getting there, buckaroo. It's a process." Arthur puts his arm around me. "See, son, when I sell somebody a car, I feel like I'm sellin' 'em a little piece of me. I'm like their daddy. So, seein' as that's how I feel, I'm gonna take the liberty of givin' you some father-son advice. You ready for me?"

"Yes, sir."

Arthur lets his tongue twirl the toothpick in his mouth for a full ten seconds. With tobacco-stained fingers, he pulls it out and pokes it at me. "A car is a lot like a woman. If you treat her right, give her what she needs when she needs it, she'll get you where you're going and not give you a peep of trouble. But if you treat her bad, she'll cut out on ya. You unnerstand me?"

That's it? That's his father-son advice? Christ.

"Yes, sir. Got it."

"Fine, fine." He claps, then rubs his hands together. "All-rightythen. Let's go see your beauty."

He leads us out through rows of gleaming cars with their orange advertising balloons tied to the windshield wipers. Gonzo looks hopefully at each car, expecting the next one to be it. I've got Balder in my arms.

"What's that there, yer mascot?" Arthur asks, pointing to Balder.

"Sort of," I say.

"Cute little feller."

Arthur turns a corner and we're on a second lot tucked away behind a service garage. The cars here are like the kids who never get adopted on those TV news programs, the ones who've been shut away in Romanian orphanages their whole lives. Arthur takes us to the very end of the lot, where a big boat of a car sits. It's a sort of gold color sprayed over a light blue, with dents in the passenger side door. On the front hood where an ornament should be sits a pair of large cattle horns. They've been rigged to the front with wire. It makes it seem like the car has a mustache.

"Gen'lemen—the Caddy Rocinante!" Arthur pries open the passenger door with a loud creak. "Slide on in. Feel 'er out, boys."

We crawl in and settle back against the cracked vinyl seats. The foam padding's coming out in spots. This car has the vehicular equivalent of mange. And an oversized boom box has been affixed to the dashboard by the previous owners. But the giant steering wheel's solid in my hands, and I love looking out past the cattle horns at the sun sparkling in bursts off the hoods of other cars.

Arthur hands me the keys. "Start 'er up."

The Rocinante grumbles, wheezes, shakes, and finally purrs into service. I've never had my own car.

"How's she feel?" Arthur shouts over the engine.

"Awesome," I say, enjoying the vibrations under my fingers.

"Dandy," Arthur says. "We're all set for the paperwork."

Reluctantly, I cut the engine and slide out. Arthur takes the keys again. "I just need your license and a parent to cosign."

"Y-you do?" I stammer. "My parents are dead."

Arthur's mustache twitches. The toothpick rolls from one side of his mouth to the other. "We-eee-lll, son, we got ourselves a sitchooashun. You ain't a legal adult, and I can only sell to legal parties."

286

Without the Caddy, we're stuck hitching or trying to get on a bus or train, where we are sitting ducks for every cop with a scanner. We need this car.

Balder waves his arm over Mr. Limbaud. "These Star Fighters are not worth the trouble," he says in a weird, artsy-fartsy voice. "You will help them escape."

Arthur's toothpick falls out of his mouth. "Did that thing just talk?"

"I . . . he . . . um," I sputter.

Balder closes his eyes and lifts a hand. "Let them go."

"Holy moley! How'dyoo get him to do that?"

"He's a . . . toy," I improvise. "A prototype."

"Well, I'll be damned," Arthur says. "What else does he say?"

"Uh, here," I say, pushing an imaginary button in Balder's back.

"Who's your Caddy!" he says, bright and chirpy.

Arthur's eyes grow to the size of quarters. He laughs, slapping his knees. "Who's your Caddy! Now don't that beat all!"

"Every Jeep's cheap!" Balder chirps.

"Amazing," Arthur says. That sharky mind of his is circling something.

"Oh yeah," Gonzo adds. "You can get 'em programmed to say all kinds of things."

"No kidding? Say, listen. I might be able to forget you're not eighteen if you could leave me this guy. Somethin' like 'is would bring in all sorts of customers. We could do commercials!"

"This one's not quite right yet," I say. "Few bugs in the system."

Arthur's face goes mean. "Well, that's a gall-darn shame. You boys sure woulda looked fine in that Caddy."

287

"You can get another! You can get another!" Balder says in his adopted parrot voice.

"Right! I can send you a brand-new one as soon as I get to Montana. To my dad's workshop. My dead dad's workshop. His workers are still there. Working. Then you can program it to say things in your voice."

"Well now. That is a fine idea. Gen'lemen, you got yourselves a car."

Ten minutes later, with the papers signed and the money in his yellowed fingers, Arthur shows us back out to the lot and the Caddy's brought round. A secretary wiggles out of the front seat. She's all in pink, like somebody who got stuck in a cotton-candy machine for a night.

"Here you go, now," she says, dropping the keys in my hand. "Y'all be careful."

Arthur takes hold of her arm. "Carol, hold on a minute. You have got to see this. These fellas have a toy—well, you just have to see it."

He pushes on Balder, hard, in the stomach. I can see that our gnomy friend is pissed. He's not going to talk. No way. But Arthur keeps pushing. "Come on, now. Say somethin', dammit!"

"Yeah, see, the bugs—" I start to explain.

"He was talkin' fine a minute ago. I'll get the sumbitch working."

Arthur picks him up and shakes so hard Balder's whole face flushes bright red. I can see from the set of Arthur's thin lips that he's determined. He's not letting our gnome down till he dances for Daddy. "Come on, now," he says, giving Balder one last, hard shake. "Do somethin' else, dangit!"

And that's when Balder pees on him.

* * *

288

We pull the Caddy into the parking lot of a Toys Mahal and duck inside. I stand guard while Gonzo rips open a Life-Sized Surfer Sammy box, switching out Balder's pee-wet pants for Sammy's black, neoprene surfer leggings complete with dragon etchings up the side. Some kid is in for a bad birthday.

"We're gonna get caught," Gonzo says, looking around like a man hunted.

"Not if you stay cool," I say.

"They'll take us to jail. It'll go down on our permanent records and we'll never go to college. We'll end up flipping burgers for the rest of our miserable, nonproductive lives."

"I'm almost in," Balder says. "There." He looks great. Like a guru of the lawn. "Take the board, too."

"That's stealing," Gonz argues.

"Who got you a Cadillac?"

"Give him the board," I say.

Balder hops on it, bending his knees, fighting imaginary waves. "Wicked."

"How did you get the idea to *Star Fighter* him?" Gonzo asks once we're on the road and sharing a drive-thru meal together in the front seat. "What if he'd seen the movie?"

"It was a calculated risk," Balder says. He's camped out in the spacious back like the king he thinks he is.

"How did you even know about *Star Fighter* in the first place?" Gonzo asks.

"One of my kidnappers was a devotee of science fiction. He took me to those—what are they called? Fields of battle where people dress as Visigoths and androids and those marauding teddy bears who are strangely lethal?"

"Teddy Vamps," Gonzo fills in. "Dude, you've been to all the cons! All right."

"Indeed. I have been photographed with the one they worship as a god, Silas, son of Fenton," he says, mentioning the name of the director revered by millions.

"Silas Fenton? You took a picture with Silas Fucking Fenton? Oh my God! Balder! You sly little kick-butt gnome. You are the man!"

Balder leans back against the seat, his arms behind his head. "Damn right."

We drive on, the Caddy and its bull-horn hood ornament cutting a colorful figure through the slick sedans and dime-a-dozen SUVs. Some little kids press their noses to the windows of their child-locked doors, gaping at us. Gonzo opens a bag of chips and hands it to Balder, who takes a handful and forwards it to Gonzo.

"Dude, I can't believe you whizzed on him."

Balder wipes his hands on the Sammy Surfer bandana he's now wearing around his neck. "He was very disrespectful. I have learned much in my current form. I have seen how those supposed to have no power can be disregarded quite easily. Just because I'm small doesn't mean I have no worth."

Gonzo nods. "Say what-what." He puts a stubby fist on the back of his seat rest.

"What-what," Balder says. He reaches up and bumps fists with Gonzo, and they go back to eating their chips in satisfied silence.

CHAPTER THIRTY-ONE

Wherein We Make Up Bumper Stickers and I Introduce the Joys of the Great Tremolo

We drive for miles. The Caddy takes us past ordinary sights that seem amazing and new glimpsed from open car windows on an unexplored road. Out in the fields that run alongside the endless highway, prisoners in orange scrubs that read PAS-SAMONTE CORRECTIONAL UNIT pick up trash with long pointed sticks and drop it into the huge Santa sacks tied to their backs. Parker Day's blindingly white teeth glare from a billboard for Rad Sport—OPTIMUM PERFORMANCE DEMANDS THE OPTIMUM SODA EXPERIENCE! Dogs stick their heads out to catch the breeze and we answer their howls with our own. An eighteen-wheeler rumbles by on the right, shaking the Caddy. UNITED SNOW GLOBE WHOLESALERS. FREEZING LIFE BEHIND GLASS. HOW'S MY DRIVING? CALL 1-800-555-1212. Above us, the clouds drift along in a blue, indifferent sea.

To pass the time, we make up bumper stickers and deliver them in movie trailer announcer voices.

"I thought I was having an existential crisis, but it was nothing."

"My honors student sells drugs to your honors student."

"I know you're stalking me."

"Please don't tailgate: body in trunk."

"Quantum physics has a problem of major gravity."

When we get hungry, we eat at greasy-spoon diners, where Balder and I order things with names like "The Count of Monte Cristo Sandwich" (a fried egg in a ham-and-toast "mask") and "Devil Dogs—hot dogs so good you'll swear you're sinning!" Gonzo always orders the grilled cheese. It's the only thing he deems safe.

We drive through interstate rainstorms that last all of ten minutes, like the weather's just in a bad mood. I like looking out through the metronome of the windshield wipers at the rain bouncing off the bull horns. When the storms pass behind us, the sun cuts through, and sometimes there's a greasy smudge of a rainbow.

At the Georgia-Alabama border, we park the car on the shoulder and Gonzo and I stand with one foot on either side of the WELCOME TO GEORGIA sign, just so we can say we were in two places at the same time. Then we hold Balder between us so he can say he did it, too. I like the way Georgia looks, so different from Texas. All those tall pine trees and that rich, red dirt, like the ground bled and scabbed over, like it's got a history you can read in the very clay.

We talk about stupid things, things that don't matter, like why no one ever has to go to the bathroom in action movies or what you'd do if you found a suitcase full of money. Gonzo wants to start a dwarf detective series called "The

Littlest PI" or "Dwarf of Destiny." Balder argues that you can never know about destiny: are the people you meet there to play a part in your destiny, or do you exist just to play a role in theirs? I tell them about my secret cartoon fantasy, the one where the coyote stops chasing the roadrunner, sells all his contraptions of death, buys a boat, and goes fishing instead.

What I don't tell them is that every time I look up at those frequent billboards for personal injury lawyers or HAMBURG-ERS NEXT FIVE MILES, I see the Small World characters smiling and waving me on. Marionette Balinese girls dancing. A Mexican boy in sombrero playing the guitar. The alligator with the umbrella. The Inuit fishing boy with his plastic fish.

It's tempting to say, "Hey, check it out—the animatronic Don Quixote on his wooden horse just winked at me."

But then they might not let me drive.

A Copenhagen Interpretation song comes on. Balder sings along.

"I didn't know you were a CI fan," Gonzo says.

"A most harmonious band," Balder says, air drumming. "They performed for my people at Breidablik."

Gonzo and I exchange glances.

"It's true!" Balder insists. "They fell from the sky with their odd instruments, and we feared that Ragnarok was upon us."

"Ragnarok." Gonzo makes a face. "Is that a musical festival?"

"The end of the world in Norse mythology," I say, remembering my mom's lessons. "The doom of the gods."

"They spoke a strange tongue, but their song was a charm against ill. While they played, peace reigned. Enemies stood as friends. The giants lay down in contentment. Even the Valkyries refused to choose the dead. We feasted. And then, the clouds opened once more. They were gone, leaving behind only the northern lights."

The sky's filling up with dark clouds. Time for an afternoon downpour. Cars flip on their headlights, bracing for the coming rain. Our rigged boom box flickers into a staticky symphony of pops, crackles, and occasional burps of words. With the precision of a code breaker, I turn the knob, listening for the sonar of life in the distance, happy when we get a sudden blurp of sound; it makes me feel like I'm moving toward something, that it's only a signal tower away and getting stronger.

"Could we please find something else? This is torture," Balder pleads.

"How do you feel about the Great Tremolo?" I ask.

"Is it static?"

"No, it's a CD," I say, feeling around on the front seat for the disc I burned.

Balder yawns. "Wonderful."

Gonzo does the honors, and soon, the car's thumping to the head-banging pleasure of Portuguese love songs on ukulele and recorder.

"What is this shit?" Gonzo asks, a smile tugging at his lips.

"The Great Tremolo. The master of love in any language."

The Great Tremolo starts to sing in his high, shaky falsetto and that's it. Gonzo is officially gone. He's crying he's laughing so hard, which of course makes me laugh, too. The Great Tremolo goes for a high note and we nearly piss our pants. Balder has chosen to ignore our immaturity. He's stretched across the backseat with his eyes closed, probably taking a little gnome snooze.

"Dude, where did you find this?" Gonzo chokes out.

I wipe away tears. "Wait—turn it up. This is his big ukulele solo!"

Gonzo slaps his leg, chortling. "He's tearing that uke up! Go, badass girly-singing man!"

"I bet the women throw their underwear," I crack.

"*I* want to throw my underwear! Pull over so I can take it off!"

A rumble of thunder rolls over us. The first big splats of rain hit the windshield, a heavy one, two-three. Four. The Great Tremolo sings out from the rigged boom box.

"Hey, Gonz, what's he saying?" I ask, catching my breath.

Gonzo snorts in disgust. "I don't know, man, it's Portuguese. I'm Mex-i-can?" he says, drawing it out. "This may come as a shock to you, *pendejo*, but not all brown people are the same."

"Sorry," I say. "I still wish I knew what he was saying." And for the first time, I really do.

"*Eu considerei a sua cara e sabia a felicidade,*" Balder murmurs from the backseat, his eyes still closed. "I looked upon your face and knew happiness."

Without further warning, the sky opens up and cries.

CHAPTER THIRTY-TWO

Of What Happens When We Take a Detour Through Hope (Georgia)

It's a soaking rain, and I decide it's better to pull off and wait it out rather than risk the Caddy's mostly bald tires on the slick highway. A sign advertising a rest area blinks white and blue in the gloom. And just behind that is a little white sign that says HOPE, GEORGIA, TWO MILES. There's a feather emblem next to it.

"Dude, why are we here?" Gonzo asks. "You know I was kidding about my underwear, right?"

"Just seems like a good place to wait out the rain," I say. I'm not mentioning the feather. Maybe it's the state mascot or something.

"Okay. I'm crashing. Wake me up if anything happens," Gonzo says, joining Balder, who's been snoring for the last half mile.

If I'm supposed to find something here, I can't imagine

what that could be. There's not much to Hope. It's a one-stoplight kind of town. They don't even have a strip mall, which I think might actually be against the law. I drive slowly past an old clapboard Church of the Nazarene. A closed gas station with a tire yard next door. A couple of houses tucked away far off the road so all I can see of them is a snatch of white or a glimpse of brick. The road veers off to the left and becomes a narrow lane that runs past a dilapidated hardware store with a chipped sign: PARTS SOLD HERE—NEW, USED, NECESSARY. And that's it. The street dead-ends at a guardrail and a wall of pine trees. There's an old man sitting on the front porch of the hardware store, his hands on his knees. I pull over and ask him how to get back to the interstate.

"What yo' lookin' fo' is just over yonder," he answers, pointing a shaky hand straight ahead at the DEAD END sign.

"There's no road there," I say.

"You can leave yo' car heah. Yo' friends be safe. You go on yonder, now. Got things to see."

"We really have to get back on the highway," I say, wishing Gonzo's door wasn't unlocked. "Thanks again. Have a nice day."

I step on the gas in reverse, and the Caddy shudders and dies.

The old man shuffles over and pops open the hood without even asking. "Go on, now. I'll take a look at yo' car."

For a second, I wonder if I should leave my friends here with a stranger. But this guy is eighty if he's a day. The worst he could do is take out his teeth and inspire us never to neglect our flossing.

I step over the aluminum guardrail and duck into the trees.

The rain's slowed to a blue-gray mist that sticks to my jacket. The ground's soft with pine needles and the occasional crunch of a cone. The air smells like it's just been born. Light bleeds through the spaces between the trees. At first, I think it's the sun coming out, but it's brighter, like someone just turned on the lights in a stadium. The water droplets on the trees; the brown carpet of pine needles under my feet; my jeans, shirt, and hands—everything glimmers in that strange white light, and then I see the small, worn path off to the right. I follow it through the maze of pines, the light getting stronger all the way, till I find the source of it—a ginormous ash tree, big as a house.

"Whoa," I murmur. The tree takes up the whole clearing. A tangle of branches sticks out in every possible direction, and every one of those branches is alive with about a million different scraps of paper.

"*Hola,* cowboy." Dulcie steps out from behind the tree. She glows like she's a part of it. I'm so happy to see her that I have the urge to scoop her up into a big bear hug, but I don't know if full-body contact with angels is cool or not, and it's not one of those things I feel like testing.

"*Hola* back. Where've you been?" I say instead.

"Places. Hey, what do you think of this, huh?" She pats the tree's milky-colored trunk.

I smirk. "It's called a tree. We have lots of 'em."

Dulcie arches an eyebrow, but that grin isn't far behind, and God, what is it about girls in general and this one in particular that I would sit in a room all day coming up with jokes just for another one of those funky smiles? "I promise you, cowboy, you haven't seen a tree like this one before. Take a closer look."

I finger one of the scraps of paper on a low-lying branch. On closer inspection, I see it's actually more like a leaf—like somebody stuck a note on the tree and it grew veins and bloomed there.

"Go on. Read it," Dulcie says.

The paper is so yellowed with age that I'm afraid it'll crumble in my hands. Even though I'm drenched, it's somehow dry. The handwriting's hard to make out.

"What does it say?" Dulcie asks.

"It says, *I wish to marry Tobias Plummer.*"

She nods. "Nice one. Read another."

I bend another leaf toward me. This one is fresher, and the words seem as if they've been printed out on a computer. *"I wish I could get a Game Guy for my birthday."*

"Huh," Dulcie says. "Good luck with that, kid." She plucks a paper leaf off.

"Should you be doing that?" I say, and just like that, it grows back.

One by one, I read them off:

I wish my daughter were cured of her sickness.

I wish I had a new job.

I wish the girl in fourth period at Bethel High School would notice me.

I wish I could feel the sun on my face. Nothing feels warm to me anymore.

I wish I knew what to wish for.

"What are these?" I ask, letting the branch snap back into place.

"Wishes. It's a wishing tree."

"A wishing tree," I repeat.

"It grants wishes," she says, like I should know this.

"So, what? People write out their hopes and dreams and

299

place them on the tree and the tree says, 'Poof! There you go. A big steaming plate of All Yours. Enjoy!'"

Dulcie wobbles her hand in an —*ish* motion. "Sort of."

"Sort of?"

"Sort of." Dulcie picks some pine needles out of her wings, which aren't decorated with flying cows or painted to look like Holsteins today. They're just normal. If wings can ever be considered normal. "I'm starving. You got any candy?"

I stick my hand in my pocket and come up with two Juicy Cute Bears stuck together like a candy sideshow act. "Just these guys."

"Fork 'em over. Minus the pocket lint."

I defuzz the bears, and Dulcie peels them apart, offers me one. When I decline, she pops the red one in her mouth and closes her eyes in a swoon. "God, I love sugar. Greatest invention ever."

"Getting back to the tree. 'Sort of' sounds pretty random, if you ask me."

"Well, you have to know what to wish for. Take this one." She plucks a wish from high on a branch. "*I wish I were famous*. Okay, first question: Why does this person want to be famous? To be worshipped? Adored? To get noticed? To make gobs and gobs of money? You have to look inside the wish and find the heart. So maybe what this person really wants, the heart of it, is to find somebody who adores her. She goes out to wherever it is people go to become famous and just gets knocked down and out and around like a pinball flipper. And one day, as she's walking on the beach totally bummed, this person comes along, and to him, she's a rock star. He adores her, and with him, she *feels* adored, famous. In a roundabout way, she's gotten what she really wanted. Wish granted."

The rain dribbles down again, hitting the ground in a soothing patter.

"What kind of self-help-philosophy-lite bullshit is that?" I ask. "Somebody puts her wish up here expecting to have it come true and this . . . *tree* makes a completely arbitrary decision about what may or may not be the 'heart' of the wish? That's retarded!"

Dulcie bites the head off the other Juicy Bear. "Your skepticism is duly noted."

"How about this? How about if the Wishing Tree grants people their freaking wishes exactly as they requested?"

"Doesn't work that way." She picks some Juicy Bear out of her back teeth.

"Well, the way it works is stupid."

Dulcie looks at me—I mean really looks at me. It's like she's seeing straight through to my cells. "No guts, no glory, cowboy," she says quietly.

"What do you mean?"

"Make a wish. See if it comes true."

She comes nearer, and I can smell her along with the rain and the pine. She has a scent that's familiar and comforting, like all the things you wish you could take with you on your travels to make you feel less alone. Dulcie tilts her face up to mine. Her eyes remind me of the ocean in winter—gray, stark, a calm surface hiding a serious undertow; something you only go into if you're sure you can handle it, and if you can't, well, too late now.

"I . . . um, I don't have any paper," I say.

She leans in. Her whisper warms my ear. "Pocket."

"Huh?"

She hops over a twig, balances on one foot. "That thing at the back of your pants."

301

I reach into my back jeans pocket and find Junior Webster's cryptic note to me: *to live*.

"Pen?" I say.

She hops to the other foot. "I don't do pens. You've got one in your jacket. It's leaking."

A large inky splotch stains the left side of my Windbreaker. Annoyed, I wipe the pen off and sit on the only dry patch of ground. For the longest time, I listen to the soft percussion of the rain while trying to word my wish airtight. None of that "I want to be famous and instead I get a guy on the beach" crap for me.

"How ya doin'?" Dulcie asks. She's stretched out on a branch Cheshire-cat style.

"Do you mind? I'm thinking. This is for the big money."

She spreads her hands in a no harm, no foul gesture. "Don't let me rush genius."

Finally, I write down the only thing I can think of and stick it on a branch. My wish disappears into the tree, and a baby leaf pokes out. In the veined paper, I can see the words struggling to be born.

Dulcie hops down. "What did you wish for?"

"Use your X-ray heat vision super angel powers to find out."

"Just a messenger, remember?" Dulcie winks. "Well, whatever it is, I'm sure it'll come true."

"Sort of," I say.

"Sort of."

Suddenly, she reaches her arms around my neck and just as quickly, she jumps back. I feel the empty space between us like an extra person.

"Got it!" she says, waving something in her hand. It's a really old one. A last plea to the universe from some weary

302

traveler passing through Hope on the road to wherever he's going.

"Ah," she says, smiling. "Now, this is brilliant."

She opens her palm, exposing the heart of some anonymous desire to me.

It reads only, *I wish* . . .

CHAPTER THIRTY-THREE

In Which I Pick Up a Necessary Part

I don't know how long I sit with Dulcie. Time seems elastic there under the Wishing Tree. We play charades, which are an exercise in the completely indecipherable and unintentionally hilarious. Mostly, Dulcie hops and twirls and makes wide-eyed faces that, I learn, could stand for anything from Bolshevik Revolution to aurora borealis. My body feels loose and light from laughing. A few feet away, Dulcie totters around like a cat with something on its tail.

"Alcoholic ballerina!" I shout, and she rolls her eyes. "Blowfish in a death spiral! The reason the dinosaurs are extinct!"

She stops, hands on her hips, and blows a lock of hair from her forehead. "Falling star!"

"Wow. You officially suck at this game. I just pwned an angel at charades. Go, me."

Two of the paper leaves drop to the ground. The ends curl up and decompose.

"What just happened?" I ask.

Dulcie plops down next to me. "Those wishes have been granted. Sort of."

There's something that's been nagging at me for the past hundred miles or so.

"Dulcie . . . ," I start. "What happens once I find Dr. X and he cures me and the wormhole is closed?"

Her eyes are closed, her head back. "The world is saved, and you are cured. Huzzah!"

"Yeah, I know. But, like, what happens to you? Do you stay here or go back to wherever it is you're from? Will I ever see you again?"

She jumps up suddenly. "Hey, wanna see me pretend to be an ice sculpture? I'm really good at it. Watch this." She stands perfectly still, hands pressed together, her left foot balanced against the inside of her right knee. "You kinda have to imagine the caviar in small bowls around my feet."

"You're avoiding the question."

"No," she says, dropping the pose. "I'm avoiding the answer."

"I just wanted to know what's next," I say.

"You people slay me," she says with a laugh, and there's an edge to it. "Always worrying, 'What will happen? What's next?' Always everywhere but where you actually are. You just don't get it."

"Get what?"

"Here. Now. This." She gestures wide, turns around. "This is it, cowboy. The whole ride. Pay attention."

"Thanks for enlightening me with your advanced angel wisdom," I snipe.

"Whatever's needed," she says, without a trace of sarcasm.

The rain picks up again. In the blink of an eye, Dulcie's stretched out on a branch above me, shielding me from the damp with a wing.

"Nice umbrella," I say.

"Like I said, whatever's needed."

My dreams kaleidoscope in and out of each other. I'm lying in my hospital bed, listening to the whirr of a respirator, Glory marking something on my chart. I'm in that house by the sea, listening to the tide come in, while the old lady arranges her lilies in a vase. Back to the hospital room, Mom and Dad reading, the TV on, forgotten, Parker Day hosting a game show. The old lady's house, a closed door. "Want to see inside?" she asks, her hand on the tarnished knob. I shake my head. She smiles, takes her hand away. "Some other time."

I'm with Dulcie. I can't hear what I've said, but she laughs. She's beautiful.

Something goes wrong. The Wizard of Reckoning grabs hold. Dulcie's arms reach out for mine, but I can't get to her. A dark hole opens in the sky, and they're pulled inside.

The fire giants lay waste to everything in their paths, and when everything's gone, they open their jagged mouths wide, one last time, and blow, engulfing me in flame.

When I wake, the woods are calm and quiet, sweet with pine. Dulcie's gone. A feather rests on my thigh. Nothing's written on it. It's blank and fresh as new snow. I bring it to my nose and breathe in her scent.

* * *

The rain has stopped by the time I get back to the Caddy where Gonzo and Balder are still crashed out and snoring away. The old man calls to me from his rocking chair on the front porch. "Got yo' car workin' fine now. Jes' needed a lil rest."

"Thank you. Um, how much . . ."

"Nevah mind that, young fella. I got som'm you need. Step on in heah."

He hobbles into the shop and the chair goes on rocking. There's nothing to do but follow him. If this shop has anything that anyone from the last century needs, I will be shocked. A layer of dust an inch thick covers every surface. The walls are filled with mismatched bins and worn storage drawers. Above each one are plates that say NEW or USED or, more mysteriously, NECESSARY. The old man shuffles along, peering at the titles, searching for something. Occasionally, he makes little sounds under his breath—"hmmm" or "uh-uh" and once an exasperated "Now, that ain't it."

The sun's starting to come out. Shafts of light break through the windows and into the dark aisle, sending the dust particles swirling. They're sort of beautiful illuminated like that. In the light, they seem like they're rising, coming together to form their own tiny Milky Way. The dust moves like it has a purpose, somewhere it wants to go.

"Heah we are," the old man says. He's standing in front of a bank of card-catalog-sized drawers with tiny knobs. The sign above them says NECESSARY. He lets his gnarled fingers drift from drawer to drawer until finally he finds the one he wants.

"Umm-*hmm*. *Ummm*-hmmm," he mutters, opening the drawer and peering in. He pulls out a long, slightly rusty screw. "Things have a way of turnin' up when you need 'em," he says in that long, slow drawl of his. He hobbles over to the counter, where he grabs a rag and works some grease onto the screw's threads. "You evah hear of a magic screw?"

I cough back a laugh. "No. No, sir."

"Weeelll, you lookin' at one. This lil thing got the power to change a life." He holds the screw up to the light to inspect it. "Jes' about right."

The thing looks like a tetanus infection waiting to happen. It sure as hell doesn't look magical.

"Hol' out yeh hand, boy," he says.

Oh fuck me, how did I get into this mess? Am I going to end up bleeding on an ER gurney while sympathetic nurses shake their heads and cluck, "Oh yeah, Pops the Impaler. We all know about him"? Is he one of those sick guys with a basement full of crawl spaces and human organs in pickle jars?

"I said, hol' out yeh hand." Pops stares at me through his bottle-thick glasses. The lenses make his eyes huge, like some prehistoric insect.

"Why?"

"If yeh don't put yo' hand out, you ain't gonna find out, now, is yeh?" He doesn't sound angry or impatient, just matter-of-fact, like it's the simplest choice in the world: you either go for it or you don't.

Slowly, I put out my hand, palm up.

"Now close yeh eyes," he drawls.

My hand snaps back by my side. "Close my eyes? Why?"

"Don't work les' you close 'em. Jes' the way it is."

Right. It would make it a whole lot easier for you to *drive that screw through my head* if I were to close my eyes, too. My feet start their backward walk. "This was really nice of you, but I should probably take off. . . ."

Pops shakes his head. "Son, if you cain't put a little faith in people, how you evah gon' git where you goin'?"

"Look, no offense, mister, but I don't know you. . . ."

"Yeah, no shit, boy. 'N I don't know you." He gives the screw one more rub with the rag. "That's why they call it trust. Now, you in or you out?"

I should just take off, get back in the car and get on the road instead of arguing with some old geezer in a broken-down hardware store about the nature of trust. But then I think of the feather emblem on the exit marker. I walk back, put out my hand again, and close my eyes, and Pops places the screw gently in my upturned palm. He covers my hand with his. His skin is leathery and warm. He's mumbling something, I can't tell what. The mumbling stops.

"This is a necessary part of your destiny. It's in your hands now. Use it well, son. You kin open yo' eyes."

I do as he says. The old man's gone and there's an old screw in my hand. It doesn't shine or sparkle or do funny tricks. I don't understand how it could be a necessary part of anything, except maybe a future bookshelf or CD rack.

Signs. Random coincidences. Trust.

I put the screw in my pocket and head out to the car.

CHAPTER THIRTY-FOUR

Which Treats of What Happens When There Is a Bounty on Our Heads and We Visit Putopia

I don't tell Gonzo and Balder about the Wishing Tree or the weird hardware store and the magic screw that's a "necessary part" of my destiny somehow. I don't want them to think I'm unraveling fast. I'd rather just freak out about that possibility solo.

Plus, my E-ticket's losing health power. Adventureland and Frontierland are gone, and the third line, Liberty Square, is fading fast. If we don't find Dr. X soon, I'm toast.

Near the outskirts of Florida, we stop to get gas. The Caddy eats a lot of it, probably getting about fifteen miles to the gallon. Efficient it is not. The guy inside rings me up. A TV above his head is fixed on an all-news channel. They're showing that WANTED flyer with the high school pictures of Gonzo and me. My legs go a little wobbly as they cut to a shot of the Church of Everlasting Satisfaction and Snack 'N' Bowl. Daniel's and Ruth's faces fill the screen. Daniel's not in mellow, don't-hurt-your-happiness mode, I can tell that much. He's practically snarling. The newscaster puts the mike in his face, and Daniel doesn't waste a minute.

"These guys are definitely armed and dangerous and on some kind of mission of total anarchy!" Daniel growls.

"They broke our smoothie machine!" Ruth interjects.

"They came in here with the full intention of disrupting our way of life, and of sowing the seeds of dissent and dissatisfaction in our community."

The camera goes to a wide shot of the parking lot, where a mob of kids pumps their fists. They hold signs saying, NO MORE VANILLA! SHAKESPEARE, NOT SMOOTHIES! and IDEAS DON'T HURT PEOPLE, PEOPLE WITHOUT IDEAS DO!

The newscaster nods grimly and tries to do his wrap-up, but Daniel grabs the mike. His pissed-off face fills the screen. "Lock them up, man. Throw away the key."

There's a quick sound bite from the mall security guard standing in front of the scorched hole that was the Konstant Kettle. "They pretended they was wrestlers—that's how they distracted us while they set the bombs. . . ." His wife squeezes his arm. "Them people are terrorists. They got absolutely no regard for human life and property and rules. No regard."

Next, the camera swings back to the TV news studio and a logo for the United Snow Globe Wholesalers along with their 1-800 number. The anchorman reads a statement: "Terrorism will not be tolerated. That's why your friends at United Snow Globe Wholesalers are offering a bounty of ten thousand dollars for the capture of these threats to our security and happiness."

"That it? Just the gas?" the guy behind the register asks, making me jump.

"Yeah, thanks," I say, grabbing my change and running for the Caddy.

"What's the matter?" Gonzo asks when I throw the car into gear and peel out.

"Just the entire fucking world is looking for us, that's all," I say, glancing at the rearview mirror. "That little asshole Daniel is over his peace, love, and smoothie crap. He wants a piece of our butts and he's taking it to the media."

"Didn't I tell you he was a craptard?" Gonzo says, vindicated at last.

"We've got other stuff to worry about. There's a reward for our capture as wanted terrorists. Our pictures are all over the news with a hotline number to call."

"Shit," Gonzo says.

"Yeah, no kidding."

There is silence from the backseat and then I hear the smile in Balder's deep voice. "Cool."

We decide to stay off the highways and stick to the back roads. There's no such thing as a GPS in the Rocinante, so we've pretty much been navigating by a ten-year-old map in the glove compartment, which is sort of like trying to make your way by a What's My Future™ fortune-telling ball: Should we take this road? *I've got such a headache. Ask me later.*

The road bumps along past tall marsh grass, rusted signs, ancient churches with the windows broken out and the kudzu taking over, railroad tracks, old barns, and a couple of empty fields where a horse or two stand around looking bored. It just keeps going until I don't have any idea where we are anymore. Under my breath, I call Dulcie's name like

312

a prayer. *Come on, Dulcie,* I say. *Throw us a bone.* A few seconds later, the Caddy jerks and twitches to a stop.

"What just happened?" Gonzo asks.

"I don't know." I turn every switch and knob. The gas gauge is stuck at half a tank. I give it a thump with my finger and it falls to E.

"Dammit!"

"What?" Gonzo sounds panicked.

"We're out of gas."

"You're Shithenging me."

"I Shithenge you not."

"Enough riding. Time for the hunt." Balder's changed back into his Viking gear and is out of the car and making his way down the road before I can stop him.

"What the hell?" Gonzo asks.

I head after Balder. Gonzo yells from the passenger side, "Shouldn't we call Friendly Tow or something, dude? Get some roadside assistance?"

"Sure," I shout back. "Just tell them the wanted terrorists with the ten-thousand-dollar bounty on their heads need gas and maybe a lift to town."

"We've been walking for a good half hour and seen a big fat nothing to help us out," Gonzo gasps. "Plus, I've got a mammoth blister on my heel. Blisters can get infected, you know. You can die from that shit."

"Just keep looking for a gas station," I say.

"I'm just saying, I don't want to die from an infected blister. That would be such a lame way to go."

About half a mile down, the road forks. I wipe the sweat from my brow, cup a hand over my eyes to block the glare. "Which way? Anybody?"

Balder consults his runes. "Left."

"Fine. We go left," I say.

"You sure?" Gonzo asks.

"No," I answer. "I'm not sure of anything. So one road's as good as another."

Left we go over a path that's little more than packed dirt winding up a hill. Finally, we reach the top.

"Whoa," Gonzo says.

Down the hill is a field of mustard-colored wheat like brushstrokes in a painting.

Everywhere I look, there are wind turbines whirling against the clean blue of the sky like alien birds ready for takeoff, or takeover, whichever comes first. Smack-dab in the center are an old farmhouse, a barn, and what looks like a futuristic gas station.

Balder drops to one knee in prayerful thanks. "The Norn have favored us."

"Great. Let's see if they'll give us some gas."

Gonzo grabs my arm. "Are you out of your mind? Dude, didn't you see *Chainsaw Motel*?"

"If I say no does that mean you'll shut up?"

"*Chainsaw Motel,* quick plot summary," Gonzo continues. "Spring break camping trip, 'Oh, man, the truck's out of gas! Bummer! Hey, look—there's a creepy old bed-and-breakfast with a gas pump.' Crunch, crunch through woods to isolated, gnarly house. 'Knock, knock—hey, there's nobody home—oh, what's this weird chair made out of? Hey, it's made out of human skin! Rrrrrnnnnnnnnnn! Oh my God, he's got a chain saw—*Aaaahhhhhh! Rrrrrnnnnnnn!* Gratuitous blood spray. Dismemberment. Death. Freezers of college-kid limbs. More screaming. And one lone, blood-spattered, forever-scarred survivor, who will spend the rest of her miserable life in psychiatric care. Roll credits." Gonzo folds his arms over his chest.

"Wow. Maybe they have that on disc. We'll ask them."

I march toward the house, down a soft slope of clover and weeds. Gonzo darts in front of me, running serpentine style.

"Not doing this, Gonz," I say, dodging him.

He sticks out his hands, moving them in bad martial-arts-movie style. "Can't let you go in there, man."

"Shall I go forward, Cameron? I would be honored to face a chain saw on your behalf, may Tyr grant me courage," Balder says.

Gonzo practically pushes Balder forward. "Good idea. Balder can go. He can't die."

"Right. Great idea. We'll send the *yard gnome* to ask for gas. No offense, Balder."

Balder bows his head. "None taken."

"Look, I'm going to knock on that door and ask for help. You can come with me or go back and stay in the car. Your choice."

Gonzo sucks down a mouthful from his inhaler.

At the door, a black cat meows a hello and winds between my legs. "Don't start," I say to Gonzo.

"It probably feasted on human fingers this morning," he whispers.

The door opens and the cat darts inside. A kid stands there, a bowl of cereal in one hand. He's maybe about ten or eleven and wears a pair of small, round glasses. His wiry dark hair is sporting some serious bedhead cowlicks.

"Careful, he might be armed," Balder deadpans.

"Let's see if you end up keeping watch over a freezer of flesh, Gnome-Man."

"Hi," I say, ignoring them both. "Our car ran out of gas

out on the road, and I was just wondering if maybe your parents have some we could buy off 'em?"

"I don't have parents," the kid says in a soft, high voice. Milk dribbles from his cereal-full mouth down his chin. "I'm an orphan."

"Is there anybody else here, like an adult?" I ask.

The kid leaves the door standing open and we follow him into the dark house. The TV's on in the living room. The kid sits down cross-legged on a beanbag chair with the name ED stitched on it and goes back to eating cereal and watching cartoons. "They're downstairs in the basement."

"Oh hell no," Gonzo whispers.

"We're not staying," I remind him. "Just getting the gas and we're outta here."

"This way." Balder opens the cellar door, and we climb down in darkness, following a short, dimly lit passageway to a pretty serious-looking door made of stainless steel. A sign beside it reads ENTERING MAGNETIZED ZONE, PLEASE REMOVE ALL METAL.

Gonzo holds his inhaler close to his chest. "This is the part in the movie where I would haul ass."

We put everything with any metal into little plastic bags we find on a nearby table. I practically have to pry Gonzo's inhaler out of his hands. There's no bell or anything that I can see, so I just throw the door open.

"Whoa," I say.

"Seconded," Gonzo whispers.

Balder gasps. "What strange new world is this?"

We've stumbled onto what could be the world's most ginormous MegaMart, if the shelves of sweat-shop-produced T-shirts and cheap-ass plastic toys were replaced by masses of long blue and red tubes, big as waterslide tunnels and connected to an intricate maze of wires, gizmos, robotics, and computers. The place seems to stretch up fifty feet or more, like we're in an airplane hangar inside a silo, and it's got enough megawatts lighting it to give a space station lightbulb envy.

Dead center is a miles-long tunnel supported by metal beams stretching out on all sides like petals on a crazy daisy. And in the center of that is a strange, bumpy door that reminds me of a cross between a seashell and a pinwheel. Two guys and one woman in white lab coats and safety goggles are gathered around a table. A third guy is strapped to a chair, his head held by a steel band.

"I'm getting a serious dwarf-tossing vibe off these guys," Gonzo whispers.

"Would you chill?" I whisper back.

"I'm just saying, if anybody goes airborne here, it's not gonna be me."

I don't want to interrupt whatever experiment they're in the middle of, so I clear my throat and hope they'll notice. When they don't, I say, "Um, hello? Excuse me?"

"Be with you in a moment," calls an older man with a pompadour of white hair. "Ready, Dr. A?"

"Ready when you are, Dr. M," the guy in the chair with his head immobilized says.

"Very well. Calabi Yau!" the white-haired man shouts.

"Calabi Yau!" the others cheer just as he lobs a grape. The guy in the chair tries to grab it with his mouth and misses.

"Ah, Heisenberg!" the white-haired man exclaims. He turns around and takes notice of us for the first time. "Oh, hello. Are you here with the pizza?"

*   *   *

After we disappoint the scientists with the news that we're not the pizza delivery guys, they take us back to the house, and we explain that we've run out of gas and how important it is that we get back on the road because I've got mad cow disease and am on my way to be cured and that we'd be eternally grateful and blah-de-blah-blah.

"I'm afraid the only fuel we have is hydrogen. Your car isn't equipped for hydrogen cell, is it?" the smiling Dr. T says.

"Honestly? We're lucky our car has seats and tires," I say.

"Well, we'll get Ed to rig you a converter, then," Dr. T explains, hooking a thumb at the kid who let us in. "He'll have you on your way by tomorrow."

The kid, Ed, doesn't look up, just continues scribbling equations on a blackboard.

"Tomorrow?" I can't keep the whine out of my voice.

"Best we can do. You're welcome to stay here for the night."

"Chainsaw Motel," Gonzo singsongs under his breath.

"Of course, there is a gas station in town if you'd care to walk," Dr. T adds.

"How far?" I ask.

The lone woman, Dr. O, shrugs. "In miles or kilometers or centimeters or what?"

"Miles would be good."

"Oh, about forty, give or take," Dr. T says.

Dr. O glares at him. "I was getting to it, Brian."

Forty miles would take us forever to walk and we're already exhausted. Then there's the little matter of the police and the United Snow Globe Wholesalers bounty on our heads. "Fine. That would be great, thanks."

"Oh, hello," Dr. M says, shaking Balder's hand. "Wonderful costume. I'm a bit of a role player myself on the weekends. Tell me, where did you get the helmet?"

"It was forged in the North, blessed by the hands of Odin, given to me by my mother, Frigg," Balder answers.

"Lovely. I got mine on the Internet."

Gonzo picks up a toy that reminds me of a kid's wacky macaroni sculpture. It's a bumpy ball constructed of these looping chutes, slides, and tubes, none of which actually seem to connect to anything else. "What is this place?"

"This? This is Putopia," says Dr. A, the tall guy with the curly hair who was trying to catch the grape in his mouth. He's wearing a T-shirt under his lab coat that reads MY BANG THEORY IS BIGGER THAN YOURS.

"Putopia?" I repeat.

"Yes. Putopia. It stands for Parallel Universe Travel Office . . . pia."

Dr. O breaks in. "We haven't figured out the whole acronym yet, but we wanted to secure the domain name before anyone else did."

"We believe our universe may be a small part of something vast—we're one house in a cosmic subdivision of houses all right next to each other. If only we could just pop in to see the neighbors, easy as opening the front door," Dr. T explains.

"You're kidding, right?" Gonzo raises an eyebrow.

"Not at all," Dr. T continues. "Why should our world be the only one? Doesn't that strike you as odd?"

"And, frankly, a little narcissistic?" Dr. M adds.

"Surely, there must be many worlds, many possibilities. Rather like these bubbles." Dr. T dips a wand into a soapy bottle, gives it a puff, and about a gazillion bubbles float out and away on the breeze. "See? Some bubbles burst immediately or don't make it far—the least-probable possibilities. But some bubbles go the distance. They float on."

"Nothing disappears. All of time is unfolding all of the

time," Dr. M continues. He picks up the macaroni-shaped toy and shifts one of the tubes. Lights flash on the toy, and now I can see another set of little shapes underneath the ones on top. "Eleven different dimensions. Most of them too small for us to see."

"Or dimensions much *larger* than our world, like a big time ship on which our universe is only a stowaway mouse," Dr. O argues.

"Whoa," Gonzo says, and really, he's got that right.

"We're trying to reach into those endless worlds now. And this little baby . . . ," Dr. A says, gesturing to the strange daisy tunnel, "is our crowbar into other realities."

"What is it?" Gonzo takes a step back. He's got one hand resting on the exit.

"Seventeen miles of magnetized tunnels with one purpose: to open a window into that house next door and the house next door to that one and so on," Dr. M tells us. He smiles broadly. "I can almost smell the coffee!"

"So it's a supercollider," I say.

"StephenfreakingHawking!" Dr. M huffs. "Super is what you call a sale. Super is the size of a hero sandwich when you upgrade for a buck. This . . ." He gestures to the weirdly shaped door. "This is an Infinity Collider."

"That's trademarked, by the way," Dr. A warns.

"Your particles colliding with the infinite in an infinite number of ways so that none of the regular quantum laws apply—backward, forward, up, down, sideways, inside out, and outside in."

Balder's eyebrows shoot up. "Time travel?"

"Parallel-world travel," Dr. T says with glee.

Gonzo leaves his post by the exit and sits next to Dr. T. "Dude! So, like, you've been to other worlds? What's it like?

Are there, like, Teddy Vamps laying waste to droids and shit? Wait—you've been, right?"

The scientists shift uncomfortably. "Not as such," Dr. A says.

"Still a few kinks to work out," Dr. T says, his smile tight.

"Kinks, like the hinges on the door need oiling or more like bad stuff I really don't want to know about?" Gonzo asks.

"We've never put a person through," Dr. A tells us.

"Except for once," Ed pipes up from his blackboard scribblings.

"Yes. Well. Best forget that one, Ed," Dr. M cautions.

"Come on. We'll show you our work. It's snack time anyway," Dr. O says. She leads us upstairs to a nice comfy game room complete with big-ass TV and sectional sofa.

"What we're about to show you is a record of all our work here at Putopia," Dr. T explains. "The Infinity Collider, String Theory, Superstring Theory, M-Theory . . ."

"Y-theory, Z-theory, Double-Z-Theory . . . ," Dr. M adds.

Dr. O chimes in. "Subatomic particles, partner particles, gravitrons, maybetrons, perhapsatrons . . ."

"The Theory of Everything . . ."

"The Theory of Nothing . . ."

"The Theory of Somewhere in Between . . ."

"What we're working on now is a supplement to the Theory of Everything," Dr. T explains. "The Theory of Everything Plus a Little Bit More."

"Because who doesn't want a little more?" Dr. O asks. "Okay, Ed—start 'er up."

The room darkens and a video burbles to life on the TV. A younger-looking Dr. M waves to the camera nervously and places an orange tabby with a purple collar inside the chamber of an earlier model of the Infinity Collider, which is half the size of the current one and not nearly as elaborate. "In you go, Schrödinger," he says to the cat. "May you find a dimension where the mice are plentiful and the tuna fresh."

Schrödinger's meowing protests are cut short by the closing of the door. Then there's a hum, and then a flash, and when the door is opened again, Schrödinger is lying inside the chamber, motionless.

"He was a good kitty," Dr. T says with a sniffle.

The clips jump around in a very disjointed history of Putopia—scientists in their younger days, mapping out equations on a blackboard. A photo of them in a band at a dance, the banner spelling out the name THE MIGHTY MIGHTY BOSONS. A soccer game in full swing. A progression of those weird macaroni toys, each one different from the last.

"What are those things?" I ask.

"Calabi Yau manifold," Dr. O says, like it's as basic as toast or socks.

"Right. I knew that," Gonzo says. He rolls his eyes at me.

Dr. M bounces the model from hand to hand. "They're geometrical models that represent the many curled-up dimensions of space we're not even aware of yet." He shrugs. "It's a math thing."

The movie plays for another minute. I notice that there are a lot of scientists in the beginning, not so many in the later shots.

"What happened to everybody else?"

Dr. T's expression is flat. "We lost our funding. More money for tanks and missiles, less for finding God particles."

"Ah—there's eternity in a kiss!"

I whip my head back to the screen. "Wait! Pause it!" I shout. The image freezes on an Asian man with surprised eyes. I point excitedly at the screen. "That's Dr. X! Do you know him? Is he here?"

The scientists shift uncomfortably.

"He was once," Dr. O says quietly.

My heart sinks. I'd hoped we'd finally found him. "Well, do you know where he went? Please, it's superimportant that I find him."

"No one's seen or heard from him since . . ." Dr. A trails off.

"Since?" I prompt.

The scientists exchange glances. Dr. T pulls a worn photo out from a bookshelf—Dr. X beside a smiling, freckle-faced woman. It's the photo I saw on his desk when I did the Internet search for the fire giants and accidentally found Dr. X instead.

"Dr. X's wife, Mrs. X," Dr. T explains. "He loved her very much. She inspired his work. He used to say, 'There is no meaning but what we assign to life, and she is my meaning.'" Dr. T puts her picture back on the shelf. "Lovely woman."

The scientists all bow their heads.

"So . . . what happened?"

"Every year for Christmas, she gifted Dr. X with a new snow globe for his collection. He loved snow globes, said they were like little worlds unto themselves. Anyway, it was the week just before Christmas, the first snow of the season. She'd gone downtown to the shop to make her final payment and collect his gift. But . . ." Dr. T shakes his head sadly.

Dr. O continues. "A bomb exploded. They never found out who did it or why. A random attack. Meaningless. Mrs. X was killed in the explosion. When they found her body, she was still clutching her husband's Christmas snow globe in one hand."

323

Balder removes his helmet. "That is a sad tale indeed."

"After his wife's death, Dr. X was a changed man," Dr. M says with a heavy sigh. "He said what did it matter if we could find the Theory of Everything Plus a Little Bit More, measure gravitrons, or prove evidence of other worlds if we could not stop such suffering in our own—the plague of the unpredictable, the terrible, the futile."

"He wanted to use the Infinity Collider not to ask questions, but to search for an answer," Dr. O says softly. "He wanted to search time and space so that he might find a way to stop death."

"So." I swallow hard. "What happened to him?"

"Dr. X had a theory that certain musical frequencies could open up portals in the fabric of time and space. Something about the vibrations. He believed that music was in fact its own dimension," Dr. T explains in that teacher voice of his.

"My friend Eubie would probably agree," I say.

"One night, he made a few secret tweaks to the Infinity Collider. Only Ed was with him." He glances at Ed, who's watching a bag of microwave popcorn expand in the microwave like it's every bit as fascinating as the Infinity Collider. "According to Ed, Dr. X reconfigured the Calabi Yau into a sort of superspeaker, which he then attached to his radio to amplify the music—"

"It was the Copenhagen Interpretation!" Ed yells from the kitchen where he's pouring the freshly popped corn into a bowl.

"—and push those musical vibrations into the universe in order to puncture a hole in the fabric of space-time and gain passage. It worked. Within minutes, he was gone. So was the Infinity Collider. We had to build this one from scratch."

Dr. M sighs. "We haven't seen or heard from Dr. X since. For all we know, he's trapped in an alternate universe."

"When was that?" I ask.

"Eleven years ago," Dr. A says. "I remember because it was the same night the Copenhagen Interpretation played their Big Benefit Concert for Peace but Against Non-Peace and People Generally Being Not Nice. Great show. I think there was an aurora borealis. That's what my girlfriend told me."

"That was also the night they disappeared," I say.

On TV, Dr. X's somber face fills the screen. "Why must we die when everything within us was born to live?" He shakes the snow globe of the angel and it blurs with fake snow.

Connections. Dulcie said everything was connected. Maybe if I can duplicate Dr. X's experiment, I can find that connection.

"Can you send me through to wherever Dr. X went?"

"Depends on whether you're deterministic or probabilistic." Dr. O laughs, but no one else does. "That's a joke," she says, rolling her eyes. "Anyway, it's possible. A record of his trip might still be imprinted there, like an echo."

"We don't know that for certain," Dr. A says. "We've never been able to duplicate Dr. X's experiment. There's the possibility we could create a small black hole. Or you could enter another world and not come back. You could cycle through worlds indefinitely, like the Flying Dutchman."

"But if he leaves an XL-gravitron—a sort of 'parallel-world footprint'—we'd have proof," Dr. M says, pacing. He lowers his voice. "It could mean funding."

"Hmmm," the scientists all say at once.

Gonzo whispers in my ear. "What if that thing pushes you into another reality where you're a Grade-A wanker with no girlfriend. Oh wait. That would be this reality. Never mind."

"Fuck off," I whisper, and Gonzo's smile widens.

"What's that?" Dr. A asks.

"Nothing," I say.

Grinning, Dr. T holds up a finger. "There's no such thing as nothing. In every nothing, there's a something. In fact, there could be everything!"

"New sales slogan," Dr. O explains. "Our research is also being funded by the Pursuit of Happiness Corp. Pursue happiness at all costs."

"Been there," Gonzo mutters. "Extreme happiness, not all it's cut out to be."

I stare at the picture of Dr. X and his wife.

"Where do I sign up?"

CHAPTER THIRTY-FIVE

**Of What Happens When I Take a Little Trip
Through Time and Space.
Calabi Yau!**

Gonzo and I sit on the porch watching the turbines spin against a night sky polka-dotted with stars. Balder's off hunting. He insisted I couldn't go into the Infinity Collider without a proper Viking feast worthy of Valhalla. For the past hour, while we wait for Gonzo's phone to charge, he's been arguing against going into the Infinity Collider.

"I'm just saying, dude, that thing doesn't look promising."

"You got a better idea?"

"Yeah," he starts. "No. Not really. But parallel universes? Dude, I'm the biggest *Star Fighter* fan on this or any other planet, but it's a movie, you know? That shit's all science fiction."

"But what if it's not? What if there *are* parallel universes where you're you, only different. You know, maybe you're a doctor or a gravedigger or a ninja. Maybe here, in *this* universe, your—your mom died when you were five"—I choke on the word "died"—"but in another world, she's alive, helping you make sand castles on the beach."

"Or maybe there's another world where you bop in from an Infinity Collider and get eaten by carnivorous house-plants."

"Don't start."

"I'm just saying it's not all sand castles and ninjas."

The turbines catch a new breeze and reverse their spin. "But all those other roads, those other choices you don't make? They must get to live somewhere. I mean, maybe . . ." I stop because it's too much to hope for and too stupid to say out loud.

"Maybe what?"

"Maybe there's a universe where I don't get this disease at all. Where none of this happens." As soon as I say it, I think of Dulcie. Of Gonzo and Balder and this whole nutty trip, how I wouldn't trade parts of it for anything.

Gonzo unwraps a piece of Juicy Chew and pops it in his mouth. "So, what, like, all of time is elastic?"

"Sure. I mean, why not?" I say, getting excited. "Maybe, right now, Junior Webster is still fighting in the war that changed him even as we're sitting on this porch watching the grass grow. The Copenhagen Interpretation is giving its forty-second comeback show and you're a kid burying toy cars in the backyard. Or you're giving a forty-second come-back concert and the Copenhagen Interpretation is hanging with your cars. It's all a big soup and it never stops cooking."

Gonzo rubs his head. "Dude, this is a stoner conversation, and we are not even high."

"I'm just saying that it's totally possible that things don't happen until you connect with an event, then the other choices you didn't make unfold in other worlds."

328

"Whatever, dude," Gonzo says, hands up. "I'm fine with this reality. In fact, it's already more reality than I can handle. I'm not ready to take on another one."

"Gonz, if, um—you know," I say softly. "Make sure Balder gets to the sea and *Ringhorn* lifts the curse, okay?"

"There is no *Ringhorn*, man."

"Just promise me."

"Yeah. Okay." Gonzo bends and folds his gum wrapper into new shapes. "So, you think maybe in another world, I'm . . . you know. Not a dwarf?"

It's hard for me to think of Gonzo as anything but Gonzo. "Or you're the Littlest PI—the Dwarf of Destiny."

Gonzo makes a gun out of his forefinger and thumb. "The dame wanted advice, but I was coming up short," he says in a hard-boiled detective voice. He sets the gum wrapper on the table. It's now a tiny silver swan. "I'd want a fedora in that other world. Can't be the Dwarf of Destiny without a sick topper."

"Indeed." The wind's died down. It's still, like the world's holding its breath. "I'm sorry," I say after a while.

"For what?"

"Dulcie told me there was something for you on this ride, but I guess it's been kind of a bust so far."

"Yeah, well." Gonzo hugs his knees. "Beats high school."

Gonzo's phone has a green light.

"You're fully charged," I say. "You wanna call your mom?"

Gonzo lets the phone lie. "Maybe later."

I find Ed in the living room in his Star Fighter pajamas. He's playing with the Calabi Yau model. The TV's on. Parker Day struts across the studio soundstage. "Just want to remind everybody back home that we are counting down to the YA!

Party House—only one more day—and we're gonna . . . what?" Parker asks.

He puts his hand to his ear as the audience chants his catchphrase back to him.

"*Smoke it!*" he joins in, and the place goes nuts.

I flip over to ConstaToons. It's the same roadrunner and coyote with all the doors.

"That one's a train," Ed says, just before coyote opens it and gets run over.

"Yeah, I know. You'd think he'd learn."

"He can't learn. He's a cartoon."

"Good point." I offer him a Corny Doodle.

He shakes his head. "I already brushed my teeth for bed."

"Gotcha." I pop it in my mouth. "So, you've lived here since you were little?"

He nods.

"That's rough, man. Sorry, you know, that your parents died."

"My parents didn't die. They left me here on the doorstep when I was three."

"Wow," I say before I can stop myself. For all my dad's assholian tendencies and my mom's spaciness, they would never do that.

Ed keeps playing with the Calabi Yau toy, arranging and rearranging the macaroni-like dimensions to make whole new shapes. Every time he does, the thing lights up like a pinball machine.

"Hey, Ed? Do you know what happened to Dr. X?" I ask. "It's really important."

"He went in the Infinity Collider," he says, not taking his eyes off the cartoon.

"Yeah, but is he lost or, like, caught in some other world? Do you know where he is right now?"

"He's gone to tomorrow. Anvil!" he warns the coyote.

I sigh. This is getting me nowhere. On the TV, the road-runner runs through the painted backdrop. Confused, coyote tries to follow and whams his whole body against a brick wall.

"You ever think about going into the Infinity Collider yourself?" I ask.

"We are infinity," Ed says, as if that settles it.

The door bangs open. Balder stands on the threshold, eyes blazing. He's dragging a stag by one hoof. "Tomorrow, we may die. But tonight we dine as heroes!"

Later, after we've polished off some deer meat and Rad soda, Balder has a blast letting the scientists test their various lasers and protoplasm pelters and even a potato gun on him. With each hit, he shouts out, "Who's your daddy?" in Norse, until, frankly, it starts to get kind of annoying. The scientists seem like they're having a little too much fun trying to obliterate my pal, but Balder's digging the chance to show off what a rocking immortal he is, so who am I to stop his fun?

The next morning, at half-past eleven, Dr. T comes in, his smile gone and his eyes anything but twinkly.

"Is it true you're terrorists?" He holds out the day's paper, and my heart nearly stops. On page four is the flyer pic of Gonz and me along with a story about the CESSNAB revolution and the supposed bombing of the Konstant Kettle, the bounty offered by United Snow Globe Wholesalers, and the number to call. "This is the sort of thing Dr. X stood against."

"No! No, I . . . just let me explain. . . ."

Gonzo ducks under my arm, starts reading. "Dude, we only made page four? That sucks! What kind of terrorists do you have to be to make page one?"

"But we are not terrorists!" I insist.

"Oh. Right. Totally not, dudes. And Dr. O."

"To quote the great Silas Fenton, 'We give our word to you: We are for honor and good, sworn to protect the galaxy until our atoms are spread among the stars,'" Balder assures them.

The professors stare at us blankly.

"Star Fighter," Gonzo prompts. "You know, *Star Fighter*? The movie?"

"Never seen it," Dr. A says with a sniff.

Gonzo takes a step back. "How can you be science nerds and not have seen *Star Fighter*? That's just wrong."

"Look, there's something I need to tell you. . . ." I explain to them about the dark energy that Dr. X accidentally set free from another universe and how it's endangering our own. All the while, they're exchanging glances and I can hear them whispering to each other: ". . . could have traveled through the Higgs Field . . . given mass to something new . . . something dangerous . . . never tried it, only a kid . . . nachos . . . had nachos yesterday, how about pasta . . . could be our breakthrough . . ."

Finally, they break from their huddle. "We will help you," Dr. A says. "In the interest of science."

Thirty minutes later, I'm standing at the entrance to the crazy-daisy door of the Infinity Collider wearing a roller derby helmet, white plastic safety goggles, and an orange padded jumpsuit with the words SCHRÖDINGER'S CAT IS A SPLIT PERSONALITY on it.

Gonzo makes a whistling sound. "Wow. Physicist humor. Who knew?"

The scientists have traded their lab coats for jumpsuits. Across the back of Dr. M's is a slogan in big white letters: EVERYONE'S A TOURIST HERE! He offers an apologetic smile. "These days, most of our research is funded by the Council of Greater Tourism. If we succeed, they want to partner with us on tours to parallel universes." He motions with his arm like he's spelling out an imaginary billboard. "Take your brain to Braneworld!"

"Lame . . . ," Dr. O singsongs under her breath, flipping switches and taking readings.

"Yes. Well. We're still working on the catchphrase," Dr. M says with a sniff.

I shift my safety goggles over my eyes. "How do I look?"

"Like you just escaped from an eighties band," Gonzo says.

"Ed, please ready our victim!" Dr. T shouts from a scaffolding above the tunnel.

I bend down so that Ed can test the security of my roller derby helmet. "Don't worry. It doesn't hurt."

"I thought nobody's come back. So how do you know it doesn't hurt?"

Ed considers this, nodding slowly. "I just know in the way you just know things." He tucks a white rabbit's foot into my pocket.

"For luck?"

"Nope." He doesn't offer any other explanation.

Balder throws his arms around me. "May Frigg spin clouds of protection around you on your travels, noble Cameron."

"Thanks, Balder."

Ed affixes the Calabi Yau manifold to the stereo speaker.

"Okay, we're ready!" Dr. T calls out. The scientists lower their safety goggles and Balder and Gonzo follow suit. Dr. T offers a sort of space-hero salute, his hand across his chest.

"To Higgs Field and beyond. Calabi Yau!"

"Calabi Yau!" they shout.

Gonzo bestows a final fist bump. "Here's to sand castles and ninjas, dude."

I give the thumbs-up, and Ed closes the door, sealing me in.

At first, it's quiet and dark. Really dark. Then I hear the Copenhagen Interpretation's music filling the space around me. *"Time is what you make of it. . . ."*

The ground hums; it vibrates till my teeth rattle. The daisy door lights up like a wheel you spin at a carnival, and that's when I nearly piss myself with fear. *Be cool, Cameron. Don't wanna trip the light fantastic with wet undies. Chafe is chafe in any dimension.*

It's like I've been shot out of a superpowered cannon. There's so much pressure bearing down on me, smashing me flat. It's like I'm a plastic toy form stuck to a plastic board along with other forms that can be moved around only on that flat board. And then I'm expanding. I can feel myself peeling off that flat board and fluffing out, and it's like I've got as many hidden dimensions as the Calabi Yau toy, all curled up and exponentially huge at the same time. Then—*kapow!*—I could swear every part of me is coming apart and being rearranged, like the ball bearings in one of those cheap plastic puzzle games you get in a birthday goody bag when you're a kid. In my ears, the Copenhagen Interpretation's getting louder. Tiny cells of time zip around me, snapshots constantly being rearranged on the blank pages of a photo album. Sometimes I look and they tell a linear story; other times they don't seem to make sense or one cell overlaps another. I can make out a few things, though: The CI playing a concert. A big black hole opening above them. Dr. X stepping into his machine. The empty stage. Dr. X and the Copenhagen Interpretation flying through space, and in their wake, something forming. A ball of fire.

I'm accelerating, and everything's getting wonky. Time bends and blends till I can't tell what's what anymore: The Copenhagen Interpretation fishing in the snow. Me falling off the Small World ride. Gonzo in a fedora, a huge stuffed albatross on his desk and a gun in his hand. Glory playing hopscotch with a little girl who looks just like her. Dr. X dancing with his wife. Dr. X all alone in his stark white room. Dad with his arm around my shoulders, two moons hanging low in the orange sky. Stars streaking over my head. A crying Dulcie out in the snow, banging her palms against a pane of glass, over and over. Junior Webster's horn in my hands. The WELCOME TO FLORIDA sign.

The music reaches a crescendo. It's so much I can't take it.

When I come to, everything's still. The Calabi Yau is smoked as a piece of Buddha Burger jerky. I can move, and since I seem to have stopped traveling, I guess the only thing left to do is open up the Infinity Collider and see what's on the other side of that door. For all I know, I could be stepping into a world where Rad soda and Parker Day don't exist, and nobody's even heard of the Copenhagen Interpretation.

The door opens with a loud *psssht* and a cloud of mist, and I hope carnivorous houseplants aren't waiting with forks and knives and tartar sauce. Blurry forms emerge from the mist. Their edges fill in; Drs. A, T, O, and M stand blinking at me. Gonzo smiles in relief, and Balder removes his helmet and sinks to his knees to offer a prayer of thanks.

"Nima Arkani-Hamed!" Dr. T whoops, jumping a full foot off the floor. The scientists hug each other in a victory huddle before running off to test for evidence of XL-gravitrons and maybetrons and perhapsatrons and whatever else they can think up.

Ed takes my helmet and goggles, offers me juice. Then he reaches into my pocket and takes out the rabbit's foot, which is now streaked with brown, though I could have sworn it was white when he put it in there.

"Huh," he says, smiling. "Thought so."

And it makes about as much sense as anything else.

Later, after the scientists have recorded everything they can, after they've high-fived each other about a gazillion times and hung up a sign that says PARALLEL UNIVERSE TRAVEL OFFICE-PIA: OPENING FOR BUSINESS SOON! they come to see us off.

"Sorry we couldn't help you find Dr. X," Dr. O says, pumping my hand. "You've been of enormous help to science."

"Hey, Gonzo—you hear that? I've been of enormous help to science!"

"Tell 'em you want a medal, a big-ass one," Gonz shouts back through a mouthful of veggie taco, because he swears he's not getting on the road without a full stomach.

"You could keep this." Ed offers me his Calabi Yau model. He puts it in the palm of my hand and it wobbles there, eleven-plus dimensions, all mine.

"You sure?"

"Yeah. We've got a ton of 'em to sell in the Putopia gift shops. People like to bring souvenirs back. It says you care."

"Cool." I stuff it in my bag. "Thanks for the veggie tacos. And if you can think of where Dr. X might be, give us a call."

"I told you where he is," Ed says.

"You said he went to tomorrow," I remind him gently.

"Yeah." He puts his taco-smudged finger on my E-ticket meter, right on top of Tomorrowland, and grins. "Get some ears. They'll even put your name on them if you want."

I trip over something by my feet. An orange tabby with a purple collar rubs against my legs with a loud purr. Dr. T scoops it up and gives it a scratch behind the ears.

"Schrödinger, you old devil. Where *have* you been? You must be starving. Come on. Let's get you some kibble."

CHAPTER THIRTY-SIX

Of What Happens When We Pick Up
Three Hitchhikers and Free the Snow Globes

The radio's warning us about wildfires blazing out of control along the roads in Florida. The brown smoke swallows us like earth. I can barely see the road ahead.

Since we left Putopia, I've been completely on edge. We're practically a big fat target driving around in the Rocinante with its bull horns front and center, and we can't stick to the back roads forever. Could Dr. X really be at Disney World? Wouldn't I have seen a sign by now?

"Do you think those really are just wildfires?" Gonzo asks. The three of us are strung so tight you could play us.

"Maybe," I answer.

Balder pulls a rune from his pouch.

"What'd you get?" Gonzo asks.

Frowning, Balder holds up a completely blank rune. "Wyrd. The beginning and the end. Fate."

I don't know what that means, but it's not doing anything to uncreep me. In another five miles, the smoke clears, and the sun glints off the asphalt in hard sparks. A siren wails behind us, and I swear I nearly choke on my heartbeat.

"Shit," I say. "Be cool, be cool."

The cop car soars past chasing somebody else, and we all let out our breath.

"We need some cover," I say, like I know what I'm talking about, like I do this all the time.

"I fear we cannot trade this car for another," Balder muses. "It hasn't enough value."

Just then I spy three guys camped out by the side of the road hoisting up a sign, PARTEE HOUSE OR BUST. It gives me an idea. I pull onto the shoulder a few feet ahead of them.

Gonzo's eyes are wide. "Dude, what are you doing?"

"Giving them a ride. We're going to Disney. We can drop them in Daytona. It's on the way."

Gonzo slaps his knee and rolls his head back to the roof like it might understand his plight. "No one ever picks up hitchers. That's, like, the kind of safety rule they don't even put on kids' milk cartons anymore because they figure everybody fucking knows it already."

"They misspelled 'party.' How evil genius can they be?"

He angles his body around to get a good look at the guys scrambling toward the car dragging their packs.

"Look," I explain. "These guys could be our cover, okay? The cops are looking for two crazy teens, not a carload of college kids on the way to spring break. With those guys on board, we just look like any other caravan on the way to Daytona for spring break. We slide under the radar."

Balder speaks up. "Cameron's battle plan is sound. But I

have seen these types before. They take pictures," he says, exhibiting a little yard-gnome post-traumatic stress disorder.

"Don't worry, Balder. Nobody's taking any pictures. You're totally safe," I say.

"Still, I think it best if I assume my enchanted form. I shall ride beside Gonzo."

Quickly, Balder scrambles over the front seat and gets gnomy with it just as this big, doughy guy throws open the back car door.

"Hey, man. Thanks for picking us up. We've been standing out there for hours."

"Because other people, sane people, know not to stop," Gonzo mutters under his breath.

"No prob," I say. "I'll pop the trunk."

Five minutes later, we're back on the interstate.

"So what school are y'all from?" the doughy guy sitting in the middle asks.

"Texas Community College," I lie. "You?"

"Gold Coast University," he says, and there's a round of earsplitting football-stadium yelling. "Coast U! Coast U! Coast Uuuuuu!"

The guy on the left says, "We call it Coast U because they coast you through."

"Amen," the guy on the right says. "You don't even have to pick a major till you're ready to graduate."

The real estate beside the highway blooms with gas stations, all-night waffle houses, home decorating centers, and gigantic all-in-one retailers. The cars line up to enter the parking lots.

A fresh billboard's just gone up. It's a picture of a little girl holding a snow globe and smiling in awe. PROTECTING YOUR SAFETY. REMOVING THE UNPREDICTABLE. ENSURING YOUR

"So do you have a major?" I ask, training my eyes back on
the road ahead.

"Not yet. I just want something that'll make me a sweet
pile of money. Some desk job where I can play Hot Hoops
or Casino Cash on my computer most of the day and still
collect a check."

"Y'all going to the Party House?" the guy on the right
asks.

"No. Just passing through," I say.

"Oh. We're going to the Party House," he says.

"Party *House*!" the guy on the right yells suddenly, startling me.

"Marisol is so fine!" Middle Guy says. "She *will* be
mine!"

"The chicks are out of control at this place," Right Guy
announces.

"So, you've been before?" I ask.

"No," he says, a little defensively. "But I've heard."

Right on cue a carload of teenage girls pulls up beside us.
They've got ponytails flapping in the wind. "Dude, roll down
your window!" Right Guy yells to Left Guy.

"Hey, y'all going to the Party House?" Right Guy shouts.

"Yeah!" the blond chick leaning out the window yells.
She's got a Diet Rad soda in her hand. The shiny silver metal
of the can glints in the sun. "You goin'?"

"You bet! We're gonna do *I Double Dog Dare You* with
Parker and Marisol!" Middle Guy promises.

The girl in the backseat has rolled down her window, too.
She shouts, "No way! Omigod, I *love* that show!"

"Yeah, Marty here already did the stunt where you run

your skateboard over a moving car. He broke five major bones but he's all right now!"

"It's all good," Marty, aka Left Guy, says, giving a little wave with his hand, I suppose to show that it still works.

The girls giggle and give each other conspiratorial looks.

"Well, we'll look for you there. Later," they say, stepping on the gas. They want us to chase them. That's the deal.

"Go on, man. Pedal to the medal," Left Guy prompts, practically coming into the front seat. I try to change lanes but an eighteen-wheeler cuts us off. We're stuck behind it while the girls zoom ahead down the road.

"Aw, man," Left Guy says, disappointed.

"No worries, bro. This is going to be a total score scene!" Right Guy notices Balder for the first time. "All right! Yard gnome. Got some buds back at the house who took one of these guys all around Barbados. How long you had him?"

"Two days." Gonzo wraps his arm around Balder.

"We should totally pose with him in front of the Party House," Right Guy says. "Be awesome."

Balder's smile twitches just slightly; he wants to go all Viking on the guy, I can tell.

"He's not that kind of yard gnome," I say.

Middle Guy snorts. " 'D'you steal him from a church or something?"

"It's one of those Last Wish things," I explain. "Some kid in Florida who's dying wanted to have his picture taken with the gnome, so we're driving him to the hospital there. For our youth group."

"That kid won't know if we get in a few shots first," Left Guy says.

"No can do," Gonzo insists. "The gnome has to be untouched. Virgin gnome."

My eyes find Balder's. *Be cool,* I silently implore him.

"I've got a cousin who's a midget," Middle Guy says to Gonzo. "We always called him Stumpy. Got any cool nicknames like that? Like Stumpy?"

"No," Gonzo says through gritted teeth. He gives me a sideways glance and I know I will pay for this later. But at least we've got some camouflage for now.

The guy stares at him for a second, and I'm afraid it's going to get ugly.

"Hey, man," he says. "Think we could make a stop? I gotta take a leak."

The only place that looks like it might have a bathroom is a roadside gift shop. It's one of those places full of useless junk—state spoons, frosted pecans with a half-life of about two hundred years, tea towels decorated with grandmas making cranky observations about life, novelty cookbooks, and trivets shaped like lighthouses because apparently the world is clamoring for cute things they can place piping hot casserole dishes on. It's hard to believe people buy this shit, and even harder to believe they give it to other people as mementos, like, "Hey, we went on this awesome vacation but we brought you back some pickled peppers in a festive, dancing jalapeño jar. Thanks for feeding our cat!" The frat guys have agreed to buy snacks in gratitude for the ride. They troll the aisles scooping up weird chip selections. Gonzo's got Balder on his shoulder. They're checking out a pen of a woman in a bathing suit and when you turn it upside down, she loses her top.

The lady behind the cash register isn't overflowing with gratitude that we're there. She reminds us that if we break something, we buy it, and goes back to reading her tabloid while occasionally flicking a suspicious glance in our direction.

When I round a corner, Dulcie's standing in the aisle pointing a potato gun at me.

"Come quietly. Don't act like a spud and we'll have no trouble."

"Hey, Dulcie. Where've you been?"

She puts the gun back, picks up a prank lollipop with a "fossil" of a baby alligator inside. "Trying to get info."

"Find out anything?"

She shakes her head. "You?"

I tell her about Putopia, the scientists and parallel universes, the Infinity Collider, seeing Dr. X, and what Ed said.

"So that's great," Dulcie says, but she doesn't sound happy.

"Yeah. I don't know. Disney? That seems like a stretch. And he was just a kid."

"You could always check for signs." Dulcie jerks her head toward the cash register up front.

I peer over the display of ceramic dog paper-towel holders at the big-haired lady sitting there. She licks her finger and turns the pages of her paper. Briefly, she looks up and squints disapprovingly at the Gold Coast U guys.

"Yeah, good luck with that," I say to Dulcie.

"Come on," she prompts.

We inch closer, past shelves displaying various curiosities—crocodile eggs, hot-sauce meat sticks, pecan logs, salt-and-pepper shakers shaped like the president and first lady—and round the corner into an entire aisle devoted to snow globes. Suddenly, Dulcie stops. I've never seen this expression on her face before. She seems sad. Her wings droop.

344

"Dulcie?"

She lifts one of the snow globes, puts her face up to it so I can see her eye through the warped glass, huge, blinking.

"Dulcie? You okay?"

"I hate these things. They're depressing." She turns it over. UNITED SNOW GLOBE WHOLESALERS is stamped on the bottom.

"What are you talking about?"

Her head snaps up. It's like she's back all of a sudden, but her eyes are still pained. "It's just that . . . you can't freeze life behind glass, you know? And . . . and take this one, for instance."

She swipes it from the shelf, turns it over in her hands. Smiling lobsters break-dance in front of a ship's wheel under a glitter-confetti rain. An empty bottle resting in the fake sand makes it seem like they got drunk and decided to cut loose.

"'Party Time,'" Dulcie says. "What a stupid thing to write on a snow globe."

"Maybe they like it there," I say.

"Poor lobsters. You should not be trapped in a glitter-water hell."

"Definitely. A fake-snow-pellet hell is better," I joke.

Dulcie ignores me. I'm used to being ignored. So why does it bother me when she does it? Why do I feel the need to try with her?

She turns away. "You should see if you can snag that paper."

"All right," I say, not sure what I did to piss her off. I go up to the counter and pretend to be very interested in the gum and mints selection. I put some Fruity Time Chews on the counter.

"Just this?" the lady asks. Her name is HELLO, MY NAME IS EMPLOYEE #3. In the corner, four rows of boxes marked UNITED SNOW GLOBE WHOLESALERS are stacked eight high. Man, people like their snow globes here.

"Yes. Thanks. And, ah, do you . . . think I could have your paper, you know, if you're finished with it?"

Her eyes narrow. "Why?"

"No reason." I swallow hard. "Just thought I'd catch the day's news."

"Papers are over by the cooler. They're three dollars and fifty cents. Here's your gum." She's still glaring.

Too late I notice the picture of Gonz and me. Apparently, it's a slow news day for the tabloids—no faces of Jesus in guacamole dip or anything—and Gonz and I have finally moved to page one right next to a picture of the president golfing on an aircraft carrier and under a lurid headline—TEENAGE TERROR PLOT HATCHED IN HIGH SCHOOL BATHROOM!

"You know, actually, it's cool. Never mind. Have a good day," I say, walking away fast.

"Hey!" she calls after me. "You stay right there. Don't you go nowhere!" Her voice goes over an intercom. "Bobby Joe, call Cyrus to come on up with the wagon. We're gettin' ourselves that fifteen large."

There's a sudden crash from aisle five. It diverts Cash Register Lady's attention. "Hey! Hey now! You stop that nonsense right this minute!"

A familiar voice rings out: "Free the snow globes!"

I rush back to Dulcie, who is standing in a puddle of sparkly water and escaped lobster toys.

"What are you doing?" I plead.

"Freeing the snow globes. Wanna help?" There's a wicked gleam in her eye that scares the crap out of me.

"No, I don't!"

"Suit yourself." With the flick of a wing, Dulcie wipes out a whole row and then another, until the dirty linoleum is awash in small plastic mermaids, floating towns, seashells, and tiny white pellets that stick to the floor like fake snow.

"I'm calling the police!" the lady screams. "I have a gun!"

She isn't kidding. A shot sails past in the other aisle, breaking open a jar of yellow-green margarita mix that splatters onto my shirt. Holy shit! I duck down next to Dulcie, who's grinning like it's the first day of summer.

"Get out of here," she says. "I'll keep her busy."

"What?"

"Don't worry about me. Just grab the paper on the way out." Dulcie picks up a snow globe and hurls it toward the soda case. Another shot shatters the glass there. Cash Register Lady starts racing in that direction, and I am off and running toward the door. Gonzo's right behind me, screaming bloody murder, Balder tucked under an arm. And the three frat guys are hot on his tail. On the way out, I grab the paper in my fist.

"Get in the car!" I scream. Everyone falls in, and I start the Rocinante up and peel out with a big screech of tread.

"I don't have my door closed!" Gonzo yells.

In the rearview mirror, I can see the lady aiming the shotgun at us.

"Then you better hold on to something, man, because I am not stopping."

"Sorry, Balder!" Gonzo yells, dropping him to the floor for safekeeping.

She fires a third shot that manages to miss the Caddy but does hit another car in the lot. Its alarm goes off with a loud, skin-crawling scream. I duck my head and floor it.

We have to clover-leaf to get back on the highway. My foot hits the gas hard, and we zoom onto the on-ramp, edging out an SUV that lays on its horn in protest. I take the first turn so fast the Caddy's airborne for a second. It comes down with a rattling whomp and then we're back on the interstate and blended into the buzzing lines of anonymous cars and trucks. We drive in total silence for a good five minutes, my knuckles white on the wheel, all of us breathing hard and sweating. Balder's on the floor in the fetal position. Gonzo's got his inhaler out. He clutches it to his chest. The guys in the backseat sit straight up, eyes wide, mouths open, not moving. We pass an overhead sign that tells us Daytona Beach is another three hundred miles.

We made it. Every part of me feels alive. I can't help it. I pound the steering wheel in victory. It was crazy. Insane. And completely awesome. Finally, Middle Guy speaks up.

"Dude, I want to party with you!"

CHAPTER THIRTY-SEVEN

In Which Dulcie Makes an Accidental Confession

By nine o'clock, we're still a hundred miles from Daytona. The Caddy's high beams are for crap and I'm dog tired, so we pull off the road and find a place to make camp. The guys have spent the last two hundred miles replaying our narrow escape. Every time, they add something new to the story, making it bigger, making it theirs. My mom used to say that's how myth is born. But it's kind of hard to resist their good-natured charms. Plus, they've provided us with a tasty meal of lime-flavored corn chips, fast-food burritos, juice, and beer bought on Left Guy's excellent fake ID. Even Balder can't resist the party atmosphere. He's come out of hiding, regaling everybody with tales of his life as a Viking.

"Whoa, your yard gnome . . . talks?" Middle Guy asks, openmouthed.

"Prototype," Gonzo and I say at the same time. Fortunately,

the guys are just drunk enough to believe our story that he's a cutting-edge computerized toy. But I hope Balder knows what he's doing.

The guys are steadily working their way through a case. Gonzo's had just two beers, but he's flying. I take a pass. Somebody has to be on the lookout for cops and fire giants and wizards, oh my. Plus, I've got a tabloid to scour, starting with the story on Gonz and me.

TEENAGE TERROR PLOT HATCHED
IN HIGH SCHOOL BATHROOM!

There's a photo of Kevin, Kyle, and Rachel showing off the fourth-floor urinals. Nice.

SHOCKNAWE NEWS—CALHOUN, TEXAS

The two teens responsible for a wave of destruction and violence across the country were notorious juvenile drug fiends who hatched their terrorist plot from a fourth-floor bathroom, Shocknawe News has learned. Were Cameron John Smith and Paul Ignacio "Gonzo" Gonzales ordinary teens who stumbled onto a dark path? Or were they human time bombs waiting to go off in the way that time bombs so often do—like time bombs, only human.

"I always knew that *pendejo* was *el problemo*," said Calhoun High's Spanish teacher, Mrs. Rector, in an exclusive interview over a pitcher of margaritas.

Smith's parents maintain that their son is very ill and needs medical treatment for his Creutzfeldt-Jakob disease, otherwise known as bovine spongiform encephalopathy or mad cow (*see box*). Paul Ignacio Gonzales's mother blamed video games and a spot on his lung for her son's sudden turn to violence. (*Do video games cause terrorism or mad cow disease? How safe are you? See other box.*)

United Snow Globe Wholesalers has raised their $10,000 bounty to $15,000 for the capture of the Teen Terror Team. Any tips should be directed to the hotline at 1-800-555-1212.

Down in the left corner is a photo of my family in happier times. It's one of the pictures from our trip to Disney, I realize. We're on line for the Small World ride. The euphoria I felt earlier falls away, and I wish I could crawl into that photo. I ball up the paper and toss it into the campfire, then rest my head on my knees and fall asleep.

A doctor is standing at the end of my hospital bed. He thrums his thumb across the sole of my foot, but I don't feel it. Mom and Dad are sitting in chairs beside the bed. Mom's eyes are red and puffy and her hair's a little greasy. Dad needs a shave. He's watching the doctor poke at me. I can't move my body at all.

The doctor says something about "tough decisions." He says something about hospice to Glory, who leaves and comes back with a business card. She gives it to Dad, who stares at the raised black lettering on the crisp white background. Glory and the doctor mumble a few words about "giving you time to think things over" as they leave the room. The respirator keeps humming. Mom and Dad sit there in their chairs, alone together.

Dad moves the card in his fingers like he wants to give it away but can't. Dad always makes all the decisions, but he can't make this one. Finally, Mom's hand comes to rest on top of Dad's. She takes the card. In the set of her shoulders there's a grim determination I've never seen before.

"It's okay," she says. "I'll do it."

When I wake up, Dulcie's perched next to me eating from a bag of jelly beans. I'm really glad to see her, and I can feel the ghosts of my dreams evaporating.

"Hey, you," I say, rubbing sleep from my eyes.

"Hey, you, back."

"Did I miss anything?" I ask, surveying the scene. Middle Guy's down to his boxers. He's telling Gonzo a story, or slurring it, mostly. Gonzo's drooling and his eyes are half-closed. Left Guy's lying on his back on the ground. He rubs his stomach and moans.

"Middle Guy dared Left Guy to down an entire package of hot dogs, which he did," Dulcie says.

"That was some stunt you pulled today," I say, stretching. "You almost got us killed."

"But I didn't."

"But you could have."

"But. I. Didn't."

Right Guy drops a log into the fire drunkenly. It hisses and sparks.

"Whatever," I say. "Thanks."

"For what?"

"For saving me back there at the Food Court of Despair."

"You're welcome."

"This has been one hell of a trip, man."

"Yuppers." She tilts her face toward the night sky and smiles in that way that makes her so very Dulcie.

"Beautiful," I mumble.

"What?"

"Oh. Um. The stars. Beautiful."

"Yeah," she says. "For ghosts." She sucks a jelly bean in her back teeth. "It takes millions of years for that light to reach us. By the time we see it, that star's probably dead and gone."

"Wow. Way to kill the mood."

One of her eyebrows lifts. "Did we have a mood?"

"Um, no. Not, I mean, not a *mood* mood."

"Hmph." Dulcie loops an arm around my shoulders. It's warm and nice. "How 'bout this, then? Somewhere out in the galaxy, right this minute, there's a big ball of gas and gravity heating up, pressing together, forming something new and bold and awesome, until finally, it can't take it anymore, and it spits out all this energy, just sending that light out into the universe. *Schoooom!*" She swooshes her other arm through the air and goes kapow with her fingers. "Even stars gotta leave home, see things, go places. Better?"

"Better," I say.

"What we're seeing right now is a twinkling farewell concert: Thanks—you've been great. Drive safe, now."

I laugh. " 'Drive safe, now'? Really? That's what they've got to say?"

"Mmmm." Dulcie nods. "Stars. Twinkly, yet surprisingly considerate."

I can't seem to stop myself from taking hold of her other hand. I lace my fingers through hers and rub my thumb over her palm. The skin there is rough, calloused, like she's been hitting it against something hard. "What happened here?"

She slips her hand out of mine. "Nothing," she says, frowning.

I don't know what I've said. I've just started to ask when

Left Guy moans louder and rolls onto his side like he's in pain.

"Is he okay? Should we do something?"

Dulcie waves it away. "He's fine. He's going to blow chow in about twenty minutes, but he's not going to die."

"I don't know. He doesn't look so good to me."

Dulcie shakes the jelly-bean bag, hunting for the right flavor. "Trust me, he doesn't die for another forty-two years."

My stomach goes cold. "Hold up—you know what's going to happen to him? You can see people's futures?"

The fire casts shadows across Dulcie's face, dulling some of the brightness. She's got a weird expression, like she swallowed a popcorn jelly bean when she thought she was getting lemon. "I didn't say that."

"Yeah, actually, you just sort of did."

"You sure you don't want to see that ice sculpture thing . . . ?"

"No. Do not change the subject. All this time, you've been feeding me bullshit about not knowing and only being a messenger when you can see the future—*my* future?"

"I told you, I didn't say that." She looks pained. "Cameron, please. Trust me."

"Why? Why should I trust you? Oh Jesus." I laugh. "I'm in the middle of fucking nowhere, no meds, no doctors, all because of you!"

"You're *alive*, Cameron."

"For how long?"

"How long does anybody have?" she asks softly.

By the campfire, the guys are really upping the ante with Balder. By my last count, he's been strangled twice, impaled four times with various objects, and had handfuls of rocks thrown at him. He's laughed off every insult with "Is that the best you can do?" I wish I felt as bulletproof.

I cross my arms and glare at Dulcie. "Tell me my future. I want to know."

"No can do. Against the rules."

"We're way beyond rules here, Dulcie."

She stands firm, and I can tell by the way she's set her chin that she's not budging on this one. Funny how you can start to know little things like that about people.

"Okay, fine. We'll take it down a notch. What about the goon brothers?" I ask. "Can you tell me theirs?"

She glances in their direction. "I'm telling you, Cameron, it's not a great idea."

"I think it's the best freaking idea I've heard in a long time. Go on. Fire away."

Dulcie fiddles with the laces on her combat boots. "No," she says quietly.

"Screw you, then." In the firelight I see Dulcie flinch. It's a small thing, but I feel lousy about it, and I wish I could take it back. She puts the jelly-bean bag to her head like a carnival magician deciphering a message from beyond through an object. "Marty—Left Guy—is going to barf hot dogs tonight."

The bag comes down, and Dulcie pops a green jelly bean in her mouth.

"You know that's not what I mean."

"Technically speaking, it *is* the future."

"Look, you got me out here, on some crazy mission, and I never know what's going to happen from one minute to the next. I don't even know if I'm going to live. The least you can do is tell me a few meaningless things—"

Her head snaps up. "Nothing's meaningless, Cameron."

"Tell me the future! Their futures. I want the real deal. Long-term stuff."

"Okay," Dulcie says, but she won't look at me. "He—Left

Guy—is going to end up running his uncle's restaurant. He'll have a serious alcohol problem and be divorced twice before he's forty. He'll think he's all chummy with the twenty-somethings who work for him, but behind his back, they'll comp all their friends and call him Chimp Brain."

I laugh. "Ha! That's amazing! Chimp Brain. What about the others?"

"Dave—Right Guy—is going to get married, have two kids, work as a computer programmer, and collect toy trains. He'll build this elaborate model train set in his basement and work on it on weekends."

Dave, Right Guy, is currently eating beans and franks out of a can with his fingers. The tomato sauce dribbles down his chin and onto his shirt.

"Sounds boring."

Dulcie watches him. "He loves it. It's his life."

"Whatever," I say, holding out my hand. Dulcie pours some jelly beans into it. I get a lime and a chocolate together. It tastes strangely good, tart and sweet at the same time. "What about Middle Guy?"

Middle Guy's singing a song about a guy named Louie while strumming his air guitar with real feeling. His goofiness is winning me over. Dulcie's gaze finds him briefly.

"Keith . . ." She stops.

"Yeah?"

"Keith—Middle Guy—is going to drop out of college next year, enlist in the army and go overseas." She picks out the green jelly beans and puts them methodically into her palm.

"And?" I say, downing the last of my candy. "That's it?"

"He'll tell everybody in his platoon about the day these guys gave him a ride to the Party House and he met Marisol and how she gave him a kiss and how it was the most rockingest time ever and that was the day he decided to quit school, which led to his joining the army. He'll be telling that story when he steps on a land mine hidden in the desert sand and gets blown to bits."

It's like the earth gives way underneath me and I have to jump up to make sure it's still there. "Whoa," I say, nearly falling over a rock behind me. "Whoa. God, Dulcie. Why the hell did you tell me that?"

"You asked. I told you it wasn't a good idea."

Middle Guy, Keith, hops around doing this goofy dance and singing loud. He's about as alive as you can get.

"That sucked, Dulcie. How do you expect me to drive this guy around knowing that?"

"Welcome to my life, cowboy."

I walk away from her, reeling, but come back. "If you know all this stuff about us . . . if you can see what's going to happen and it's already in motion, why bother? Why should we try to do anything? We can't change it."

She hops up, opens her arms wide. "Did I say that you couldn't change it?"

"No, but . . ."

"What I see is the course as it stands now. Today. At 10:27:07 p.m. Relatively Standard Time. Tomorrow, Keith could pick up a book, read a sentence there that completely alters the course of his life, and decide he wants to become an English professor and that's it. New ball game. Destiny isn't fixed, Cameron."

"A butterfly flaps his wings in South America and they get snow in Chicago," I say, repeating something I learned from my dad.

"Right. Exactly. The snow comes down in Chicago, and a seventeen-year-old kid's mom tells him to shovel the walk.

357

He's in the front yard just as this new girl walks by. She slips on a patch of ice, but he catches her, and that's how they start dating. And on and on, a revolving door of action-reaction, of interconnection. Things can change, Cameron. It's the one constant of this universe."

"So now, just by randomly picking Keith up on the side of the road, I've altered the course of his life?"

"And he's altered yours."

"But which way?"

She shakes her head. "That I really don't know."

"What if I told Keith not to enlist? That he'll die if he does?"

"You can try it, but he'll probably think you're crazy. Haven't you ever watched any TV sci-fi? People think they can warn other people and it always backfires."

"So I'm just supposed to sit with this information for the next one hundred miles to the Party House?"

"You feel responsible for his life choices?"

"Well, I didn't until a minute ago, till you sprung your little news on me."

"Sorry I upset you."

"Forget this, man. I'm gonna tell him," I say.

"Do whatever you need to do," she says, flopping to the ground. She opens the jelly-bean bag again and picks out two pink ones.

I make my way over to where Keith is sitting with Balder. "Hey, um, Keith, right?"

"Yeah, that's me." He goes back to singing his song and Balder joins in on the chorus. Balder, it turns out, is a very happy drunk.

I don't exactly know how to begin this conversation. How do you tell a guy you know how he's gonna die? "So what do you think you'll do, you know, after college and stuff?"

"I don't know. Can't think that far ahead."

"Maybe you'll meet somebody at the Party House."

"I have a house!" Balder slurs. "It is called Breidab . . . Bradeblack . . . Braeder . . . it is called Balder's house, and it is very, very nice. You should come and try to kill me again there."

"Awesome, dude." Keith fist-bumps Balder.

"You could totally meet somebody at the Party House," I say, trying to get Keith back on track. "And, you know, maybe she lives there and you'll want to stay."

Keith scratches his chin. "Yeah. Maybe. I hear Daytona's nice. I could be a beach bum for the rest of my life. Stay by the ocean."

"That sounds great, man. You should do that." Ha! Take that, Dulcie, you angel of doom.

"I don't know," Keith says. "Daytona's expensive, and my money for school just ran out. But I got a cousin in the army. He says they really take care of you. I was thinking of enlisting this summer."

Balder nods. "Man is the augmentation of the dust. Great is the claw of the hawk."

"Okay, Balder? Could you and your Norse goodness do me a solid and take a hike? I need a minute here."

Balder bows. "As you wish, Cameron the Noble. This Twist My Brains beer is worthy. I shall have more."

"You do that."

Balder stops to wrap a meaty arm around my neck. You wouldn't think a yard gnome would be so butch, but I can barely breathe. "What is your battle cry again?" Balder asks Keith. "Oh yes. *I love you. Man.*"

"Love you, too, B," I squeak out.

Balder releases my thankful neck. As he stumbles off, he crumples a beer can against his skull and it sticks there. One of the logs sinks deeper into the campfire, sending out a shower of sparks that flare in the dirt and vanish. It's getting a little chilly. I stick my hands in my pockets to warm them. Something sharp sticks me. I pull out the screw.

"What's that?" Keith asks.

"This? It's kind of a funny story. This old guy at a hardware store gave it to me. It's supposed to be important. Actually, he said it was a magic screw," I say, rolling my eyes so he doesn't think I take that shit seriously.

"A magic screw?" Keith repeats, grabbing it from me.

"Yeah? I know. Like I said, I didn't believe the guy. . . ."

Keith laughs so hard I'm afraid he'll burst something. "Hey, guys! Guess what Bonehead here has? A magic screw!"

Everybody's laughing now. Gonzo rouses from his stupor and makes high-pitched snorting noises.

"Hey, *I* didn't say it was magic," I argue. "Just that it's . . . a necessary part. That's what he told me. It's a necessary part."

"Necessary part of what?" Keith chokes out.

"I . . . don't know. He was old. A little senile."

"Dude, you totally believed him. Admit it." It's Gonzo. He's forgotten that these guys wanted to give him demeaning nicknames and has practically joined their fraternity.

"Laugh it up, Stumpy," I say.

Gonzo can't stop laughing long enough to be insulted. All I hear from him is a high-pitched "Magic screw!"

Keith's slapping Left Guy on the back. "Hey, baby. You wanna screw? No, it'll be magic, I swear." He breaks into a kind of chortling that comes out of his nose in snorts and honks. It's the sort of contagious laughing that ripples out to everyone.

"Yeah, yeah, okay. I was joking. . . ."

"No, no, I'm sorry, man. Here, let me make it up to you," Keith says, putting his arm around me and trying to get his breathing under control. There are tears streaming from his eyes. "You want a screw?"

That's all it takes for the whole crew to fall out again like a pack of deranged hyenas, their laughing punctuated only by guttural gasps of "magic" and "screw." I can see this will be the joke played out at my expense for the next one hundred miles.

"I'm gonna get some more firewood."

Dulcie follows me out of the campground. "You can get mad. It's okay. It won't kill you to say it, Cameron."

"I'm not—" I whip around. "Okay. Fine. Yes. I am mad at you, Dulcie. Satisfied?"

She curls herself up in her wings. "See? You're still here."

"I'm serious."

"I know. It's making me swoon. Tell me more."

"I'm mad because you came into my life and totally messed with it so I don't know what's what anymore."

"Uh-huh."

"I'm mad because you told me about those guys and now I have to care. I'm mad because you won't tell what's going to happen to me. Because you don't give guarantees."

"True, true." Her wings open up again.

"Jesus. I'm mad because you make me feel like things are possible when they probably aren't, or maybe they are, I don't know. I'm mad because . . ."

"Because?"

"Because you make me give a shit."

Dulcie gets really quiet. "Yeah. Sorry about that."

Her feathers smell like rainwater after a drought. She's so close I could kiss her. If I weren't so pissed off at her right now, I might try it. I want to fight with her, then kiss her. "And . . . and that's why I'm, you know. Mad."

"Thanks for telling me."

"You're . . . welcome."

"Cameron," she says, her face tilted toward mine. "It's about time."

"Time for what?" My mouth has gone dry.

"Time. Exactly twenty minutes."

With a thunderous groan, Left Guy sits up, dazed, and barfs hot dogs everywhere.

"Destiny's not fixed, huh?" I say. Dulcie doesn't answer. "Fuck this."

I tear off the E-ticket wristband and toss it in the weeds.

"Cameron, wait!" Dulcie calls out, but I'm already running.

I walk in circles for hours, until I'm exhausted. When I come back, the others are passed out. I feed some twigs to the dwindling campfire and sit to think. What Dulcie said has me all messed up inside. Why didn't she tell me this before? Can she see what's going to happen?

I rub my wrist where the E-ticket used to be. My muscles burn, and I feel a spot of fear laced with hopelessness growing larger.

There's a rustling sound. At first I think it's some animal, but then Balder drops next to me by the fire. He's got Keith's jacket around his shoulders and a bag of marshmallows in one hand. In his other is the E-ticket, which he places on the thin strip of dirt between us. He squints up at the night sky. "Ah. Do you see Hati chasing Mani? It is the ravenous wolf in relentless pursuit!"

Thin wisps of gray cloud stretch their jaws across the moon.

"That's the moon. And that's a cloud. No wolf."

"You're mistaken!" Balder says cheerily. "It is the—"

I slap my hand against the ground making the E-ticket jump. "They're just fucking stories, okay? Like Santa Claus and the Tooth Fairy. It's bullshit we tell ourselves so we don't feel afraid."

Balder turns back to the fire, and I'm sorry for yelling at him. He threads a stick with marshmallows. "Shall *I* tell you a story?" he asks softly. "You don't have to believe it if you don't want to."

I want to say no. Or maybe yes. But my throat's too tight to make a sound. And then, as if he can read my thoughts, Balder begins.

"I wish you could see my homeland. In the winter, the snows greet you with vigor. Every breath you take is a warrior's breath, fighting against that worthy adversary, the cold. Ice floes drift past our longboats, and the sails are as ghosts in the mist. But in the spring! In the spring, the land is the green of a ribbon plaited in the golden hair of a village girl you've glimpsed only once, fleetingly, as your horses lead you on toward battle, but whose face you remember the rest of your days. Golden-grass fields rise and fall to the sea. There are mountains! Great, slumbering giants of rock who wake with a frightful noise from time to time, shaking the earth, belching heat, reminding us that change is always at hand. At the great ash tree, Yggdrasil, which holds our nine worlds, the Norn tend the roots, keeping them nourished that they not decay, deciding men's fates with a length of string. Above it all, Frigg spins clouds that float in the ever-blue like giants' eyes watching from a careful distance. And there is Breidablik, where all are welcome and no lies may enter through its stones. My great, gleaming hall." His voice falters. "My home."

Balder's eyes twinkle with pride and sadness. I think of my dusty Texas town. Other than Eubie's, there's not much to miss.

"You're not the only one who feels such pain, Cameron. There have been many times during my captivity that I dearly wished I were not immortal, that I could die. But then you came. This quest has renewed my hope."

His eyes search mine. I nod toward the blackened marshmallows. Balder shakes them off, lets the fire take them, and starts over with fresh ones.

"You are like the Allfather, Odin," he says after a while.

"What do you mean?"

Balder turns the stick in the fire. "When Odin heard of the coming of Ragnarok, of the end to the days of gods, he found no more joy. The foreknowledge of our fate was too much to bear. He refused all food and sank into despair."

"I'm not that dramatic," I say, because he's making me feel like a wuss.

"You miss the point. Like Odin, you see only the coming doom and lose faith in what is here, what is good."

I lean my head back. The moon bleeds a hole into the night sky, a wound that seems beyond healing. "So what should I believe in?"

"That I cannot say. For me, it is the dream that *Ringhorn* waits for me on the sea. That I shall sail through the eternal mist until Breidablik gleams in the distance. That I will return home. Here." Balder offers me the gooey browned mess at the end of his stick. "You must have sustenance."

"That's a marshmallow," I say, but Balder insists. Gingerly,

I pry the bubbling thing loose, blow, then drop it in my mouth where it coats my tongue in scorched sweetness. "Thanks."

In the firelight, Balder's features are sharply illuminated. I've never noticed the tiny lines at the corners of his eyes, the weariness etched there. "The dark does not weep for itself because there is no light. Rather, it accepts that it is the dark. It is said that even the gods must die." He winks. "But not without one hell of a fight."

"Can I have another marshmallow?" I ask.

Balder cooks me up another one, and it's as good as the first. "If you are in need of more guidance, I could draw a rune." He tugs the pouch free from under his tunic. It sits in his palm, heavy with destiny.

I shake my head. "Let's just see what comes."

He pushes the E-ticket meter a little closer to me. He thinks he's being clever. Vikings. Not great at subtlety. With a sigh, I pick it up and he helps me fasten it on my wrist again. The cloud shifts into a shapeless blot. A raccoon comes sniffing for food. For a few seconds, it skirts the edge of the fire, nose up, smelling. And then it scurries off into the brush.

CHAPTER THIRTY-EIGHT

Wherein We Discover What Assholes These Mortals Be

The hundred miles to Daytona are a rough, quiet affair. Everybody's hungover but Balder and me. Every eight miles or so, I have to pull over and let somebody puke.

The guys are splayed out in the backseat sleeping when they're not sick. Up front, Gonzo's curled on the front seat with his head against the door and the seat belt lax across his middle like a mom's arm around you when you're a kid. He's got on a pair of little-girl sunglasses we bought at a convenience mart. They're bright orange cat's-eyes with rhinestones on the winged part. He wanted the mirrored aviators but the adult size was too big for his face. Fortunately, when you're extremely hungover and the sun is torturing your eyes, you'll wear any old damn thing.

The land's flattening out the closer we get to the beach. It's like we're going to drive off the edge of the world. On the sides of the road, the ground's gone patchy as an old man's beard, half sand, half scrub. The air pushing past my open car window is thick with that salt-spray smell. I stick my head out and let it coat my face.

The thing is, I can't stop obsessing over what Dulcie told me about Keith stepping on that land mine. Why do I care? He's a jerk. A week ago, I would have said, hey, natural selection, man. Stupid people, out of the gene pool. But now I know that in addition to being a boneheaded jerk, Keith also has a mom and a dad and two younger sisters he takes out for ice cream whenever he gets home. I know he sings goofy, off-key songs and has a habit of kissing the top of your head when he's really drunk.

The exit for South Daytona Beach puts us in a line of cars that's backed up for miles. A melting pot of different songs flows out of open car windows. Girls stick their feet out windows. Surfboards are attached to car roofs. Some idiot is actually lying on the car roof with one of those silver reflector pads, trying to get a tan. The guys are awake now and ready for action. They scope each car we crawl past. If it's a girl car, they pile their faces out the windows and chat them up, make jokes—anything to try to score their digits or hotel info. We've been in this line for thirty minutes and have only gone a half a mile. At this rate, we'll be stuck in traffic for hours, and that's time I just can't spare.

"Hey, guys," I say as we get close to a side-road escape route. "I don't want to be a jerk, but we've gotta get on the road."

"Oh hey, it's cool," Left Guy says. "We can make it from here. Can you just pop the trunk?"

With the engine still running, I get out and open the trunk. Right and Left Guy pull out their gear. Keith waits his turn, holding his jacket and a bag of snacks. He looks sleepy and content, and an image of him tromping through the desert weighs me down.

"Dude, you're the best. Thanks, man." He gives me a manly hug.

"You're welcome," I say. Before getting back in the car, I add, "You should definitely kick it on the beach as long as you can."

I promise I'll tell Gonzo they said goodbye, since he's sleeping off his two beers. There's the inevitable "Stay cool" and "Party hard" well wishes, even though those two things seem like a contradiction, and they hurry down the road asking everybody for a ride.

An hour later, Gonzo wakes up in desperate need of food. We opt for a twenty-four-hour breakfast joint. I go to wake Balder, but he's no longer nestled in my Windbreaker. He's not in the car at all. He's just gone. We call his name. Nothing.

"Where could he be?" Gonzo asks, checking under the seat for the fortieth time.

"I don't know. He was in the car when we started on the road this morning and . . ." I flash back to the traffic jam. The trunk hood up like a shield. Keith coming around from the front with his hands full and his face flushed and smug. Sonofabitch.

"What's the matter?" Gonzo asks.

"Those assholes kidnapped Balder."

CHAPTER THIRTY-NINE

In Which Gonzo and I Make
an Unscheduled Visit to the Party House

We're back in that traffic jam that stretches a full ten miles out of Daytona. I keep scanning the horizon of heat squiggle and cars, looking for the guys, but no luck. The Caddy's revving into the red zone. It smells like hot oil. I keep turning the engine on and off so it doesn't overheat and die on us.

"We gave them a ride and they took Balder," I grumble.

"Sucks," Gonzo agrees. He's got his orange little-girl sunglasses perched on top of his head like an extra pair of eyes.

"What a bunch of total punks."

"Totally." Gonzo's smiling like a crazy man, and it's annoying me.

"What's got you in such a good mood?"

He slips the glasses back over his eyes. "Dude, we're going to the Party House!"

The Caddy can't take the heat, so we leave it by the side of the road about two miles from the Party House. The entire road is jam-packed with hotels.

"Can we just rent a room for the night? I need a shower," Gonzo says. He sniffs his shirt and makes a face.

"You'll live," I say. We're getting Balder back and hitting the road, no stops.

Gonzo sniffs my shirt and grabs his throat like he's choking. "Dude, *you* reek!"

"I'm not that bad," I argue.

"Not that bad? Fucking A, dude! Have you had your olfactory sense removed? Seriously, man, you are not going to see any action if you don't clean up, you know?"

"I'm not looking for action. I'm looking for our yard gnome."

Two girls in bikinis and navel rings pass us. One of the girls has a skateboard tattoo on her arm. Mr. Happy rises, unbidden, to say hello, like he's the sheriff in this here town. When they move on, I give myself a quick sniff. Holy cow. I could kill someone with my BO.

"Did I warn you or what? Dude, just for the night. Come on. It's the Party House!" He's jumping up and down, pulling on my stink shirt and whining like a kid brother.

"Okay," I say. "But it'll have to be someplace dirt cheap."

It takes some doing, but we find a no-frills bungalow motel. I hate using the credit card, but since we should be long gone before they can trace it, I figure we're safe. And the shower feels amazing.

Gonzo bursts through the door. "Dude! You should see how many people are here! It's awesome!"

The beach is swarming. Volleyball and Hacky Sack games have sprung up here and there. Girls sun themselves on beach towels with their bikini tops untied in the back. The Party

House—a sprawling, ultramodern megamansion made of glass—shimmers on the horizon. They've built a couple of stages in and around the place. I think they're filming something. Camera crews are everywhere, and we have to step over tons of wires.

A group of television-perfect teens in headsets and bathing suits work the crowd.

"Hey, would you like to be on our TV show?" a girl in a yellow flowered bikini and an edgy black haircut asks. She's got a clipboard in her hands and a kitty-cat pen that looks like it should belong to a third grader.

"We have to find somebody . . . ," I say, craning my neck.

"Can you just answer some quick questions, then? Please? It would totally help me out?"

"Go for it. Don't worry about me," Gonzo says. He's looking over at a group of tattooed guys smoking cigarettes. His video-game geek monitor must have picked up their signals.

The girl smiles at me. "Please?"

"Just a sec," I tell her. To Gonzo I say, "Okay. But keep a low profile. We'll meet up in an hour over there by the stage. Got it?"

"Stage. One hour," he says. He walks right over to those guys and starts talking. It's the amazing thing about Gonzo. For all his weird-ass phobias about dying, he's absolutely fearless about people.

"Ready?" the girl asks, taking my arm.

"Guess so," I say, following her into the Party House.

"What's your name?" she asks, leading me into a gigantic, glassed-in living room where we have to squeeze between sweaty dancers. I can barely hear her over the thumping bass line of the music.

"Cameron," I say. "What's yours?"

"Iphigenia," she shouts.

We leave the living room and enter a kitchen area, where some kids are reading from scripts for a table of three judges. The judges give them notes about reading "more pissed-off" or "let's create drama."

"What's that?" I whisper.

"Oh," Iphigenia says. "We're casting for a realitymercial. It's like a reality TV show mixed with an infomercial. If you like what you see happening here, you can call the 1-800 number and order up any of the custom-made lives demonstrated by the characters and, you know, try them on for size."

"Custom-made lives?"

"Yeah. We send you the clothes and the name and the backstory. So you can be the troubled kid from the trailer park who comes with the *Wrestle Craziness!* package. Or the bright, hopeful inner-city kid of *Dope I. Am.* The wardrobe and sound track for that one are killer. Or the rich heiress of *Envy Me.* That one comes complete with a small dog and a cell phone that you can have surgically attached to your wrist. And there's *Gosh, I'm Lucky,* which is the innocent country girl with the awesome singing voice. That tested huge."

Iphigenia pushes open a door to a small office space and offers me a chair in front of a desk. She slips into the chair behind the desk. Something's ringing.

"Excuse me for a sec." She locates the ringing device and attaches herself to a headset. "This is Iphigenia. Uh-huh . . . uh-huh . . . do you want the Rad XL, the Rad Diet, the Rad Sport, or the Rad Clear and Brite?" Iphigenia makes some notes on a pad with her kitty pen. "Nuclear!" she says brightly, and hangs up.

I'm still puzzling over the realitymercial thing. "I don't get it. Why would anybody want to order up somebody else's life?"

Iphigenia looks at me like I'm an idiot. "Why? Because figuring out who you really are is hard work. Why do all that if somebody else has done it for you, if they can tell you who to be? It's like me with Iphigenia." She whispers, "That's not my real name."

"No?"

"No. My real name? Ann. Jones." She rolls her eyes and giggles. "Can you imagine anything more boring? Yeah, Ann Jones is not going to get behind the velvet rope. So I changed it. I read that name in some Fake It! Notes and liked it."

"You know, the Greeks sacrifice Iphigenia. So they can get home."

She lights up. "Hey, so it has a tragic feel to it? Big drama name. I love that!"

"But why not just be who you are?"

"Hello!" she says, pushing away from the desk and twirling around in the rolling chair till she's facing me again. "Nobody wants to be themselves. That's why there's TV. So you know what to want and who to be. That's what I did. I mean, Ann Jones? Ann Jones played flute in marching band, okay? Ann Jones's future was going to include a good state college and a few boyfriends and, you know, like maybe a used compact car to get to her job at a yogurt shop. But Iphigenia, one name, is, like, a totally different person. She's ethnically ambiguous—you're like, 'Is she Afro-Greek-Japo-Indian chic?' She has a dad who had a slight alcohol problem, which gives her street cred, and a mom who used to model in her native country, wherever that is, which makes her hot. She wears the latest jeans and everybody copies her. Everybody

373

listens to her and sees her and wants to be her. I mean, you're nobody unless everybody knows who you are."

I nod, speechless.

She grabs her pen, all business. "Questionnaire time. Where are you from, Cameron?"

"Texas."

"Ride 'em, cowboy!" she says, apropos of nothing. "So, who are your best friends?"

"Gonzo and Balder," I say. I like the way it sounds.

"What do you guys like to do?"

Go on insane road trips dictated by personal ads in tabloids. Search for fugitive, time-traveling doctors. Evade the cops. Steal money from low-rent druggies. Fight beings from parallel worlds.

"Hang out," I answer.

"Mm-kay. Good. Anything interesting you want to add?"

I should tell her a bunch of bullshit, but for some reason, I want to be honest.

"I've got a fatal illness. Creutzfeldt-Jakob."

Iphigenia writes something, then scratches it out. "How do you spell that?"

"Just put mad cow disease."

"Great!" She jots it down. "Now for the really important questions. Do you drink Rad soda? And if so, how often? Frequently. Often. Rarely. Never."

"Rarely."

The kitty pen bounces across the page like a deranged pet. "Which of these situations would most increase your thirst for a Rad soda? Hanging with friends. Talking with Mom and Dad. Playing a game of hoops. Going to the mall. Doing homework. Attending a funeral . . ."

"Attending a funeral?"

She shows me the paper and I see the question right there. "New marketing strategy. They're getting ready to launch a new teen drink? Rad Grief—'For those times when your thirst needs a friend.' So, do you think you would drink Rad Grief?"

Death and soda don't really go together in my head, but it's getting late and I need to find Gonzo. "Sure. You bet."

Iphigenia lets out a little squeak and bops in her chair. "Excellent! You're my first yes. Hey, Cameron, you're so nice. Would you like me to get you on one of the shows? They need players for *What's Your Category?* today. Whaddaya say?"

"I don't think . . ."

"I could totally hook you up with the producers. You can win a lot of money," she singsongs.

My brain does a cost analysis: could I win us some cash, find Balder, and get our butts out of here before we're found out? The Party House crowd doesn't really watch the news, and the bounty hunters probably aren't watching YA! TV. It's a risk, but a risk with a lot of money attached, and we desperately need the money.

"Sign me up."

"Nuclear!" Iphigenia says. "Okay, we need to figure out what category you go in."

"Category."

"Yeah, like are you a techno gadgetronic, a Saturday cinephile, sports authority, sex machine, audio boss, comics crusader, party hopper? You know. Where do you fit in?"

"What's an audio boss?"

Iphigenia gives herself two big twirls in the rolling chair, first going left, then going right. "Somebody who's obsessed with music. Is that you? You seem sort of audio savvy to me."

"Well, there's this music store I like back home called Eubie's Hot—"

She brings the chair to a dead stop. "Great. So audio boss."

"Wait! I don't know that that's how I want to be categorized. I mean, maybe I'm a sex machine."

Iphigenia taps her pen while looking me up and down. "Doubtful."

"Or a techno gadg-a . . . gadge . . ."

"Gadgetronic. It's somebody who's way into electronics and wants the latest gears gear." Iphigenia's mouth forms an excited O. "Didya hear me say that? 'Gears Gear.' Omigod. No one's ever said that here before. So it's mine! I made it up. I have to fill out the form to make it officially my trademark phrase. Hold on a sec, 'kay?"

Iphigenia's fingers fly over the keyboard. She hits Send. "Done. God, that would be so cool, wouldn't it? I could probably turn that into a clothing line—Gears Gear. Anyway, back to you. So would you say you're a techno gadgetronic, then?"

"No. I mean, not really."

Iphigenia's getting antsy. She taps her fake nails against the tabletop. "Well, you have to be something."

"What if I'm a lot of different somethings?"

"No can do. It messes with the marketing plan. Just one thing. If we can't categorize you, then you can't play."

"What category are you?"

Iphigenia smiles. "Oh! I'm a trendinator."

"Trendinator?"

"Yeah. That's somebody who's totally ahead of the curve on trends. Like, we sort of predict what's going to be hot next. Trendinators are sort of the top. God! I wish I had trademarked that phrase, because the merch is out of control. The handbags alone go for two fifty a pop."

"Just because they say trendinator on them?"

"No! They don't say anything at all on them! That's the genius of it. It's like, you're so far ahead of the curve that all there is is blankness."

Iphigenia's feather sparkle pen with the One Love Kitty hovers over the page. She's itching to categorize me.

"Audio boss," I say.

"Cool! Hey, you wanna see the rest of the Party House? We've got a pool that shoots Rad XL Soda—'The Soda for Our Generation'—out of a fountain in the back. It is so nuclear." She sighs. "I've been trying to get 'nuclear' to catch on for ages—like, at least three weeks—but so far, all the feedback forms say it's just not time for it yet. Sometimes I'm so far ahead of the curve that no one gets me."

When we leave the office I'm officially signed up as a contestant for *What's Your Category?* to film at three-thirty. Iphigenia takes me to meet the show people and I sign a form saying I won't sue them for anything that happens to me as a result of being on their show. Ten feet away, Parker Day sits in his chair getting his hair and makeup done by a stylist while arguing with his agent on a cell phone that some poor schmuck assistant holds up to his ear. A bank of TVs above his head broadcasts live from the Party House, where Marisol interviews some shirtless jocks down by the pool before introducing a new video clip. Keith wasn't lying about Marisol. She is seriously fine, with coffee-brown skin, hazel eyes, and long, curly black hair. I keep hoping I'll see the guys and Balder in the crowd, but they cut to the video and there's nothing to do but hook up with Gonzo again and try our luck together.

* * *

Gonzo is ten minutes late. "Dude," he yells, running up to me all out of breath. "This place is amazing!"

"You're late," I say.

"Sorry," Gonzo says, even though I can tell he's not.

I fill him in about *What's Your Category?*

"Awesome!" Gonzo says. "Look, this guy just gave me his card. He said I'd be perfect for a show they've got in development where a bunch of rich, spoiled kids live with kids who have abnormalities. It's called *Freaks Versus Fantastics.*"

I snort. "Who's the sadistic shithead who thought that up?"

"Dude—I could be on TV! They've already got this kid with flippers for hands. He hates Little People. He'd be my roommate. They said the potential for drama is off the charts."

"Gonzo. Reality check. We're not staying. We still have to find Dr. X." I hold up my E-ticket meter. Fantasyland is losing color fast. "We're only here long enough to score some cash and find Balder."

Gonzo looks let down, and I feel like the asshole who just told him Santa's a front.

"Look, after that, if you wanna come back, that's cool. In the meantime," I say, showing him my contestant's backstage pass, "we have access to the green room and free food. Let's eat."

CHAPTER FORTY

Of What Happens When I Take My Chances on TV

At three o'clock, the *What's Your Category?* assistants come to the green room and escort me to makeup. Parker Day's sitting in the chair getting a touch-up, a phone pressed to his ear. I can hear him making deals with this soda company, that shoe corporation, arguing with his agent, telling an assistant that he shouldn't have to *ask* her to pick up his dry cleaning, she should just *know.* Our chairs are less than five feet from each other, and while the makeup lady does her thing, I keep stealing glances at Parker, trying to dissect what makes him a star. There's the short brown hair with subtle blond tips. A worked-out body under a form-fitting vintage rocker tee. The year-round tan. The roughed-up jeans that probably cost more than I could make from twelve Buddha Burger shifts. No doubt about it, he's a good-looking guy, but in a generic way, like some kind of human wallpaper you'll want to change out for something else in a few years.

Once I'm camera-ready, the assistants lead me to my spot on the re-created beach stage complete with grass huts and tiki torches on the sides. The director downloads info about the camera, which I can't take in because in front of me is a sea of people and my stomach is in free fall. Down in front, I see Gonzo giving me a thumbs-up and a nervous smile. Off to the side of the stage, Parker examines his notecards while a wardrobe lady steams the creases out of his jeans. The director calls for places. The cameraman gives us a three, two, one. The little light goes on and Parker Day walks out to a thunderous roar from the crowd. He works it, shaking hands and giving a big "Ho-oh!" into the mike, which everybody repeats to him.

"Hel-lo! I'm Parker Day, coming to ya live from the Party House in Daytona Beach, Flo-ri-da!"

The crowd goes wild, and Parker gives them a moment while he mugs for the camera. "Brought to you in living madness by Rad Soda—the Soda of Our Generation." Parker takes a slug from his Rad XL can and hands it to an assistant. "Today on *What's Your Category?* we've got a new challenger, Cameron, an audio boss from *Te-jas*. Cameron, come on down, my man."

I move to my appointed spot beside Parker, who has a cheat sheet with all my info filled in, courtesy of Ann "Iphigenia" Jones. "Cam—it says here that you have mad cow disease. Is that right?"

"Yeah." Man, I hope we're long gone before this airs.

"So how's that going for you?"

"Uh . . . it sucks?" I say.

Everybody laughs and Parker slaps me on the back. "You're funny, Cameron. I like that. Okay, Cam, as you know, on *What's Your Category?* we ask you questions about your area of expertise, which is . . ." He puts his mug right up in the camera and drops his voice low. "Audio boss!" I've seen Parker Day enough to know that they're doing some cheesy reverb action on his voice when he says "audio boss." It gets the whoops and hollers from the audience, though. They're expecting it. "So. I will ask you the questions printed out on these white cards in my hands. If you answer successfully, you will advance to the next round of questions, where the cash values are even higher. But if you miss a question, we'll be forced to take a toe. Just kidding."

The crowd laughs at his lame joke. I glance down at Gonzo, who mouths the word *pendejo,* which makes me feel a little better.

"No, if you miss a question, you'll be forced to sit in the . . ."

"Dunking chamber!" the audience screams.

A couple of stagehands in black T-shirts and jeans hustle a portable potty with a big red HIT ME button on its side onto the stage. Parker opens the door so that everyone can see inside. The smell knocks me back. A rickety platform is poised above the open latrine. Somebody's placed a shoe on the platform.

Parker pinches his nose with his free hand. "Yes, ladies and gentlemen and Cameron. Once you're placed in the Dunking Chamber you will be asked an all-or-nothing question. If you answer correctly, we will double your winnings and you will not need to shower with a household pine cleaner for a week. But if you answer it incorrectly . . ."

Parker hits the HIT ME button. The chair above the potty releases the shoe into the latrine with a loud flushing sound. The shoe is sucked down into a hose large enough to hold a person and flushed out into God only knows where. The camera zooms in on the clear plastic tube so that the fans back home don't miss a single disgusting minute of human waste. In the front row, Gonzo looks like he might be sick, and I'm wondering what the hell I've gotten myself into.

"You've had all your shots, right?" The audience laughs and Parker gives one of those dazzling smiles he's so famous for.

A stagehand helps me up the ladder and gets me in position on the platform. It smells like the kind of farts your grandfather lays down. The lights are hot, and all I can see in front of me is a mass of tanned, half-dressed bodies in various stages of drunkenness.

Parker shields his eyes with the card-holding hand to look up at me. "Cam, you okay up there? That mad cow disease kicking in?" He leans in to the camera and uses that low voice everyone loves. "Moo."

There's a lot of foot stomping, clapping, and cheering. I just want to win some cash and find my yard gnome. It's not a lot to ask.

"Okay, let's do it. Cameron, who sings the Rad soda anthem, 'Make Mine an XL'?"

The Rad soda anthem is only on TV or the radio every fifteen minutes. He's starting with the easy ones.

"Uh, that would be Big Philly Cheese Steak."

"You are absolutely right. And a big one hundred dollars goes into the *What's Your Category?* account."

The light-up board rings and flips over a flashing one hundred sign. The crowd cheers. Somebody screams out, "Dunk him!"

"Question number two, Camster. What album does the coyote use to trick the roadrunner into thinking there's a stampede of elephants after him? Take your time."

"El—" I start.

Parker holds up a hand. "Take your time. Don't rush."

Oh. Right. He wants me to milk it for the home audience. Create suspense.

"Uh," I say, screwing up my face like I'm trying to solve one of my dad's quantum physics equations. "I'm not sure, but I think, I think it's *Elephants Are After Me, Volume One*?"

"Cameron," Parker says, looking very serious. "You . . . *smoked* it!" People go wild.

"Okay, Cam. Getting serious now. Big money time. Two-part question. Part one: Who composed the highly influential 'Cypress Grove Blues'?"

"Junior Webster."

There's a murmur of appreciation in the crowd.

"Cam-my-man is on fire. Part numero dos: What does Cypress Grove refer to?"

I am about to hand Parker Day his stylist-assisted ass on a platter. "A cemetery in New Orleans."

Parker raises that much-photographed eyebrow. "You sure about that?"

"Yeah."

"You're ab-so-lutely sure?"

"Well . . . yeah. I guess so."

"You don't sound so sure."

"No. I mean, yeah. Yeah, I'm sure."

He strokes his chin meaningfully. "Oh, Cam-Cam-Cam. I am sorry but that . . . is incorrect."

"Incorrect? No way. I've been there. I met him . . ."

"You met Junior Webster. Sure you did, sponge brain. The correct answer is, the town of his birth. See? Town of his birth. Right here. On the card." He presents the card to the camera for a close-up. "Camtoid, I'm going to have to ask you to take a seat in the . . ." Parker leans toward the audience, his hand cupping his ear.

"Dunking chamber!" they shout, right on cue.

I climb up the rickety ladder to the platform. As I do, I hear Gonzo's lone voice. "You da man, Cam!"

My head's swimming, both from the smell and my thoughts: if Cypress Grove wasn't the cemetery he meant, then maybe I went to the wrong place, which would mean I got the wrong message, which would mean this whole trip is wrong and I'm doing this for nothing. There's no way to know for certain. I'm choked by a panic that has nothing to do with the Dunking Chamber.

"Cam, you okay up there? Need some help?"

"Huh?" I realize I've stopped at the top of the ladder. I scoot out and take a seat on the platform over the cesspool.

"You comfy up there, Cam-man?" Parker asks. It would be so easy to swing a foot out and kick him in that photogenic head.

"Like a bug in a rug," I answer. This actually gets a laugh from the crowd.

"Okay. Last question. For all the money. We're going to play a sound bite from a song. You have to tell me the song and the artist. Get it right, and you win six hundred bucks. Get it wrong, and it is down the flusher with the Cam-a-lama-ding-dong. You ready?"

I nod.

The speakers crackle to life. A song wafts out. A haunting melody on recorder and ukulele. And then that helium-high Portuguese vibrato floats over the crowd. It's possible I have the biggest shit-eating grin in the history of television.

"Oh, Cam. Do I sense you're in trouble?" Parker asks, moving toward the HIT ME button. "Time for your answer."

"Oh, dude," I say, shaking my head and sighing. They want some good television, I'm happy to oblige. "Gimme a minute."

"Ten seconds on the clock, Big Cam."

In the audience, people start counting down, "Ten, nine, eight, seven . . ." Gonzo's eyes are huge, his lips barely moving as he counts with them. I let them get to "zero." The buzzer goes off. The ruffing dog noise spreads through the crowd like a wave.

"Time's up, Cameron. Have you got an answer?" Parker's licking his lips. His palm hovers over the button, just itching to dunk me into a nasty pond of muck.

"Yes, Parker. I believe I do. That would be *'Viver É Amar, Amar É Viver'* by the Great Tremolo."

Parker's smug smirk vanishes. He looks back down at his cards as if he can't believe what's written there. The crowd goes quiet. They want dunking action, and they don't know why it's taking Parker so long to satisfy them.

"Cameron, Cameron, Cameron," Parker says, shaking his head. The crowd's on edge. "You. Are." He sighs, and his hand gets closer to the button before he pulls it away completely. "*Absolutely right!* Come on down, Cam-my-man."

An assistant helps me down the ladder to the huge applause from the audience and a few jeers. "You've just won six hundred dollars and a case of Rad Mellow—keep it on the chill-low with Rad Mel-low."

An assistant pulls out a wagon filled with Rad Mellow six-packs, and Parker counts off six hundred dollars, which I immediately stick in my pocket. We're back in the black. Now all we have to do is find Balder.

When I get offstage, Gonzo welcomes me with double high-fives. "Dude, you rocked the house!"

"Thanks, Gonz. Have you seen the goons who stole Balder?" I ask. The hot sun and my nerves have gotten the best of me. I'm starting to cramp up again, and my vision's a little blurry.

Gonzo shakes his head. "Not yet, man. Hey, you okay? You don't look so good."

I'm sweating freakin' bullets. "I'm just overheated."

We're pushed along with the crowd down to the beach, where they've built a large, open-air platform designated STAGE THREE. It's a Marisol event. In her bright pink sarong and half-shirt, she's waving to the crowd and blowing kisses, her long black curls shining under the sun. If we've found Marisol, we'll probably find the goons.

"Hey," I ask a girl who's on her way in. "What's this show?"

"Some kind of auction for charity," she says. "They let people come up onstage to auction off their most valuable or weird possessions. The more bizarre you are, the better chance you've got of getting on."

We thank her and push through the crowd. On stage, this chubby guy's standing there with an autograph he got from some movie star. A few bids are traded back and forth and the gavel comes down on a final price of $125. They usher the next idiot onstage. I can't believe it. It's Keith. And he's holding Balder, who's been outfitted in a frilly pink dress, pantaloons, and a white lace bonnet.

"Gonzo," I say, pointing.

He starts to laugh but stops when he sees I'm not in a joking mood. "Dude, they put him in a dress."

A security guard the size of a compact car steps in front of us. He puts out a hand to stop our progress. "You can't go in unless you're part of the auction."

"That's our gnome! They stole him from us!" Gonzo yells.

The guy pushes us back, away from the stage. "Fine. You have the winning bid, you can get him back."

I stick my hand in my pocket, feeling the slickness of those six one-hundred-dollar bills. "Fine. We're in," I say.

The guy hands us paddles and we push our way up to the front. Keith is blabbing on and on about how he and his buddies kidnapped the gnome from the dean's house in the dead of night, making up a bullshit story so he'll sound hot. Marisol acts all enchanted. She flips her long, dark hair and gives Balder a kiss, then lifts his dress to show off his pantaloons.

Balder's bearing up with his usual stoic grace, but I know under that Zen master expression is a seething cauldron of gnome rage.

"I can't believe that guy. What a freakin' poser," Gonzo snarls.

Two supertall dudes crowd next to us, making it hard for us to be seen.

"Here. Climb up and get ready to bid," I say, boosting Gonzo onto my shoulders.

"Are you sure it's safe?" Gonzo asks. "You strong enough to hold me?"

"I can hold you long enough to win back Balder. You just be quick on that paddle." Gonzo's heavier than I thought, and my muscles feel the strain, but I can hold him for the five minutes this should take.

"How much we got?" Gonzo yells down.

"Six hundred," I croak back. My neck's killing me.

Keith finishes his shout-outs to a million buddies back home, and the bidding starts. It's fast and furious at first. Bids fly out from all over. But when it reaches three hundred bucks, most people drop out. It's just us and some other guys, bidding back and forth in twenty-five-dollar increments.

"Do I hear three fifty?" Marisol shouts to the crowd. "I've got three fifty!"

"Gonz! Who's bidding against us?" I say with effort. For a Little Person he is solid.

"Those assholes from the car. His buddies," he says.

Gonzo's paddle goes up. The bidding goes back and forth, till we reach $525. We've still got $75 in the bank. I'm sweating like a mofo. My muscles are getting stiff and twitchy. Man, not now. Please not now.

"They're weakening," Gonzo yells.

His paddle goes up. Marisol calls out $525. The twitch travels down my arms and into my legs. My knees are buckling.

"G-Gonzo," I sputter. "I can't hold you."

"Just one second, dude."

The guys make a counterbid of $600. Marisol wants it over. She yells going once, going twice, just as my legs give out and I fall to the ground with Gonzo on top. I hear Marisol shout, "Sold!" We've lost Balder.

"Dude, what the hell?" Gonzo yells, rubbing his head.

A guy with massively tattooed arms crouches down and asks Gonzo if he's okay. *Yeah, I'm fine, thanks. No need to check here. Just leave me on the ground, watch your step.*

"You all right?" Gonzo asks me, almost as an afterthought.

"No," I say, standing with effort. "We lost Balder."

"We'll get him back," he says, checking his head with his hands. "I'll be in the first-aid tent."

"Yeah. Got it," I snap, practically pushing him toward the tent with tattoo boy.

Keith welcomes his friends up onstage. He gives Marisol the gnome as a gift. She squeals and collects her prize, holding our gnome over her head, showing him to the crowd.

"He's so cuuuuute!" she yelps. "We're going to use him for the new ad campaign for *I Double Dog Dare You!*" The crowd loves this. They go wild. I remember the last TV spots they did for that show. It involved a stuffed bear. In one spot, they hacked his arm off with a chain saw. In another, they put a firecracker in his mouth and set it on fire. By the end of the five spots, he was nothing but a few pieces of dirty, scorched fluff attached to one glass eye.

"Hey, get a picture!" Keith Middle Guy Asshole Taker of Other People's Yard Gnome Friends yells out to his buddies. He puts his arm around Marisol. And she gives him a big kiss on the mouth.

"Whooo-hooo! This is the rockingest day of my life!" Keith yells. The guys make that weird dog sound they do when they want to show their support. My heart sinks, both because I've lost Balder and because I've somehow put Keith on a path to certain doom. I hate that I know this. I hate that I can't just hate him.

"Hey, Marisol!" Keith grins from ear to ear. "Wanna screw?"

There's a collective stunned gasp from the crowd. Marisol's mouth hangs open. Keith pulls my magic screw from his pocket and hands it to her. "Here. It's a magic screw. Supposed to bring you good luck."

People laugh now, even though it's about the stupidest thing I've ever heard. Marisol seems like she still wants to hit him but, hey, she's on TV and she needs to at least pretend to be cool, so she laughs, too, and says, "Omigosh, you are too funny!" The crowd yells "Magic screw!" over and over, and then Marisol signs off with her trademarked "I'm Marisol, over and outie—later days!" Thumping house music blares out of the speakers for the part where they roll credits on TV. Marisol does a silly dance with Balder and the screw, one in each hand, so that nobody gets the idea that she takes this—or anything else, for that matter—seriously. It's all one big laugh, one big party house. No need to care. Or get involved. No risk, no mess, no hassle.

A couple of suits meet Keith when he comes offstage. They shake hands and offer cards. "We loved what you did with that magic screw business," they say. "The kids loved it, too."

"Yeah?" Keith grins. "I didn't plan it or anything. It just happened."

"Yeah, great. Listen, we were just talking about building some YA! TV promos around you. You could be the wacky Magic Screw Guy. What do you say to that?"

"I'd be on TV?" Keith punches the air with his fist. "All right! Sign me up, man!"

"Great! We'll go fill out the paperwork. Listen, you like Rad soda?"

And just like that, something in the cosmos shifts. A butterfly flaps its wings in South America. Snow falls in Chicago. You give an idiot a stupid magic screw and it turns out to be a necessary part after all.

CHAPTER FORTY-ONE

In Which Gonzo Makes a Life-or-Yard-Gnome Decision

A hundred bucks of my prize money has gotten us intel about Balder. He's currently in Marisol's dressing room, where she's using him as a jewelry tree. Another hundred bucks has gotten us badges that allow us backstage access. The minute Marisol leaves her dressing room for the beach stage to film a spot, we duck inside. We find Balder buried under a collection of colorful scarves. His face is red and he looks tired.

"Thank the gods you've found me," he says with a sheepish smile. "I've never been so humiliated in all my life. Do you know she let her friends put makeup on me?"

Balder is indeed sporting some sparkly blue eye shadow and glossy lipstick.

"It's cool," Gonzo says. "You look pretty glam rock."

"Let's just get you out of here, okay?" I bundle Balder up

in one of the scarves and we head for the door just as Parker walks in.

"Cameron! The Cam-right-answer-man. What are you doing here?"

"Um, nothing."

"You smoked it today. Good job. Is that the gnome?" The scarf has fallen off Balder's face. Parker eyes us suspiciously. "What are you up to?"

"We . . . ah . . . they told us to bring it to the stage," I lie.

"Bullshit. I'm calling security." Parker reaches for his phone.

"Okay!" I shout. "You totally busted us. We just wanted to take some pictures. School prank. You know?"

"Yeah. I know. I know that you're trying to make off with YA! TV property. Gonna need this little guy for promos." He flicks his finger at Balder's nose. Balder flinches, but Parker doesn't notice.

"Parker. Please. Just let us take him for pictures." I fan out the bills in my hands.

Balder's eyes get huge.

"Come on, dude," Gonzo adds. "Don't make us go home empty-handed. There's bills riding on this in the locker room. Reputations."

Parker tries on a pair of expensive sunglasses and checks himself out in the mirror. "You can have the gnome," he says, taking off the glasses and pocketing them. "On one condition."

"Anything. You name it," I say.

He points to Gonzo. "Your friend here does *I Double Dog Dare You.*"

We are so screwed. Balder shuts his eyes. He knows his fate as a cross-dressing object of destruction has just been sealed.

"He can't, but I can," I say.

Parker shakes his head. He pokes through the food tray, taking some grapes and a hunk of cheese. "You've already been on. Besides, we've never had a dwarf."

I put the four hundred dollars on the table.

"I make that in an hour."

"What if I let you dunk me? You could put me back on the show and I'll miss the question on purpose and . . ."

"I'll do it," Gonzo announces with a look of grim determination on his face.

Parker grins at me and slaps Gonzo hard on the back. "Excellent! Little man, you just bought yourself a yard gnome."

He puts his arm around Gonzo's shoulders and ushers him down the hall.

Gonzo looks back at me. "It'll be okay," he says, puffing like a dying man on his inhaler.

"You okay, Balder?" I ask, once we're out of Marisol's room and sneaking our way out of the Party House.

"I have suffered the humiliation of capture, and I am what you call cranky, but I am okay. Thank you," he says. "I saw you bidding."

"You're welcome," I say. "I'm sorry I didn't realize they'd taken you till we were an hour down the road."

"Neither did I at first. I was asleep. Next thing I knew I woke up in a strange hotel room with those three idiots. They took photographs of me on top of the minibar and e-mailed them to all their friends. Posing me with chocolate bars and soda cans. Can you imagine?"

"Shake it off, man. You're okay now."

"Cameron?" A familiar voice stops me cold. Standing five feet in front me is my sister, Jenna. She's got on her white capris and a striped shirt. For once, her hair is not in a ponytail but down and curled. She looks different. Older, maybe. Less like a kid.

"Cameron!" she shouts, smiling. She runs over and throws her arms around me. "Oh my God! It is you!"

"Jenna, hey," I say, hugging her back as best I can with an armful of yard gnome. I'm not putting Balder down for anything.

"What are you doing here?" she says. Her eyes are wet. She rubs them with the back of her hand.

"Top-secret mission," I say, trying to make her laugh. It's what I used to do when we were kids.

"Cameron . . ."

I hold up a hand. "I know, I know. I'll explain everything. I promise. But first I've got to drop something off in my room. Wait right here."

I try to break away, but she pulls me back. Either I'm really weakening or she's got a grip that's even manlier than Chet King's. "No way," she says with a determined smile. "I'm going with you."

It would be impossible to fight her. "Fine."

We make our way downstairs and push through the packed bodies on the dance floor they've built on the beach, walking through the warm sand till we're at the crappy motel.

"Yikes," Jenna says, taking a look around at the seedy décor—the stained carpet, butt-ugly floral bedspreads, and lack of any amenity, like a minibar or even an ice bucket. She doesn't step inside.

"It's sixty-five dollars a night and free cable," I explain. "I'll be out in one second."

She nods and I enter the hazy room with Balder. I turn on the bedside lamp. "Balder, I've gotta deal with my sister. Will you be okay here by yourself?"

"Just lock the door, please," he says. "I don't care to have any more adventures."

"Sure thing."

"Cameron."

"Yeah?"

"That was a very brave thing you did today, rescuing me, offering all your money."

"Well, I couldn't let them turn one of my best buds into a promo snuff reel," I say.

Balder gives me a self-satisfied little smile. "I've told you, I can't be harmed."

"Yeah. Sure. I know that. But still."

"Will Gonzo be okay?"

Gonzo. Shit. "Don't worry. The show doesn't tape till late tonight. I'll rescue him before then and we'll all be long gone by morning."

Balder nods. For the first time, he looks worried. "What's up?" I ask.

"Sometimes, I dream of my ship, of *Ringhorn*. It shines like the sun after rain, and I'm running toward it."

"Sounds like a good dream."

His face is thoughtful. "But I never reach it."

"We'll get there," I promise him. "We'll make it to the ocean."

I help him up into Gonzo's bed, pour him a soda, and give him the remote. When I close the door behind me, he's lying there, happily channel surfing, a Viking warrior on spring break.

CHAPTER FORTY-TWO

Wherein I Have a Conversation with My Sister and the Fates Throw Me a Bone

Jenna and I find a place to sit in the loud, packed beach lounge. Every television is turned to YA! TV except one, which shows the ConstaToons channel. The sound has been muted on all of them. A succession of musical acts plays on the tiny stage—bands, acoustic-guitar girls, comics who sing, rappers. Partiers wander in from the mosh pit scene outside, carrying cups of beer. Some have flasks that they hide in their swim trunks and pull out when they think no one's looking. They're all checking each other out.

I buy Jenna and me a couple of sodas. It takes half an hour just to make it to the bar. "Here you go," I say, handing her a cup.

"It's diet, right?"

I roll my eyes. "Don't worry."

Some guy shoves another guy, who sort of half falls onto our table, nearly spilling Jenna's soda.

"Sorry," he says, laughing. "Look what you did, man!" he screams to his friends as he runs over and grabs one in a drunken headlock.

Jenna gives me a frogger in the arm, not hard, just like she used to do when we were eight.

"Ow."

"Cameron, I am so mad at you!" she says. "Why did you run away from the hospital? Have you really been doing all those things?"

I rub the sore spot on my arm. "It's hard to explain."

"Try me." She's got her all-business face on, the one that has seen her through countless cheerleader tryouts and student council elections. I'm defenseless against the Face. I take a deep breath and dive in. By the end of it, I'm exhausted and Jenna looks like somebody's secretly replaced her reality with a different one, which I suppose is one hundred percent true.

"You know this sounds crazy," Jenna says finally.

I shake my head. "Believe me, I know. But I'm not going back, Jenna. I can't. Not yet."

The guys goofing around near our table get a little too physical again, and the same guy bumps our table hard. He doesn't apologize this time.

"Do you mind?" Jenna says, and the guy moves away. "Cameron, how do you know this is all true?"

"I don't."

"That scares me."

"Yeah. It scares me, too." I need to change the subject, and fast. "So, spring break at the Party House, huh? How'd that happen? Weren't you supposed to go skiing with the Lord?"

She makes a face.

397

"I meant Chet. I get those two mixed up sometimes."

Jenna fiddles with her straw. "Chet and I broke up."

"Oh. Sorry."

"No you're not," she says, laughing.

Okay, I'm not. But I am sorry she's sorry. "He didn't mess with you or anything, did he?"

She rolls her eyes. "No. He just kept pressuring me to be more like him, and if I wasn't like him, he didn't know what to do with me. He's dating some girl from his church now. They like all the same things."

"Did you come here by yourself?" I ask. I can't imagine that. Dad wouldn't allow it, and Jenna can't go anywhere without at least two other girls in tow. It's against her personal bill of rights.

"I came with Staci and those guys. Mom said it would be good for me to get away." Jenna takes a drink of her soda, and we sit for a minute watching some punk-poser band in cutoff work pants and tattoos hop around onstage screaming out a song.

"Everybody's completely freaked out. I mean, Cam, those bounty hunters aren't fooling around, and Mom and Dad . . ."

"I know. I'm sorry. I promise I'll be back as soon as I can and make everything right. You're not going to tell them, are you?"

She gives me a hard look, like I'm material on the blackboard she needs to understand, classify, and master for the test. I never realized how much she's like Dad in that way. "Yeah. I am. I have to, Cameron. But I'll give you a head start. I'll wait till tomorrow when I call in again."

"Fair enough," I say.

Somebody's done the unthinkable and changed the channel to the news and our story. They cut from our flyer to

Arthur Limbaud at the lot of his Resale Beauties. He's sitting on the hood of one of his best, shiniest models, with his secretary by his side, not missing an opportunity to work it. It doesn't matter that the sound's muted, because I know what he's saying. He's telling them about us, about the car. They flash a picture of the Caddy up there, and we are in deep shit now.

The drunken idiot guys have stopped playing. They've broken out into a real fight. Other people are getting in on it now, either trying to break it up or land a few punches, too. Two guys fall into our table, and the crowd falls with them. Somebody pulls Jenna out of the mix on her side, a big dude in a Midgard University shirt. He's a good-looking guy.

"Careful there," he says.

"Thanks," Jenna says.

He sticks a hand out. "Name's David Morae."

"Jenna Smith."

"Nice to meet you, Jenna Smith."

Jenna laughs and shakes his hand. He's got her full attention, and that's just the opening I need to slip away.

Rescue Gonzo, pack up, and leave. Now. Immediately. That's the plan as I make my way through the hordes of spring breakers, trying to find a three-foot-six-inch dwarf sporting the world's most ridiculous mustache. I don't see him anywhere. It's wall-to-wall people. I bump into a blond chick.

"Sorry," I say, trying to move past her.

"Cameron? Is that you? Oh. My. God." Staci Johnson's standing right in front of me, holding a beer in a plastic cup.

"You look so hot!" The next thing I know, Staci Johnson kisses me, and it's like a mind eraser. "Where were you going?" she asks.

"Nowhere," I say.

"Want a beer?"

"You bet."

CHAPTER FORTY-THREE

In Which I Discover Eleven Dimensions
All in One Person

My whole body has that light, early-drunk feel. I've had three beers—not enough to get ugly or sick, just enough to be riding out a pleasant, mellow groove. Staci's only had two. She's very giggly. We dance for a few songs, and then Staci suggests we go back to my room. She wants to "see it."

"So, this is it," I say, letting her in. Balder's not on the bed. I guess he went out. The bedside lamp is still on; so's the TV. I flip it off.

"Great room," Staci says, flopping onto the bed.

"Thanks," I say, like I have anything to do with this shithole.

"You know I always liked you." She bites her lip. Her shirt's fallen off her shoulder. She's wearing a black bra. "But you seemed like you only went out with those smart, punker kinda girls. Remember when we were lab partners in seventh grade?"

"Yeah."

She traces a circle on my leg. "I gave you my school picture with *Love, Staci* on it. You were so nice. Hey, you're not drinking." She puts her still-full cup to my lips. "Drink, drink, drink."

The beer's warm and a little flat. Some of it dribbles down my chin and onto my shirt.

"Oops," she giggles.

I abandon the cup on the nightstand. Staci leans back on her elbows, giving me a calculated shy look. "So . . . did you ever think about me?"

"Yeah, sure."

"Shut up!" She swats at me playfully. "For real? Did you ever think about asking me out?"

I shrug apologetically. "I thought you only went out with the Über Genetic Specimen types."

"The what?"

"The Chet King guys."

"That is so not true!" She hits me on the leg again, and I wonder if I'm going to be completely bruised by the end of the night. She gets a serious look on her face. I'm not sure what to do, so I sit there and hope something brilliant comes to me. After a minute, she says, "Do you remember when I was dating Tommy?"

"Sure." Everybody remembers that. For a year, they were like one name, StaciandTommy, with daily hallway PDA. When school started again, they had become Staci. And Tommy.

"You know how he went to Dallas for the summer, for football camp?"

"Uh-huh," I say, like I follow Tommy's every move.

"He stopped calling me, and I knew, I just knew he was

with somebody else. He'd hooked up with this skank from Plano." Staci looks really small sitting on the cheap bedspread with her shirt falling down. "You know how I found out? I heard him talking to Bobby Wender and David Mack about her. He said she was the best he'd ever had."

I think about my dad and Raina, and I wonder if they've ever done it, and if so how many times? I wonder if Dad feels guilty. Or maybe he feels great. I wonder if my mom knows and if she cares. How do people stay in love, anyway? Is it a choice? Or is it like those plants we studied in biology that mutate into something new and totally different but are still part of the same plant family?

I've never been in love. I will die without knowing what it feels like to need to see one person's face when you go to sleep at night, to crave seeing it when you wake up. I wish I knew.

"Hey, Staci?" I say. "You okay?"

She tries to smile. "He'll be sorry. I've got big ideas. You know?"

"Oh. Sure. I mean, of course you do." We're in that weird no-man's-land. I'm not sure if I'm supposed to kiss her or just keep listening.

"Can I tell you something?" she asks.

"Sure."

"I've got this idea." She sucks on a strand of her hair in a way that gets a rise in my pants. "Are you sure you wanna hear it? I mean, it's probably stupid."

I put the pillow over my crotch. "I absolutely want to hear it."

Staci takes a sip of her beer and puts it back on the edge of the nightstand. "Okay. You know how, like, when you go to a restaurant they always have a host or hostess to seat you?"

I nod.

"Well, I was thinking of doing a reality show where people compete for a shot at being the host or hostess of a nice restaurant. We could call it *The Hostess*. Or *The Host* if a guy wins. Or, no, no! We'll do girls first and call it *The Hostess* and then guys and call it, *The Host*. I'm not talking about some cheesy restaurant like they've got in our shitty town. Like good restaurants in Dallas or Atlanta or something. I've already got all these ideas for stuff they'd have to do in the competition. . . . Am I boring you?"

"No. God, no."

Staci gives me a big, slurpy kiss on the cheek. "You are so friggin' cute, Cam! Okay, so, like, they would have to deal with problems, like if a homeless couple came in and wanted a table—but, like, they'd have money that we'd give them as a setup and a reservation, so what do you do? Do you seat them and gross out everybody in the restaurant and piss off your boss? Or do you tell them you can't find the reservation and wait for them to flip out on you? Stuff like that. And every week, somebody gets voted off until there's a winner.

"I was a hostess for a summer at Hooray, It's Wednesday's and it's not easy. People yell at you or they wanna switch tables all the time or sometimes, sometimes they just seat themselves even though there's a big friggin' sign up front that says HOSTESS WILL SEAT YOU."

"Sounds tough."

"Exactly." Staci crawls across the bed and kisses me. "You're so cute," she whispers. I hear a weird sound in the room. A snort or a cough. Something. There's Balder, sitting in a chair by the window, taking in the whole scene.

"Uh, excuse me for a minute," I say, removing Staci's arms. "Just a sec."

Balder's sitting stone-still with that cheery grin. "Sorry, buddy," I whisper. Before he can protest, I put him in the back of the closet.

"Now, where were we?" I ask, slipping back to the bed.

Staci crawls on top of me again. We kiss some more. I'm getting hard. I feel Staci up and she doesn't object, but that doesn't necessarily mean anything in girl language. Any second now, I could do "the wrong thing" and "the wrong thing" could end with me getting my face slapped and an evening spent in solo gratification. Since the feeling up has gone okay, I venture out a little more and find the buckle on her bra. There's no face slap. My fingers struggle to liberate the hooks, which were no doubt made by a group of nuns in a convent factory somewhere. Staci sits up. Shit, I did "the wrong thing."

"Here," Staci says, giggling. "Let me help you out with that." She gives me a coy grin, bites her bottom lip, and puts her hands behind her back so that her breasts are practically in my face. Two seconds later, the bra is flung across the room, landing on the TV. She's still got her shirt on, though. "Hold on. I have to pee." She stumbles off to the bathroom.

Oh my God. I think I'm about to have sex. With Staci Johnson.

I don't know what to do. Should we have music? I feel like we should have music. But all I've brought are those Great Tremolo CDs. I'd kill for a Junior Webster album right about now. But Tremolo will have to do. I put in *"Viver É Amar, Amar É Viver"* and push play.

The toilet flushes. Staci comes back out and practically falls into the bed. This makes her laugh some more. "What's this?" she says, meaning the music.

"The Great Tremolo. You ever hear it?"

Staci wrinkles her nose. "No. Wait, are they one of those Scottish bands? Is he singing in Scottish right now?"

"It's not a band. The Great Tremolo is a guy who sings Portuguese love songs that always end badly."

"Oh." Staci straddles my lap. She's brushed her teeth with my toothbrush in the bathroom. Between the toothpaste and the beer, her breath has a weird scent—mint mixed with grapes gone bad.

"He plays the ukulele, too." I'm losing my mojo. Like the bathroom break was just enough to make me nervous again. "So do you wanna hear some more of his stuff?"

Staci licks her lips. "Is that what you wanna do?" She slips her hands up my shirt and rubs them over my nipples. It seems like something she's read in a magazine and wants to try out. Jesus, she's going to town. My nipples are in danger of being erased.

"Here, just listen to one song," I say. I grab her wrists and take her hand off my chest. I turn up the volume as Tremolo whisper-sings the line about looking at his lover's face and seeing happiness. It's sort of beautiful. Cheesy, but heartfelt and sad and happy all at once.

Staci laughs so hard I think she'll fall off the bed. "Omigod. This guy sucks so bad. It's hilarious. You should totally put this on your MyNet page or something."

I nod, suddenly wishing she weren't here. *I looked upon your face and knew happiness.* I wonder if my dad has ever felt that about my mom or if my mom has ever felt that about Jenna and me. I feel kind of shitty for leaving them behind like I did, without a note or any kind of goodbye. I don't know, for the first time, the song hits me in the gut. Under the recorder, beneath the sort of bizarre lyrics is that pain Eubie talked about. This longing for something, for someone, all your atoms dreaming toward somebody else's. And just like that, Dulcie's face flashes in my mind. The way the light's all soft around her face, the goofy expressions she makes, the look of wonder when she smiles.

"Amor, amor, o meu amor," the Great Tremolo sings, and for the first time, I feel every note of it.

"What a retard," Stacy laughs.

I turn the music off. Suddenly, I don't want her to hear any more of this. I don't want to make fun of the Great Tremolo.

"What's wrong?" she asks, sitting up on her knees. Her shirt's half off.

"Nothing," I say. I kiss her hard on the mouth. I want to blot out everything.

Staci giggles. "Cam, I didn't know you had it in you." Her eyes are half closed and her mouth opens. I kiss her again and again. I keep kissing her, chasing a feeling that's staying just out of reach.

Staci fumbles with the buttons on my Levi's. Her warm hand slips inside my boxers, and I don't want her hand to go away, ever.

"Um, I don't have anything on me. . . ."

"It's okay," Staci says, kissing me some more.

This goes against all the responsible You Can Get Knocked Up the First Time/Don't Drink and Drive/This Is Your Brain on Drugs/STDs Don't Discriminate programming I've gotten through years of "very special guest speaker" assemblies in the auditorium. But then I remember I'm dying and it doesn't really seem like the time for caution.

"You sure?" I ask. I'm practically panting when I say it.

In answer, Staci pushes me back on the bed. We shed clothes like we're setting a land speed record. Her body feels soft but awkward against mine, like we don't quite fit. Then I'm inside, and I'm not thinking anymore. I couldn't if I wanted to. I try to say something to Staci but her eyes are closed and wherever she is, I don't think she's really with me. Maybe she's thinking about Tommy. It's like we're alone together, and it doesn't seem like that's how it should be. And then something explodes inside me.

"Oh shit," I say, teeth clenched.

The dust clears. I come back to my body. The digital clock flips over a few white numbers: 11:11. The whole thing has lasted three minutes. But I'm not going to die a virgin.

I roll onto my back, gasping for air, trying to come back to my body. Staci slides out of bed and stumbles around for her clothes.

I prop myself up on my elbows. "Hey, where ya going?"

"I hafta meet the girls in the bar," she explains, pulling on her shorts.

"Do you have to go now?" I touch the bony xylophone of her spine and she moves away.

"I need to shower first."

I pull the sheets up to my neck and watch her dress. "Maybe I'll see you later," she says. An afterthought. Like when you sign somebody's yearbook *See you this summer.*

"Yeah, maybe," I say.

She opens the door. Light bleeds in from the hall. Then she's gone and the room is dark and empty.

It's after midnight, but I can't sleep. I've got night sweats. The sheets are drenched and a little pool of perspiration gathers in the hollow of my throat.

Dulcie's leaning over me. Her face is a small, glowing

nightlight in the dark. "Hey, cowboy. You don't look so good."

"Can't breathe."

"Yes you can. You're just having a bad dream. Relax."

I try to take a deep breath, but it's like there's a Goddamn elephant on my chest, and my muscles are doing their twitch-and-spaz disco routine. For a minute, I hear Glory saying, "Relax, baby. Just need your blood pressure."

"I can't sleep," I say.

I hear sounds. Beep. Whirr. Muffled voices. I don't see Gonzo. The bed next to me is empty. Glory's holding my wrist, checking my pulse, a frown one more line on her face. When she's through, she wipes my brow with a washcloth.

"Sweet boy. Get some rest." She clicks the bolus, giving me a new bump of morphine.

"Glory, I can't go to sleep. I'm afraid I'll die."

She gives it another click, and my body feels light as goose down.

"Cameron, wake up. It's Dulcie."

"Huh?"

I'm back in the hotel room, away from dreams. Dulcie's stroking my face. "What did you mean, you were afraid you'd die if you went to sleep?"

"I saw Glory. In the hospital."

"Cam, you're with me, okay?"

I look around and see that she's right. The light from the parking lot cuts through the thin curtains in harsh streaks.

"I can't go to sleep, Dulcie. Now that . . ." I can't finish it. Can't tell her that since I'm no longer a virgin, I'm sure I'll die.

"How was it?" she asks in a voice soft as a prayer.

"Good."

"Liar." Dulcie gives me a small smile, but she looks sad.

Somebody's puking out in the parking lot. His friends are laughing in a grossed-out way.

"I thought I would feel different."

"Do you?" Dulcie asks.

Yes. No. I don't know. I feel emptied. Lost. A little sad. Like I was expecting a package that never arrived. Maybe if I had more time, I could've shrugged it off and said, hey, pal, better lay next time. But this was pretty much my one shot, and I blew it. It's not just the sex, though. It's the whole damn unfairness of it all. Like I'm just starting to understand how amazing this whole crazy ride is going to be and now it's coming to the end.

"Cameron?" Dulcie's staring at me in the strangest way. She reaches out and strokes my face. She has the lightest touch I've ever felt as she wipes away my tears.

"Go away."

"No," she says.

"Please. Okay?"

"Cameron, look at me. . . ."

The room's getting brighter. Dulcie's wings unfurl, exposing her bare body by degrees. Shoulders. Stomach. Arms. Thighs. Her skin glistens.

"Dulcie?" I say, not taking my eyes off her. She is such a bright thing.

"Shhh . . ."

"If we do this, will I die?"

She puts her fingers to my lips, and this is the part of her that I see most.

"Everyone's dying, Cameron. A little, every day. Make it count."

Without another word, she pulls me to her. Those huge,

soft wings fold around me like I'm being held for the first time. Like I'm drifting toward that black hole in the sky and I'm not afraid. I want to be pulled in. I want to hear it sing. I want to hear that B-flat in an octave no human being can really hear. I want to keep feeling. I want her.

Something brushes against my bare skin. Fingers? Lips? Wings? I can't say, but the sensation is incredible. It's like I'm accelerating through those eleven dimensions at once, and my body is both wave and particle. We're colliding, making our own universe, something new and unnamed and full of every possibility. It's so intense, this happiness—there is no escape velocity from this kind of feeling. And for once, I'm not looking for a way out.

I trace kisses from the hard calluses of her palms to the soft pads of her fingertips. She reaches up and cups my face in those small hands. They're warm as the first sun in spring.

"Cameron, look at me," she whispers.

I do. I see her. Really see her. And in that moment, I know she sees me.

She smiles, and in her smile is everything I could ever want. Her face looms closer, closing the impossible distance. Her lips are near mine.

And when it comes, her kiss is like something not so much felt as found.

CHAPTER FORTY-FOUR

Of What Happens to Gonzo
When We Aren't Looking

When I wake up, it's after noon. The sun's trying to break through the crack in the curtains, so I get out of bed and let it in. The harsh white of it hurts my eyes, but only for a second. In fact, nothing really hurts on me right now. No tics. No muscle weakness or shortness of breath. I feel great. I feel whole.

"Dulcie?" I call. Already, I miss the feel of her skin against mine.

The sheets are a rumpled mess. I slept hard. On the pillow is one pink-tinged feather. It smells like rain and laughter and the unexpected. It smells like Dulcie. There's no note on it this time. No secret code. I don't need it. My jeans are on the floor; I slip the feather into my back pocket for safekeeping.

There's a racket coming from the closet. Balder's way pissed. "If I wanted to be ignored and abused, I could have stayed on the cul-de-sac or with those wretched TV people," he says when I slide open the doors. I pick him up and put him on the table in the sun.

"Sorry, Balder."

"Can I help it if you bring your lady friends back to the room? Were you successful?" he asks, arching an eyebrow.

I grin. "No kiss-and-tell action."

"Ah, a true gentleman," he says, nodding sagely.

"I'll make it up to you," I say, filling up one of the complimentary glasses with water from the tap. It's got a harsh taste, but it quenches my thirst.

"How?"

"I'll buy you a camera. You can take pictures of us in front of landmarks to send to all your friends."

This pleases Balder. "And where is our illustrious Gonzo? I trust you were able to rescue him?"

Gonzo. Holy crap. I totally forgot about him. I left him to the mercy of Parker Day and his team of we'll-do-anything-for-ratings assholes. There's no telling what they did to him.

"Stay here!" I shout, grabbing my jacket and racing out the door.

I scour the beach and the Party House, searching for any sign of Gonzo. Most people are sleeping off whatever went down the night before. Things are just waking up. There's a guy selling T-shirts from a booth on the beach. The shirts say BRING BACK THE DWARF! On the back is a picture of Gonzo's terrified face.

"What size, bro?" the guy asks me when I grab one.

"When did you make these?"

413

"Last night, right after they filmed *I Double Dog Dare You*. It was outrageous, man. A dwarf and an electric chair."

I'm running fast on the beach. An electric chair? Panic has completely overtaken my senses. I run till I can't run another step. Then I go back to the room, trembling and spent.

"What's wrong? What's the matter?" Balder asks the minute I walk in.

I slump down in one of the chairs. "I fucked up, Balder. I forgot about Gonzo last night. I think something happened to him. Something bad."

Someone's banging on the door. "Open up! Police!"

Jenna promised me a head start.

"I said, open up!"

Balder nods gravely. I open the door.

"Dude, you are so *busted*!" Gonzo races in, beaming. "You look like you just dropped a load, man."

I grab him in a full body hug. "Gonzo!"

"Aaahh!" He winces. "Watch the shoulder."

"Oh my," Balder says. "You've a warrior's countenance now."

I put Gonzo down and take a good look.

"Well. What do you think?" he asks, beaming. His clothes are torn and grungy and covered in some kind of dye. His hair is blue-black, and he's sporting a new Mohawk.

"Holy Shiite Muslim," I say, circling him, checking out the back.

"You like it? It's cool, right?"

"It's insane!"

"Yeah, I know. Check out the tattoo."

"You got a tattoo?"

"Yeah. Shoulder. Check it out, dude." He pulls down his shirt to show me his shoulder, and there it is in new ink, the Buddha Cow above the words *How Now Mad Cow?*

414

"What the hell happened?"

"Dude, it was so kick-ass. I was at the Party House with Parker and Marisol and these two other people who are supposed to go on before me. I am totally freaked-the-hell-out. They keep showing these promos from *I Double Dog Dare You*, and it is just the gnarliest shit you can imagine. People bungee jumping into horse manure. Guys getting their whole bodies waxed, screaming in pain. The first one to go up is this chick. They double dog dared her to eat a dung beetle . . ."

"A dung beetle? Where did they get—"

"Put a cap on it for a sec. So they dared her but she wouldn't do it, man. No go. Same with the guy who was supposed to get his butt shaved and shocked with a cattle prod. He was a total *cabrón*, anyway. He let them shock him on the arm, but it's not the same, you know? The crowd booed him. They thought he was completely lame. Next thing I know, Drew—remember Drew? Guy who took me to the first-aid tent at the auction?"

"Yeah," I say.

"Turns out he works on the show. Anyway, he sits down next to me and says, 'Don't worry. You'll be great.' Like he totally believed I could do it. I can see Parker waving me up and everybody yelling and shit, but it's like I don't even hear it. And right then, I thought, what the hell. What. The. Hell. I never do anything. *Boom!* These two *huge* dudes come strap me into an old electric chair, and right then, at that moment, I had no idea what was going to happen. I thought I was going to shit my pants."

My heart's thumping hard just hearing this. Balder's on the edge of his seat.

"And?" Balder prompts.

"I hear this *rrrrrrnnnnn-nnnn-nnnnn*, and I think, Oh

shit, man. They are revving this baby up. I started thinking about all the things I've never done, like surf or get a tattoo or tell my mom off. Mostly I think that I've never gotten to be myself. Ever. I hear that *rrrrrnnnn-nnn-NNNN-nnn* near my ear, and I vowed to myself, Dude, if you make it out of this alive, you are going to do it, whatever it is. The big guys wrap their paws around my throat. Parker pulls out a razor, lowers it to my head. And thirty seconds later, I'm a Mohawk man."

He pops the top on a warm can of soda. "People went *insane*! They're shouting my name, 'Gon-*zo*! Gon-*zo*! Gon-*zo*!' And they're passing me around over their heads. It was, like, the greatest day of my life. And then I just . . . disappeared."

Gonzo guzzles soda. He wipes his mouth on his arm.

"Wow. That's . . . wow. And the tattoo?" I ask.

"First thing I did when I left the chair. Me and Drew."

It bothers me that Gonzo's got a new friend, somebody who sounds a lot cooler than me.

"So, I guess you're all famous now, huh?" I say.

"Yeah. Guess so." He beams again, drinks his soda.

"You saved me, my son," Balder says, embracing Gonzo. "You fought with honor. You are truly Gonzo the Great."

Gonzo blushes. "Gonzo the Great. Sweet. I'm getting me a T-shirt with that on it soon as we hit a mall."

Balder gives Gonzo a fist bump. "Word."

There's a knock on the door, and my pulse zooms into the red zone again. Maybe it is the cops this time. Gonzo must think it's Santa, from the shit-eating grin he's sporting. He runs to open it. Drew's standing there in a white muscle tee, a mop of dirty blond hair framing his choirboy face. His arms are inked from his wrists to his biceps.

"Hey," Drew says. He shoves his hands in his pockets and gives us a wary nod.

"It's okay. They're cool," Gonzo says. Drew leans down and gives him a kiss right on the mouth. I've never seen Gonzo so happy. I swear it's like he's just gotten a brand-new inhaler with Captain Carnage sticker decals. And now I know: Drew isn't a threat to our friendship. He's something else entirely.

"Hey, Drew. Cameron," I say, shaking his hand so he knows I'm okay with the whole You're My Best Friend's Slightly Juvenile-Delinquentish Spring Break Boyfriend.

"I was just telling them about last night," Gonzo says.

"Aw, man," Drew says in a thick Southern drawl. "Y'all shoulda seen my boy, here. Nerves of steel. He eats fear for breakfast."

"Yeah, that's our Gonzo," I say, without missing a beat. "He's a wild man."

"A warrior spirit," Balder chimes in.

"Hey, you must be Balder. Cool. I brought this for you. Freebie from the show," he says, handing off a camera. Balder's eyes gleam with mischief.

We step out blinking into the new day. Something's going on at the Party House, because there must be forty camera crews lined up, and hordes of people are streaming toward the stage.

"What's going on?" I ask a passing guy. He's wearing a shirt that says, MY PARENTS WENT TO SHITHENGE AND ALL I GOT WAS THIS CRAPPY T-SHIRT.

"You haven't heard?" he says excitedly.

"No. What's up?"

"The Copenhagen Interpretation!" he shouts, racing on. "They're back!"

CHAPTER FORTY-FIVE

In Which the World's Most Famous Band Plays the Most Important Comeback Concert Ever

With the news of the Copenhagen Interpretation's sudden reappearance, the Party House is complete pandemonium. Practically every camera in the state is trained on the stage where the band is scheduled to talk to the world for the first time in eleven years. Because of Gonzo's new celebrity status, we're able to push our way to the front.

"That's right, I'm bad," Gonzo singsongs. Drew laughs and wraps him in his tattooed arms. He gives Gonz a big kiss and the Gonz-man gets all blushy.

Reporters flank out along the front of the stage down in the security area. They hold their mikes and stare into the cameras as if they're filing the most important news stories of their lives.

". . . no clue yet as to where they've been, why they disappeared, and why they've come back at this moment, in this place . . ."

". . . unsubstantiated rumors of travel through a wormhole to other worlds . . ."

". . . backstage requests for fresh fish and a toy piano fueled speculation—Copenhagen Interpretation: disappearing divas? . . ."

". . . finally answer the question why *do* they have so many words for snow? . . ."

"This is history-making shit, yo!" Gonzo says. "Totally awesome."

"Yeah," I say, looking around for Dulcie, because if she were here, it *would* be awesome.

It seems like forever that we wait for the Copenhagen Interpretation to take the stage. Finally, there's a new feeling of excitement. People cheer as the curtain parts. There's deafening applause. Wolf whistles. Flashes go off like fireworks. A surge in the crowd pushes us against the security barrier, but we don't care. About ten feet in front of us, the Copenhagen Interpretation files out—five people in mukluks and long, hooded parkas that nearly hide their faces. They stop center stage and stand perfectly still.

A balding guy in a Hawaiian shirt walks to a microphone center stage.

"That's totally their interpreter," a girl with a lip ring informs us. "Even though they totally record their music in English, they totally speak in Inuktitut. Totally."

The interpreter clears his throat, ready to deliver the band's message. The crowd quiets in anticipation. The Copenhagen Interpretation speaks softly to their interpreter, who then relays their words in English through the mike:

Murmurmur. Stop.

"Hello."

Murmurmurmurmurmur. Stop.

"We have been gone a while, it seems."

Murmurmurmurmurmur. Stop.

"Wow. You all got so big!"

MurmurmurmurmurmurMurmurmurMurmurmurmur.
Stop.

"We have traveled through space and time. We have been many places. Visited many worlds. And there is good news: the acoustics everywhere are terrific."

Murmur. Murmur. Mur. Mur. Stop.

"There is one last thing we would like to address."

Murmurmurmur. "You say we have . . ." *Murmurmurmurr.* ". . . so many words . . ." *Murmur.* ". . . for snow."

Mur? Murmur? "Well? Wouldn't you?"

"Totally." The girl behind us sighs.

Without delay, the Copenhagen Interpretation launches into the opening notes of their first song. People go nuts. I've been to a few concerts here and there, but nothing like this. I feel like I've swallowed this music whole. It's pretty fucking amazing the way it connects you to everybody else, makes you part of the same experience at the same time. Drew and Gonzo sway to each song, singing along word for word. Balder closes his eyes and stands perfectly still.

"It's as if I can hear the soft grass rustling in the wind on the hill toward Breidablik," he murmurs.

By the fifth song, the crowd's dancing, body surfing, and singing along. Even though I don't know the words, I join in, too, managing to hit one or two right. Some kid rushes the stage and dives into the crowd. Security guards scowl. And all I can think is *Man, I want to do that.* Yeah, why not?

"Here goes nothing," I say, and rush the stage. I've got maybe four seconds tops, no time to think, only time to do. Arms out, I fall backward into the concert crowd.

"Holy shit!" I scream.

And then the most amazing thing happens. There are fingers under my body, passing me along. It's incredible, like floating on a sea of hands. Nobody drops me. It's absolute trust. It takes about ten minutes to work me to the back of the crowd, where I'm lowered gently to the ground.

I hug the nearest person, a patchouli-scented girl in braids, who hugs me right back. "That. Was. Awesome!" I shout.

She smiles. Her eyes are bloodshot slits. "You look like a dancing bear," she says.

"That's because I am a dancing bear," I say back.

"Wow. Cool."

A group of college kids yank me over to join their huddle. They lock arms around my shoulders, and we sway together, holding each other up and singing along.

"Because there's so many, words for snow . . . so many, words for snow . . ."

When I look again, Dulcie's sidled up next to me. Grinning, I throw my arms around her neck and we wobble over to a spot at the back. She leans against the weathered side of a beer shack and I lean into her.

"Hey, cowboy," she says. "How's the sky treating you?"

"Like I'm hauling a cargo ship full of trouble," I answer in perfect *Star Fighter* response.

"Sounds like fun."

My lips are on hers and there's nothing but us and the music.

Dulcie and I take in the concert from our private spot in the back. But I don't want to lose the others, so we start threading our way through the capacity crowd to the front. By the time we rejoin Gonzo, Drew, and Balder, the first set's nearly over. My friends don't notice Dulcie, but I've stopped worrying about that. I see her and she sees me, and that's what matters.

The band finishes their song. The interpreter steps to the mike again. The band speaks. *Murmur. Murmur. Murmur.* Stop.

"We would like to play more for you. But first, there are sandwiches backstage. Do you know how long it's been since we had a sandwich? We will come back in thirty minutes."

Amid whooping and hollering and stomping, the band is ushered to the side of the stage. One of the band members turns, puts a hand up to block the glare of the lights. He sees Balder and waves. Balder waves right back.

"Dude," Gonzo says in awe.

Balder's expression is smug satisfaction. "I told you."

The interpreter comes over to us. Balder says something in Norse, and he and the interpreter chitchat. At one point, they're both chuckling. Gonzo, Drew, and I exchange glances. I look over at Dulcie, who shrugs. The next thing I know, we're being whisked backstage to eat sandwiches with this world's—and possibly some other world's—favorite band.

The minute we step into the green room we're bombarded. Reporters asking questions. Assistants offering Rad soda. Fans asking for autographs, which they clutch to their chests, then cry. The band takes it all in, answering in cryptic fashion: Yes. No. Maybe. Seals are shoplifters—you really have to watch them at parties.

Parker Day comes running up and pumps the hands of each band member. "Great to meet you. Big fan. Don't know if you caught my special on *The Backside of Music?* We could totally do a follow-up."

The band keeps walking.

"Call me!" Parker shouts after them.

Security takes us to a roped-off area. As promised, there are sandwiches and they are good. Balder makes introductions. Gonzo and Drew are so stoked they take the opportunity to sing one of the band's songs to them at top decibel level. At one point, the Copenhagen Interpretation waves to somebody behind me, and I see it's Dulcie. She wiggles her fingers back. To me, she shrugs. No one else even notices. And then the Copenhagen Interpretation tells us what they know about the night they disappeared.

"It was the Big Concert for Peace and Against Non-Peace," the interpreter relays. "It had been a good show. Very good. Dinlitla's guitar work was exemplary."

He looks over at his bandmate, who smiles and goes back to her sandwich.

"And then, in the middle of 'Words for Snow,' the sky began to frown. The clouds knotted together the way my grandmother scowls at my grandfather when he passes wind and blames the dog."

Gonzo snickers.

"What happened next?" I prompt, ignoring him.

"The sky swirled over our heads. A hole opened. And then we were sucked up and tumbling through tunnels of light, falling into other dimensions."

"Did you ever come across a Dr. X? A scientist?"

There's more murmuring. The interpreter wants to be sure he's gotten it right.

"At one point," he says. "We came upon a man in a white lab coat the color of snow you cannot shake from your shoe."

"Dr. X!" I blurt out. "Had to be. Were you guys ever in the same universe at the same time? Do you know where he ended up?"

"We did not speak. Only passed each other. You know. The way people do in space."

My heart sinks at this. I'm out of my chair, pacing. "At Putopia, they told us Dr. X had a theory about music. That it was its own dimension. That the vibrations could punch holes through space and time. Dr. X was playing 'Words for Snow' when he stepped into the Infinity Collider. He used this"—I pull the Calabi Yau manifold from my backpack— "to amplify the sound."

Thule murmurs to the interpreter, who says, "Looks like macaroni art."

"What if he stepped into the Infinity Collider at the precise moment you were playing at the concert—the same song at the same time, a supersynchronized vibration opening up a passage?"

I look to my friends. Balder strokes his beard. Gonzo's squinting like he's trying to pay attention in algebra class. Drew laces his fingers with Gonzo's. Dulcie's eyes shine.

The keyboard player leans forward and whispers in the interpreter's ear. "Interesting," the interpreter says. "Do you want to try the peanut butter? It's very good."

Just then, a bunch of YA! TV suits show up. It's time for the second set, and we have to leave. I have so many more questions—about parallel dimensions, Dr. X, time travel, and the wormhole we're supposed to close—but our audience with the Copenhagen Interpretation is officially over for now.

We all shake hands, and Balder gives the lead singer Thule, a fist bump.

When we come out again, it's gotten darker.

"What's that?" A girl points to thick black smoke in the distance. Just behind it is a fierce orange glow. "Is it the wildfires?"

"Should we close down?" an assistant asks someone next to him.

"Nah, here comes a storm. That should take care of it," the other guy answers.

The crowd boos at the coming rain. I get a tingly feeling up my arms. The clouds are moving fast, swirling, pulling.

"Dulcie . . . ," I say.

Her eyes are wide. "Yeah."

"You think those are wildfires and a passing storm?"

She shakes her head. Down on the beach, the wind rips away a hotel awning. It tumbles down the beach before zipping up toward the sky and disappearing.

"Dulcie!" I shout over the wind and fire sirens. "I don't think we can wait. I think we have to try to re-create what happened the night the wormhole was opened."

Lightning crackles overhead. Dulcie gives me a push. "Go."

By the time we reach the stage, the beach is black with smoke and the sky is as dark as a night without stars. A voice comes over the loudspeaker. "Ah, folks, I'm afraid those wildfires are getting a little too close for comfort, and the weather isn't cooperating too much, either. We're gonna have to shut down the concert."

People boo loudly. A hulking security guard with a shaved head and biceps the size of giant poodles pushes people away from the stage. There's no way to get closer.

"Shit! What do we do now?"

Dulcie looks around quickly. "I'll get the crowd stirred up. You try to get the Copenhagen Interpretation to come out for one more song."

Just like that, Dulcie starts zigzagging through the crowd, shouting, "Encore! Encore! 'Words for Snow!' C'mon!"

A few people take up a chant—"Words for Snow!"—and it

swells. I try to slip under the security ropes. The big guy hauls me out without even breathing hard.

"I have to talk to the Copenhagen Interpretation!"

"Pal, everybody needs to talk to the Copenhagen Interpretation. Back off." He pushes me back. Lightning zaps one of the hotels and then again near the stage. Car alarms go off. People get a little nervous.

I hold up my E-ticket bracelet, blocking the words with my fingers. "I'm press."

The guy peers at it. "Aren't you a little young to be press?"

"I won it. One of those Last Wish things." I cough for effect.

"Oh, I'm so sorry," the guy says. "I didn't know."

"Yeah. My last wish was to see the Copenhagen Interpretation play. And meet them."

He shakes his head, slips me under the ropes, and points me toward the band huddled just offstage.

"Hello again," the interpreter relays. "The sky is frowning."

"Yes. It's frowning big-time," I say. Sweat beads on my forehead. "And it's gonna get worse unless we stop it."

As quickly as possible, I tell them my plan. They exchange glances.

"Will we end up in the shit again?"

I shake my head. "I don't know. I don't even know if this will work. But if we don't try, the world's gonna end very shortly."

A tech guy makes his way over. "Sorry, guys. With the storm, it's not safe to go back out. The concert's been canceled."

"What?" I shout. "No! You have to uncancel it!"

The tech guy shrugs in apology. "We just got these guys back. Can't have 'em going up in smoke."

"Please," I beg, ignoring him. "Just one song."

The Copenhagen Interpretation forms a tight huddle. Their heads bob in discussion. They call for their interpreter. *Murmur. Mur. Murmur.* Stop.

"It's like fishing in fake snow, checking your line."

"Right." I nod. I have no idea what they mean.

Against the advice of everyone at YA! TV, the Copenhagen Interpretation agrees to play one last song in the hopes it will send the fire giants and the wizard back through the Higgs Field to wherever they came from and close the wormhole so they can't come back. A roadie ushers me out onstage. People cheer until they realize I'm not anybody. Down in the pit, Gonzo, Drew, and Balder shout my name anyway.

"Cameron! Save the universe, *pendejo!*"

Soon, the crowd's chanting, "Save the universe, *pendejo!*" and they have no idea.

The blaze has gotten even closer. In the distance, I hear fire-truck sirens. I take the Calabi Yau toy from my backpack and rig it to one of the amplifiers as best I can. It sags like a half-emptied piñata. "Please," I whisper. "Just . . . please."

That sky's looking really ominous. The clouds start to pull in. Lightning shoots out like loose electrical lines. Now people are getting nervous. They turn to leave. Any minute we'll have a stampede on our hands. I can't see Dulcie and I hope wherever she is, she's okay. I run into the wings just as the Copenhagen Interpretation takes the stage again, and for one second, the crowd explodes with manic happiness. But it's quickly replaced by fear. They don't know if they should stay or go. On the one hand, it's the Copenhagen Interpretation. On the other, there's the fire and the sky.

The interpreter steps to the microphone.

Murmurmrumumurmurmurmurmuuuurmrrrrmmrurr. Long stop.

"In our travels, we have come across many equations—math for understanding the universe, for making music, for mapping stars, and also for tipping, which is important. Here is our favorite equation: Us plus Them equals All of Us. It is very simple math. Try it sometime. You probably won't even need a pencil."

"Hey. Hey! What is that?" a girl screams.

The fire giants have reached us. We're completely sealed off by a circle of them, an angry army looking to be satisfied, except they can never be satisfied, and so they just keep burning. Those bottomless black eyes make my throat dry. The crowd screams and cowers together, holding each other up. But the Copenhagen Interpretation doesn't flinch. They stand firm; they have more to say, and the interpreter relays every word.

Murmur. Murmurmurrmrururmmmururururmmmmmmrururururu. Stop.

"Please. We know. These are hard times. The world hurts. We live in fear and forget to walk with hope. But hope has not forgotten you. So ask it to dinner. It's probably hungry and would appreciate the invitation."

The fire giants throw their heads back and howl for all they're worth—the horrible screech makes my skin crawl. In the crowd, people scream in fear. The interpreter has to shout into the microphone. "This is a song. It is called 'Small World.'"

The drummer clicks the sticks together—two, three,

four—and knocks the Calabi Yau off the speaker. Fuck. They're playing, but without the amplification, it's not enough.

I rush the stage. Security comes after me, but the guitar player blocks me with his body. "Here goes everything," I shout, and hold the Calabi Yau to the speaker with both hands, shifting it into place. The sound that comes out nearly knocks me flat, and for a minute, I feel like I'm back in the Infinity Collider. It's more than music; it's a living thing, a portal into dimensions I've never even thought about. The music actually drifts high above our heads; I can see it swirling there—an aurora borealis of light and notes and vibrating strings. It drifts into the black hole, and the hole narrows bit by bit. The fire giants howl as the sonic waves push them back. Soon, people begin loosening their death grips on one another. They join hands and sing along. The fire giants grow smaller. With each note, they shrink down to pissant little flickers and then to smoke, which is pulled up into the swirling clouds. The hole is only a dot.

Onstage, the Copenhagen Interpretation has stopped playing. The singer looks up, says five words in English. "Shit. Here we go again."

That hole in the sky sucks them and the Calabi Yau toy right up and closes over. The clouds disperse. It's an unearthly quiet. The concertgoers are dazed. Slowly, as people realize they're okay, that we're all still here, they whoop and hug each other in relief. Then they notice the empty stage.

I drop down into the crowd and help Gonzo up, and he helps Balder.

"What was that?" Gonzo asks when he finds his voice again.

I peer up at the hint of rainbow. "I think we might have just saved the universe."

I look around for Dulcie, but she's gone. I start to panic. What if she's been sucked up, too? But then I see her in the crowd, pink and white.

I run to her.

CHAPTER FORTY-SIX

Of What Happens When
Balder Has His Day at the Beach

After a fuel-up of convenience-store corn dogs and soda, we're packed and ready to head out. Drew's managed to fix the Caddy, but it looks tired. It's coated in sand and road dust. Somebody has finger-written WASH ME across the back window. I wish it were coated in more dust. Every cop in Florida's probably looking for that car now, and I just hope we can stay one step ahead of them.

Gonzo's wearing Drew's I GOT CRABS AT JOE'S SURF & TURF T-shirt.

"Mohawk's cool," I say.

Gonzo runs his hand over his head, watching Drew who's letting Balder take his picture with the Party House in the background.

"Hey, you don't have to come with me, you know," I say. "If you wanna stay, ride out the rest of spring break, it's cool."

"He's got my e-mail and cell and all that."

"Seems like a cool guy," I say.

"He is," Gonzo says, and there's a little sigh under it.

"You sure you don't want to stay?"

Gonzo elbows me in the side. I elbow him back. He elbows me again till I cry "Ow."

"I said I'm riding shotgun, I'm riding shotgun," he says.

I nod, and we stand there watching Balder bark out orders to Drew to crouch lower and lower, till I know his head will be nothing more than a small human icon down in the left-hand corner of the photo.

Dulcie waves to me from behind a green station wagon. I slip away from the guys and go to her. "You coming along?"

"I'll catch up," she answers. When I look disappointed, she adds, "Don't worry. I'll be sticking close."

"Because I'm a badass who saved the universe, princess?" I brace myself for the smackdown to come.

"Yeah." She laughs and kisses me on the nose. "Something like that."

I made a promise to Balder back on the cul-de-sac that we would get him to the ocean to search for *Ringhorn* so he could try to get back to his own world. I just didn't know we'd be so short on time. My E-ticket meter is down to its last bar—Tomorrowland—and fading.

"Do not worry about me, Cameron. You must do what is right for your mission." Balder's expression is stoic.

Gonzo gives him a little pat on the back. "You could stay with us, dude. I could teach you to play Captain Carnage."

"Yes. Thank you," Balder says, trying to smile.

But I can see in Balder's eyes that he's homesick, and we're by the beach right here, right now. "Who wants to play in the surf?" I ask.

Balder's eyes light up. "But your mission, Cameron?"

"Can wait for a few hours," I lie.

"When I am once again in the company of Odin and Freya, I shall tell them of the two bravest souls I ever met. Your names shall ring in the golden hall of the gods," Balder says, sniffling a little.

"Just don't tell 'em you keep your runes near your gnomy bits, amigo," Gonzo jokes. "'Cause that is seriously off-putting."

We drive down a few miles to a quiet part of the beach. No college revelers here. Just a few families with their kids, a handful of old people camped in their beach chairs facing the late-day sun. We move far away from them, not that they're watching us anyway. They're enjoying their own paradise bubbles.

Balder's back in his surfer uniform. He pulls up the leggings, takes off his flip-flops, and wades out to the edge of the water. A wave nudges his toes.

"Oh my," Balder says. I've never seen him so happy. "That is . . . wonderful." He cups his hands over his eyes to cut the glare and keeps watch for his ship.

A piece of driftwood has washed up on shore. I take it and write my name in the sand. The water rushes over my name, makes it into some new word, then erases it completely. Using the driftwood as a walking stick, I hike along the shore, thinking about Dulcie, about the way her wings felt, smooth and soft except for the spines in each feather. Nestled into all that velvety down was something solid but supple, something hard to break, hundreds of them fanning out around me like the softest, most improbable shell. It makes me smile to know she's in the world. That's all.

A feather drops onto my head, followed by another, and another. Feathers fall like snow from the sky. A great big pillow fight of feathers coating my skin, the beach, the water, till all I can do is twirl and laugh in them, a character in my own broken snow globe.

We stay longer than we should, probably. The day is spent talking and building badass sand castles, taking Balder for rides on the waves. It's all been so nice just being together that I haven't wanted to leave. Now the sun's low in the sky, and Gonzo and I sit in the sand while Balder finishes constructing a moat around his castle, waiting for *Ringhorn,* which he assures us will come with the evening tide.

"Thirty more minutes," I tell him.

"It will come," Balder insists, and goes back to looking.

"Hey, you wanna see if we can crash that shit by the taco stand?" Gonzo nods in the direction of a small party that's sprung up off to our right.

"Nah," I say.

A wave rushes over my toes and back out. The sand goes soft and sucks at my foot. Seagulls congregate on a dune, pecking at a piece of bread. An old couple parks their chairs near the boardwalk. The wind shifts, carrying the sounds of a volleyball game down the shore.

"Seems like we should be doing something," Gonzo says.

"We are doing something."

"Yeah. Guess so."

We sit staring out at that vast ocean, Gonzo and I, just watching the sky colors drip into the sea like a giant percolator, making something sweet and strong, something to keep you going when all you've got left are fumes.

Maybe there's a heaven, like they say, a place where everything we've ever done is noted and recorded, weighed on the big karma scales. Maybe not. Maybe this whole thing is just a giant experiment run by aliens who find our human hijinks amusing. Or maybe we're an abandoned project started by a deity who checked out a long time ago, but we're still hardwired to believe, to try to make meaning out of the seemingly random. Maybe we're all part of the same unconscious stew, dreaming the same dreams, hoping the same hopes, needing the same connection, trying to find it, missing, trying again—each of us playing our parts in the others' plotlines, just one big ball of human yarn tangled up together. Maybe this is it.

Or maybe there's something to what Junior said about those black holes singing. That B-flat? Maybe that's the last sound we make when we join the universe, something to say, I was here. One last "Whoo-hoo!" before we're pulled into the vast, dark unknown and shot out into some other galaxy, some other world, where we have the chance to do it differently. I don't know. It's something to think about, though.

"This is pretty fucked up, dude," Gonz says, giving me that big, lovable lopsided grin.

I know what he means, and I want to say something back, but I can't find the words for how incredible this is any more than I can pin the sky in place. I'm happy to be right here, right now. And I know, even as I'm surrounded by this feeling, that it will take its arms away soon enough. Tears sting my eyes. I turn my head so Gonzo can't see.

"Hey, new bumper sticker," Gonzo announces. "This car powered by the Dwarf of Destiny!"

I wipe my face against my shoulder. "Everyone says you're paranoid."

"The Norse like to keep things Wyrd," Balder chimes in.

"Good one," Gonzo says, giggling.

"Free the snow globes!" I shout to the sky.

"Free-ee the snow globes, free-ee the snow globes . . ." Balder turns it into an opera riff, and we join in till we're laughing too hard to continue.

We've left the moment. It's gone. We're somewhere else now, and that's okay. We've still got that other moment with us somewhere, deep in our memory, seeping into our DNA. And when our cells get scattered, whenever that happens, this moment will still exist in them. Those cells might be the building block of something new. A planet or star or a sunflower, a baby. Maybe even a cockroach. Who knows? Whatever it is, it'll be a part of us, this thing right here and now, and we'll be a part of it.

And if it's a cockroach? Well, that will be the happiest fucking cockroach on the planet. I can tell you that.

CHAPTER FORTY-SEVEN

In Which We Are Unprepared for the Unexpected

"I . . . I believe I see it!" Balder gasps. "There on the horizon, where the sun bleeds—it's my ship. It's *Ringhorn*!"

Gonz and I squint out at the ocean going golden-hot with fading sun. The glare's bad, but I don't see a ship. Balder runs along the shore speaking excitedly in Norse. "I must have my possessions," he says, a note of worry in his voice. "I left them in the car."

"Relax. I'll get them. You just keep your eye on your ship," I say, and hoof it to the parking lot. Two cops on bikes patrol the sand, blocking my way to the car. Crap.

I turn and run smack into a guy with a mustache, mirrored sunglasses, and a baseball cap. "Hi there! Can I take a minute of your time to talk to you about safety?" he asks.

"Uh, you know, right now's not a good time—"

"It's always a good time to be prepared for the unexpected.

How will you protect your loved ones in the event of the eventful?" he asks.

I've got my eyes on the cops. They're biking away. Yes!

"Hey, what's your name?"

"Junior. Junior Webster."

"Really? 'Cause I think you're Cameron Smith and you're in some deep trouble." He grabs my wrist in an iron-tight grip. His baseball cap reads UNITED SNOW GLOBE WHOLE-SALERS. "This is Employee number four fifty-seven calling base," he says into a walkie-talkie. "Terror suspect in custody. Got the other two in my sights. Request backup. Over."

A muffled voice worthy of a drive-thru window answers him.

"Roger that. Let's go get your friends," he says, yanking my arm up and behind my back.

"Please," I say, swallowing hard. "You're making a big mistake. I've been trying to save the world—you guys included!"

He angles for some cuffs. "Just hold still."

I didn't come this far to go back now with some armchair vigilante who spends his days stocking snow globe emporiums. "You're not my daddy!" I shout. "I won't get in your van! You're not my daddy!"

"What?" he says.

"Hey! Leave that kid alone!" In the parking lot, a hulking tattooed biker gets off his motorcycle and rolls up his sleeves.

"This is a terrorist!" Employee #457 shouts back.

"Don't make me come kick your ass!"

Employee #457's grip goes a little slack, and I take this opportunity to break for the beach.

"Hey! *Hey!*" The vigilante walkie-talkies for immediate backup.

Gonzo's stretched out, relaxing in the sand. He sees me

438

hauling ass toward him. "Gonzo—the water! Get to the water!"

"Dude!" Gonzo shouts, pointing. I chance a glance behind me and count two more guys in baseball caps and sunglasses running toward us. Then three and four. Five big guys in mirrored sunglasses and United Snow Globe Wholesalers hats.

"Shit," I mutter. Behind us is only ocean. And what would we swim to?

"Okay. Evasive maneuver," I say, eyes searching. "Gonz, you break left for the taco shack. I'll duck right and try to make it to the pier. And Balder—"

He stands firm in the sand. "I stay right here to wait for *Ringhorn*."

"But Balder—"

"I shall wait!" he insists. "Those men cannot harm me. I shall be a worthy distraction. Do what you must and leave me to it."

"All right," I say. "Two . . . three . . . go!"

Gonzo and I run in opposite directions. With a war cry, Balder advances on the snow globers, wielding that piece of driftwood like the badass warrior he is inside. One guy's coming after me full speed.

My legs and lungs burn, and I stumble. I try to get back up, but I'm having a hard time. My E-ticket meter's nearly blank—there's just a tiny shred of Tomorrowland hanging on.

"Cameron!" Dulcie's here, reaching out. "Hold on!"

I grab her hand and we're flying over the beach. I wrap my legs around her. "Whoa!"

Dulcie turns my face to hers. "Just don't look down and don't let go."

"Trust me. I will not do either of those things."

439

Something zips past. Dulcie cries out and we're tumbling through the air. We land in the sand. Dulcie's curled up.

"You okay?"

"Bad landing." She sits up, grabbing her shoulder. Singed feathers fall from her wing.

"What happened?"

In answer, a bullet zips past. A USGW employee is making his way through the sand, gun glinting in the sun.

"Grab hold," Dulcie croaks.

"You can't fly like that. Can you?"

Dulcie doesn't wait. She draws me to her and we sort of half fly, half trot on the beach. But with Dulcie's injured wing, we can't get enough lift.

"Ahhhh!" A bullet grazes Dulcie's other wing and we drop onto the pier. "Run out!" Dulcie instructs.

This time I pull her. We're bordered on all sides by the ocean.

She tries to smile, but I can see the pain in her eyes. "The water, Cameron."

"No. No water," I say.

"You'll be okay."

"Is that a sure thing or a destiny-can-be-changed thing?"

She doesn't answer. "Cameron," she whispers. It's like the cooing of doves. Her wings smell of rain and smoke. She pushes me hard and I fly backward into the ocean. The water's cold and heavy, like being wrapped in a blanket soaked with snow. Feels like I'm going to drown, like when I was five. Dulcie's on the edge of the pier. United Snow Globe Employee #457 aims a long gun with a spray nozzle at her. "Gotcha," he growls.

Dulcie closes her eyes as he hits the trigger. There's a blinding flash. When it clears, Dulcie's gone. Where she was standing, there's nothing but a snow globe.

"Dulcie!" I scream. "Dulcie!"

"You're next." Employee #457 aims the nozzle at my head.

I take a deep breath and let the ocean carry me down.

"Cameron? Look at that! Isn't it wonderful?"

Mom's pointing to a marionette Inuit boy pulling a fish out of the hole again and again. The snow glistens. A kids' choir sings that it's a small world after all. It's the most amazing thing, this ride. I love it. I want to go on it again and again and again.

"I want to play in the snow!" I tell Mom.

"We have to stay in the boat, honey."

I notice a tiny door behind the igloo. "Where does that door go?"

"Oh, I don't know. Somewhere. Oooh, isn't that cute?" Mom points out a dancing girl to Jenna. Dad puts his arm around me. I'm here and I'm safe with my mom and dad and sister. But I can't help it. I want to know where the door goes. I want to play. Over there.

And then I'm in the water, going under. Above me the surface gleams with color and light. Muffled screaming filters down. But it's peaceful here, and I could just reach out and touch that other shore. My lungs can't hold back anymore. I open my mouth and the water rushes in.

With a loud gasp, I break the waves and stagger toward the sand. Employee #457 is waiting with the weird gun in one hand and the Dulcie snow globe in the other. "Knew you couldn't stay down there forever."

"Give . . . her . . . back," I pant.

"Sorry. She's a threat that must be contained. Now. Smile pretty. Maybe we'll call this one *Beach Break*."

He lowers the nozzle. I hear it making a weird *wheeeeee* sound as it fires up.

"That's the creep!" The motorcycle guy is back with the bicycle cops. "He was trying to kidnap a kid."

"Officer, you've got it wrong. I'm working with United Snow Globe Wholesalers." The vigilante points to his cap. "We're working to protect your safety!"

The wail of sirens fills my ears. Cops scramble down the dunes and cuff the snow globe guy.

"Dude!" Gonzo waves to me from his protected spot behind a parked car. But I can't stop staring at the snow globe. It's got an angel inside. Her hands are pressed against the glass and her tiny plastic mouth is open in a scream.

"Dude! Now!"

I'm dazed and my body hurts. Gonzo half drags me behind a dune, leaving the snow globe behind. I try to fight him to go back, but I don't have the strength, and the beach is crawling with USGW employees.

Down on the beach, Balder's still kicking ass. No matter what they throw at him, it bounces off. They can't catch him, and they can't kill him. Suddenly, Balder looks out to the horizon, and with a shout of glee, drops the driftwood.

"Ringhorn!"

In a flash, USGW Employee #457 grabs the stick and plunges it into Balder's back. It comes straight through his chest. Balder looks surprised, especially when he can't pull it out. But it doesn't stop him; he runs straight for the water, ducking under the waves, disappearing from sight.

I want to run after him, but we can't chance it, so we stay hidden behind the dune, watching. Two of the vigilantes wade out and drag Balder back in, laying him on the sand. More cops are on the scene now. One kicks Balder with his foot.

"There's your terrorist," the cop snickers. "A yard gnome."

Statements are taken, witnesses' phone numbers given. The last people to leave the scene are the vigilantes.

"Should we take the gnome in for processing?" Employee #458 asks.

"Nah. Just leave it," answers Employee #456. "Let's go back to the hotel. They have Casino Cash on the channel options."

"Can I have him?" a little girl with a plastic shovel asks.

"Sure," Employee #458 says, and the kid starts burying our yard gnome in the sand.

"At least we got this one." Employee #458 flips the snow globe in his hand, and my heart flips along with it.

As I watch, frozen, they cover Dulcie in bubble wrap, pack her away in a box of other snow globes, and load it into their truck. I memorize the license plate number: USGW 3111. They drive it across the street and park in the lot of the Ancient Mariner hotel. They secure the door with two different combination locks, and my heart sinks.

"Dude," Gonzo says quietly. "Balder." And I know there's nothing else I can do right now.

We run out to rescue our valiant Viking, who is buried up to his neck, the driftwood still sticking out on the sides.

I offer the kid ten bucks. "For the yard gnome."

We carry Balder to a more secluded spot. "I saw it. I saw . . . *Ringhorn*." We help him to his feet. He winces. "Cameron? Are you . . . all right?" he asks.

"They got Dulcie. They turned her into a snow globe." I'm trying not to cry. My eyes sting.

"I am . . . sorry," Balder says. He pulls on the driftwood spear but can't dislodge it.

It's really wedged in there. "Could you?"

Together, we manage to yank it free. The end is slippery and it stains my hands red.

"Oh. My," Balder says. He stands there, arms wide, gazing at his chest in total wonder. And that's when I see it: a small trickle of blood burbling up and spilling down the front of his shirt. Balder is bleeding.

Gonzo's eyes are wide.

"Oh my," Balder repeats. He puts a hand to his chest and the blood seeps between his closed fingers, a thin red waterfall. "That stick . . ." He examines the end. A small cluster of white berries sprouts from a tiny knob. Balder rubs the berries between his fingers, inhales their scent. "Mistletoe."

"Balder!" I shout as his legs give out. I grab hold and we drop to the sand, Balder cradled in my arms, as his warm, sticky blood pools in my hands. "Balder."

Our Viking's breath comes fast and shallow. "All pledged no harm to Balder . . . save for the mistletoe, who was too young. But Loki, Loki the trickster . . . he must have known. . . ."

"Shhh, don't talk. We'll get you in the car."

"No," he says, and coughs. "No. Leave me here on the beach. For *Ringhorn*."

It's gotten dark. The fishing boats are heading in. Their lights cast lonely pools of white on the water. There's no *Ringhorn*.

"We'll come back for your ship," I lie. "You need a doctor."

"No. *Ringhorn* will come. Wait. Wait with me," Balder urges.

When I look over, Gonzo's got his arms crossed. He's kicking at the ground and crying without making a noise except for a little strangled sob deep in his throat.

"Wait with me," Balder asks again.

We keep our vigil through the night, checking on the truck when we can. Sometimes, Balder mumble-sings a few words in Norse. He grabs at the air for something we can't see, something just out of reach. "The dark does not weep," he whispers. Toward dawn, he gets so quiet I'm afraid. Early-morning surfers take to the waves. Seagulls circle us.

"I like . . . that sound," Balder says, his words pushing out on shallow gasps.

At first I think he means Gonzo's sniffling. "What sound, Balder?"

"The gulls. Cry. And the waves. Answer. They wash . . . over the shore. Say, it is all . . ." His eyes move back and forth in his head like he's searching for the word, the thought. He looks at me as if he's said it. "Right?"

I listen, but the only thing I can hear are those damn birds wailing. One starts and the rest follow. They're all crying at once. It's a terrible sound.

"Balder . . . ," I say.

His mouth is still open in that weird little smile. His eyes are fixed and staring. The gulls fly off, leaving nothing but the soothing whoosh of the tide rushing up, washing back out, again and again. *All. Right. All. Right. All. Right.*

It takes us a while to get everything we need. Scavenging along the beach, we find a surfboard, a cardboard Taco Shack tray, an abandoned T-shirt, seashells, and handfuls of seaweed and small sticks. We duct-tape the cardboard tray to the surfboard and rig the Caddy's bull horns to the front. We load the tray with his Sammy the Surfer outfit and all my Great Tremolo CDs. When it's ready, we place Balder's lifeless body gently on top of the tray, in his chain mail and helmet, just

445

like a Viking warrior on his way to Valhalla. Last, we add a hand-lettered sign: RINGHORN.

"What do you think?" I ask Gonzo.

"Good." His eyes are red. He takes a puff off his inhaler and puts it in Balder's hands. "The air might be crap there."

He hands me a disposable blue lighter we found half-buried by the Taco Shack. I put it to the dry seaweed, which starts to smoke immediately. The flames eat through the cardboard pretty fast. In seconds, they surround Balder in a hot orange halo. I lift my foot, Gonzo gives the surfboard a final push, and the sea does the rest. The water's pretty choppy. It buffets our makeshift pyre back and forth, and finally over, till the only thing left on the peach-pink horizon are those crazy bull horns.

And then, even those are gone.

An hour later, the United Snow Globe Wholesalers truck, license plate number USGW 3111, pulls out of the hotel parking lot. One minute after that, we follow.

CHAPTER FORTY-EIGHT

In Which the Coyote and the Roadrunner Go Again

"You still see him?"

"Yeah. He's four cars up," Gonzo answers. "Dude, shouldn't we be going after Dr. X and your cure?"

"Not going," I say.

"What do you mean?"

"I'm going after Dulcie."

"Cameron, this is crazy."

"Just keep an eye on that truck."

For the next hour, we drive in silence. No talk. No music. Nothing but the white noise of asphalt under tires. The road sways in the afternoon sun. Little waves of clear heat spiral dance in front of me, bathing everything in shimmery motion. I keep glancing in the rearview mirror, expecting to see Balder in the backseat, and the emptiness of it presses down on me, along with the last sight I had of Dulcie. The signs are starting to blur into big globs of reflective green and white that hurt my eyes. Sometimes on the sides of the roads I see things that aren't there: Mom and Dad holding each other. Balder running through the grass toward a glimmering hall. Glory switching out the bag on an IV pole. The old lady with her garden shears; she waves to me. The coyote. The road-runner. The Copenhagen Interpretation playing Hacky Sack with the Calabi Yau. Just a bunch of travelers on the same road. But I don't see Dulcie, no matter how hard I try to make her appear.

The Caddy veers over the yellow line, nearly hitting a big truck, whose horn blast has me swerving back into our lane with a jerk.

"Holy shit," Gonzo says, putting his hands on the dash.

"Sorry," I say. I pull the car over to the shoulder and rest my head on the steering wheel. I'm clammy, and my muscles ache.

"You okay?" Gonzo asks.

"Yeah," I lie.

USGW 3111 turns on his blinker and hits the exit, stop-ping at a Freedom Waffles. There's a salvage yard on a dusty yellow road to the right of the diner. I park beside the chain-link fence and the mile-high towers of tires and cut the engine.

"Can you keep watch?" I ask, and then I remember how Gonzo got our asses stranded by not looking out for the bus. Seems like years ago. "Never mind. I'll keep an eye out."

"No, man. It's okay. Get some sleep. I'm on it." And I can tell he is.

"Thanks. You know, for everything. You're a great wing-man," I say.

Gonzo smirks. "Yeah. Well. That's what you get when you sign up the Dwarf of Destiny, *cabrón*."

I climb into the backseat, shut my eyes, and go to sleep.

I'm a roadrunner. I look down and see those big bird feet and that's when I know I'm dreaming. I'm standing in the middle of a cartoon desert landscape. It's two-dimensional, a bunch of squiggly lines and paint. There are no anvils rigged over my head. No fake holes painted on a backdrop. No explosives rigged to a fuse that will trigger a domino effect of roadrunner-snuffing devices. Nope. I'm alone out here. Just me. And then I see the coyote sitting in a chair, watching TV, his paw in a big bowl of popcorn, like he could care less. At first I think it's a trap, but then I realize that he really doesn't care about chasing me. I say, "Beep, beep," and he keeps flipping channels with his remote. Finally, I give up and hop over to him.

"Aren't you going to chase me?" I ask.

He looks at me. His yellow eyes are weary. "What's the point?"

He's got me there. "I don't know," I say, sitting on the edge of his chair. "Because it's what we do."

"Huh," he says. He offers me some popcorn. I peck at it because I'm a bird now.

We sit watching cartoons. A tumbleweed rolls past. It's really just a bunch of angry pencil marks made to look like motion, an illusion. I guess this is nice, but what I really want to do is run. But without the coyote chasing me, I don't have a reason to run. Knowing he wants to catch me makes me keep going; and knowing I'm just out of reach makes him keep coming after me. We can't really live without each other. That's how it works.

"Come on," I whisper in my bird voice. "Chase me. Just one more time."

"Dude. Wakey-wakey." Gonzo's face looms over mine. "We got movement."

I wipe the sleep from my eyes. Through the windshield I can see Employees #457 and #458 opening the back of the truck and loading a box onto the dolly. Two minutes later, they come out of the diner with the empty dolly, climb into the truck's cab, and head back toward the interstate.

"Dude, aren't we following them?" Gonzo asks.

"Gotta check the diner first," I say, making my way toward the door. My legs have really stiffened up.

A shining, bright-smiled hostess greets us at the door, a couple of menus the size of atlases in her hands. "Joining us for breakfast today? Will that be smoking or nonsmoking?"

"I'm sorry," I say. "We're sort of in a hurry. We were just wondering about that box of snow globes that was delivered? Could we check them, please?"

Her thumb hovers over the silent alarm button near the cash register. Buddha Burger had one of those. "We don't let people just check out our snow globes till they been inventoried."

"Inventoried?" Gonzo mouths.

My eyes flash a Don't Go There signal. I've got to see if Dulcie's in that box. "I'm sorry. I'm with quality control. We think you may have gotten one of our tainted shipments."

"Tainted?" the hostess repeats, her smile gone. "What's that mean?"

"There might be something wrong with them. Really wrong. Like laced-with-poison wrong."

Her hand flies to her mouth. "Omigosh. We better call the police, then."

"No!" I say too quickly.

The hostess's eyes narrow. She looks from me to Gonzo and back again. "Is this some kind of prank? Are y'all with a fraternity?"

I shake my head. "You got us. It is a prank"—I steal a look at her name tag—"Freedom LaToya. Actually, we're casting for a new reality TV show."

Freedom LaToya's eyes get very big. "For real?"

"You bet. I probably shouldn't tell you this, but . . ." I make a show of craning my neck left and right. "It's set in a restaurant and it's all about finding the perfect restaurant hostess. In fact, it's called *The Hostess*. United Snow Globe Wholesalers is the sponsor. You know, you'd make a great candidate. I'm gonna let them know."

"Wow. Thanks. TV. Oh wow."

"Yeah. But we do need to get some footage of me looking through that box. For the show."

"Oh sure! Go right ahead!"

Freedom LaToya takes us to the stockroom. "I'll just leave you to it, then."

"You do that. Thanks."

We cut through the tape, open the box, and pull the bubble wrap from all ten snow globes. Not one of them is Dulcie.

"Let's go," I say, running for the car.

"Dude, that was awesome," Gonzo says, fastening his seat belt. "How did you think of something as stupid as a reality show about restaurant hostessing?"

I gun the engine. "You don't want to know."

* * *

It takes us about ten minutes of driving like a bat out of hell before we have the truck in our sights again. We follow it to each drop-off—gas stations, restaurants, gift shops, churches—until it's late afternoon and the Caddy Rocinante starts kicking up that hot oil smell again. Shit. Hold together, pal. I might as well be talking to myself. The twitches are back, and I really don't know how much longer I can safely drive with my arms ready to break-dance. Green and white signs pass overhead, telling us where we are, where we're headed.

ORLANDO. INTERSTATE 4. NORTH EXIT 62. OSCEOLA PKWY.

The green dreads of the palm trees dance in the breeze. Gleaming hotels play peekaboo with the crisscross of highways. Streetlights crane their necks over the roads like metal flamingos.

536 EAST. TO INTERNATIONAL DR S. LAKE BUENA VISTA. CENTRAL FLORIDA PKWY. The signs change from green-and-white to blue-and-red. MAGIC KINGDOM. WORLD DRIVE. Up ahead is a huge archway with the world's most beloved mouse attached.

"No way," Gonzo says as the truck makes the turnoff.

Every cell in my body is on high alert.

"Welcome to Disney World," I say.

CHAPTER FORTY-NINE

Of What Happens When We Hit Fantasyland

Finding a parking spot for the Caddy in the cavernous Disney World lot proves challenging. Every white-striped piece of asphalt for a mile is taken. The tops of the cars are like colored circuits on some huge motherboard. I end up parking the Caddy on a strip of grass that I'm sure will get it towed. It doesn't matter now.

We take the parking-lot tram to the Monorail, which zips us to the front gates of America's favorite amusement park. It takes most of the rest of our money to get our tickets. And then we're inside, standing on Main Street. All around us, life-sized furry cartoon characters wave and dance and pose for pictures.

I stagger into Gonzo, who pushes me back up with a grunt. My forehead's beading with cold sweat. His eyes widen. "Dude," he says softly, nodding at my wristband.

The E-ticket's lost all but a thin line of color below Tomorrowland. I'm almost out of health. My lungs feel like they've been tied up with shoelaces.

"Be okay," I pant. "Gotta find Dulcie."

"Where are we?"

"Main Street."

Up ahead, Cinderella's Castle shines like a mirage in the late-afternoon haze. An old-fashioned car *putt-putt*s past. Visitors crowd the sidewalks and street. It all seems unreal—except for the security guards patrolling with their walkie-talkies. Gonzo nods toward the guards.

"I see them," I say. "We need disguises."

In one of the four zillion gift shops, we buy a giant knight's helmet, a wizard's cape and an Ultimate Peace Weapon for me and a droopy-eared dog hat and matching costume for Gonzo.

"I feel like a complete asshat," Gonzo mutters through the mask.

"Better than being a snow globe," I remind him. "Here."

I press the remainder of our stash—four hundred dollars—into his paw.

"What's this for?"

"Bus ticket to New York. Say hi to Drew for me. Go see the Empire State Building. I always wanted to do that."

"You say that like you're not coming back, dude."

"I don't know what's gonna happen. Look, just take the money, okay?"

"Okay," he says softly. He pats himself with his paws. "Does this thing have a fucking pocket?" Gonzo unzips the costume on the side and tucks the wad of cash into his jeans.

The two of us hoof it down Main Street, keeping a lookout for anybody pushing a dolly of snow globes. In each gift shop, we stop to check their inventory, with no luck. It's a nice day, and the park is crammed with people. Families on vacation. Honeymoon couples wearing mouse-ear top hats and veils. Grandmas and grandpas indulging their grandkids with souvenirs.

Dulcie, where are you?

By the time we reach Fantasyland, I'm so tired I'm hallucinating. I think I see Glory walking past me with her IV pole. She smiles, but when I look again, it's just some lady pushing a stroller. Gonzo's eyes are huge. His face radiates awe. He's digging Disney—the character parades, the rides, the crazy light-up toys.

Gonzo's cell rings. Hurriedly, he unzips his costume and roots around in his pocket, which looks really pervy.

"Hello?" he says, a big smile breaking. "Hey," he says, all flirty. "Nuttin' much, what're you doin'?" He mouths the word "Drew" to me.

"Can you call him back?" I snipe.

"Oh. Sure," he says. "Hey, baby, can I call you back? We're kinda at Disney World."

I sigh.

"An arcade? We are so there." Gonzo pulls away from the phone for a second. "Drew says Space Mountain is, like, *ridonculous*. What's that?" Gonzo says into the phone again. "Uh-huh. Yeah, I miss you, too. . . ."

I start to tell Gonzo to hang up, that we need to find Dulcie, but I realize that *I'm* the one who needs to find Dulcie. He's found what he came for. So I let him talk for a minute longer while I keep a lookout for guys in mirrored sunglasses pushing dollies of boxed snow globes to secret destinations. I wander over to the Small World ride and wait in a small patch of shade. Faint music floats out. People load into the boats and drift off into the dark, happy underworld of Disney.

455

"Line starts over there," somebody says.

"That's okay. I'm just waiting."

"Suit yourself," she says. And when I look, it's the old lady from the hospital. She gets on line.

"Hey." I stumble after her, but when I get there, it's a different woman altogether. "Sorry," I say. "Thought you were someone else."

She smiles. "That happens to me all the time."

People come and go. Moms walking fast pull little kids toward bathroom entrances, sounding pissed. *Why didn't you go before we got in line?* The kids are crying or whining. Sometimes the dads wait outside. The moms try to hand bags and stuffed animals and shit to the dads, but the dads don't do it right; they don't get it and the moms get all pissy. They say things like, *Well, I thought we decided not to do Splash Mountain this time,* while the dads stick their hands in their pockets.

All I can think is *This is the place where I spent the happiest day of my life?* Why? The lines are all crazy long, and I think, *There is no way I would wait around in the sun for some lousy ride that's over too quick.*

But then the kids come pouring out of the exit, and what I see makes me want to cry. Their faces are pure wonder. They're all lit up and talking a mile a minute. The parents trail behind them, smiling, too. A contagious joy.

Something plops onto my shoulder. A feather. "Dulcie?" I call, but on closer examination, it's a pigeon feather, perfectly ordinary. A United Snow Globe Wholesalers employee pushes past me with a box on a dolly. The side of the box is stamped TOMORROWLAND.

A tingle works its way up my neck. Dulcie's here. I know it. And so is Dr. X. Like Dulcie said, the only thing that

456

makes sense in this world is the random. I have to tell Gonzo.

I turn and run smack into a guy in mirrored sunglasses and a baseball cap.

He grins. "Excuse me, could I talk to you a minute about safety?"

I try to run, but he kicks my legs out from under me and I hit the ground with an audible smack. "We've got him," the guy says to no one I can see. Security starts coming from the character pin booths and gift shops.

While startled tourists watch and snap pictures for the albums back home, USGW Employee #221 hauls me to the side of the Small World ride.

"Where's your accomplice? Where's Paul?" he asks, and it takes me a minute to realize he means Gonzo. From the corner of my eye, I see Gonzo over by the bathroom in his dog disguise. He's sipping a soda and laughing, the phone still pressed to his ear.

"It's not his fault," I say. "I forced him to come with me. At gunpoint."

Employee #221 seems to take this in, and I just roll for all I'm worth. "Do you know how many times that crazy kid tried to escape? He even tried to pass a note to the waitress at the Konstant Kettle."

Gonzo's turning around, walking toward us. *Please. Please do not come any closer, Gonzo,* I silently plead. As if he hears me, Gonzo looks up from his call and freezes. I crane my neck barely perceptibly toward the impressively mustachioed USGW agent in front of me. Gonzo plays quick charades with me: *Eye. Kung fu kick. Agent. Butt.* I kung fu agent in butt? He repeats his charades slowly.

I kick his butt?

457

I shake my head very slowly. "Live to fight another day," I shout, startling everyone around me. "For you are the Dwarf of Destiny!"

"What's that for?" Employee #741 is on the scene now. He presses the barrel of his gun into my side.

"He's crazy," Employee #221 says. "Call security again."

"Roger that." Employee #741 speaks into his walkie-talkie.

Gonzo has heard. He looks a little sad as he nods. There's not much I can do without alerting the guys to his presence. And so I put up my palm. It's not really a wave, not a goodbye or a hello, just a hand, a *Hey, I see you*. He gives me a palm right back. *I see you, too*. And then he does what he should; he folds into the swarm of people trying to have a good time and make a few memories, just another face in the crowd.

"We're taking him in for processing," Employee #741 says, and I know what that means.

My throat is tight and my eyes sting. I'm close to crying. I've gotten all the way here just to fail at the last minute.

"Can I ask you something? What do you guys think you're going to accomplish with all this? I mean, honestly, how can you prepare for the unpredictable?"

"Just shut up."

They sit me down, and suddenly, I'm pissed. Fuck this. I will not shut up. *"It's a small world after all . . . ,"* I sing. *"It's a small world after all. . . ."*

"What are you doing? Stop singing," the agent commands, and it just makes me angrier.

". . . a small, small world!" I sing even louder.

"Oh, I love it when they give you entertainment in line," a lady in a big sun hat says.

The guy hits me hard with the gun. I double over.

"Hey," a guy in line says. "What are you doing? He's a kid."

"Sir, we're with United Snow Globe Wholesalers, working to protect you."

"Stay out of it, pal. Let the pros handle it," another guy in line advises the first.

"Exactly," Employee #457 says. "This is a matter of security."

"No. It's a matter of abuse," the dad says.

I keep singing. *". . . world of laughter, a world of tears . . ."*

The kids don't know what's going on. But they know the song. And they start to sing along.

"That's it, kids!" I shout. "We're putting this on TV, so everybody needs to grab a partner and sing really, really loud!"

At the mention of TV, the line goes nuts. The USGW vigilantes aren't expecting this. And that's all I need. *Okay, coyote mofo man. Get your anvil ready. Come and get my road-runner ass.*

I bolt for Tomorrowland and hope my legs hold out.

"Hey! Stop!" the agents yell behind me. "Don't make us shoot!"

He can't shoot me. I'm a kid. And this is Disney World. There's no shooting at Disney World. Beside me, there's a blinding flash, and a family of four buying cotton candy becomes an instant plastic tableaux behind glass.

Fast as I can, I duck around the Mad Tea Party ride; darting in and out of the crowds, I make it past the Speedway, and finally I can see colorful planets of Tomorrowland. Shit. I'm gasping for breath. Vision's blurry. Behind me, I can hear screaming and shouts. The snow globe men are close.

The lines for everything are twenty minutes deep at least. Except for the Tomorrowland Transit Authority.

"Excuse me!" I shout, staggering up the ramp, pushing past the few people in line. Before anyone can object, I hop onto the moving conveyor belt, past the attendant, who can only get out a lame "Hey, watch it" as I fall into the seat of the tram. I stay low, out of sight as the little tram glides into a tunnel toward the Carousel of Progress.

My heart's beating as fast as the drum break in "Cypress Grove Blues." I'm alert, eyes peeled, ears open, totally awake and alive. I'm waiting for a signal, a sign that I'm in the right place. A narrator's voice drones into the darkness. He sounds like he should be selling cars in an old newsreel. The train slows in front of a window showing a diorama of Tomorrowland. The narrator tells us this is a vision of the future: a place where people can live, work, and play in harmony. Some posters show machines that do things for you. Robots. The standard-issue sci-fi stuff. I guess at one point this was cutting-edge. It was a dream.

The tram jolts around a corner, and suddenly, the tunnel goes totally dark. I can't see my hand in front of my face. It makes my pulse jump in my throat. Is this it? Are they coming for me?

"Dulcie?" I say into the darkness. It's silent. And then the meteor shower starts. Like the dark is crying tears of colored light.

The tram slows to a crawl, and I'm pretty sure they're stopping it to look for me. They can't be too far behind now. Trails of light blink over our faces, and for a second, I swear I see the neon outline of a door off to my right. Another streak breaks the dark and I see it again. It's most definitely a door, and right in the center is a feather. The ride starts jerking forward again. It's now or never.

"Hey, I don't think you're supposed to be doing that," the

man behind me says as I clamber over the side and step out onto a small platform. I turn around as carefully as I can on the narrow ledge, trying not to lose my footing. The narrator's voice thunders in the dark like some forgotten god. I push through the door, and the sudden whiteness nearly blinds me.

CHAPTER FIFTY

Wherein I Visit Tomorrowland

It takes a minute for my eyes to adjust. Far above me I can see the grinding motion of huge gears in operation, keeping the ride going. Behind me is the door. Ahead of me is a long tunnel.

I start walking. "Dulcie?" I call out. "Dulcie!"

The tunnel winds around and stops at a door with a big X on it. I push it open. Inside is a stark white laboratory with a ginormous movie screen. A messy desk and chair sit in the middle. I've seen a glimpse of this room before, on my computer. Followthefeather.com. There's a man in a lab coat sitting in a folding chair at the desk. He's reading a tabloid and eating a bowl of jelly beans. On the screen behind him is the exact same image.

"Dr. X?" I whisper.

He looks down at me from the screen, and in person,

squints. "Yes? Can I help you?" He's smaller than he seemed in the videos and pictures, but otherwise he looks exactly the same, like he hasn't aged a day. A small, tinny radio plays the Copenhagen Interpretation.

"I—I've been looking for you."

"You have?"

"Yes. Yes!" I say, laughing with some weird mix of relief and happiness. "I've been reading the papers and checking the personals, looking for clues and signs, making sense of the random—all to get to you."

Dr. X's eyebrows knit together in confusion. "Why?"

"You're Dr. X," I say. "You're going to cure me."

"I don't even know your name."

"It's Cameron. Cameron Smith."

"And why should I save you, Cameron Smith? What makes you so special?" Dr. X asks in a tired voice.

"I . . . I don't know. It's just that Dulcie said you would and it'd be kind of terrible if—"

Dr. X interrupts me. "Terrible things happen all the time. Don't you know that? And there's no reason, no reason at all. No god holding us in his hands like a benevolent parent. This suffering is meaningless. Well, someone should do something about it! There should be some way to stop the pain, the loneliness, the uncertainty. And I've found the answer—a way to stop death. Go on. Pull that curtain over there."

My footsteps echo in the mostly empty room. I pull aside the curtain. Floor-to-ceiling shelves hold the most impressive snow globe collection I've ever seen. Each one is marked UNITED SNOW GLOBE WHOLESALERS.

His hand encloses a globe. "This is the answer: To stop yearning. Our atoms sleeping, content."

"You brought something back from your travels in the

Infinity Collider," I say. "You unleashed dark energy on our world."

"Did I? Oh. Sorry."

"Sorry?" I laugh. "Sorry? Jeez. I closed the wormhole, by the way. You can thank me later."

"You can thank me later," Dr. X muses. "That's from *Star Fighter*, isn't it?"

"Yeah," I say, a little impressed. Then I remember that he's being a complete asshole. "You used to be a scientist. You were doing amazing things! I mean, parallel worlds, time travel—that's huge. I don't think it gets any huger than that."

"What does all that matter if we cannot stop the one injustice of life: everything within us is born to live, and yet, we die. And what we love can be taken from us in the blink of an eye." He blinks, and on the movie screen, his eyes seem huge, a confused owl. "That is why I created United Snow Globe Wholesalers. To take away the uncertainty. The pain. No. I must continue my work. You can show yourself out."

"Not without Dulcie," I say.

"Who is this Dulcie person?"

"A friend. I think she's part of your collection now. I just want her back. That's all."

"Very well." Dr. X clasps his hands together. "If you can tell me one true thing you've learned, one thing worth living for, you may have your friend back."

I don't know what to say. I could say anything—fish, popcorn, unicycles. What has meaning to me might not mean a damn thing to Dr. X. I'm so tired my muscles are shaking and I feel like crying. And so I say the only thing that comes to mind, the truest thing I can think of. "To live is to love, to love is to live."

On the screen, Dr. X blinks, thinking. And then, suddenly,

464

the Dulcie snow globe is on the desk in the room. Her plastic fists are pressed against the glass, and her red, painted mouth is open in a scream.

"Set her free," I say.

"Ah," Dr. X says softly. "That I cannot do."

"You have to turn her back!" I say.

"I could freeze you, too. Then you'd feel nothing."

"I don't want to feel nothing."

"That's wonderful," he murmurs, and the screen goes to static.

In the room, I hear someone clapping. The Wizard of Reckoning's moving toward me, applauding. He's a good six feet tall, just my height. Hooked to his belt is a scabbard with a gleaming sword poking out. Those gloved hands reach up and remove his helmet.

"Hey, Cameron. Remember me?" The Wizard of Reckoning grins, and I'd know that grin anywhere. I've been staring at it in the mirror for the past sixteen years. "Big surprise, huh? Bet you didn't know you had that zit on your chin."

"This can't be happening."

"And yet it is. Nice cape, by the way. Though it is a little copycat."

Off to the right is a long hallway dotted with doors. I stumble-run toward the safety of it.

"Won't work!" the wizard calls after me as I run smack into the wall. "It's painted. Sorry, my little roadrunner. No escaping this."

He unzips his space-armor jacket. Underneath he's wearing an orange tee: MY PARENTS WENT TO SHITHENGE AND ALL I GOT WAS THIS CRAPPY T-SHIRT.

"But we got rid of you. You can't be here," I say, looking for an exit.

The wizard's smile hardens. "I'm always here, Cameron.

465

You people, I tell ya. Always looking for signs, for meaning. This is what you keep at bay—chaos, disorder, the irrational and unexplainable, death looming on the horizon, a big dark hole sucking up everything in its path, no escape." He takes a seat on the edge of the desk. "You always seemed to have that figured out: Why try? We're just gonna die in the end. Sensible attitude. I liked that about you, Cameron. That's why I'm a little surprised by this third act filled with heroics. So much *effort*. Really, you're making it much harder than it needs to be."

"Making what harder than it needs to be?" *Where is the door I came in through?*

"Dying, of course."

"I'm not gonna die. Dr. X is going to cure me!" I shout.

"There is no Dr. X, sponge brain," the wizard says. "See, this whole thing—it's in your head. A fantasy jerry-rigged from your life's scrap-metal heap, dude."

"Then who's that?" I point to Dr. X's image on the screen.

"Why must we die when everything within us was born to live?" Dr. X says, like a loop of tape that's gone back to the beginning. "It's a tragedy cloaked in a comedy."

"Some guy you saw on the Internet once."

"That's not true. Those United Snow Globe employees—"

The Wizard of Reckoning's hand comes down hard, rattling the snow globes. "Do. Not. Exist. Just a figment of your spongiform mind. They're stand-ins—the coyote on your ass."

"No." I look around the room frantically.

"Oh, Cameron. Don't tell me you still don't get it." He knocks on my head. "Hello? Is any of this getting through?"

"Ow. Quit it."

"Sorry. My bad." He sighs and picks some lint off his shiny

466

pants, and I make a vow that if I live through this, I will never wear pants like that. "Cameron. What do you think this whole trip has been about, man? Searching for a cure? Saving the universe? Dude. Please. It's about this."

He throws a crumpled piece of paper at my feet. I pick it up and smooth it out. It's Junior's message that I stuck on the Wishing Tree back in Hope with Dulcie.

"Read it out loud, man."

"I wish to live."

"There you go." He smiles.

"But . . . Dr. X was supposed to give me the cure. . . ."

"There is no cure for this life." The wizard takes a seat on the folding chair for a minute. He stretches his long legs out in front of him, removes the sword from its scabbard, and polishes it with the edge of his shirt. "You live it to the best of your ability."

"This is bullshit! I was supposed to get my wish!" I can't help it. I'm crying.

The Wizard of Reckoning keeps polishing. "Sort of."

"Huh?"

He makes a sound in his throat, a cross between a grunt and a sigh. He's tiring of me. "So. Right. To review," he says, putting the weapon down and lacing his fingers together, resting them on the back of his head. My head. His head. Shit, I don't know anymore. "Did you live these past two weeks?"

"I live every week!" I argue.

"No. You exist. The question is, did you live?"

For a second, I stop fighting and think about what he's asking me. Did I live? I made a best friend. Lost another. Cried. Laughed. Lost my virginity. Gained a piece of magic, gave it away. Possibly changed a man's destiny. Drank beer.

Slept in cheap motels. Got pissed off. Laughed some more. Escaped from the police and bounty hunters. Watched the sun set over the ocean. Had a soda with my sister. Saw my mom and dad as they are. Understood music. Had sex again, and it was pretty mind-blowing. Not that I'm keeping score. Okay, I'm keeping score. Played the bass. Went to a concert. Wandered around New Orleans. Freed the snow globes. Saved the universe.

"Well?" the wizard asks.

Dulcie, my mind answers.

"So you're saying none of this is real?" I ask.

He checks his reflection in the cool steel of his blade. "I'm not saying that at all. Reality is what you make of it."

Dulcie.

"Then I make it that," I say, pointing to Dulcie.

"That?" The wizard flicks his finger at Dulcie's glass prison and I want to punch him. "That's a snow globe, Cameron."

"No," I say, swiping at the tears. "I don't believe that. I won't. She's real."

He holds out his hand. "Join me, Cameron."

I start to laugh. The Wizard of Reckoning tries to smirk, but I can tell he's confused.

"Hold up," I say. "I know this bit. You're *Star Fighter*-ing me. You're going to tell me to become one with you and the universe and then fold in on yourself."

He nods appreciatively. "Not going for it, huh?"

I cross my arms. "No."

He shrugs. "Okay. Plan B." His sword comes down swift and hard as justice. It leaves a bloody cut on my arm, and I gasp in pain.

"Holy crap!" I fall down and scramble away from him. The blood leaves spots on the pristine white floor, like stars in a forming universe.

"Oooh, dude. That looks nasty. You might want Glory to take a look at that."

I'm on my knees on the white floor, holding my hand over my bleeding arm. "Glory's back at the hospital."

"Yeah? Where the hell do you think you are?"

"What the hell are you talking about, freak face? I'm at Disney World!" God, my arm hurts.

The wizard advances in little dance steps, swinging his sword and catching it like a partner. "No, man. You never left St. Jude's."

The edges of the scene buckle. The room wavers and blurs till we're back in the hospital. Nurses and doctors bustle about. Glory walks past, a cup of coffee in her hand.

"Glory?" I blink twice, but there she is in her pink scrubs, her angel pins clinking.

I glare at the wizard, who's got a smug little smile. "This isn't happening. You're making it up."

The hospital fades as the Wizard of Reckoning shrugs. "Suit yourself." He swings the sword and slices at my other arm.

"Aaah!" I wince. I raise my Ultimate Peace Weapon and whack at him. It collapses in on itself.

"Dude. That's a toy. I'm carrying the real deal."

His blade comes down again, narrowly missing me. I've got to get away from this guy. He's too much for me.

"Those prions should be ripping you apart right about now, buddy, destroying what's left of your tenuous grasp on reality."

My E-ticket meter has gone to empty. In its place is my hospital ID bracelet. SMITH, CAMERON JOHN.

"Whatcha dreaming about now, Cam-my-man?"

Dreaming. Dreams. Do atoms dream of more? That's what Dr. X wanted to know. I wish he were here so I could tell

469

him yes. Yes, they do. Mine have been dreaming for weeks now. Every one of those freaking atoms catching a wave through the universe and laughing.

"What?" The Wizard of Reckoning's looking at me funny, his sword dangling at his side.

There is no meaning but what we assign. We create our own reality. I can live with that.

"I said, 'Catch me if you can.'"

With that, I leap up and run for the corridor, fast as a road-runner, and open the first door I see.

CHAPTER FIFTY-ONE

In Which Coyote and Roadrunner Meet One Last Time

It's quiet on the other side of that door. Daylight's streaming in, landing in bright patches on familiar green-flowered wallpaper. I'm standing in our old kitchen watching the eight-year-old me at the table eating sugary cereal and reading a comic book. Mom walks by with her coffee. She looks young. And happy. She rubs a hand across my head, tousling my hair. I rub it back into messy place.

"Love you, crankmuffin," she says.

"I'm not a crankmuffin. Don't mess with my hair," I grumble. It seems like a bratty thing to say, but Mom laughs.

"You are a crankmuffin, but you're *my* crankmuffin." She sits beside me with her paper, and there we are, reading and sipping and slurping. I want to tell her she's a good mom. That I *am* her crankmuffin and I like it.

The Wizard of Reckoning steps out of the bathroom that's

off the kitchen. I don't know how he got there. "Hey, dude," he says, smirking. "Nice moment, huh? What was your thing about your hair, though? Kinda teen girl of you, if you don't mind my saying."

He twirls the blade like a threat and I dash back out the door and into that long white hallway where all the doors are like vibrating strings. I try the next door. I'm in Dad's office. Dad's at his desk, hunched over some papers. Raina's pacing around the office. They're not looking at each other. Raina's telling Dad about some guy she met at a concert. She says he asked her out on a date, and Dad's telling her she should go. She looks a little hurt. She says, "Maybe I will." Dad says, "I think you should." Then it's quiet for a minute and Dad says, "Well, I've got a lot of paperwork to catch up on." Raina says, "Sure." And that's it. She's gone. I don't know if this is something that's going to happen, something that's happening now, or something that will never happen. It's hard to tell.

"Cam-er-on! Where are you, you slippery little road-runner?" The wizard's hot on my tail. I leap back into the corridor and through another door.

I'm in the studio audience of some TV show. Staci Johnson's front and center on the soundstage, wearing a really hot dress, and I think, *Whoa, I had her.* Or maybe she had me. She reads from a teleprompter. "Tonight, on *The Hostess* . . . will Freedom best Jackie in the not-enough-menus challenge? Or will they both have to turn in their name tags when the reservation book goes missing . . . ?"

"Dude, she is pretty hot." The wizard's sitting a row over.

"Stop chasing me!" I shout.

He shrugs. I take off again, ducking in and out of doors. I run past the Small World ride.

"Oh my God!" a lady cries. "A little boy drowned! He just jumped overboard!"

Open the next door, and I'm in somebody's backyard. Swing set. Toys. A little girl toddles over to a yard gnome, pounds its head with her pudgy hands. "Cameron, over here," her mom calls, her arms open wide. It's Jenna. Jenna's a mom.

"Meep-meep!" The Wizard of Reckoning taunts, and I scramble back into that endless corridor. He pops out from behind a door in front of me. "Hot-cha!" he says, waving his spirit fingers.

"Stop doing that—it's annoying!" I yell as I dive through a different door and find myself in a desert, a gun in my hands. I'm wearing camouflage.

"Move it, soldier. There's a war on." A guy barks, and slaps my back, and then we're marching forward.

"Keith, tell that story again—the one about the Party House," one of the soldiers calls out.

"Oh, man! You would not believe how fine Marisol is, I'm telling you," the other soldier turns and says. His uniform reads PVT. KEITH WASHINGTON. "It was the rockingest day—"

"Hey," I shout. "Wait—"

His foot comes down. "—of my life—"

The sand explodes in a mile-high fireball. There's shouting. Orders. Chaos. Explosions. Gunfire. I toss the gun and run pushing out into the safety of the hall. Except that it's not safe. Another door. More sand. But this is a beach, not a war zone.

"Can I help you?" Behind me is a shack. The Magic Screw Guy Boat Repair. The man at the counter holds out his hands as if to say, *I don't have all day, pal.* His hat reads KEITH.

"I said, can I help you?"

"You already did," I say, and dart for the next door.

I keep running, trying doors. In one, Eubie's onstage in New Orleans drumming for Junior Webster; in another, he's playing Junior's albums and guiding college kids toward good music in his shop. The Copenhagen Interpretation plays a futuristic, Tomorrowland-worthy palace in a sky where three moons shine, and you know, the acoustics *are* really good. I see the busy streets of New Orleans and the quiet peace of the graveyards. I see people coming and going from the Wishing Tree, pinning their hopes to it so it's always in bloom. In another, Gonzo and Justin ride a coaster together. When it plunges, they raise their arms and scream in happiness. I walk through all kinds of landscapes. Past. Present. Future. Alternatives. At first, I try hard to figure out what's real and what's not. But after a while, it doesn't matter anymore.

Door after door after door. I open one and am surrounded by the sight of gases twirling, stars swirling. Something fires and the whole thing is set in motion. A universe is being born. It's so cool. It's a thing that should be shared. I wish Dulcie were here to see it.

"Cool, huh?" It's the wizard. I know that without even looking.

"Yeah," I say.

The room falls away and we're in that corridor again, but it looks different. It's still really white, but the ceiling is lower. It has spongy acoustic tiles. I hear the beep of the heart monitor, the whirr of a respirator.

"You're out of doors, Cameron."

Just like that, we're back in the room by the desk. There's nothing on it now but the Wizard of Reckoning holding the angel snow globe.

"Any last words?"

I shrug. "Only what I've already said."

"Oh right. 'To live is to love, to love is to live.' That's your great insight?"

"Yeah."

He starts laughing. It's really weird to watch yourself laugh. Like I never knew my mouth went up higher on one side. "Oh, Cameron! Dude. That is soooo lame."

"Yeah." I'm laughing, too, because really, the whole thing strikes me as hilarious all of a sudden.

"Come on, buddy. You're not exiting stage left on that, are you? Give me something else—'And don't forget my soda, punk.' Something."

"Sorry," I giggle. "That's all I got."

The me who's the Wizard of Reckoning sets his mouth in a grim line. "That's too bad. 'Cause you're gonna die."

I stop laughing. "Yeah. I know."

"There's nothing else."

Nothing else.

"*Meep-meep!* That's all for now, kids," the wizard taunts.

Nothing else. Nothing.

"Time to say goodbye."

Nothing else. Isn't that what Junior said back in New Orleans? Man, that seems so long ago. *You take this horn and someday, when you gotta, when there's nothin' else, you play it.*

I try to run for my backpack and fall flat on my stomach. My legs have stopped working. So I crawl. Every inch is an exercise in will and pain.

"Oh, Cameron. Crawling? Dude, that's an icky way to go out."

Backpack. Just need to reach my backpack.

"Here comes the big bad coyote!"

Fingers are so stiff. Shit. Not now. Please not now. Fumble with the zipper.

"Owooooooeeeeee!" the wizard howls.

Zipper's open. Reach in. Feel the cold metal. It's in my hands.

"Hey. Whaddaya got there, buddy?"

"Just this." I raise Junior Webster's horn and blow for all I'm worth.

Nothing.

I hear nothing.

The Wizard of Reckoning chuckles, then stops. "Hey, I heard that. B-flat. Hey . . ." He's starting to fold in on himself, everything disappearing, pulling in. Just before his face crumbles, he looks right at me. "Well, shit."

All at once, the snow globes shatter. The water rises and I'm caught in it. It pushes me along, down that hallway, toward one last door. My face is reflected in the knob, all distorted. I open it wide and step in.

The ocean. A house. And there's the old lady in her garden. She looks up briefly, nods, and goes right back to planting her garden. So I go on in the house. Walk upstairs. It smells sweet. There's lily of the valley in a jar on the dresser. And the window looks out on the ocean, where the sun and its shadow hang low in the sky. The bed's been turned down, and I realize I'm really tired. But a good tired, like I've spent all day at the beach. The sheets are cool and welcoming as I slip in.

It's like everything is slowing down inside me. *Beep. Beep. Whirr. Whirr.* The ceiling. White like the moon. Like snow with all its words. The angel picture on the wall.

Beep. Whirr.

Mom, Dad, and Jenna are gathered around me. Glory

steps over to the respirator and flicks a switch. She turns off the EKG and the heart monitor, too, flipping switches till the room is perfectly quiet. I'm sort of floating here. It's not bad. It's not anything, really.

Mom and Dad each take one of my hands. Jenna sits beside me. Everything slows. The room gets darker, and I feel like I'm being pulled toward something I can't see. Things streak past me. Stars. Gases. Satellites. Whole planets wobble and careen away. Universes, too. It makes me feel vast and impossibly small at the same time. Connected.

Just before the room falls completely away, Glory puts a hand over my eyes and just like that, the world disappears.

CHAPTER ONE

Wherein . . .

I know two things for sure.

1. I'm floating.

And 2. It's really fucking dark. No, really, man. You have no idea.

I'm trying to be okay with it. Really, I am. But frankly, it's freaking me out. Plus, it's boring. I hope this isn't the whole package, because jeez, I'll have to learn a craft or something to keep from going mental.

There's a soft sound coming from up ahead, and just the faintest light, like an old TV being turned on and warming up. The light reaches me enough so that I can see I'm in a boat on a river.

I hear singing. I know that song.

The boat floats out of the darkness, and I start laughing. The Bollywood puppets are singing to me. *It's a world of laughter, a world of tears.* Up ahead, I can see her for real, whatever that means. In her torn fishnets and black combat boots, she's hanging with the fishing Inuit boy.

"Hey, cowboy," she calls, waving from the snowy white shore. Her wings have been spray-painted with Buddha cows. They look awesome. "Thanks for showing up. What took you so long?"

"Took a detour, princess!" It's getting brighter.

She dances a little jig. "This would make a hell of a TV show, huh?"

"Yeah. But no one would believe it." I should let it go. But it's like the hole, like the door, and I have to know. Or at least, I have to ask. "Hey, Dulcie, was any of that real?"

She finishes her dance and the wings come to rest. "Who's to say what's real or not?"

"Yeah, but—my barometer on reality, not so good since I started going crazy."

"Yeah, well, who but the mad would choose to keep on living? In the end, aren't we all just a little crazy?"

"So. This place," I say, whistling.

"Yeah. It's a great ride, isn't it?" she says wistfully while the Inuit boy pulls the same fish from the hole, puts it back, pulls it up again, smiling the whole while.

"You know what? It really is. Definitely E-ticket."

She brushes my hair off my forehead with those soft fingers. "Wanna go again?"

"Maybe."

I'm not really thinking about that, about what happens next, or if anything does. All I know is what I'm feeling right now. I want to kiss Dulcie. After that, I don't know.

"What are you thinking about?" she says, laughing.

I smile. "Nothing."

"Good. I like 'em big and stupid."

The boat drifts to the glittering plastic shore of its own accord. I take her hand and step onto the snowbank. It's cold against my feet, and when I reach down, the snow comes up in my fingers icy and wet.

"Awesome," I murmur, scooping it up. It's so bright it hurts my eyes. There's a splashing sound. The fish on the end of the hook is struggling against its fate. The Inuit boy laughs and throws him back in the hole.

Dulcie bumps me with her shoulder. "Hey."

"Hey, yourself," I say, bumping her back.

She opens her wings and takes me in. The song plays on and the lights are so bright they seem to be alive. Dulcie parts her lips to kiss me and there's music. It's a note in an octave I've never heard before but that I somehow know has always been there. A note of endings, of beginnings. A note you have to be ready to hear.

"You ready?" she asks.

"Sure."

"Are you really?"

"No," I say. "Not at all."

She grins wide then. It's like the sky can't take anymore and it explodes, all particles and partner-particles and perhapsatrons, something new being born—a whole universe of yes and no and why the hell not? Sparks fly out past us, a zooming show of charged light that catches Dulcie's face in midlaugh.

And there's nothing to say but wow. Wow. The same word backward and forward.

Dulcie sighs in happiness. "That's always my favorite part."

And I can see why.

about the author

LIBBA BRAY is the author of the *New York Times* bestselling
Gemma Doyle Trilogy, which comprises the novels *A Great and
Terrible Beauty*, *Rebel Angels*, and *The Sweet Far Thing*. She has
written short stories about everything from Cheap Trick concerts
to *The Rocky Horror Picture Show* devotees to meeting Satan
worshippers on summer vacation. Libba lives in Brooklyn, New
York, with her husband, son, and two cats. Her dream is to stop
sucking so badly at drums in Rock Band. You may visit her at
www.libbabray.com and you don't even have to call first.